THE GOLDEN APPLES

By Eudora Welty

Eudora Welty

THE GOLDEN APPLES

A Harvest Book
Harcourt Brace & Company
San Diego   New York   London

To Rosa Farrar Wells
and Frank Hallam Lyell

CONTENTS

MAIN FAMILIES IN MORGANA, MISSISSIPPI

King MacLain
Mrs. MacLain (nee Miss Snowdie Hudson)
Ran and Eugene

Comus Stark
Mrs. Stark (nee Miss Lizzie Morgan)
Jinny Love

Wilbur Morrison
Mrs. Morrison
Cassie and Loch

Mr. Carmichael
Mrs. Carmichael (Miss Nell)
Nina

Felix Spights
Mrs. Spights (Miss Billy Texas)
Woodrow, Missie, and Little Sister

Old Man Moody
Mrs. Moody (Miss Jefferson)
Parnell

Miss Perdita Mayo
Miss Hattie Mayo

Fate Rainey
Mrs. Fate Rainey (Miss Katie)
Victor and Virgie

Also Loomises, Carlyles, Holifields, Nesbitts, Bowles-
es, Sissums *and* Sojourners. *Also* Plez, Louella, *and* Tellie
Morgan; Elberta, Twosie, *and* Exum McLane; Blackstone
and Juba, *colored*

THE GOLDEN APPLES

1.

SHOWER OF GOLD

That was Miss Snowdie MacLain.

She comes after her butter, won't let me run over with it from just across the road. Her husband walked out of the house one day and left his hat on the banks of the Big Black River.—That could have started something, too.

We might have had a little run on doing that in Morgana, if it had been so willed. What King did, the copy-cats always might do. Well, King MacLain left a new straw hat on the banks of the Big Black and there are people that consider he headed West.

Snowdie grieved for him, but the decent way you'd grieve for the dead, more like, and nobody wanted to think, around her, that he treated her that way. But how long can you humor the humored? Well, always. But I could almost bring myself to talk about it—to a passer-by, that will never see her again, or me either. Sure I can churn and talk. My name's Mrs. Rainey.

You seen she wasn't ugly—and the little blinky lines to her eyelids comes from trying to see. She's an albino but nobody would ever try to call her ugly around here—with that tender, tender skin like a baby. Some said King figured out that if the babies started coming, he had a chance for a nestful of little albinos, and that swayed him. No, I don't say it. I say he was just willful. *He* wouldn't think ahead.

Willful and outrageous, to some several. Well: he married Snowdie.

Lots of worse men wouldn't have: no better sense. Them Hudsons had more than MacLains, but none of 'em had enough to count or worry over. Not by then. Hudson money built that house, and built it for *Snowdie* . . . they prayed over that. But take King: marrying must have been some of his showing off—like man never married at all till *he* flung in, then had to show the others how he could go right on acting. And like, "Look, everybody, this is what I think of Morgana and MacLain Courthouse and all the way between"—further, for all I know—"marrying a girl with pink eyes." "I swan!" we all say. Just like he wants us to, scoundrel. And Snowdie as sweet and gentle as you find them. Of course gentle people aren't the ones you lead best, he had that to find out, so know-all. No, sir, she'll beat him yet, balking. In the meantime children of his growing up in the County Orphan's, so say several, and children known and unknown, scattered-like. When he does come, he's just as nice as he can be to Snowdie. Just as courteous. Was from the start.

Haven't you noticed it prevail, in the world in general? Beware of a man with manners. He never raised his voice to her, but then one day he walked out of the house. Oh, I don't mean once!

He went away for a good spell before he come back that time. She had a little story about him needing the waters. Next time it was more than a year, it was two—oh, it was three. I had two children myself, enduring his being gone, and one to die. Yes, and that time he sent her word ahead: "Meet me in the woods." No, he more invited her than told her to come—"Suppose you meet me in the woods." And it was night time he supposed to her. And Snowdie met him without asking "What for?" which I would want to know of Fate Rainey. After all, they were married—they had a right to sit inside and talk in the light and comfort, or lie down easy on a good goosefeather bed, either. I would even consider he might not be there when I came. Well, if Snowdie went without a question, then I can tell it without a question as long as I love Snowdie. Her version is that in the woods they met and both decided on what would be best.

Best for him, of course. We could see the writing on the wall.

"The woods" was Morgan's Woods. We would any of us know the place he meant, without trying—I could have streaked like an arrow to the very oak tree, one there to itself and all spready: a real shady place by *day*, is all I know. Can't you just see King MacLain leaning his length against that tree by the light of the moon as you come walking through Morgan's Woods and you hadn't seen him in three years? "Suppose you meet me in the woods." My foot. Oh, I don't know how poor Snowdie stood it, crossing the distance.

Then, twins.

That was where I come in, I could help when things got to there. I took her a little churning of butter with her milk and we took up. I hadn't been married long myself, and Mr. Rainey's health was already a little delicate so he'd thought best to quit heavy work. We was both hard workers fairly early.

I always thought twins might be nice. And might have been for them, by just the sound of it. The Mac-Lains first come to Morgana bride and groom from MacLain and went into that new house. He was educated off, to practice law—well needed here. Snowdie was Miss Lollie Hudson's daughter, well known. Her father was Mr. Eugene Hudson, a storekeeper down at Crossroads past the Courthouse, but he was a lovely man. Snowdie was their only daughter, and they give her a nice education. And I guess people more or less expected her to teach school: not marry. She couldn't see all that well, was the only thing in the way, but Mr. Comus Stark here and the supervisors overlooked that, knowing the family and Snowdie's real good way with Sunday School children. Then before the school year even got a good start, she got took up by King MacLain all of a sudden. I think it was when jack-o'-lanterns was pasted on her window I used to see his buggy roll up right to the schoolhouse steps and wait on her. He courted her in Morgana and MacLain too, both ends, didn't skip a day.

It was no different—no quicker and no slower— than the like happens every whipstitch, so I don't need to tell you they got married in the MacLain Presbyterian Church before you could shake a stick at it, no matter how surprised people were going to be. And once they dressed Snowdie all in white, you know she was whiter than your dreams.

So—he'd been educated in the law and he traveled for somebody, that was the first thing he did —I'll tell you in a minute what he sold, and she stayed home and cooked and kept house. I forget if she had a Negro, she didn't know how to tell one what to do if she had. And she put her eyes straight out, almost, going to work and making curtains for every room and all like that. So busy. At first it didn't look like they would have any children.

So it went the way I told you, slipped into it real easy, people took it for granted mighty early—him leaving and him being welcomed home, him leaving and him sending word, "Meet me in the woods," and him gone again, at last leaving the hat. I told my husband I was going to quit keeping count of King's comings and goings, and it wasn't long after that he did leave the hat. I don't know yet whether he meant it kind or cruel. Kind, I incline to believe. Or maybe she was winning. Why do I try to figure? Maybe because Fate Rainey ain't got a surprise in him, and proud of it. So Fate said, "Well now, let's have the women to settle down and pay attention to homefolks a while." That was all he could say about it.

So, you wouldn't have had to wait long. Here come Snowdie across the road to bring the news. I seen her coming across my pasture in a different walk, it was the way somebody comes down an aisle. Her sun-

bonnet ribbons was jumping around her: springtime.
Did you notice her little dainty waist she has still? I
declare it's a mystery to think about her having the
strength once. Look at me.

I was in the barn milking, and she come and took
a stand there at the head of the little Jersey, Lady
May. She had a quiet, picked-out way to tell news.
She said, "I'm going to have a baby too, Miss Katie.
Congratulate me."

Me and Lady May both had to just stop and look
at her. She looked like more than only the news had
come over her. It was like a shower of something had
struck her, like she'd been caught out in something
bright. It was more than the day. There with her eyes
all crinkled up with always fighting the light, yet she
was looking out bold as a lion that day under her
brim, and gazing into my bucket and into my stall
like a visiting somebody. Poor Snowdie. I remember
it was Easter time and how the pasture was all spotty
there behind her little blue skirt, in sweet clover. He
sold tea and spices, that's what it was.

It was sure enough nine months to the day
the twins come after he went sallying out through
those woods and fields and laid his hat down on the
bank of the river with "King MacLain" on it.

I wish I'd seen him! I don't guess I'd have stopped
him. I can't tell you why, but I wish I'd seen him!
But nobody did.

For Snowdie's sake—here they come bringing the
hat, and a hullabaloo raised—they drug the Big
Black for nine miles down, or was it only eight, and
sent word to Bovina and on, clear to Vicksburg, to
watch out for anything to wash up or to catch in the
trees in the river. Sure, there never was anything—
just the hat. They found everybody else that ever
honestly drowned along the Big Black in this neighborhood. Mr. Sissum at the store, he drowned later
on and they found him. I think with the hat he ought
to have laid his watch down, if he wanted to give it
a better look.

Snowdie kept just as bright and brave, she didn't seem to give in. She must have had her thoughts and they must have been one of two things. One that he was dead—then why did her face have the glow? It had a glow—and the other that he left her and meant it. And like people said, if she smiled *then*, she was clear out of reach. I didn't know if I liked the glow. Why didn't she rage and storm a little—to me, anyway, just Mrs. Rainey? The Hudsons all hold themselves in. But it didn't seem to me, running in and out the way I was, that Snowdie had ever got a real good look at life, maybe. Maybe from the beginning. Maybe she just doesn't know the *extent*. Not the kind of look I got, and away back when I was twelve year old or so. Like something was put to my eye.

She just went on keeping house, and getting fairly big with what I told you already was twins, and she seemed to settle into her content. Like a little white kitty in a basket, making you wonder if she just mightn't put up her paw and scratch, if anything was, after all, to come near. At her house it was like Sunday even in the mornings, every day, in that cleaned-up way. She was taking a joy in her fresh un-tracked rooms and that dark, quiet, real quiet hall that runs through her house. And I love Snowdie. I love her.

Except none of us felt very *close* to her all the while. I'll tell you what it was, what made her different. It was the not waiting any more, except where the babies waited, and that's not but one story. We were mad at her and protecting her all at once, when we couldn't be close to her.

And she come out in her pretty clean shirt waists to water the ferns, and she had remarkable flowers—she had her mother's way with flowers, of course. And give just as many away, except it wasn't like I or you give. She was by her own self. Oh, her mother was dead by then, and Mr. Hudson fourteen miles down the road away, crippled up, running his store

in a cane chair. We was every bit she had. Everybody tried to stay with her as much as they could
spare, not let a day go by without one of us to run in
and speak to her and say a word about an ordinary
thing. Miss Lizzie Stark let her be in charge of raising
money for the poor country people at Christmas that
year, and like that. Of course we made all her little
things for her, stitches like that was way beyond her.
It was a good thing she got such a big stack.

The twins come the first day of January. Miss
Lizzie Stark—she hates all men, and is real important: across yonder's her chimney—made Mr. Comus
Stark, her husband, hitch up and drive to Vicksburg
to bring back a Vicksburg doctor in her own buggy
the night before, instead of using Dr. Loomis here,
and stuck him in a cold room to sleep at her house;
she said trust any doctor's buggy to break down on
those bridges. Mrs. Stark stayed right by Snowdie,
and of course several, and I, stayed too, but Mrs.
Stark was not budging and took charge when pains
commenced. Snowdie had the two little boys and
neither one albino. They were both King all over
again, if you want to know it. Mrs. Stark had so
hoped for a girl, or two *girls*. Snowdie clapped the
names on them of Lucius Randall and Eugene Hudson, after her own father and her mother's father.

It was the only sign she ever give Morgana that
maybe she didn't think the name King MacLain had
stayed beautiful. But not much of a sign; some
women don't name after their husbands, until they
get down to nothing else left. I don't think with
Snowdie even *two* other names meant she had
changed yet, not towards King, that scoundrel.

Time goes like a dream no matter how hard you
run, and all the time we heard things from out in the
world that we listened to but that still didn't mean
we believed them. You know the kind of things.
Somebody's cousin saw King MacLain. Mr. Comus
Stark, the one the cotton and timber belongs to, he
goes a little, and he claimed three or four times he

saw his back, and once saw him getting a haircut in Texas. Those things you will hear forever when people go off, to keep up a few shots in the woods. They might mean something—might not.

Till the most outrageous was the time my husband went up to Jackson. He saw a man that was the spit-image of King in the parade, my husband told me in his good time, the inauguration of Governor Vardaman. He was right up with the big ones and astride a fine animal. Several from here went but as Mrs. Spights said, why wouldn't they be looking at the Governor? Or the New Capitol? But King Mac-Lain could steal anyone's glory, so he thought.

When I asked the way he looked, I couldn't get a thing out of my husband, except he lifted his feet across the kitchen floor like a horse and man in one, and I went after him with my broom. I knew, though. If it was King, he looked like, "Hasn't everybody been wondering, though, been out of their minds to know, where I've been keeping myself!" I told my husband it reasoned to me like it was up to Governor Vardaman to get hold of King and bring something out of him, but my husband said why pick on one man, and besides a parade was going on and what all. Men! I said if I'd been Governor Vardaman and spied King MacLain from Morgana marching in my parade as big as I was and no call for it, I'd have had the whole thing brought to a halt and called him to accounts. "Well, what good would it have done you?" my husband said. "A plenty," I said. I was excited at the time it happened. "That was just as good a spot as any to show him forth, right in front of the New Capitol in Jackson with the band going, and just as good a man to do it."

Well, sure, men like that need to be shown up before the world, I guess—not that any of us would be surprised. "Did you go and find him after the Governor got inaugurated to suit you then?" I asked my husband. But he said no, and reminded me. He went for me a new bucket; and brought me the wrong size. Just like the ones at Holifield's. But he said he saw King or his twin. What twin!

Well, through the years, we'd hear of him here or there—maybe two places at once, New Orleans and Mobile. That's people's careless way of using their eyes.

I believe he's been to California. Don't ask me why. But I picture him there. I see King in the West, out where it's gold and all that. Everybody to their own visioning.

II.

Well, what happened turned out to happen on Hallowe'en. Only last week—and seems already like something that couldn't happen at all.

My baby girl, Virgie, swallowed a button that same day—later on—and that *happened*, it seems like still, but not this. And not a word's been spoke out loud, for Snowdie's sake, so I trust the rest of the world will be as careful.

You can talk about a baby swallowing a button off a shirt and having to be up-ended and her behind pounded, and it sounds reasonable if you can just see the baby—there she runs—but get to talking about something that's only a kind of *near* thing—and hold your horses.

Well, Hallowe'en, about three o'clock, I was over at Snowdie's helping her cut out patterns—she's kept on sewing for those boys. Me, I have a little girl to sew for—she was right there, asleep on the bed in the next room—and it hurts my conscience being that lucky over Snowdie too. And the twins wouldn't play out in the yard that day but had hold of the scraps and the scissors and the paper of pins and all, and there underfoot they were dressing up and playing ghosts and boogers. Uppermost in their little minds was Hallowe'en.

They had on their masks, of course, tied on over their Buster Brown bobs and pressing a rim around the back. I was used to how they looked by then—but I don't like masks. They both come from Spights' store and cost a nickel. One was the Chinese kind, all yellow and mean with slant eyes and a dreadful thin mustache of black horsy hair. The other one was a lady, with an almost scary-sweet smile on her lips. I never did take to that smile, with all day for it. Eugene Hudson wanted to be the Chinaman and so Lucius Randall had to be the lady.

So they were making tails and do-lollies and all kinds of foolishness, and sticking them on to their little middles and behinds, snatching every scrap from the shirts and flannels me and Snowdie was cutting out on the dining room table. Sometimes we could grab a little boy and baste something up on him whether or no, but we didn't really pay them much mind, we was talking about the prices of things for winter, and the funeral of an old maid.

So we never heard the step creak or the porch give, at all. That was a blessing. And if it wasn't for something that come from outside us all to tell about it, I wouldn't have the faith I have that it come about.

But happening along our road—like he does every day—was a real turstworthy nigger. He's one of Mrs. Stark's mother's niggers, Old Plez Morgan everybody calls him. Lives down beyond me. The real old kind, that knows everybody since time was. He knows more folks than I do, who they are, and all the *fine* people. If you wanted anybody in Morgana that wouldn't be likely to make a mistake in who a person is, you would ask for Old Plez.

So he was making his way down the road, by stages. He still has to do a few people's yards won't let him go, like Mrs. Stark, because he don't pull up things. He's no telling how old and starts early and takes his time coming home in the evening—always stopping to speak to people to ask after their health and tell them good evening all the way. Only that day, he said he didn't see a soul *else*—besides you'll hear who in a minute—on the way, not on porches

or in the yards. I can't tell you why, unless it was
those little gusts of north wind that had started blowing. Nobody likes that.

But yonder ahead of him was walking a man. Plez
said it was a white man's walk and a walk he knew
—but it struck him it was from away in another year,
another time. It wasn't just the walk of anybody supposed to be going along the road to MacLain right
at that *time*—and yet it was too—and if it was, he
still couldn't think what business that somebody
would be up to. That was the careful way Plez was
putting it to his mind.

If you saw Plez, you'd know it was him. He had
some roses stuck in his hat that day, I saw him right
after it happened. Some of Miss Lizzie's fall roses,
big as a man's fist and red as blood—they were nodding side-to-side out of the band of his old black hat,
and some other little scraps out of the garden laid
around the brim, throwed away by Mrs. Stark; he'd
been cleaning out her beds that day, it was fixing to
rain.

He said later he wasn't in any great hurry, or he
would have maybe caught up and passed the man.
Up yonder ahead he went, going the same way Plez
was going, and not much more interested in a race.
And a real familiar stranger.

So Plez says presently the familiar stranger paused.
It was in front of the MacLains'—and sunk his
weight on one leg and just stood there, posey as
statues, hand on his hip. Ha! Old Plez says, accord-
ing, he just leaned himself against the Presbyterian
Church gate and waited a while.

Next thing, the stranger—oh, it was King! By then
Plez was calling him Mr. King to himself—went up
through the yard and then didn't go right in like anybody else. First he looked around. He took in the
yard and summerhouse and skimmed from cedar to
cedar along the edge of where he lived, and under
the fig tree at the back and under the wash (if he'd
counted it!) and come close to the front again,

sniffy like, and Plez said though he couldn't swear to seeing from the Presbyterian Church exactly what Mr. King was doing, he knows as good as seeing it that he looked through the blinds. He would have looked in the dining room—have mercy. We shut the West out of Snowdie's eyes of course.

At last he come full front again, around the flowers under the front bedroom. Then he settled himself nice and started up the front steps.

The middle step sings when it's stepped on, but we didn't hear it. Plez said, well, he had on fine tennis shoes. So he got across the front porch and what do you think he's fixing to do but knock on that door? Why wasn't he satisfied with outdoors?

On his own front door. He makes a little shadow knock, like trying to see how it would look, and then puts his present behind his coat. Of course he had something there in a box for her. You know he constitutionally brought home the kind of presents that break your heart. He stands there with one leg out pretty, to surprise them. And I bet a nice smile on his face. Oh, don't ask me to go on!

Suppose Snowdie'd took a notion to glance down the hall—the dining room's at the end of it, and the folding-doors pushed back—and seen him, all "Come-kiss-me" like that. I don't know if she could have seen that good—but *I* could. I was a fool and didn't look.

It was the twins seen him. Through those little bitty mask holes, those eagle eyes! There ain't going to be no stopping those twins. And he didn't get to knock on the door, but he had his hand raised the second time and his knuckles sticking up, and out come the children on him, hollering "Boo!" and waving their arms up and down the way it would scare you to death, or it ought to, if you wasn't ready for them.

We heard them charge out, but we thought it was just a nigger that was going by for them to scare, if we thought anything.

Plez says—allowing for all human mistakes—he seen on one side of King come rolling out Lucius Randall all dressed up, and on the other side, Eugene Hudson all dressed up. Could I have forgotten to speak of their being on skates? Oh, that was all afternoon. They're real good skaters, the little fellows, not to have a sidewalk. They sailed out the door and circled around their father, flying their arms and making their fingers go scarey, and those little Buster Brown bobs going in a circle.

Lucius Randall, Plez said, had on something pink, and he did, the basted flannelette teddy-bears we had tried on on top of his clothes and he got away. And said Eugene was a Chinaman, and that was what he was. It would be hard to tell which would come at you the more outrageous of the two, but to me it would be Lucius Randall with the girl's face and the big white cotton gloves falling off his fingers, and oh! he had on *my hat*. This one I milk in.

And they made a tremendous uproar with their skates, Plez said, and that was no mistake, because I remember what a hard time Snowdie and me had hearing what each other had to say all afternoon.

Plez said King stood it a minute—he got to turning around too. They were skating around him and saying in high birdie voices, "How do you do, Mister Booger?" You know if children *can* be monkeys, they're going to be them. (Without the masks, though, those two children would have been more polite about it—there's enough Hudson in them.) Skating around and around their papa, and just as ignorant! Poor little fellows. After all, they'd had nobody to scare all day for Hallowe'en, except one or two niggers that went by, and the Y. & M. V. train whistling through at two-fifteen, they scared that.

But monkeys—! Skating around their papa. Plez said if those children had been black, he wouldn't hesitate to say they would remind a soul of little nigger cannibals in the jungle. When they got their papa in their ring-around-a-rosy and he couldn't get out, Plez said it was enough to make an onlooker a little uneasy, and he called once or twice on the Lord. And after they went around high, they crouched down and went around low, about his knees.

The minute come, when King just couldn't get out quick enough. Only he had a hard time, and took him more than one try. He gathered himself together and King is a man of six foot height and weighs like a horse, but he was confused, I take it. But he got aloose and up and out like the Devil was after him—or in him—finally. Right up over the bannister and the ferns, and down the yard and over the ditch and gone. He plowed into the rough toward the Big Black, and the willows waved behind him, and where he run then, Plez don't know and I don't and don't nobody.

Plez said King passed right by him, that time, but didn't seem to know him, and the opportunity had gone by then to speak. And where he run then, nobody knows.

He should have wrote another note, instead of coming.

Well then, the children, I reckon, just held open-mouth behind him, and then something got to mounting up after it was all over, and scared them. They come back in the dining room. There were innocent ladies visiting with each other. The little boys had to scowl and frown and drag their skates over the carpet and follow us around the table where we was cutting out Eugene Hudson's underbody, and pull on our skirts till we saw.

"Well, speak," said their mother, and they told her a booger had come up on the front porch and when they went out to see him he said, "I'm going. You stay," so they chased him down the steps and run him off. "But he looked back like this!" Lucius Randall said, lifting off his mask and showing us on his little naked face with the round blue eyes. And

Eugene Hudson said the booger took a handful of pecans before he got through the gate.

And Snowdie dropped her scissors on the mahogany, and her hand just stayed in the air as still, and she looked at me, a look a minute long. And first she caught her apron to her and then started shedding it in the hall while she run to the door—so as not to be caught in it, I suppose, if anybody was still there. She run and the little glass prisms shook in the parlor —I don't remember another time, from *her*. She didn't stop at the door but run on through it and out on the porch, and she looked both ways and was running down the steps. And she run out in the yard and stood there holding to the tree, looking towards the country, but I could tell by the way her head held there wasn't nobody.

When I got to the steps—I didn't like to follow right away—there was nobody at all but old Plez, who was coming by raising his hat.

"Plez, did you see a gentleman come up on my porch just now?" I heard Snowdie call, and there was Plez, just ambling by with his hat raised, like he was just that minute passing, like we thought. And Plez, of course, he said, "No'm, Mistis, I don't recollect one soul pass me, whole way from town."

The little fellows held on to me, I could feel them tugging. And my little girl slept through it all, inside, and then woke up to swallow that button.

Outdoors the leaves was rustling, different from when I'd went in. It was coming on a rain. The day had a two-way look, like a day will at change of the year—clouds dark and the gold air still in the road, and the trees lighter than the sky was. And the oak leaves scuttling and scattering, blowing against old Plez and brushing on him, the old man.

"You're real positive, I guess, Plez?" asks Snowdie, and he answers comforting-like to her, "*You* wasn't looking for nobody to come today, was you?"

It was later on that Mrs. Stark got hold of Plez and

got the truth out of him, and I heard it after a while, through her church. But of course he wasn't going to let Miss Snowdie MacLain get hurt now, after we'd all watched her so long. So he fabricated.

After he'd gone by, Snowdie just stood there in the cool without a coat, with her face turned towards the country and her fingers pulling at little threads on her skirt and turning them loose in the wind, making little kind deeds of it, till I went and got her. She didn't cry.

"Course, could have been a ghost," Plez told Mrs. Stark, "but a ghost—I believe—if he had come to see the lady of the house, would have waited to have word with her."

And he said he had nary doubt in his mind, that it was Mr. King MacLain, starting home once more and thinking better of it. Miss Lizzie said to the church ladies, "I, for one, trust the Negro. I trust him the way you trust me, old Plez's mind has remained clear as a bell. I trust his story implicitly," she says, "because that's just what I *know* King MacLain'd do —run." And that's one time I feel in agreement about something with Miss Lizzie Stark, though she don't know about it, I guess.

And I live and hope *he* hit a stone and fell down running, before he got far off from here, and took the skin off his handsome nose, the devil.

And so that's why Snowdie comes to get her butter now, and won't let me bring it to her any longer. I think she kind of holds it against me, because I was there that day when he come; and she don't like my baby any more.

And you know, Fate says maybe King did know it was Hallowe'en. Do you think he'd go that far for a prank? And his own come back to him? Fate's usually more down to earth than that.

With men like King, your thoughts are bottomless. He was going like the wind, Plez swore to Miss Lizzie

Stark; though he couldn't swear to the direction—so he changed and said.

But I bet my little Jersey calf King tarried long enough to get him a child somewhere.

What makes me say a thing like that? I wouldn't say it to my husband, you mind you forget it.

2.

JUNE RECITAL

Loch was in a tempest with his mother. She would keep him in bed and make him take Cocoa-Quinine all summer, if she had her way. He yelled and let her wait holding the brimming spoon, his eyes taking in the whole ironclad pattern, the checkerboard of her apron—until he gave out of breath, and took the swallow. His mother laid her hand on his pompadour cap, wobbled his scalp instead of kissing him, and went off to her nap.

"Louella!" he called faintly, hoping she would come upstairs and he could devil her into running to Loomis's and buying him an ice cream cone out of her pocket, but he heard her righteously bang a pot to him in the kitchen. At last he sighed, stretched his toes—so clean he despised the very sight of his feet —and brought himself up on his elbow to the window.

Next door was the vacant house.

His family would all be glad if it burned down; he wrapped it with the summer's love. Beyond the hackberry leaves of their own tree and the cedar row and the spready yard over there, it stretched its weathered side. He let his eyes rest or go flickering along it, as over something very well known indeed. Its left-alone contour, its careless stretching away into that deep backyard he knew by heart. The house's side was like a person's, if a person or giant would lie sleeping there, always sleeping.

A red and bottle-shaped chimney held up all. The roof spread falling to the front, the porch came around the side leaning on the curve, where it hung with bannisters gone, like a cliff in a serial at the Bijou. Instead of cowboys in danger, Miss Jefferson Moody's chickens wandered over there from across the way, flapped over the edge, and found the shade cooler, the dust fluffier to sit in, and the worms thicker under that blackening floor.

In the side of the house were six windows, two upstairs and four down, and back of the chimney a small stair window shaped like a keyhole—one made never to open; they had one like it. There were green shades rolled up to various levels, but not curtains. A table showed in the dining room, but no chairs. The parlor window was in the shadow of the porch and of thin, vibrant bamboo leaves, clear and dark as a pool he knew in the river. There was a piano in the parlor. In addition there were little fancy chairs, like Sunday School chairs or children's drug store chairs, turned this way and that, and the first strong person trying to sit down would break them one after the other. Instead of a door into the hall there was a curtain; it was made of beads. With no air the curtain hung still as a wall and yet you could see through it, if anybody should pass the door.

In that window across from his window, in the back upper room, a bed faced his. The foot was gone, and a mattress had partly slid down but was holding on. A shadow from a tree, a branch and its leaves, slowly traveled over the hills and hollows of the mattress.

In the front room there, the window was dazzling in afternoon; it was raised. Except for one tall post with a hat on it, that bed was out of sight. It was true, there was one person in the house—Loch would recall him sooner or later—but it was only Mr. Holifield. He was the night watchman down at the gin, he always slept all day. A framed picture could

be seen hanging on the wall, just askew enough so
that it looked straightened every now and then.
Sometimes the glass in the picture reflected the light
outdoors and the flight of birds between branches
of trees, and while it reflected, Mr. Holifield was
having a dream.

Loch could look across through cedars that missed
one, in the line, and in a sweeping glance see it all
—as if he possessed it—from its front porch to its
shedlike back and its black-shadowed summerhouse
—which was an entirely different love, odorous of
black leaves that crumbled into soot; and its shade
of four fig trees where he would steal the figs if July
ever came. And above all the shade, which was dark
as a boat, the blue sky flared—shooting out like a
battle, and hot as fire. The hay riders his sister went
with at night (went with against their father's will,
slipped out by their mother's connivance) would ride
off singing, "Oh, It Ain't Gonna Rain No More."
Even under his shut eyelids, that light and shade
stayed divided from each other, but reversed.

Some whole days at a time, often in his dreams
day and night, he would seem to be living next door,
wild as a cowboy, absolutely by himself, without his
mother or father coming in to feel his skin, or run a
finger up under his cap—without one parent to turn
on the fan and the other to turn it off, or them both
together to pin a newspaper around the light at night
to shade him out of their talk. And there was where
Cassie could never bring him books to read, miserable
girls' books and fairy tales.

It was the leaky gutter over there that woke Loch
up, back in the spring when it rained. Splashy as a
waterfall in a forest, it shook him with that agony of
being *made* to wake up from a sound sleep to be
taken away somewhere, made to go. It made his heart
beat fast.

They could do what they wanted to to him but
they could not take his pompadour cap off him or

take his house away. He reached down under the
bed and pulled up the telescope.

It was his father's telescope and he was allowed to
look through it unmolested as long as he ran a temperature. It was what they gave him instead of his
nigger-shooter and cap pistol. Smelling of brass and
the drawer of the library table where it came from, it
was an object hitherto brought out in the family
group for eclipses of the moon; and the day the air-
plane flew over with a lady in it, and they all waited
for it all day, wry and aching up at the sky, the telescope had been gripped in his father's hand like a
big stick, some kind of protective weapon for what
was to come.

Loch fixed the long brass tubes and shot the telescope out the window, propping the screen outward
and letting more mosquitoes in, the way he was forbidden. He examined the size of the distant figs:
like marbles yesterday, wine-balls today. Getting
those would not be the same as stealing. On the other
side of fury at confinement a sweet self-indulgence
could visit him in his bed. He moved the glass lov-
ingly toward the house and touched its roof, with the
little birds on it cocking their heads.

With the telescope to his eye he even smelled the
house strongly. Morgana was extra deep in smell this
afternoon; the magnolias were open all over the
tree at the last corner. They glittered like lights in the
dense tree that loomed in the shape of a cave opening at the brought-up-close edge of the Carmichael
roof. He looked at the thrush's nest, Woodrow
Spights' old ball on the roof, the drift of faded election handbills on the porch—the vacant house again,
the half of a china plate deep in the weeds; the chickens always went to that plate, and it was dry.

Loch trained the telescope to the back and caught
the sailor and the girl in the moment they jumped
the ditch. They always came the back way, swinging

hands and running low under the leaves. The girl
was the piano player at the picture show. Today she
was carrying a paper sack from Mr. Wiley Bowles'
grocery.

Loch squinted; he was waiting for the day when
the sailor took the figs. And see what the girl would
hurry him into. Her name was Virgie Rainey. She
had been in Cassie's room all the way through
school, so that made her sixteen; she would ruin any
nice idea. She looked like a tomboy but it was not
the truth. She had let the sailor pick her up and carry
her one day, with her fingers lifting to brush the
leaves. It was she that had showed the sailor the
house to begin with, she that started him coming.
They were rusty old fig trees but the figs were the
little sweet blue. When they cracked open their pink
and golden flesh would show, their inside flowers,
and golden bubbles of juice would hang, to touch
your tongue to first. Loch gave the sailor time, for
it was he, Loch, who was in command of leniency
here; he was giving him day after day.

He swayed on his knees and saw the sailor and
Virgie Rainey in a clear blue-and-white small world
run sparkling to the back door of the empty house.

And next would come the old man going by in
the blue wagon, up as far as the Starks' and back to
the Carmichaels' corner.

> "Milk, milk,
> Buttermilk.
> Fresh dewberries and—
> Buttermilk."

That was Mr. Fate Rainey and his song. He would
take a long time to pass. Loch could study through
the telescope the new flower in his horse's hat each
day. He would go past the Starks' and circle the cemetery and niggertown, and come back again. His cry,
with a song's tune, would come near, then far, and
near again. Was it an echo—was an echo that? Or
was it, for the last time, the call of somebody seek-

ing about in a deep cave, "Here—here! Oh, here am I!"

There was a sound that might have been a blue jay scolding, and that was the back door; they were just now going in off the back porch. When he saw the door prized open—the stretched screen billowing from being too freely leaned against—and let the people in, Loch felt the old indignation rise up. But at the same time he felt joy. For while the invaders did not see him, he saw them, both with the naked eye and through the telescope; and each day that he kept them to himself, they were his.

Louella appeared below on their steps and with a splash threw out the dirty dish water in the direction of the empty house. But she would never speak, and he would never speak. He had not shared anybody in his life even with Louella.

After the door fell to at the sailor's heel, and the upstairs window had been forced up and propped, then silence closed over the house next door. It closed over just as silence did in their house at this time of day; but like the noisy waterfall it kept him awake—fighting sleep.

In the beginning, before he saw anyone, he would just as soon have lain there and thought of wild men holding his house in thrall, or of a giant crouched double behind the window that corresponded to his own. The big fig tree was many times a magic tree with golden fruit that shone in and among its branches like a cloud of lightning bugs— a tree twinkling all over, burning, on and off, off and on. The sweet golden juice to come—in his dream he put his tongue out, and then his mother would be putting that spoon in his mouth.

More than once he dreamed it was inside that house that the cave had moved, and the buttermilk man went in and out the rooms driving his horse with its red rose and berating its side with a whip that unfurled of itself; in the dream he was not singing. Or the horse itself, a white and beautiful one,

was on its way over, approaching to ask some
favor of him, a request called softly and intelligibly
upward—which he was not decided yet whether to
grant or deny. This call through the window had not
yet happened—not quite. But someone had come.

He turned away. "Cassie!" he cried.

Cassie came to his room. She said, "Didn't I tell
you what you could do? Trim up those Octagon
Soap coupons and count them good if you want that
jack-knife." Then she went off again and slammed
her door. He seemed to see her belatedly. She had
been dressed up for whatever she was doing in her
room like somebody in the circus, with colored spots
on her, and hardly looked like his sister.

"You looked silly when you came in!" he called.

But over at the empty house was a stillness not of
going off and leaving him but of coming nearer.
Something was coming very close to him, there
was something he had better keep track of. He had
the feeling that something was being counted. Then
he too must count. He could be wary enough that
way, counting by ones, counting by fives, by tens.
Sometimes he threw his arm across his eyes and
counted without moving his lips, imagining that
when he got to a certain amount he might give a
yell, like "Coming, ready or not!" and go down by
the hackberry limb. He never had yelled, and his
arm was a heavy weight across his face. Often that
was the way he fell asleep. He woke up drenched
with the afternoon fever breaking. Then his mother
pulled him and pushed him as she put cool pillow
cases on the pillows and pushed him back straight.
She was doing it now.

"Now your powder."

His mother, dressed up for a party, tilted the little
pinked paper toward his stuck-out, protesting
tongue, and guided the glass of water into his grop-
ing hand. Every time he got a powder swallowed,
she said calmly, "Dr. Loomis only gives you these
to satisfy me you're getting medication." His father,

when he came home from the office, would say,
"Well, if you've got malaria, son . . ." (kissing him)
". . . you've got malaria, that's all there is to it. Ha!
Ha! Ha!"

"I've made you some junket, too," she said with a
straight face.

He made a noise calculated to sicken her, and she
smiled at him.

"When I come back from Miss Nell Carlisle's I'll
bring you all the news of Morgana."

He could not help but smile at her—lips shut.
She was almost his ally. She swung her little reticule
at him and went off to the Rook party. By leaning
far out he could see a lackadaisical, fluttery kind of
parade, the ladies of Morgana under their parasols,
all trying to keep cool while they walked down to
Miss Nell's. His mother was absorbed into their
floating, transparent colors. Miss Perdita Mayo was
talking, and they were clicking their summery heels
and drowning out—drowning out something. . . .

A little tune was playing on the air, and it was
coming from the piano in the vacant house.

The tune came again, like a touch from a small
hand that he had unwittingly pushed away. Loch
lay back and let it persist. All at once tears rolled
out of his eyes. He opened his mouth in astonish-
ment. Then the little tune seemed the only thing in
the whole day, the whole summer, the whole season
of his fevers and chills, that was accountable: it was
personal. But he could not tell why it was so.

It came like a signal, or a greeting—the kind of
thing a horn would play out in the woods. He halfway closed his eyes. It came and trailed off and was
lost in the neighborhood air. He heard it and then
wondered how it went.

It took him back to when his sister was so sweet,
to a long time ago. To when they loved each other
in a different world, a boundless, trustful country all
its own, where no mother or father came, either

through sweetness or impatience—different altogether from his solitary world now, where he looked out all eyes like Argus, on guard everywhere.

A spoon went against a dish, three times. In her own room Cassie was carrying on some girls' business that, at least, smelled terrible to him, as bad as when she painted a hair-receiver with rosebuds and caught it on fire drying it. He heard Louella talking to herself in the lower hall. "Louella!" he called, flat on his back, and she called up for him to favor her with some rest or she would give up the ghost right then. When he drew up to the window again, the first thing he saw was someone new, coming along the walk out front.

Here came an old lady. No, she was an old woman, round and unsteady-looking—unsteady the way he felt himself when he got out of bed—not on her way to a party. She must have walked in from out in the country. He saw her stop in front of the vacant house, turn herself, and go up the front walk.

Something besides countriness gave her her look. Maybe it came from her having nothing in her hands, no reticule or fan. She looked as if she could even be the one who lived in the house and had just stepped outside for a moment to see if it was going to rain and now, matter-of-factly, a little toilsomely with so much to do, was going back in.

But when she began to hasten, Loch got the idea she might be the sailor's mother come after her son. The sailor didn't belong in Morgana anyhow. Whoever she was, she climbed the steps and crossed the wobbly porch and put her hand to the front door, which she opened just as easily as Virgie Rainey had opened the back door. She went inside, and he saw her through the beady curtain, which made her outline quiver for a moment.

Suppose doors with locks and keys were ever locked—then nothing like this would have the chance to happen. The nearness of missing things, and the possibility of preventing them, made Loch narrow his eyes.

Three party ladies who were late and puffing, all hurrying together in a duck-like line, now passed. They just missed sight of the old woman—Miss Jefferson Moody, Miss Mamie Carmichael, and Miss Billy Texas Spights. They would have stopped everything. Then in the middle of the empty air behind everybody, butterflies suddenly crossed and circled each other, their wings digging and flashing like duelers' swords in the vacuum.

Though Loch was gratified with the outrage mounting—three people now were in the vacant house—and could consider whether the old woman might have come to rout out the other two and give them her tirade, he was puzzled when the chandelier lighted up in the parlor. He ran the telescope out the window again and put his frowning eye to it. He discovered the old woman moving from point to point all around the parlor, in and out of the little chairs, sidling along the piano. He could not see her feet; she behaved a little like a wind-up toy on wheels, rolling into the corners and edges of objects and being diverted and sent on, but never out of the parlor.

He moved his eye upstairs, up an inch on the telescope. There on a mattress delightfully bare—where he would love, himself, to lie, on a slant and naked, to let the little cottony tufts annoy him and to feel the mattress like billows bouncing beneath, and to eat pickles lying on his back—the sailor and the piano player lay and ate pickles out of an open sack between them. Because of the down-tilt of the mattress, the girl had to keep watch on the sack, and when it began to slide down out of reach that was when they laughed. Sometimes they held pickles stuck in their mouths like cigars, and turned to look at each other. Sometimes they lay just alike, their legs in an M and their hands joined between them, exactly like the paper dolls his sister used to

cut out of folded newspaper and unfold to let him
see. If Cassie would come in now, he would point
out the window and she would remember.

And then, like the paper dolls sprung back
together, they folded close—the real people. Like a
big grasshopper lighting, all their legs and arms drew
in to one small body, deadlike, with protective color-
ing.

He leaned back and bent his head against the
cool side of the pillow and shut his eyes, and felt
tired out. He clasped the cool telescope to his side,
and with his fingernail closed its little eye.

"Poor old Telescope," he said.

When he looked out again, everybody next door
was busier.

Upstairs, the sailor and Virgie Rainey were running
in circles around the room, each time jumping with
outstretched arms over the broken bed. Who chased
whom had nothing to do with it because they kept
the same distance between them. They went around
and around like the policeman and Charlie Chaplin,
both intending to fall down.

Downstairs, the sailor's mother was doing something just as fanciful. She was putting up decorations. (Cassie would be happy to see that.) As if she
were giving a party that day, she was dressing up
the parlor with ribbons of white stuff. It was newspaper.

The old woman left the parlor time and time again
and reappeared—in and out through the beads in
the doorway—each time with an armful of old
Bugles that had lain on the back porch in people's
way for a long time. And from her gestures of eating
crumbs or pulling bits of fluff from her bosom, Loch
recognized that mother-habit: she had pins there.
She pinned long strips of the newspaper together,
first tearing them carefully and evenly as a school
teacher. She made ribbons of newspaper and was
hanging them all over the parlor, starting with the

piano where she weighted down the ends with a
statue.

When Loch grew tired of watching one animated
room he watched the other. How the two playing
would whirl and jump over the old woman's head!
That was the way the bed fell to begin with.

As Loch leaned his chin in his palm at the window
and watched, it seemed strangely as if he had seen
this whole thing before. The old woman was dec-
orating the piano until it rayed out like a Christmas
tree or a Maypole. Maypole ribbons of newspaper
and tissue paper streamed and crossed each other
from the piano to the chandelier and festooned again
to the four corners of the room, looped to the backs
of chairs here and there. When would things begin?

Soon everything seemed fanciful and beautiful
enough to Loch; he thought she could stop. But the
old woman kept on. This was only a part of something in her head. And in the splendor she fixed and
pinned together she was all alone. She was not con-
nected with anything else, with anybody. She was
one old woman in a house not bent on dealing punishment. Though once when Woody Spights and his
sister came by on skates, of course she came out
and ran them away.

Once she left the house, to come right back. With
her unsteady but purposeful walk, as if she were on
a wheel that misguided her, she crossed the road to
the Carmichael yard and came back with some green
leaves and one bloom from the magnolia tree—carried in her skirt. She pulled the corners of her skirt
up like a girl, and she was thin beneath in her old
legs. But she zigzagged across the road—such a
show-off, carefree way for a mother to behave, but
mothers sometimes did. She lifted her elbows—as if
she might skip! But nobody saw her: his forehead
was damp. He heard a scream from the Rook party
up at Miss Nell's—it sounded like Miss Jefferson
Moody shooting-the-moon. Nobody saw the old
woman but Loch, and he told nothing.

She brought the bunch of green into the parlor and put it on the piano, where the Maypole crown would go. Then she took a step back and was as admiring as if somebody else had done it—nodding her head.

But after she had the room all decorated to suit her, she kept on, and began to stuff the cracks. She brought in more paper and put it in all the cracks at the windows. Now Loch realized that the windows in the parlor were both down, it was tight as a box, and she had been inside in the suffocating heat. A wave of hotness passed over his body. Furthermore, she made her way with a load of *Bugles* to the blind part of the wall where he knew the fireplace was. All the load went into the fireplace.

When she went out of the parlor again she came back slowly indeed. She was pushing a big square of matting along on its side; she wove and bent and struggled behind it, like a spider with something bigger than he can eat, pushing it into the parlor. Loch was suddenly short of breath and pressed forward, cramped inside, checkerboarding his forehead and nose against the screen. He both wanted the plot to work and wanted it to fail. In another moment he was shed of all the outrage and the possessiveness he had felt for the vacant house. This house was something the old woman intended to burn down. And Loch could think of a thousand ways she could do it better.

She could fetch a mattress—that would burn fine. Suppose she went upstairs now for the one they played on? Or pulled the other one, sheet and all, from under Mr. Holifield (whose hat had imperceptibly turned on the bedpost; it changed like a weathercock)? If she went out of sight for a minute, he watched at the little stair window, but she did not go up.

She brought in an old quilt that the dogs there once slept on, that had hung over the line on the back porch until it was half light-colored and half dark. She climbed up on the piano stool, the way women climb, death-defying, and hung the quilt over the front window. It fell down. Twice more she climbed up with it and the third time it stayed. If only she did not block the window toward him! But if she meant to, she forgot. She kept putting her hand to her head.

Everything she did was wrong, after a certain point. She had got off the track. What she really wanted was a draft. Instead, she was keeping air away, and let her try to make fire burn in an airless room. That was the conceited thing girls and women would try.

But now she went to the blind corner of the parlor and when she came out she had a new and mysterious object in her hands.

At that moment Loch heard Louella climbing the back stairs, coming to peep in at him. He flung himself on his back, stretched out one arm, his hand on his heart and his mouth agape, as he did when he played dead in battle. He forgot to shut his eyes. Louella stood there a minute and then tiptoed off.

Loch then leapt to his knees, crawled out the window under the pushed-out screen, onto the hackberry branch, and let himself into the tree the old way.

He went out on a far-extending limb that took him nearest the vacant house. With him at their window the sailor and girl saw him and yet did not see him. He descended further. He found his place in the tree, a rustling, familiar old crotch where he used to sit and count up his bottle tops. He hung watching, sometimes by the hands and sometimes by the knees and feet.

The old woman was dirty. Standing still she shook a little—her hanging cheeks and her hands. He could see well now what she was holding there like a lamp. But he could not tell what it was—a small brown wooden box, shaped like the Obelisk. It had a door—she opened it. It made a mechanical sound. He heard it plainly through the boxed room which was like a sounding board; it was ticking.

She set the obelisk up on the piano, there in the crown of leaves; she pushed a statue out of the way. He listened to it ticking on and his hopes suddenly rose for her. Holding by the knees and diving head down, then swaying in the sweet open free air and dizzy as an apple on a tree, he thought: the box is where she has the dynamite.

He opened his arms and let them hang outward, and flickered his lashes in the June light, watching house, sky, leaves, a flying bird, all and nothing at all.

Little Sister Spights, aged two, that he had not seen cross the street since she was born, wandered under him dragging a skate.

"Hello, little bitty old sweet thing," he murmured from the leaves. "Better go back where you came from."

And then the old woman stuck out a finger and played the tune.

He hung still as a folded bat.

II.

Für Elise.

In her bedroom when she heard the gentle opening, the little phrase, Cassie looked up from what she was doing and said in response, "Virgie Rainey, *danke schoen.*"

In surprise, but as slowly as in regret, she stopped stirring the emerald green. She got up from where she had been squatting in the middle of the floor and stepped over the dishes which were set about on the matting rug. She went quietly to her south window, where she lifted a curtain, spotting it with her wet fingers. There was not a soul in sight at the MacLain house but Old Man Holifield asleep with his gawky hightop shoes on and his stomach full as a robin's. His presence—he was the Holifield who was night watchman at the gin and slept here by day— never kept Cassie's mother from going right ahead and calling the MacLain house "the vacant house."

Whatever you called it, the house was something you saw without seeing it—it was part of the world again. That unpainted side changed passively with the day and the season, the way a natural place like the river bank changed. In cooler weather its windows would turn like sweetgum leaves, maroon when the late sun came up, and in winter it was bare and glinty, more exposed and more lonesome even than now. In summer it was an overgrown place. Leaves and their shadows pressed up to it, arc-light sharp and still as noon all day. It showed at all times that no woman kept it.

That rainless, windless June the bright air and the town of Morgana, life itself, sunlit and moonlit, were composed and still and china-like. Cassie felt that now. Yet in the shade of the vacant house, though all looked still, there was agitation. Some life stirred through. It may have been *old* life.

Ever since the MacLains had moved away, that roof had stood (and leaked) over the heads of people who did not really stay, and a restless current seemed to flow dark and free around it (there would be some sound or motion to startle the birds), a life quicker than the Morrisons' life, more driven probably, thought Cassie uneasily.

Was it Virgie Rainey in there now? Where was she hiding, if she sneaked in and touched that piano? When did she come? Cassie felt teased. She doubted for a moment that she had heard *Für Elise*—she doubted herself, so easily, and she struck her chest with her fist, sighing, the way Parnell Moody always struck hers.

A line of poetry tumbled in her ears, or started to tumble.

"Though I am old with wandering . . ."

She banged her hands on her hipbones, enough to hurt, flung around, and went back to her own business. On one bare foot with the other crossed over it, she stood gazing down at the pots and dishes in which she had enough colors stirred up to make a sunburst design. She was shut up in here to tie-and-dye a scarf. "Everybody stay out!!!" said an envelope pinned to her door, signed with skull and crossbones.

You took a square of crepe de Chine, you made a point of the goods and tied a string around it in hard knots. You kept on gathering it in and tying it. Then you hung it in the different dyes. The strings were supposed to leave white lines in the colors, a design like a spiderweb. You couldn't possibly have any idea what you would get when you untied your scarf; but Missie Spights said there had never been one yet that didn't take the breath away.

Für Elise. This time there were two phrases, the *E* in the second phrase very flat.

Cassie edged back to the window, while her heart sank, praying that she would not catch sight of Virgie Rainey or, especially, that Virgie Rainey would not catch sight of her.

Virgie Rainey worked. Not at teaching. She played the piano for the picture show, both shows every night, and got six dollars a week, and was not popular any more. Even in her last year in consolidated high school—just ended—she worked. But when Cassie and she were little, they used to take music together in the MacLain house next door, from Miss Eckhart. Virgie Rainey played *Für Elise* all the time. And Miss Eckhart used to say, "Virgie Rainey, *danke schoen.*" Where had Miss Eckhart ever gone? She had been Miss Snowdie MacLain's roomer.

"Cassie!" Loch was calling again.

"What!"

"Come here!"

"I can't!"

"Got something to show you!"

"I ain't got time!"

Her bedroom door had been closed all afternoon. But first her mother had opened it and come in, only to exclaim and not let herself be touched, and to go out leaving the smell of rose geranium behind for the fan to keep bringing at her. Then Louella had moved right in on her without asking and for ages was standing over her rolling up her hair on newspaper to make it bushy for the hayride that night. *"I cares if you don't."*

With her gaze at a judicious distance from the colors she dipped in, Cassie was now for a little time far away, perhaps up in September in college, where, however, tie-and-dye scarves would be out-of-uniform, though something to unfold and show.

But with *Für Elise* the third time, her uncritical self of the crucial present, this Wednesday afternoon, slowly came forward—as if called on. Cassie saw herself without even facing the mirror, for her small, solemn, unprotected figure was emerging staring-clear inside her mind. There she was now, standing scared at the window again in her petticoat, a little of each color of the rainbow dropped on her —bodice and flounce—in spite of reasonable care. Her pale hair was covered and burdened with twisty papers, like a hat too big for her. She balanced her head on her frail neck. She was holding a spoon up like a mean switch in her right hand, and her feet were bare. She had seemed to be favored and happy and she stood there pathetic—homeless-looking— horrible. Like a wave, the gathering past came right up to her. Next time it would be too high. The poetry was all around her, pellucid and lifting from side to side,

> *"Though I am old with wandering*
> *Through hollow lands and hilly lands,*
> *I will find out where she has gone . . ."*

Then the wave moved up, towered, and came drowning down over her stuck-up head.

Through the years Cassie had come just before Virgie Rainey for her music lesson, or, at intervals, just after her. To start with, Cassie was so poor in music and Virgie so good (the opposite of themselves in other things!) that Miss Eckhart with her methodical mind might have coupled them on purpose. They went on Mondays and Thursdays at 3:30 and 4:00 and after school was out and up until the recital, at 9:30 and 10:00 in the morning. So punctual and so formidable was Miss Eckhart that all the little girls passed, one going and one coming, through the beaded curtains mincing like strangers. Only Virgie would let go the lights of mockery from her eyes.

Though she was tireless as a spider, Miss Eckhart waited so unbudgingly for her pupils that from the back she appeared asleep in her studio. How much later had it occurred to Cassie that "the studio" itself, the only one ever heard of in Morgana, was nothing more than a room that was rented? Rented because poor Miss Snowdie MacLain needed the money?

Then it seemed a dedicated place. The black-painted floor was bare even of matting, so as not to deaden any sound of music. There was in the very center a dark squarish piano (ebony, they all thought) with legs twisted like elephant legs, bearing many pounds of sheet music on its back—just to look heavy there, Cassie thought, for whose music was it? The yellow keys, some split and others in the bass coffee-colored, always had a little film of sweat. There was a stool spun up high, with a seat worn away like a bowl. Beside it, Miss Eckhart's chair was the kind of old thing most people placed by their telephones.

There were gold chairs, their legs brittle and set the way pulled candy was, sliding across the floor at a touch, and forbidden—they were for the recital audience; their fragility was intentional. There were taboret tables with little pink statuettes and hydrangea-colored, horny shells. Beaded curtains in the doorway stirred and clicked now and then during a lesson, as if someone were coming, but it signified no more than the idle clicking redbirds made in the free outdoors, if it was not time for a pupil. (The MacLains lived largely upstairs, except for the kitchen, and came in at the side.) The beads were faintly sweet-smelling, and made you think of long strings of wine-balls and tiny candy bottles filled with violet liquid, and licorice sticks. The studio was in some ways like the witch's house in *Hansel and Gretel*, Cassie's mother said, "including the witch." On the right-hand corner of the piano stood a small, mint-white bust of Beethoven, all softened around the edges with the nose smoothed down, as if a cow had licked it.

Miss Eckhart, a heavy brunette woman whose age was not known, sat during the lessons on the non-descript chair, which her body hid altogether, in apparent disregard for body and chair alike. She was alternately very quiet and very alert, and sometimes that seemed to be because she hated flies. She held a swatter in her down-inclined lap, gracefully and tenderly as a fan, her hard, round, short fingers surprisingly forgetful-looking. All at once as you played your piece, making errors or going perfectly it did not matter, smack down would come the fly swatter on the back of your hand. No words would be passed, of triumph or apology on Miss Eckhart's part or of surprise or pain on yours. It did hurt. Virgie, her face hardening under the progress of her advancing piece, could manage the most oblivious look of all, though Miss Eckhart might strike harder and harder at the persistent flies. All her pupils let the flies in, when they trailed in and out for their lessons; not to speak of the MacLain boys, who left their door wide open to the universe when they went out to play.

Miss Eckhart might also go abruptly to her little built-on kitchen—she and her mother had no Negro and didn't use Miss Snowdie's; she did not say "Ex-

cuse me," or explain what was on the stove. And
there were times, perhaps on rainy days, when she
walked around and around the studio, and you
felt her pause behind you. Just as you thought she
had forgotten you, she would lean over your head,
you were under her bosom like a traveler under a
cliff, her penciled finger would go to your music, and
above the bar you were playing she would slowly
write "Slow." Or sometimes, precipitant above you,
she would make a curly circle with a long tail, as if
she might draw a cat, but it would be her "P" and the
word would turn into "Practice!!"

When you could once play a piece, she paid scant
attention, and made no remark; her manners were all
very unfamiliar. It was only time for a new piece.
Whenever she opened the cabinet, the smell of new
sheet music came out swift as an imprisoned spirit,
something almost palpable, like a pet coon; Miss
Eckhart kept the music locked up and the key down
her dress, inside the collar. She would seat herself
and with a dipped pen add "$.25" to the bill on the
spot. Cassie could see the bills clearly, in elaborate
handwriting, the "z" in Mozart with an equals-sign
through it and all the "y's" so heavily tailed they
went through the paper. It took a whole lesson for
those tails to dry.

What was it she did when you played without a
mistake? Oh, she went over and told the canary
something, tapping the bars of his cage with her finger. "Just listen," she told him. "Enough from *you* for
today," she would call to you over her shoulder.

Virgie Rainey would come through the beads
carrying a magnolia bloom which she had stolen.

She would ride over on a boy's bicycle (her
brother Victor's) from the Raineys' with sheets of
advanced music rolled naked (girls usually had port-
folios) and strapped to the boy's bar which she strad-
dled, the magnolia broken out of the Carmichaels'
tree and laid bruising in the wire basket on the han-

dlebars. Or sometimes Virgie would come an hour late, if she had to deliver the milk first, and sometimes she came by the back door and walked in peeling a ripe fig with her teeth; and sometimes she missed her lesson altogether. But whenever she came on the bicycle she would ride it up into the yard and run the front wheel bang into the lattice, while Cassie was playing the "Scarf Dance." (In those days, the house looked nice, with latticework and plants hiding the foundation, and a three-legged fern stand at the turn in the porch to discourage skaters and defeat little boys.) Miss Eckhart would put her hand to her breast, as though she felt the careless wheel shake the very foundation of the studio.

Virgie carried in the magnolia bloom like a hot tureen, and offered it to Miss Eckhart, neither of them knowing any better: magnolias smelled too sweet and heavy for right after breakfast. And Virgie handled everything with her finger stuck out; she was conceited over a musician's cyst that appeared on her fourth finger.

Miss Eckhart took the flower but Virgie might be kept waiting while Cassie recited on her catechism page. Sometimes Miss Eckhart checked the questions missed, sometimes the questions answered; but every question she did check got a heavy "V" that crossed the small page like the tail of a comet. She would draw her black brows together to see Cassie forgetting, unless it was to remember some nearly forgotten thing herself. At the exact moment of the hour (the alarm clock had a green and blue waterfall scene on its face) she would dismiss Cassie and incline her head toward Virgie, as though she was recognizing her only now, when she was ready for her; yet all this time she had held the strong magnolia flower in her hand, and its scent was filling the room.

Virgie would drift over to the piano, spread out her music, and make sure she was sitting just the way she wanted to be upon the stool. She flung her skirt behind her, with a double swimming motion.

Then without a word from Miss Eckhart she would start to play. She played firmly, smoothly, her face at rest, the musician's cyst, of which she was in idleness so proud, perched like a ladybug, riding the song. She went now gently, now forcibly, never loudly.

And when she was finished, Miss Eckhart would say, "Virgie Rainey, *danke schoen.*"

Cassie, so still her chest cramped, not daring to walk on the creaky floor down the hall, would wait till the end to run out of the house and home. She would whisper while she ran, with the sound of an engine, "*Danke schoen, danke schoen, danke schoen.*" It wasn't the meaning that propelled her; she didn't know then what it meant.

But then nobody knew for years (until the World War) what Miss Eckhart meant by "*Danke schoen*" and "*Mein liebes Kind*" and the rest, and who would dare ask? It was like belling the cat. Only Virgie had the nerve, only she could have found out for the others. Virgie said she did not know and did not care. So they just added that onto Virgie's name in the school yard. She was Virgie Rainey *Danke schoen* when she jumped hot pepper or fought the boys, when she had to sit down the very first one in the spelling match for saying "E-a-r, ear, r-a-k-e, rake, ear-ache." She was named for good. Sometimes even in the Bijou somebody cat-called that to her as she came in her high heels down the steep slant of the board aisle to switch on the light and open the piano. When she was grown she would tilt up her chin. Calm as a marble head, defamed with a spit-curl, Virgie's head would be proudly carried past the banner on the wall, past every word of "It's Cool at the Bijou, Enjoy Typhoons of Alaskan Breezes," which was tacked up under the fan. Rats ran under her feet, most likely, too; the Bijou was once Spights' Livery Stable.

"Virgie brings me good luck!" Miss Eckhart used to say, with a round smile on her face. Luck that

might not be good was something else that was a
new thought to them all.

Virgie Rainey, when she was ten or twelve, had
naturally curly hair, silky and dark, and a great deal
of it—uncombed. She was not sent to the barber
shop often enough to suit the mothers of other children, who said it was probably dirty hair too—what
could the children see of the back of her neck, poor
Katie Rainey being so rushed for time? Her middy
blouse was trimmed in a becoming red, her anchor
was always loose, and her red silk lacers were actually ladies' shoestrings dipped in pokeberry juice.
She was full of the airs of wildness, she swayed and
gave way to joys and tempers, her own and other
people's with equal freedom—except never Miss Eckhart's, of course.

School did not lessen Virgie's vitality; once on a
rainy day when recess was held in the basement
she said she was going to butt her brains out against
the wall, and the teacher, old Mrs. McGillicuddy,
had said, "Beat them out, then," and she had really
tried. The rest of the fourth grade stood around
expectant and admiring, the smell of open thermos
bottles sweetly heavy in the close air. Virgie came
with strange kinds of sandwiches—everybody
wanted to swap her—stewed peach, or perhaps banana. In the other children's eyes she was as exciting
as a gypsy would be.

Virgie's air of abandon that was so strangely en-
dearing made even the Sunday School class think of
her in terms of the future—she would go somewhere,
somewhere away off, they said then, talking with
their chins sunk in their hands—she'd be a mission-
ary. (Parnell Moody used to be wild and now *she*
was pious.) Miss Lizzie Stark's mother, old Mrs.
Sad-Talking Morgan, said Virgie would be the first
lady governor of Mississippi, that was where she
would go. It sounded worse than the infernal regions.
To Cassie, Virgie was a secret love, as well as her

secret hate. To Cassie she looked like an illustration by Reginald Birch for a serial in Etta Carmichael's *St. Nicholas Magazine* called "The Lucky Stone." Her inky hair fell in the same loose locks—because it was dirty. She often took the very pose of that inventive and persecuted little heroine who coped with people she thought were witches and ogres (alas! they were not)—feet apart, head aslant, eyes glancing up sideways, ears cocked; but you could not tell whether Virgie would boldly interrupt her enemies or run off to her own devices with a forgetful smile on her lips.

And she smelled of flavoring. She drank vanilla out of the bottle, she told them, and it didn't burn her a bit. She did that because she knew they called her mother Miss Ice Cream Rainey, for selling cones at speakings.

Für Elise was always Virgie Rainey's piece. For years Cassie thought Virgie wrote it, and Virgie never did deny it. It was a kind of signal that Virgie had burst in; she would strike that little opening phrase off the keys as she passed anybody's piano—even the one in the café. She never abandoned *Für Elise;* long after she went on to the hard pieces, she still played that.

Virgie Rainey was gifted. Everybody said that could not be denied. To show her it was not denied, she was allowed to play all through school for the other children to march in and to play for Wand Drill. Sometimes they drilled to "Dorothy, an Old English Dance," and sometimes to *Für Elise*—everybody out of kilter.

"I guess they scraped up the money for music lessons somehow," said Cassie's mother. Cassie, when she heard Virgie running her scales next door, would see a vision of the Rainey dining room—an interior which in life she had never seen, for she didn't go home from school with the Raineys—and sitting around the table Miss Katie Rainey and Old Man Fate Rainey and Berry and Bolivar Mayhew, some cousins, and Victor who was going to be killed in the war, and Virgie waiting; with Miss Katie scraping up nickels and pennies with an old bone-handled knife, patting them into shape like her butter, and each time—as the scale went up—just barely getting enough or—as it went down—not quite.

Cassie was Miss Eckhart's first pupil, the reason she "took" being that she lived right next door, but she never had any glory from it. When Virgie began "taking," she was the one who made things evident about Miss Eckhart, her lessons, and all. Miss Eckhart, for all her being so strict and inexorable, in spite of her walk, with no give whatsoever, had a timid spot in her soul. There was a little weak place in her, vulnerable, and Virgie Rainey found it and showed it to people.

Miss Eckhart worshiped her metronome. She kept it, like the most precious secret in the teaching of music, in a wall safe. Jinny Love Stark, who was only seven or eight years old but had her tongue, did suggest that this was the only thing Miss Eckhart owned of the correct size to lock up there. Why there had ever been a real safe built into the parlor nobody seemed to know; Cassie remembered Miss Snowdie saying the Lord knew, in His infinite workings and wisdom, and some day, somebody would come riding in to Morgana and have need of that safe, after she was gone.

Its door looked like a tin plate there in the wall, the closed-up end of an old flue. Miss Eckhart would go toward it with measured step. Technically the safe was hidden, of course, and only she knew it was there, since Miss Snowdie rented it; even Miss Eckhart's mother, possibly, had no expectations of getting in. Yes, her mother lived with her.

Cassie, out of nice feeling, looked the other way when it was time for the morning opening of the safe. It seemed awful, and yet imminent, that because she was the first pupil she, Cassie Morrison, might be the one to call logical attention to the absurdity of a safe in which there were no jewels, in which there was the very opposite of a jewel. Then Virgie, one day when the metronome was set going in front of her—Cassie was just leaving—announced simply that she would not play another note with that thing in her face.

At Virgie's words, Miss Eckhart quickly—it almost seemed that was what she'd wanted to hear—stopped the hand and slammed the little door, bang. The metronome was never set before Virgie again.

Of course all the rest of them still got it. It came out of the safe every morning, as regularly as the canary was uncovered in his cage. Miss Eckhart had made an exception of Virgie Rainey; she had first respected Virgie Rainey, and now fell humble before her impudence.

A metronome was an infernal machine, Cassie's mother said when Cassie told on Virgie. "Mercy, you have to keep moving, with that infernal machine. I want a song to *dip.*"

"What do you mean, dip? Could you have played the piano, Mama?"

"Child, I could have *sung,*" and she threw her hand from her, as though all music might as well now go jump off the bridge.

As time went on, Virgie Rainey showed her bad manners to Miss Eckhart still more, since she had won about the metronome. Once she had a little *Rondo* her way, and Miss Eckhart was so beset about it that the lesson was not like a real lesson at all. Once she unrolled the new *Étude* and when it kept rolling back up, as the *Étude* always did, she threw it on the floor and jumped on it, before Miss Eckhart had even seen it; that was heartless. After such showing off, Virgie would push her hair behind her ears and then softly lay her hands on the keys, as she would take up a doll.

Miss Eckhart would sit there blotting out her chair in the same way as ever, but inside her she was lis-

tening to every note. Such listening would have made
Cassie forget. And half the time, the piece was only
Für Elise, which Miss Eckhart could probably have
played blindfolded and standing up with her back
to the keys. Anybody could tell that Virgie was
doing something to Miss Eckhart. She was turning
her from a teacher into something lesser. And if she
was not a teacher, what was Miss Eckhart?

At times she could not bring herself to swat a summer fly. And as little as Virgie, of them all, cared if
her hand was rapped, Miss Eckhart would raise her
swatter and try to bring it down and could not. You
could see torment in her regard of the fly. The
smooth clear music would move on like water, beautiful and undisturbed, under the hanging swatter and
Miss Eckhart's red-rimmed thumb. But even boys hit
Virgie, because she liked to fight.

There were times when Miss Eckhart's Yankeeness,
if not her very origin, some last quality to fade, almost faded. Before some caprice of Virgie's, her
spirit drooped its head. The child had it by the lead.
Cassie saw Miss Eckhart's spirit as a terrifying gentle water-buffalo cow in the story of "Peasie and
Beansie" in the reader. And sooner or later, after
taming her teacher, Virgie was going to mistreat
her. Most of them expected some great scene.

There was in the house itself, soon, a daily occur-
rence to distress Miss Eckhart. There was now a second roomer at Miss Snowdie's. While Miss Eckhart
listened to a pupil, Mr. Voight would walk over
their heads and come down to the turn of the stairs,
open his bathrobe, and flap the skirts like an old turkey gobbler. They all knew Miss Snowdie never sus-
pected she housed a man like that: he was a sewing
machine salesman. When he flapped his maroon-
colored bathrobe, he wore no clothes at all underneath.

It would be plain to Miss Eckhart or to anybody
that he wanted, first, the music lesson to stop. They
could not close the door, there was no door, there

were beads. They could not tell Miss Snowdie even
that he objected; she would have been agonized. All
the little girls and the one little boy were afraid of
Mr. Voight's appearance at every lesson and felt
nervous until it had happened and got over with.
The one little boy was Scooter MacLain, the twin
that took the free lessons; he kept mum.

Cassie saw that Miss Eckhart, who might once
have been formidable in particular to any Mr.
Voights, was helpless toward him and his antics—as
helpless as Miss Snowdie MacLain would have been,
helpless as Miss Snowdie was, toward her own little
twin sons—all since she had begun giving in to Virgie Rainey. Virgie kept the upper hand over Miss
Eckhart even at the moment when Mr. Voight
came out to scare them. She only played on the stronger and clearer, and never pretended he had not
come out and that she did not know it, or that she
might not tell it, no matter how poor Miss Eckhart
begged.

"Tell a soul what you have seen, I'll beat your
hands until you scream," Miss Eckhart had said. Her
round eyes opened wide, her mouth went small. This
was all she knew to say. To Cassie it was as idle as a
magic warning in a story; she criticized the rhyme.
She herself had told all about Mr. Voight at breakfast, stood up at the table and waved her arms, only
to have her father say he didn't believe it; that Mr.
Voight represented a large concern and covered
seven states. He added his own threat to Miss Eckhart's: no picture show money.

Her mother's laugh, which followed, was as usual
soft and playful but not illuminating. Her laugh,
like the morning light that came in the window each
summer breakfast time around her father's long head,
slowly made it its solid silhouette where he sat
against the day. He turned to his paper like Douglas
Fairbanks opening big gates; it was indeed his; he
published the *Morgana-MacLain Weekly Bugle* and
Mr. Voight had no place in it.

"Live and let live, Cassie," her mother said, meaning it mischievously. She showed no repentance, such as Cassie felt, for her inconsistencies. She had sometimes said passionately, "Oh, I hate that old MacLain house next door to me! I hate having it there all the time. I'm worn out with Miss Snowdie's cross!" Later on, when Miss Snowdie finally had to sell the house and move away, her mother said, "Well, I see Snowdie gave up." When she told bad news, she wore a perfectly blank face and her voice was helpless and automatic, as if she repeated a lesson.

Virgie told on Mr. Voight too, but she had nobody to believe her, and so Miss Eckhart did not lose any pupils by that. Virgie did not know how to tell anything.

And for what Mr. Voight did there were no ready words—what would you call it? "Call it spontaneous combustion," Cassie's mother said. Some performances of people stayed partly untold for lack of a name, Cassie believed, as well as for lack of believers. Mr. Voight before so very long—it happened during a sojourn home of Mr. MacLain, she remembered— was transferred to travel another seven states ending the problem; and yet Mr. Voight had done something that amounted to more than going naked under his robe and calling alarm like a turkey gobbler, it was more belligerent; and the least describable thing of all had been a look on his face; that was strange. Thinking of it now, and here in her room, Cassie found she had bared her teeth and set them, trying out the frantic look. She could not now, any more than then, really describe Mr. Voight, but without thinking she could *be* Mr. Voight, which was more frightening still.

Like a dreamer dreaming with reservations, Cassie moved over and changed the color for her scarf and moved back to the window. She reached behind her for a square of heavenly-hash in its platter and bit down on the marshmallow.

There was another man Miss Eckhart had been

scared of, up until the last. (Not Mr. King MacLain. They always passed without touching, like two stars, perhaps they had some kind of eclipse-effect on each other.) She had been sweet on Mr. Hal Sissum, who clerked in the shoe department of Spights' store.

Cassie remembered him—who didn't know Mr. Sissum and all the Sissums? His sandy hair, parted on the side, shook over his ear like a toboggan cap when he ambled forward, in his long lazy step, to wait on people. He teased people that came to buy shoes, as though that took the prize for the vainest, most outlandish idea that could ever come over human beings.

Miss Eckhart had pretty ankles for a heavy lady like herself. Mrs. Stark said what a surprise it was for Miss Eckhart, of all people, to turn up with such pretty ankles, which made it the same as if she didn't have them. When she came in she took her seat and put her foot earnestly up on Mr. Sissum's stool like any other lady in Morgana and he spoke to her very nicely. He generally invited the bigger ladies, like Miss Nell Loomis or Miss Gert Bowles, to sit in the children's chair, but he held back, with Miss Eckhart, and spoke very nicely to her about her feet and treated them as a real concern; he even brought out a choice of shoes. To most ladies he brought out one box and said, "There's your shoe," as though shoes were something predestined. He knew them all so well.

Miss Eckhart might have come over to his aisle more often, but she had an incomprehensible habit of buying shoes two or even four pairs at a time, to save going back, or to take precaution against never finding them again. She didn't know how to do about Mr. Sissum at all.

But what could they either one have done? They couldn't go to church together; the Sissums were Presbyterians from the beginning of time and Miss Eckhart belonged to some distant church with a previously unheard-of name, the Lutheran. She could not

go to the picture show with Mr. Sissum because he
was already at the picture show. He played the
music there every evening after the store closed—
he had to; this was before the Bijou afforded a piano,
and he could play the cello. He could not have refused Mr. Syd Sissum who bought the stable and
built the Bijou.

Miss Eckhart used to come to the political speakings in the Starks' yard when Mr. Sissum played with
the visiting band. Anybody could see him all evening
then, high on the fresh plank platform behind his
cello. Miss Eckhart, the true musician, sat on the
damp night grass and listened. Nobody ever saw
them really together any more than that. How did
they know she was sweet on Mr. Sissum? But they
did.

Mr. Sissum was drowned in the Big Black River
one summer—fell out of his boat, all alone.

Cassie would rather remember the sweet soft
speaking-nights in the Starks' yard. Before the speakings began, while the music was playing, Virgie and
her older brother Victor ran wild all over everywhere, assaulting the crowd, where couples and
threes and fives of people joined hands like paperdoll
strings and wandered laughing and turning under
the blossoming China trees and the heavy crape
myrtles that were wound up in honeysuckle. How
delicious it all smelled! Virgie let herself go completely, as anyone would like to do. Jinny Love Stark's
swing was free to anybody and Virgie ran under the
swingers, or jumped on behind, booting and pumping. She ran under sweethearts' twining arms, and
nobody, even her brother, could catch her. She rolled
the country people's watermelons away. She caught
lightning bugs and tore out their lights for jewelry.
She never rested as long as the music played except
at last to throw herself hard and panting on the
ground, her open mouth smiling against the trampled
clover. Sometimes she made Victor climb up on the
Starks' statue. Cassie remembered him, white face

against dark leaves, a baseball cap turned backwards with the bill behind, and long black-stockinged legs wound over the snowy limbs of the goddess, and slowly, proudly sliding down.

But Virgie would not even watch him. She whirled in one direction till she fell down drunk, or turned about more slowly when they played *Vienna Woods*. She pushed Jinny Love Stark into her own lily bed. And all the time, she was eating. She ate all the ice cream she wanted. Now and then, in the soft parts of *Carmen* or before the storm in *William Tell* —even during dramatic pauses in the speaking— Mrs. Ice Cream Rainey's voice could be heard quickly calling, "Ice cream?" She had brought a freezer or two on Mr. Rainey's wagon to the foot of the yard. This time of year it might be fig. Sometimes Virgie whirled around with a fig ice cream cone in each hand, held poised like daggers.

Virgie would run closer and closer circles around Miss Eckhart who sat alone (her mother never came out that far) on a *Bugle*, all four pages unfolded on the grass, listening. Up above, Mr. Sissum—who bent over his cello in the Bijou every night like an old sewing woman over the machine, like a shoe clerk over another foot to fit—shone in a palm beach coat and played straightbacked in the visiting band, and as fast as they did. The lock of hair was no longer hiding his eyes and nose; like the candidate for supervisor, he looked out.

Virgie put a loop of clover chain down over Miss Eckhart's head, her hat—her one hat—and all. She hung Miss Eckhart with flowers, while Mr. Sissum plucked the strings up ·above her. Miss Eckhart sat on, perfectly still and submissive. She gave no sign. She let the clover chain come down and lie on her breast.

Virgie laughed delightedly and with her long chain in her hand ran around and around her, binding her up with clovers. Miss Eckhart let her head roll back,

and then Cassie felt that the teacher was filled with
terror, perhaps with pain. She found it so easy—ever
since Virgie showed her—to feel terror and pain in
an outsider; in someone you did not know at all well,
pain made you wonderfully sorry. It was not so easy
to be sorry about it in the people close to you—it
came unwillingly; and how strange—in yourself, on
nights like this, pain—even a moment's pain—
seemed inconceivable.

Cassie's whole family would be at the speakings,
of course, her father moving at large through the
crowd or sometimes sitting on the platform with Mr.
Carmichael and Mr. Comus Stark with the rolling
head and Mr. Spights. Cassie would try to stay in
sight of her mother, but no matter how slightly she
strayed, only to follow Virgie around the backyard
and find croquet balls in the grass, or down the hill
to get a free cone, when she got back to their place
her mother would be gone. She always lost her
mother. She would find Loch there, rolled in a ball
asleep in his sailor suit, his cheek holding down the
ribbon of her softly removed hat. When she was back
again, "I've just been through yonder to speak to
my candidate," she said. "It's you that vanishes, Lady
Bug, you that gets away."

It appeared to Cassie that only the figure of Miss
Eckhart, off there like a vast receptacle in its island
of space, did not move or sway when the band
played *Tales of Hoffmann*.

One time Mr. Sissum gave Miss Eckhart something,
a Billikin. The Billikin was a funny, ugly doll that
Spights' store gave free to children with every pair
of Billikin shoes. Never had Miss Eckhart laughed so
hard, and with such an unfamiliar sound, as she
laughed to see Mr. Sissum's favor. Tears ran down
her bright, distorted cheeks every time one of the
children coming into the studio picked the Billikin
up. When her laughter was exhausted she would sigh
faintly and ask for the doll, and then soberly set it

down on a little minaret table, as if it were a vase of fresh red roses. Her old mother took it one day and cracked it across her knee.

When Mr. Sissum was drowned, Miss Eckhart came to his funeral like everybody else. The Loomises invited her to ride with them. She looked exactly the same as ever, round and solid, her back a ramrod in her dress that was the wrong season's length and her same hat, the home-made one with cambric flowers sticking up on it. But when the coffin was lowered into Mr. Sissum's place in the Sissum lot under a giant magnolia tree, and Mr. Sissum's preacher, Dr. Carlyle, said burial service, Miss Eckhart broke out of the circle.

She pressed to the front, through Sissums from everywhere and all the Presbyterians, and went close to get a look; and if Dr. Loomis had not caught her she would have gone headlong into the red clay hole. People said she might have thrown herself upon the coffin if they'd let her; just as, later, Miss Katie Rainey did on Victor's when he was brought back from France. But Cassie had the impression that Miss Eckhart simply wanted to see—to see what was being done with Mr. Sissum.

As she struggled, her round face seemed stretched wider than it was long by a feeling that failed to match the feelings of everybody else. It was not the same as sorrow. Miss Eckhart, a stranger to their cemetery, where none of her people lay, pushed forward with her unstylish, winter purse swinging on her arm, and began to nod her head—sharply, to one side and then the other. She appeared almost little under the tree, but Mr. Comus Stark and Dr. Loomis looked more shrunken still by the side of her as they —sent by ladies—reached for her elbows. Her vigorous nods included them too, increasing in urgency. It was the way she nodded at pupils to bring up their rhythm, helping out the metronome.

Cassie remembered how Miss Snowdie MacLain's grip tightened on her hand and stayed tightened until

Miss Eckhart got over it. But Cassie remembered her manners better than to seem to watch Miss Eckhart after one look; she stared down at her Billikin shoes. And her mother had slipped away.

It was strange that in Mr. Sissum's life Miss Eckhart, as everybody said, had never known what to do; and now she did this. Her sharp nodding was like something to encourage them all—to say that she knew now, to do this, and that nobody need speak to her or touch her unless, if they thought best, they could give her this little touch at the elbows, the steer of politeness.

"*Pizzicato.*"

Once, Miss Eckhart gave out the word to define in the catechism lesson.

"*Pizzicato* is when Mr. Sissum played the cello before he got drowned."

That was herself: Cassie heard her own words. She had tried—she was as determined as if she'd been dared—to see how that sounded, spoken out like that to Miss Eckhart's face. She remembered how Miss Eckhart listened to her and did nothing but sit still as a statue, as she sat when the flowers came down over her head.

After the way she cried in the cemetery—for they decided it must have been crying she did—some ladies stopped their little girls from learning any more music; Miss Jefferson Moody stopped Parnell.

Cassie heard noises—a thump next door, the antiquated sound of thunder. There was nothing she could see—only Old Man Holifield's hat that idly made a half-turn on the bedpost, as if something, by a long grapevine, had jolted it.

One summer morning, a sudden storm had rolled up and three children were caught at the studio— Virgie Rainey, little Jinny Love Stark, and Cassie— though the two bigger girls might have run their short way home with newspapers over their hair.

Miss Eckhart, without saying what she was going

to do, poked her finger solidly along the pile of music on top of the piano, pulled out a piece, and sat down on her own stool. It was the only time she ever performed in Cassie's presence except when she took the other half in duets.

Miss Eckhart played as if it were Beethoven; she struck the music open midway and it was in soft yellow tatters like old satin. The thunder rolled and Miss Eckhart frowned and bent forward or she leaned back to play; at moments her solid body swayed from side to side like a tree trunk.

The piece was so hard that she made mistakes and repeated to correct them, so long and stirring that it soon seemed longer than the day itself had been, and in playing it Miss Eckhart assumed an entirely different face. Her skin flattened and drew across her cheeks, her lips changed. The face could have belonged to someone else—not even to a woman, necessarily. It was the face a mountain could have, or what might be seen behind the veil of a waterfall. There in the rainy light it was a sightless face, one for music only—though the fingers kept slipping and making mistakes they had to correct. And if the sonata had an origin in a place on earth, it was the place where Virgie, even, had never been and was not likely ever to go.

The music came with greater volume—with fewer halts—and Jinny Love tiptoed forward and began turning the music. Miss Eckhart did not even see her —her arm struck the child, making a run. Coming from Miss Eckhart, the music made all the pupils uneasy, almost alarmed; something had burst out, unwanted, exciting, from the wrong person's life. This was some brilliant thing too splendid for Miss Eckhart, piercing and striking the air around her the way a Christmas firework might almost jump out of the hand that was, each year, inexperienced anew.

It was when Miss Eckhart was young that she had learned this piece, Cassie divined. Then she had almost forgotten it. But it took only a summer rain to start it again; she had been pricked and the music came like the red blood under the scab of a forgotten fall. The little girls, all stationed about the studio with the rushing rain outside, looked at one another, the three quite suddenly on some equal footing. They were all wondering—thinking—perhaps about escape. A mosquito circled Cassie's head, singing, and fastened on her arm, but she dared not move.

What Miss Eckhart might have told them a long time ago was that there was more than the ear could bear to hear or the eye to see, even in her. The music was too much for Cassie Morrison. It lay in the very heart of the stormy morning—there was something almost too violent about a storm in the morning. She stood back in the room with her whole body averted as if to ward off blows from Miss Eckhart's strong left hand, her eyes on the faintly winking circle of the safe in the wall. She began to think of an incident that had happened to Miss Eckhart instead of about the music she was playing; that was one way.

One time, at nine o'clock at night, a crazy nigger had jumped out of the school hedge and got Miss Eckhart, had pulled her down and threatened to kill her. That was long ago. She had been walking by herself after dark; nobody had told her any better. When Dr. Loomis made her well, people were surprised that she and her mother did not move away. They wished she had moved away, everybody but poor Miss Snowdie; then they wouldn't always have to remember that a terrible thing once happened to her. But Miss Eckhart stayed, as though she considered one thing not so much more terrifying than another. (After all, nobody knew why she came!) It was because she was from so far away, at any rate, people said to excuse her, that she couldn't comprehend; Miss Perdita Mayo, who took in sewing and made everybody's trousseaux, said Miss Eckhart's *differences* were why shame alone had not killed her and killed her mother too; that differences were reasons.

Cassie thought as she listened, had to listen, to the

music that perhaps more than anything it was the
nigger in the hedge, the terrible fate that came on her,
that people could not forgive Miss Eckhart. Yet
things divined and endured, spectacular moments,
hideous things like the black nigger jumping out of
the hedge at nine o'clock, all seemed to Cassie to be
by their own nature rising—and so alike—and crossing the sky and setting, the way the planets did. Or
they were more like whole constellations, turning at
their very centers maybe, like Perseus and Orion and
Cassiopeia in her Chair and the Big Bear and Little
Bear, maybe often upside down, but terribly recognizable. It was not just the sun and moon that traveled. In the deepening of the night, the rising sky
lifted like a cover when Louella let it soar as she
made the bed.

All kinds of things would rise and set in your own
life, you could begin now to watch for them, roll back
your head and feel their rays come down and reach
your open eyes.

Performing, Miss Eckhart was unrelenting. Even
when the worst of the piece was over, her fingers like
foam on rocks pulled at the spent-out part with un-
stilled persistence, insolence, violence.

Then she dropped her hands.

"Play it again, Miss Eckhart!" they all cried in star-
tled recoil, begging for the last thing they wanted,
looking at her great lump of body.

"No."

Jinny Love Stark gave them a grown-up look and
closed the music. When she did, the other two saw it
wasn't the right music at all, for it was some bound-
together songs of Hugo Wolf.

"What were you playing, though?"

That was Miss Snowdie MacLain, standing in the
door, holding streams of bead curtains in both hands.

"I couldn't say," Miss Eckhart said, rising. "I have
forgotten."

The pupils all ran out in the slackening rain without another word, scattering in three directions by the mimosa tree, its flowers like wet fur, which once grew in the yard of the now-vacant house.

Für Elise. It came again, but in a labored, foolish way. Was it a man, using one finger?

Virgie Rainey had gone straight from taking music to playing the piano in the picture show. With her customary swiftness and lightness she had managed to skip an interval, some world-in-between where Cassie and Missie and Parnell were, all dyeing scarves. Virgie had gone direct into the world of power and emotion, which was beginning to seem even bigger than they had all thought. She belonged now with the Gish and the Talmadge sisters. With her yellow pencil she hit the tin plate when the tent opened where Valentino lived.

Virgie sat nightly at the foot of the screen ready for all that happened at the Bijou, and keeping pace with it. Nothing proved too much for her or ever got too far ahead, as it certainly got ahead of Mr. Sissum. When the dam broke everywhere at once, or when Nazimova cut off both feet with a saber rather than face life with Sinji, Virgie was instantly playing *Kamennoi-Ostrow*. Missie Spights said only one thing was wrong with having Virgie to play at the Bijou. She didn't work hard enough. Some evenings, she would lean back in her chair and let a whole forest fire burn in dead silence on the screen, and then when the sweethearts had found each other, she would switch on her light with a loud click and start up with creeping, minor runs—perhaps *Anitra's Dance*. But that had nothing to do with working hard.

The only times she played *Für Elise* now were for the advertisements; she played it moodily while the slide of the big white chicken on the watermelon-pink sky came on for Bowles' Gro., or the yellow horn on the streaky blue sky flashed on for the *Bugle,* with Cassie's father's picture as a young man inserted in the wavy beam of noise. *Für Elise* never got finished any more; it began, went a little way, and was interrupted by Virgie's own clamorous hand. She could do things with "You've Got to See Mama Every Night," and "Avalon."

By now, it was not likely she could play the opening movement of her Liszt concerto. That was the piece none of the rest of them could ever hope to play. Virgie would be heard from in the world, playing that, Miss Eckhart said, revealing to children with one ardent cry her lack of knowledge of the world. How could Virgie be heard from, in the world? And "the world"! Where did Miss Eckhart think she was now? Virgie Rainey, she repeated over and over, had a gift, and she must go away from Morgana. From them all. From her studio. In the world, she must study and practice her music for the rest of her life. In repeating all this, Miss Eckhart suffered.

And all the time, it was on Miss Eckhart's piano that Virgie had to do her practicing. The Raineys' old borrowed piano was butted and half-eaten by the goats one summer day; something that could only happen at the Raineys'. But they had all known Virgie would never go, or study, or practice anywhere, never would even have her own piano, because it wouldn't be like her. They felt no less sure of that when they heard, every recital, every June, Virgie Rainey playing better and better something that was harder and harder, or watched this fill Miss Eckhart with stiff delight, curious anguish. The very place to prove Miss Eckhart crazy was on her own subject, piano playing: she didn't know what she was talking about.

When the Raineys, after their barn got blown away in a big wind, had no more money to throw away on piano lessons, Miss Eckhart said she would teach Virgie free, because she must not stop learning. But later she made her pick the figs off the trees in the backyard in summer and the pecans off the ground in the front yard in winter, for her lessons. Virgie said Miss

Eckhart never gave her a one. Yet she always had nuts in her pocket.

Cassie heard a banging and a running next door, the obvious sound of falling. She shut her eyes.

"Virgie Rainey, *danke schoen.*" Once that was said in a dreadful voice, condemning. There were times in the studio when Miss Eckhart's mother would roll in; she had a wheelchair. The first years, she had kept to herself, rolling around no closer than the dining room, round and round with a whining wheel. She was old, and fair as a doll. Up close, her yellowish hair was powdery like goldenrod that had gone forgotten in a vase, turned white in its curls like Miss Snowdie's. She had wasting legs that showed knifelike down her long skirt, and clumsy-shaped, suffering feet that she placed just so out in front of her on the step of her chair, as if she wanted you to think they were pretty.

The mother rolled in to the studio whenever she liked, as time went on; with her shepherdess curls she bobbed herself through the beads that opened to her easier than a door. She would roll a certain distance into the room, then stop the wheels and wait there. She was not so much listening to the lesson as watching it, and though she was not keeping time, it was all the more noticeable the way her hands would tip, tap against her chair; she had a brass thimble on one finger.

Ordinarily, Miss Eckhart never seemed disturbed by her mother's abrupt visits. She appeared gentler, more bemused than before, when old Mrs. Eckhart made Parnell Moody cry, just by looking at Parnell too hard. Should daughters *forgive* mothers (with mothers under their heel)? Cassie would rather look at the two of them at night separated by the dark and the distance between. For when from your own table you saw the Eckharts through their window in the light of a lamp, and Miss Eckhart with a soundless ebullience bouncing up to wait on her mother, some- times you could imagine them back far away from

Morgana, before they had troubles and before they had come to you—plump, bright, and sweet somewhere.

Once when Virgie was practicing on Miss Eckhart's piano, and before she was through, the old mother screamed, *"Danke schoen, danke schoen, danke schoen!"* Cassie heard and saw her.

She screamed with a shy look still on her face, as though through Virgie Rainey she would scream at the whole world, at least at all the music in the world and wasn't that all right? Then she sat there looking out the front window, half smiling, having mocked her daughter. Virgie, of course, kept on practicing—it was a Schumann "forest piece." She had a pomegranate flower (the marbelized kind, from the Moodys') stuck in her breast-pin, and it did not even move.

But when the song was smoothly finished, Miss Eckhart made her way among the little tables and chairs across the studio. Cassie thought she was going for a drink of water, or something for herself. When she reached her mother, Miss Eckhart slapped the side of her mouth. She stood there a moment more, leaning over the chair—while it seemed to Cassie that it must, after all, have been the mother that slapped the daughter—with the key from her bosom, slipped out, beginning to swing on its chain, back and forth, catching the light.

Then Miss Eckhart, with her back turned, asked Cassie and Virgie to stay for dinner.

Enveloping all that the pupils did—entering the house, parting the curtains, turning the music page, throwing up the wrist for a "rest"—was the smell of cooking. But the smell was wrong, as the pitch of a note could be wrong. It was the smell of food nobody else had ever tasted.

Cabbage was cooked there by no Negro and by no way it was ever cooked in Morgana. With wine. The wine was brought on foot by Dago Joe, and to the front door. Some nice mornings the studio smelled like a spiced apple. But it was known from Mr. Wiley

Bowles, the grocer, that Miss Eckhart and her mother (whose mouth was still held crooked after the slap) ate pigs' brains. Poor Miss Snowdie!

Cassie yearned—she did want to taste the cabbage —that was really the insurmountable thing, and even the brains of a pig she would have put in her mouth that day. With that, Missie Spights might be flouted. But when Miss Eckhart said, "Please—please, will you stay to dinner?" Virgie and Cassie twined arms and said "No" together.

The war came and all through it and even after 1918 people said Miss Eckhart was a German and still wanted the Kaiser to win, and that Miss Snowdie could get along without her. But the old mother died, and Miss Snowdie said Miss Eckhart needed a friendly roof more than she did herself. Miss Eckhart raised the price of her lessons to six dollars a month. Miss Mamie Carmichael stopped her girls from taking, for this or for one thing or another, and then Miss Billy Texas Spights stopped Missie to be like her. Virgie stopped taking her free lessons when her brother Victor was killed in France, but that might have been coincidence, for Virgie had a birthday: she was fourteen. It might have been Virgie's stopping that took away Miss Eckhart's luck for good.

And when she stopped, Virgie's hand lost its touch —that was what they said. Perhaps nobody wanted Virgie Rainey to be anything in Morgana any more than they had wanted Miss Eckhart to be, and they were the two of them still linked together by people's saying that. How much might depend on people's being linked together? Even Miss Snowdie had a little harder time than she had had already with Ran and Scooter, her bad boys, by being linked with roomers and music lessons and Germans.

The time came when Miss Eckhart had almost no pupils at all. Then she had only Cassie.

Her mother, Cassie had long known in her heart,

could not help but despise Miss Eckhart. It was just for living so close to her, or maybe just for living, a poor unwanted teacher and unmarried. And Cassie's instinct told her her mother despised herself for despising. That was why she kept Cassie taking just a little longer after Miss Eckhart had been deserted by all the other mothers. It was more that than the money, which would go to Miss Snowdie on the rent bill. The child had to make up for her mother's abhorrence, to keep her mother as kind as she really was. While Miss Snowdie could stay kind through always being far away in her heart.

Cassie herself was well applauded when she played a piece. The recital audience always clapped more loudly for her than they did for Virgie; but then they clapped more loudly still for little Jinny Love Stark. It was Cassie who was awarded the Presbyterian Church's music scholarship that year to go to college —not Virgie. It made Cassie feel "natural"; winning the scholarship over Virgie did not surprise her too much. The only reason for that which she put into words, to be self-effacing, was that the Raineys were Methodists; and yet she did not, basically, understand a slight. And now stretching ahead of her, as far as she could see, were those yellow Schirmer books: all the rest of her life.

But Miss Eckhart sent for Virgie and gave her a present that Cassie for many days could close her eyes and see. It was a little butterfly pin made of cut-out silver, like silver lace, to wear on her shoulder; the safety-catch wasn't any good.

But that didn't made Virgie say she loved Miss Eckhart or go on practicing as she told her. Miss Eckhart gave Virgie an armful of books that were written in German about the lives of the masters, and Virgie couldn't read a word; and Mr. Fate Rainey tore out the Venusberg pictures and fed them to the pigs. Miss Eckhart tried all those things and was strict to the last in the way she gave all her love to Virgie Rainey and none to anybody else, the way she was strict in music;

and for Miss Eckhart love was just as arbitrary and one-sided as music teaching.

Her love never did anybody any good.

Then one day, Miss Eckhart had to move out.

The trouble was that Miss Snowdie had had to sell the house. She moved with her two boys back to MacLain where she came from, seven miles away, and where her husband's people came from too. She sold the house to Mrs. Vince Murphy. And soon Miss Eckhart was put out, with Mrs. Vince Murphy retaining the piano and anything Miss Eckhart had or that Miss Snowdie had left for Miss Eckhart.

It was not long before Mrs. Vince Murphy was struck by lightning and left the house to Miss Francine, who always kept meaning to fix up the house and take boarders, but had a beau then. She temporized by putting Mr. Holifield in to see that nobody ran off with the bathtubs and what furniture there was. And the house "ran down"—as they said alike of houses and clocks, thought Cassie, to put the seal on inferiority and carelessness and fainting hopes alike, and for ever.

Then stories began to be told of what Miss Eckhart had really done to her old mother. People said the old mother had been in pain for years, and nobody was told. What kind of pain they did not say. But they said that during the war, when Miss Eckhart lost pupils and they did not have very much to eat, she would give her mother paregoric to make sure she slept all night and not wake the street with noise or complaint, for fear still more pupils would be taken away. Some people said Miss Eckhart killed her mother with opium.

Miss Eckhart, in a room out at the old Holifields' on Morgan's Wood Road, got older and weaker, though not noticeably thinner, and would be seen from time to time walking into Morgana, up one side of the street and down the other and home. People said you could look at her and see she had broken. Yet she still had authority. She could still stop young,

unknowing children like Loch on the street and ask
them imperative questions, "Where were you throwing that ball?" "Are you trying to break that tree?"
. . . Of course her only associates from first to last
were children; not counting Miss Snowdie.

Where did Miss Eckhart come from, and where in
the end did she go? In Morgana most destinies were
known to everybody and seemed to go without saying. It was unlikely that anybody except Miss Perdita
Mayo had asked Miss Eckhart where the Eckharts
came from, where exactly in the world, and so received the answer. And Miss Perdita was so unde-
pendable: she couldn't tell you now, to save her life.
And Miss Eckhart had gone down out of sight.

Once on a Sunday ride, Cassie's father said he bet
a nickel that was old lady Eckhart hoeing peas out
there on the County Farm, and he bet another nickel
she could still do the work of ten nigger men.

Wherever she was, she had no people. Surely by
this time, she had nobody at all. The only one she
had ever wanted to have for "people" was Virgie Rainey *Danke schoen*.

Missie Spights said that if Miss Eckhart had allowed herself to be called by her first name, then she
would have been like other ladies. Or if Miss Eckhart
had belonged to a church that had ever been heard
of, and the ladies would have had something to invite
her to belong to . . . Or if she had been married to
anybody at all, just the awfullest man—like Miss
Snowdie MacLain, that everybody could feel sorry
for.

Cassie knelt, and with hurrying hands untied all
the knots in her scarf. She held it out in a square.
Though she was not thinking of her scarf, it did surprise her; she didn't see indeed how she had ever
made it. They had told her so. She hung it over the
two posts of a chair to dry and as it fell softly over
the ladder of the back she thought that somewhere,
even up to the last, there could have been for Miss

Eckhart a little opening wedge—a crack in the door. . . .

But if I had been the one to see it open, she thought slowly, I might have slammed it tight for ever. I might.

Her eyes lifted to the window where she saw a thin gray streak go down, like the trail of a match. The humming-bird! She knew him, one that came back every year. She stood and looked down at him. He was a little emerald bobbin, suspended as always before the opening four-o'clocks. Metallic and misty together, tangible and intangible, splendid and fairy-like, the haze of his invisible wings mysterious, like the ring around the moon—had anyone ever tried to catch him? Not she. Let him be suspended there for a moment each year for a hundred years—incredibly thirsty, greedy for every drop in every four-o'clock trumpet in the yard, as though he had them numbered—then dart.

"Like a military operation."

Cassie's father always said the recital was planned that way, in all its tactics and dress. The preparations went on for many hot, secret weeks—all of May. "You're not to tell anyone what the program is to be," Miss Eckhart warned at every lesson and rehearsal, as if there were other music teachers, other classes, rivaling, and as if every year the program didn't begin with "The Stubborn Rocking Horse" by the one boy and end with "Marche Militaire" for eight hands. What Virgie played in the recital one year, Cassie (gradually improving) would come to the next, and Missie Spights had it one more step in the future.

Miss Eckhart decided early in the spring what color each child should wear, with what color sash and hair ribbon, and sent written word to the mother. She explained to the children that it was important which color followed which. "Think of God's rainbow and its order," and she would shake her pencil in abrupt

little beats in an arch overhead; but they had to think
of Spights' store. The quartet, with four dresses in
view at one time and in close conjunction, pushing
one another, made Miss Eckhart especially appre-
hensive.

Account was kept in a composition book of each
child's assigned color; Miss Eckhart made a little "v"
beside the name in token of the mother's agreement
and regarded it as a promise. When the dress was re-
ported finished, starched, and ironed, a line was
drawn through that name.

In general, mothers were scared of Miss Eckhart
then. Miss Lizzie Stark laughed about it, but she was
as scared as anybody else. Miss Eckhart assumed that
there would be a new dress for every pupil for the
recital night, that Miss Perdita Mayo would make it,
or if not Miss Perdita, who even with her sister could
not make them all, then the pupil's own mother. The
dress must be made with the fingers and the edges of
bertha and flounce picoted, the sash as well; and—
whatever happened—the costume must be saved for
recital night. And this was the kind of thing that both
Miss Perdita and most mothers understood immediately.

And it could seldom be worn again; certainly not
to another recital—by then an "old" dress. A recital
dress was fuller and had more trimming than a Sunday
dress. It was like a flower girl's dress in a wedding;
once little Nina Carmichael's *was* a flower girl's dress,
after Etta's wedding, but this was special dispensation. The dress should be organdie, with ruffles on
skirt, bertha, and sleeves; it called for a satin or taf-
feta sash tied in a back bow with long tails, pointed
like the tails of arrows, to hang over the stool and,
if it could be afforded, to reach the floor.

All through May, Miss Eckhart would ask how far
along the dresses had come. Cassie was uneasy, for
her mother's way was to speak too late for Miss Perdita's list and plan to run the dress up herself at the
last minute; but Cassie had to encourage Miss Eck-

hart. "She's just evening my hem," she would report, when the material would still be lying folded up with the newspaper-pattern borrowed from Miss Jefferson Moody, in the *armoire*.

As for the program, that was no problem; it existed readymade without discussion. Far back in the winter, Virgie Rainey would have been allotted a piece that was the most difficult Miss Eckhart could find in the music cabinet. Sometimes it was not as showy a thing as Teensie Loomis always had to have (before she got old and stopped taking), but always it was the hardest piece of all. It would be the test of what Virgie could do, to learn it; an ordeal was set for her each year and each year it was accomplished, with no yielding sign from Virgie that she had struggled. The rest of the program would lead up to this, and did not matter enough to be altered seriously from one year to the next. Just so everybody had a piece to play, and a new dress finished in time, and kept the secrets, there was nothing to do but endure May.

A week ahead of the night, the gold chairs were set in a solid row across the room, to look as if all were gold, and the extra chairs would appear one by one behind them until the room was filled. Miss Eckhart must have carried them in from the dining room first, and then, as she could get hold of them, from elsewhere. She carried them downstairs from Miss Snowdie's freely, of course, and then even from Mr. Voight's, for no matter what Miss Eckhart thought of Mr. Voight, she wouldn't hesitate to go in and take his chairs for the recital.

A second piano had to be rented from the Presbyterian Sunday School (through the Starks), hauled over in time for rehearsing the quartet all together, and of course tuned. There were programs to be printed (through the Morrisons), elaborate enough to include the opus numbers, the first, middle, and last name of each pupil, and flowing across the top in a script which resembled, as if for a purpose, Miss Eckhart's writing in the monthly bills, the full name

of Miss Lotte Elisabeth Eckhart. Some little untal-
ented Maloney would give the programs out at the
door from a pink fruit plate.

On the day, gladiolas or carnations in princess-baskets were expected to arrive for each child, duly ordered from some Loomis florist-connections in Vicksburg and kept in buckets of water on the MacLains'
shady back porch. They would be presented at the
proper time—immediately after the bow—by Miss
Eckhart. The pupil could hold the basket for the
count of three—this had been rehearsed, using a black
umbrella—then present it back to Miss Eckhart, who
had in mind a crescent moon design on the floor
which she would fill in basket by basket on the night.
Jinny Love Stark always received a bouquet of Parma
violets in a heart of leaves, and had to be allowed to
keep it. She said, "Ta-ta." She never did give it up a
single year, which hurt the effect.

For the recital was, after all, a ceremony. Better
than school's being let out—for that presupposed ex-
aminations—or the opening political fireworks—the
recital celebrated June. Both dread and delight were
to come down on little girls that special night, when
only certain sashes and certain flowers could possibly
belong, and with only smart, pretty little girls to carry
things out.

And Miss Eckhart pushed herself to quite another
level of life for it. A blushing sensitivity sprang up in
her every year at the proper time like a flower of the
season, like the Surprise Lilies that came up with no
leaves and overnight in Miss Nell's yard. Miss Eckhart stirred here and there utterly carried away by
matters that at other times interested her least—
dresses and sashes, prominence and precedence,
smiles and bows. It was strange, exciting. She called
up the pictures on those little square party invita-
tions, the brown bear in a frill and the black poodle
standing on a chair to shave at a mirror . . .

With recital night over, the sensitivity and the drive
too would be over and gone. But then all trials

would be ended. The limitless part of vacation would have come. Girls and boys could go barefooted alike in the mornings.

The night of the recital was always clear and hot; everyone came. The prospective audience turned out in full oppression.

Miss Eckhart and her pupils were not yet to be visible. It was up to Miss Snowdie MacLain to be at the door, and she was at the door staunchly, as if she'd been in on things the whole time. She welcomed all female Morgana there in perfect innocence. By eight o'clock the studio was packed.

Miss Katie Rainey would always come early. She trembled with delight, like a performer herself, and she had milked with that hat on. She laughed with pleasure as she grew accustomed to it all, and through the recital she would stay much in evidence, the first to clap when a piece was over, and pleased equally with the music she listened to and the gold chair she sat on. And Old Man Fate Rainey, the buttermilk man, was the only father who came. He remained standing. Miss Perdita Mayo, who had made most of the recital dresses, was always on the front row to see that the bastings had all been pulled out after the dresses got home, and beside her was Miss Hattie Mayo, her quiet sister who helped her.

As the studio filled, Cassie, peeping around the sheet curtain (*they* were all herded in the dining room), bore the dread that her mother might not come at all. She was always late, perhaps because she lived so near. Miss Lizzie Stark, the most important mother there, who was just waiting for Jinny Love to get a little older to play better, would turn around in her chair down front to spot each of the other mothers. Knowing that too, and dressed beautifully in a becoming flowery dress just right for a mother on recital night, Cassie's mother could not walk across the two yards on time to save her life. And Cassie's *Rustle of Spring*, for instance, was very hard, harder than Missie Spights' piece; but it appeared that everything Miss Eckhart planned for, Cassie's mother could let go for nothing.

In the studio decorated like the inside of a candy box, with "material" scalloping the mantel shelf and doilies placed under every movable object, now thus made immovable, with streamers of white ribbons and nosegays of pink and white Maman Cochet roses and the last MacLain sweetpeas dividing and re-dividing the room, it was as hot as fire. No matter that this was the first night of June; no electric fans were to whir around while music played. The metronome, ceremoniously closed, stood on the piano like a vase. There was no piece of music anywhere in sight.

When the first unreasoning hush—there was the usual series—fell over the audience, the room seemed to shake with the agitation of palmetto and feather fans alone, plus the occasional involuntary tick of the metronome within its doors. There was the mixture together of agitation and decoration which could make every little forthcoming child turn pale with a kind of ultimate dizziness. Whoever might look up at the ceiling for surcease would be floundered within a paper design stemming out of the chandelier, as complicated and as unavailing as a cut-out paper snowflake.

Now Miss Eckhart came into the room all changed, with her dark hair pulled low on her brow, and gestured for silence. She was wearing her recital dress which made her look larger and closer-to than she looked at any other times. It was an old dress: Miss Eckhart disregarded her own rules. People would forget that dress between times and then she would come out in it again, the untidy folds not quite spotlessly clean, gathered about her bosom and falling heavy as a coat to the sides; it was a tawny crepe-back satin. There was a bodice of browning lace. It was as rich and hot and deep-looking as a furskin. The unexpected creamy flesh on her upper arms gave her a look of emerging from it.

Miss Eckhart, achieving silence, stood in the shadowy spot directly under the chandelier. Her feet, white-shod, shod by Mr. Sissum for good, rested in the chalk circle previously marked on the floor and now, she believed, perfectly erased. One hand, with its countable little muscles so hard and ready, its stained, blue nails, went to the other hand and they folded quite still, holding nothing, until they lost their force by lying on her breast and made a funny little house with peaks and gables. Standing near the piano but not near enough to help, she presided but not with her whole heart on guard against disaster; while disaster was what remained on the minds of the little girls. Starting with the youngest, she called them out.

So they played, and except Virgie, all played their worst. They shocked themselves. Parnell Moody burst into tears on schedule. But Miss Eckhart never seemed to notice or to care. How forgetful she seemed at exactly the moments she should have been agonized! You expected the whip, almost, for forgetting to repeat before the second ending, or for failing to count ten before you came around the curtain at all; and instead you received a strange smile. It was as though Miss Eckhart, at the last, were grateful to you for *anything*.

When Hilda Ray Bowles' turn came and Miss Eckhart herself was to bend down and move the stool out twelve inches, she did it in a spirit of gentle, uninterrupted abstraction. She might be not moving a stool out for an overgrown girl at all, but performing some gentle ministration to someone else, someone who was not there; perhaps it was Beethoven, who wrote Hilda Ray's piece, and perhaps not.

Cassie played and her mother—not betraying her, after all—was seated among the rest. At the end, she had creased her program into a little hat, for which Cassie could have fallen at her feet.

But recital night was Virgie's night, whatever else it was. The time Virgie Rainey was most wonderful in her life, to Cassie, was when she came out—her

turn was just before the quartet—wearing a Christ-
mas-red satin band in her hair with rosettes over the
ears, held on by a new elastic across the back; she
had a red sash drawn around under the arms of a
starched white swiss dress. She was thirteen. She
played the *Fantasia on Beethoven's Ruins of Athens,*
and when she finished and got up and made her bow,
the red of the sash was all over the front of her waist,
she was wet and stained as if she had been stabbed in
the heart, and a delirious and enviable sweat ran
down from her forehead and cheeks and she licked
it in with her tongue.

Cassie, who had slipped around to the front, was
spellbound still when Miss Katie Rainey put a hand
on her sash and to her pure terror said, "Oh, but I
wish Virgie had a sister!"

Then there was only the quartet, and with the last
chord—sudden disintegration itself—laughter and
teasing broke loose. All the children got a kiss or a
token spank in congratulation and then ran free. Ladies waved and beckoned with their fans, conversation opened up. Flowers were lifted high, shown off,
thrown, given, and pulled to giddy pieces by fingers
freed for the summer. The MacLain twins, now crashing restraint, rushed downstairs in identical cowboy
suits, pointing and even firing cap pistols. Two fans
were set rumbling and walking on the floor, from
which the dropped programs flew up like a flock of
birds, while the decorations whipped and played all
over. Neither piano was gone near except for punch-
ing out "Sally in Her Shimmie Tail." Little Jinny
Stark, after all, fell, skinned her knee and bled pro-
fusely. It was like any other party.

"Punch and *Kuchen!*" Miss Eckhart came announc-
ing.

The big MacLain dining room at the back, where
Miss Snowdie only wintered her flowers for the most
part, was thrown open tonight. Punch was being
served from the MacLain punch bowl, one of Miss
Snowdie's gifts from her husband—served impromptu

by Miss Billy Texas Spights who sprang for the ladle, and they drank it out of the twenty-four MacLain cups and the twelve Loomis. The little cakes that Miss Eckhart tirelessly brought out were sweet, light, and warm, their tops sprinkled with colored "shot" that came (or so they'd thought) only out of glass pistols sold on trains. When the plate was empty, you saw it was decorated with slipping flower garlands and rowdy babies, sprinkled with gold and now with golden crumbs.

Miss Eckhart's cheeks flooded with color as the guests accepted her sugar cookies and came back to lift their punch cups, with the drowned fruit in the bottom, again to her quick, brimming ladle. ("*I'll* give you more punch!" she cried, when Miss Billy Texas started counting.) Her hair was as low on her forehead as Circe's, on the fourth-grade wall feeding her swine. She smiled, not on any particular one but on everyone, everywhere she looked and everywhere she went—for the party had spread out—from studio to dining room and back and out on the porch, where she called, "What is this out here? You little girls come back inside and stay till you eat my *Kuchen* all up! The last crumb!" It made them laugh to hear her, when strictness was only a pretense.

Miss Lizzie Stark, although she had occasionally referred to Miss Eckhart as "Miss Do-daddle," did not spare herself from wearing her most elaborate hat, one resembling a large wreath or a wedding cake, and it was constantly in the vision, turned this way and that like a floating balloon at a fair over the heads of the crowd. The canary sang; his cover was lifted off. Gradually the Maman Cochets bowed their little green stems over the vase's edge.

At the close of the evening, saying goodnight, people congratulated Miss Eckhart and her mother. Old Mrs. Eckhart had sat near the door during the whole evening—had sat by Miss Snowdie at the door, when she welcomed them in. She wore a dark dress too, but it was sprigged. In the path of the talking and laughing mothers and the now wild children she sat blinking her eyes, but amenable, like a baby when he is wheeled out into the sunlight. While Miss Snowdie watched her kindly, she would hold her mouth in one evening-long smile; she was letting herself be looked at and herself, at the end, be thanked.

Miss Eckhart, breasting the pushing, departing children, moving among the swinging princess-baskets and the dropped fans of the suddenly weakened mothers, would be heard calling, "Virgie Rainey? Virgie Rainey?" Then she would look down ceremoniously at the sleepiest and smallest child, who had only played "Playful Kittens" that night. All her pupils on that evening partook of the grace of Virgie Rainey. Miss Eckhart would catch them running out the door, speaking German to them and holding them to her. In the still night air her dress felt damp and spotted, as though she had run a long way.

Cassie listened, but *Für Elise* was not repeated. She took up her ukulele from the foot of the bed. She screwed it into tune and played it, slurring the chords expertly and fanning with her fingers. She strolled around her scarf hanging up to dry, playing a chorus or two, and then wandered back to the window.

There she saw Loch go hanging on all fours like a monkey down the hackberry limb. Far on the other side of the tree he hung by his hands, perfectly still, diver-like—not going into any of his tricks. That was the way he stayed in bed taking quinine.

He was concerned not with tricks but with watching something inside the vacant house. Loch could see in. Cassie opened her mouth to cry out, but the cry wouldn't come.

Except for once, she had not answered Loch all day when he called her, and now the sight of his spread-eagled back in the white night drawers seemed as far from her as the morning star. It was gone from her, any way to shield his innocence, when his innocence was out there shining at her, cavorting

—for Loch calmly reversed himself and hung by his knees; plunged upside down, he looked in at the old studio window, with his pompadour cap falling to earth and his hair spiking out all over his young boy's head.

Once Loch wandered over their house in a skirt, beating on a christening cup with a pencil. "Mama, do you think I can ever play music too?" "Why, of course, dear heart. You're *my* child. Just you bide your time." (He was her favorite.) And he never could—bide or play. How Cassie had adored him! He didn't know one tune from another. "Is this *Jesus Loves Me?*" he'd ask, interrupting his own noise. She looked out at him now as stricken as if she saw him hurt, from long ago, and silently performing tricks to tell her. She stood there at her window. Softly she was playing and singing, "By the light, light, light, light, light of the silvery moon," her favorite song.

She could never go for herself, never creep out on the shimmering bridge of the tree, or reach the dark magnet there that drew you inside, kept drawing you in. She could not see herself do an unknown thing. She was not Loch, she was not Virgie Rainey; she was not her mother. She was Cassie in her room, seeing the knowledge and torment beyond her reach, standing at her window singing—in a voice soft, rather full today, and halfway thinking it was pretty.

III.

After a moment of blackness, upside down, Loch opened his eyes. Nothing had happened. The house he watched was all silence but for the progressing tick-tock that was different from a clock's. There were outer sounds. His sister was practicing on her ukulele again so she could sing to the boys. He heard from up the street the water-like sounds of the ladies' party, and off through the trees where the big boys were playing, sounds of the ball being knocked out—gay and removed as birdsong. But the tick-tock was sharper and clearer than all he could hear just now in the world, and at moments seemed to ring close, the way his own heartbeat rang against the bed he came out of.

His mother, had it been she in the vacant house, would have stopped those two Negroes straggling home with their unsold peas and made them come in off the street and do all that for her, and finish up in no time. But the sailor's mother was doing her work alone. She wanted things to suit herself, nobody else would have been able to please her; and she was taking her own sweet time. She was building a bonfire of her own in the piano and would set off the dynamite when she was ready and not before.

Loch knew from her actions that the contrivance down in the wires—the piano front had been taken away—was a kind of nest. She was building it like a thieving bird, weaving in every little scrap that she could find around her. He saw in two places the mustached face of Mr. Drewsie Carmichael, his father's candidate for mayor—she found the circulars in the door. The litter on his bed, the Octagon Soap coupons, would have pleased her at that moment, and he would have turned them over to her.

Then Loch almost gave a yell; pride filled him, like a second yell, that he did not. Here down the street came Old Man Moody, the marshal, and Mr. Fatty Bowles with him. They had taken the day off to go fishing in Moon Lake and came carrying their old fishing canes but no fish. Their pants and shoes were heavy with mud. They were cronies of old Mr. Holifield and often came to wake him up, this time of day, and hound him off to the gin.

Loch skinned the cat over the limb and waited head down as they came tramping, sure enough, across the yard. In his special vision he saw that they could easily be lying on their backs in the blue sky and waving their legs pleasantly around, having nothing to do with law and order.

Old Man Moody and Mr. Fatty Bowles divided at

the pecan stump, telling a joke, joined, said "Bread and butter," and then clogged up the steps. The curtain at the front window flapped signaling in their faces. They looked at each other anew. Their bodies and their faces grew smooth as fishes. They floated around the porch and flattened like fishes to nose at the window. There were round muddy spots on the seats of their pants; they squatted.

Well, there it is, thought Loch—the houseful. Two upstairs, one downstairs, and the two on the porch. And on the piano sat the ticking machine. . . . Directly below Loch a spotted thrush walked noisily in the weeds, pointing her beak ahead of her straight as a gun, just as busy in the world as people.

He held his own right hand ever so still as the old woman, unsteady as the Christmas angel in Mrs. McGillicuddy's fourth-grade pageant, came forward with a lighted candle in her hand. It was a kitchen tallow candle; she must have taken it out of Mr. Holifield's boxful against all the times the lights went out in Morgana. She came so slowly and held the candle so high that he could have popped it with a nigger-shooter from where he was. Her hair, he saw, was cropped and white and lighted up all around. From the swaying, farthest length of a branch that would hold his weight, he could see how bright her big eyes were under their black circling brows, and how seldom they blinked. They were owl eyes.

She bent over, painfully, he felt, and laid the candle in the paper nest she had built in the piano. He too drew his breath in, protecting the flame, and as she pulled her aching hand back he pulled his. The newspaper caught, it was ablaze, and the old woman threw in the candle. Hands to thighs, she raised up, her work done.

Flames arrowed out so noiselessly. They ran down the streamers of paper, as double-quick as freshets from a loud gully-washer of rain. The room was crisscrossed with quick, dying yellow fire, there were pinwheels falling and fading from the ceiling. And up above, on the other side of the ceiling, they, the first two, were as still as mice.

The law still squatted. Mr. Fatty's and Old Man Moody's necks stretched sideways, the fat and the thin. Loch could have dropped a caterpillar down onto either of their heads, which rubbed together like mother's and child's.

"So help me. She *done* it," Mr. Fatty Bowles said in a natural voice. He lifted his arm, that had been hugging Old Man Moody's shoulders, and transferred to his own back pocket a slap that would have cracked Old Man Moody's bones. "Bless her heart! She done it before our eyes. What would you have bet?"

"Not a thing," said Old Man Moody. "Watch. If it catches them old dried-out squares of matting, Booney Holifield's going to feel a little warm ere long."

"Booney! Why, I done forgot him!"

Old Man Moody laughed explosively with shut lips.

"Wouldn't you say it's done caught now," said Mr. Fatty, pointing into the room with his old fishing knife.

"The house is on fire!" Loch cried at the top of his voice. He was riding his limb up and down and shaking the leaves.

Old Man Moody and Mr. Fatty might have heard, for, a little as if they were insulted, they raised up, moved their fishing poles along, and deliberately chose the dining room window instead of the parlor window to get to work on.

They lifted the screen out, and Mr. Fatty accidentally stepped through it. They inched the sash up with a sound that made them draw high their muck-coated heels. They could go in now: they opened their mouths and guffawed silently. They were so used to showing off, they almost called up Morgana then and there.

Mr. Fatty Bowles started to squeeze himself over the sill into the room, but Old Man Moody was ready for that, pulled him back by the suspenders, and went first. He leap-frogged it. Inside, they both let go a holler.

"Look out! You're caught in the act!"

In the parlor, the old lady backed herself into the blind corner.

Old Man Moody and Mr. Fatty made a preliminary run around the dining room table to warm up, and then charged the parlor. They trod down the barrier of sparky matting and stomped in. They boxed at the smoke, hit each other, and ran to put up the window. Then Loch heard their well-known coughs and the creep and crack of fire inside the room. The smoke mostly stayed inside, contained and still.

Loch skinned the cat again. Here came somebody else. It was a fine day! Presently he thought he knew the golden Panama hat, and the elastic spareness of the man under it. He used to live in that vacant house and had at that time promised to bring Loch a talking bird, one that could say "Rabbits!" He had left and never returned. After all the years, Loch still wanted a bird like that. It was to his taste today.

"Nobody lives there now!" Loch called out of the leaves in an appropriate voice, for Mr. Voight turned in just like home at the vacant house. "If you go in, you'll blow up."

There was no talking bird on his shoulder yet. It was a long time ago that Mr. Voight had promised it. (And how often, Loch thought now with great surprise, he had remembered and cherished the promise!)

Mr. Voight shook his head rapidly as though a faraway voice from the leaves bothered him only for a moment. He ran up the steps with a sound like a green stick along a fence. He, though, instead of running into the flapping barrier over the door, drifted around the porch to the side and leisurely took a look through the window. Everything made his shout alarming.

"Will you please tell me why you're trespassing here?"

"So help me!" said Mr. Fatty Bowles, who was looking right at him, holding a burning hat.

Old Man Moody only said, "*Good* evening. Now I don't speak to you."

"Answer me! Trespassing, are you?"

"Whoa. Your house is afire."

"If my house is afire, then where's my folks gone?"

"Oh, *'tain't* your house no more, I forgot. It's Miss Francine Murphy's house. You're late, Captain."

"What antics are these? Get out of my house. Put that fire out behind you. Tell me where they went. Never mind, I know where they went. All right, burn it down, who's to stop you?"

He slapped his hands on the boarding of the house, fanfare like, and must have glared at them between, at the window. He had inserted himself between Loch and what happened, and to tell the truth he made one too many.

Old Man Moody and Mr. Fatty, exchanging murderous looks, ran hopping about the parlor, clapping their hats at the skittering flames, working in a team mad at itself, the way two people try to head off chickens in a yard. They jumped up and knocked at the same flame. They kicked and rubbed under their feet a spark they found by themselves, sometimes imaginary. Maybe because they'd let the fire almost go out, or because Mr. Voight had come to criticize, they pretended this fire was bigger than it had ever been. They bit their underlips tightly as old people do in carrying out acts of rudeness. They didn't speak.

Mr. Voight shook all over. He was laughing, Loch discovered. Now he watched the room like a show. "That's it! That's it!" he said.

Old Man Moody and Mr. Bowles together beat out the fire in the piano, fighting over it hard, banging and twanging the strings. Old Man Moody, no matter how his fun had been spoiled, enjoyed jumping up and down on the fierce-burning magnolia leaves. So they put the fire out, every spark, even the matting, which twinkled all over time and again before it went out for good. When a little tongue of flame started up for the last time, they quenched it together; and with a whistle and one more stamp each, they dared it, and it stayed out.

"That's it, boys," said Mr. Voight.

Then the old woman came out of the blind corner. "Now who's this?" cried Mr. Voight. In the center of the room she stopped. Without the law to stand over her, she might have clasped her empty hands and turned herself this way and that. But she did not; she was more desperate still. Loch hollered out again, riding the tree, his branch in both fists.

"Why don't you step on in, Captain?" called Mr. Fatty Bowles, and he beckoned the old lady to him.

"Down to business here. Now I'd appreciate knowing why you done this, lady," Old Man Moody said, rubbing his eyes and rimming them with black. "Putting folks to all this trouble. Now what you got against us?"

"Cat's got her tongue," said Mr. Fatty.

"I'm an old man. But you're an old woman. *I* don't know why you done it. Unless of course it was for pure lack of good sense."

"Where you come from?" asked Mr. Fatty in his little tenor voice.

"You clowns."

Mr. Voight, who said that, now went lightly as a dragonfly around the porch and entered the house by the front door: it was not locked. He might have been waiting until all the beating about had been done by others—clowns—or perhaps he thought he was so valuable that he could burn up in too big a hurry.

Loch saw him step, with rather a flare, through the beads at the hall door and come into the parlor. He gazed serenely about the walls, pausing for a moment first, as though something had happened to them not that very hour but a long time ago. He was there and not there, for he alone was not at his wit's end.

He went picking his feet carefully among the frills and flakes of burned paper, and wrinkled up his sharp nose; not from the smell, it seemed, but from wider, dissolving things. Now he stood at the window. His eyes rolled. Would he foam at the mouth? He did once. If he did not, Loch might not be sure about him; he remembered Mr. Voight best as foaming.

"Do you place her, Captain?" asked Old Man Moody in a cautious voice. "Who's this here firebug? You been places."

Mr. Voight was strolling about the room, and taking the poker he poked among the ashes. He picked up a seashell. The old lady advanced on him and he put it back, and as he came up he took off his hat. It looked more than polite. There close to the old lady's face he cocked his head, but she looked through him, a long way through Mr. Voight. She could have been a lady on an opposite cliff, far away, out of eye range and earshot, but about to fall.

The tick-tock was very loud then. Just as Mr. Fatty had forgotten Mr. Booney Holifield, Loch had forgotten the dynamite. Now he could go back to expecting a blast. The fire had had a hard time, but fire could manage to connect itself with an everlasting little mechanism that could pound like that, right along, right in the room.

("Do you hear something, Mr. Moody?" Loch could cry out right now. "Mr. Voight, listen."—"All right, say—do you want your bird this minute?" might be the reply. "We'll call everything off.")

"Man, what's that?" asked Mr. Fatty Bowles, and "Fatty boy, do you hear something ugly?" Old Man Moody asked at the same instant. At last they cocked their ears at the ticking that had been there in the room with them all this time. They looked at each other and then with hunched shoulders paraded around looking for the source of it.

"It's a rattlesnake! No, it ain't! But it's close," said Mr. Fatty.

They looked high and low all over the room but

they couldn't see it right in front of their eyes and up just a little, on top of the piano. That was honestly not a fair place, not where most people would put a thing. They looked at each other harder and hurried faster, but all they did was run on each other's heels and tip the chairs over. One of the chair legs snapped like a chicken bone.

Mr. Voight only got in their way, since he did not move an inch. He was still standing before the eyes of the sailor's mother, looking at her with lips puckered. It could be indeed that he knew her from his travels. He looked tired from these same travels now.

At last Old Man Moody, the smarter one of those two, spied what they were looking for, the obelisk with its little moving part and its door open. Once seen, that thing was so surely *it* that he merely pointed it out to Mr. Fatty. Mr. Fatty tiptoed over and picked the obelisk up and set it down again quickly. So Old Man Moody stumped over and picked it up and held it up on the diagonal, posing, like a fisherman holding a funny-looking fish to have come out of Moon Lake.

The old woman lifted her head and walked around Mr. Voight to Old Man Moody. She reached up and took the ticking thing right out of his hand, and he turned it loose agreeably; Old Man Moody seemed not taken by surprise by women.

The old woman held her possession to her, drawn to her big gray breast. Her eyesight returned from far to close by. Then she stood looking at the three people fixedly, as if she showed them her insides, her live heart.

And then a little whir of her own voice: "See . . . See, Mr. MacLain."

Nothing blew up, but Mr. Voight (but she called him MacLain) groaned.

"No, boys. I never saw her in my life," he said.

He walked stiffly out of the room. He walked out of the house and cater-cornered across the yard toward the MacLain Road. As he reached the road itself, he put his hat on, and then he did not look as shabby, or as poor.

Loch clasped a leafy armful of the tree and sank his head in the green cool.

"Let *me* see your play-pretty," Mr. Fatty Bowles was saying with his baby-smile. He took the obelisk away from the old woman, and with a sudden change on his face threw it with all his might out the open window. It came straight toward Loch, and fell into the weeds below him. And still it ticked.

"You could have been a little too quick there, Fatty boy," said Old Man Moody. "Flinging evidence."

"You ought to think about us. Listen and you'll hear it blow up. I'd rather have it blow up your wife's chickens."

"Well, I wouldn't."

And while they talked, the poor old woman tried it again. She was down on her knees cradling the lump of candle and the next moment had it lighted. She rose up, agitated now, and went running about the room, holding the candle above her, evading the men each time they tried to head her off.

This time, the fire caught her own hair. The little short white frill turned to flame.

Old Man Moody was so quick that he caught her. He came up with a big old rag from somewhere, and ran after the old woman with it. They both ran extraordinarily fast. He had to make a jump. He brought the cloth down over her head from behind, grimacing, as if all people on earth had to do acts of shame, some time. He hit her covered-up head about with the flat of his hand.

Old Man Moody and Mr. Bowles brought the old woman between them out on the porch of the vacant house. She was quiet now, with the scorched black cloth covering her head; she herself held it on with both hands.

"Know what I'm going to have to do with you?"
Old Man Moody was saying gently and conversa-
tionally, but she only stood there, all covered in
wrinkled cloth with her little hands up, clawed, the
way a locust shell would be found clinging to that
empty door in August.

"It don't signify nothing what your name is now,
or what you intended, old woman," Mr. Bowles told
her as he got the fishing canes. "We know where
you belong at, and that's Jackson."

"Come on ladylike. I'm sure you know how," Old
Man Moody said.

She came along but she did not answer either man
anything.

"Maybe she aimed mischief at King MacLain after
all," said Mr. Fatty Bowles. "She's a she, ain't she?"

"That'll be enough out of you for the rest of the
day," said Old Man Moody.

Among the leaves, Loch watched them come
down the walk and head towards town. They went
slowly, for the old woman took short, hesitant steps.
Where would they take her now? Not later, to Jackson, but now? After they passed, he let go his hands
and jumped out of the tree. It made a good noise
when he hit ground. He turned a forward and a
backward somersault and started walking on his
hands around the tree trunk. He made noises like a
goat, and a bobwhite, like the silly Moody chickens,
and like a lion.

On his hands he circled the tree and the obelisk
waited in the weeds, upright. He stood up and
looked at it. Its ticker was outside it.

He felt charmed like a bird, for the ticking stick
went like a tail, a tongue, a wand. He picked the
box up in his hands.

"Now go on. Blow up."

When he examined it, he saw the beating stick to
be a pendulum that instead of hanging down stuck
upwards. He touched it and stopped it with his fin-

ger. He felt its pressure, and the weight of the obelisk, which seemed about two pounds. He released the stick, and it went on beating.

Then he turned a little key in the side of the box, and that controlled it. The stick stopped and he poked it into place within the box, and shut the door of the thing.

It might not be dynamite: especially since Mr. Fatty thought it was.

What was it?

He opened his shirt and buttoned it in. He thought he might take it up to his room. It was this; not a bird that knew how to talk.

The sand pile was before him now. He planed away the hot top layer and sat down. He held still for a while, while nothing was ticking. Nothing but the crickets. Nothing but the train going through, ticking its two cars over the Big Black bridge.

IV.

Cassie moved to the front window, where she could see Old Man Moody and Mr. Fatty Bowles carrying off the old woman. The old woman was half sick or dazed. She held on her head some nameless kitchen rag; she had no purse. In a gray housedress prophetic of an institution she was making her way along, about to be touched, prodded, any minute, but not worrying about it. She wore shoes without stockings—and she had such white, white ankles. When she saw the ankles, Cassie flung herself in full view at the window and gave a cry.

No head lifted. Cassie rushed out of her room, down the stairs and out the front door.

To Loch's amazement his sister Cassie came running barefooted down the front walk in her petticoat and in full awareness turned toward town, crying, "You can't take her! Miss Eckhart!"

She was too late for anybody to hear her, of course, but he creaked up out of the sand pile and

ran out after her as if they had heard. He caught up
with her and pulled at her petticoat. She turned, with
her head still swimming high in the air, and cried
softly, "Oh, Mother!"

They looked at each other.

"Crazy."

"Crazy yourself."

"Back yonder," said Loch presently, "I can show
you how ripe the figs are." They withdrew as far
as the tree.But it was only in time to see the sailor
and Virgie Rainey run out, trying to escape by the
back way. Virgie and the sailor saw them. Back into
the house they ran, and then, in utter recklessness
out the front, the sailor first. The Morrisons had nowhere to go.

Old Man Moody's party was only now progressing
again, for the old woman had fallen down and they
had to hold her on her feet. Further along, the ladies'
Rook party was coming out of Miss Nell's with a
pouring sound. The sailor faced both these ranks.

The marshal tagged him but he ran straight on
into the wall of ladies, most of whom cried "Why,
Kewpie Moffitt!"—an ancient nickname he had outgrown. He whirled about-face and ran the other way,
and since he was carrying his blouse and was naked
from the waist up, his collar stood out behind him
like the lowest-hung wings. At the Carmichael corner,
he tried east and took west, and ran into the shadows
of the short-cut to the river, where he would
just about meet with Mr. King MacLain, if he was
not too late.

"Look at that!" Miss Billy Texas Spights called
clearly. "I see you, Virgie Rainey!"

"Mother!" Cassie called, just as clearly. She and
Loch found themselves out in front again.

The front door of the empty house fell to with
a frail sound behind Virgie Rainey. A haze of the old
smoke lifted unhurryingly over her, brushed and hid
her for a moment like a gauzy cloud. She was coming
right out, though, in a home-made dress of apricot

voile, carrying a mesh bag on a chain. She ran down the steps and walked clicking her heels out to the sidewalk—always Virgie clicked her heels as if nothing had happened in the past or behind her, as if she were free, whatever else she might be. The ladies hushed, holding onto their prizes and folded parasols. Virgie faced them as she turned toward town.

It was the hour, of course, for her to go to work. Once past the next corner, she could drink a Coca-Cola and eat a box of cakes at Loomis's drug store, as she did every evening for her supper; then she could vanish inside the Bijou.

She passed Cassie and Loch, cutting them, and kept going and caught up, as she had to, with the marshal, Fatty Bowles, and the old woman.

"You're running the wrong way!" Miss Billy Texas Spights called loudly. "Better run after that sailor boy!"

"Isn't he visiting the Flewellyns out in the country?" Miss Perdita Mayo was pleading to everybody. "What ever became of his mother? I'd forgotten all about him!"

Pinning Loch tightly by the arms in front of her, Cassie could only think: we were spies too. And nobody else was surprised at anything—it was only we two. People saw things like this as they saw Mr. MacLain come and go. They only hoped to place them, in their hour or their street or the name of their mothers' people. Then Morgana could hold them, and at last they were this and they were that. And when ruin was predicted all along, even if people had forgotten it was on the way, even if they mightn't have missed it if it hadn't appeared, still they were never surprised when it came.

"She'll stop for Miss Eckhart," breathed Cassie.

Virgie went by. There was a meeting of glances between the teacher and her old pupil that Cassie knew. She could not be sure that Miss Eckhart's eyes closed once in recall—they had looked so wide-open at everything alike. The meeting amounted only to Virgie Rainey's passing by, in plain fact. She clicked by Miss Eckhart and she clicked straight through the middle of the Rook party, without a word or the pause of a moment.

Old Man Moody and Fatty Bowles, dirty, their faces shining like the fish they didn't catch, took advantage of the path Virgie cut through the ladies and walked Miss Eckhart, unprotesting, on. Then the ladies brought their ranks safely to, and Miss Billy Texas, suddenly beside herself, cried once more, "He went the *other* way, Virgie!"

"That's enough, Billy Texas," said Miss Lizzie Stark. "As if her mother didn't have enough on her, just burying her son."

The noise of tin pans being beaten came from the distance, then little children's and Negro nurses' cries, "Crazy! Crazy!"

Cassie turned on Loch, pulled him to her and shook him by the shoulders. He was wet as a dishrag. A row of those big salt-and-pepper-colored mosquitoes perched all along his forehead. "What were you doing out of your bed, anyway?" she asked in a matter-of-fact, scolding voice. Loch gave her a long, gratified look. "What have you got there inside your nighties, crazy?"

"None of your business."

"Give it to me."

"It's mine."

"It is not. Let go."

"You make me."

"All right, I know what it is."

"What is it? You do not."

"You can't have that."

"Get away from me."

"I'll tell Mama and Papa.—You hit me! You hit a girl where she's tender."

"Well, you know you can't have it."

"All right then—did you see Mr. MacLain? He's been gone since you were born."

"Why, sure," said Loch. "I saw Mr. MacLain."

"Oh, Loch, why don't you beat off those mosquitoes!" She wept. "Mother!" Even Loch flew from her, at once.

"Well, here I am," said her mother.

"Oh!" After a moment she raised her head to say, "And Mr. King MacLain was here, and now he's gone."

"Well. You've seen him before," said her mother after a moment, breaking from her. "That's no excuse for coming outdoors in your petticoat to cry."

"You knew it would be this way, you were with them!"

There was no answer then either, and Cassie trudged through the yard. Loch stood near the sandpile. His lips clamped down, he held his bulging nightie and regarded it. She ran him back under the tree and into the house by the back door.

"What orphan-lookin' children is these here?" said Louella. "Where yawl orphan come from? Yawl don't live here, yawl live at County Orphan. Gawn back."

Cassie pushed Loch through the kitchen and then pulled him to a stop in the back hall. It was their father coming home.

"What's going on here! The house is on fire, the MacLain house! I see smoke!"

They could see him coming up the front walk, waving the rolled-up *Bugle* he brought home every night.

"Holifield! Holifield!"

Mr. Holifield must have come to the window, for they heard, "Did I hear my name called?" and they sighed with foreboding.

"It's gone out, Wilbur," said their mother at the door.

"That house has been on fire *and* gone out, sir." Their father was speaking loudly as he did from the platform at election time. "You can read about it in tomorrow's *Bugle*."

"Come in, Wilbur."

They could see her finger tracing a little pattern

on the screen door as she stood there in her party dress. "Cassie says King MacLain was here and gone. That's as interesting as twenty fires."

Cassie shivered.

"Maybe this will bestir Francine Murphy to take a step. *There's* a public guardian for you: Booney Holifield."

Cassie was glad her father kept on. If there was anything that unsettled him it was for people not to be on the inside what their outward semblances led you to suppose. "MacLain came to the wrong place this time. It might have caught *our* house: Booney Holifield!"

Their mother laughed. "That old monkey," she said. As far as she was concerned, the old man next door had just come alive, redeemed himself a little from being a Holifield.

The six-o'clock summer light shone just as usual on their father and mother meeting at the door.

"Come on."

Cassie and Loch running up the back stairs heard the sigh of the door and the old, muffled laugh that came between their parents at this moment. No matter what had happened, or had started to happen, around them, they could come in the house and laugh about the old thing. Theirs was a laugh that hinted of some small but interesting object, a thing even their deliberate father could find—something that might be seizable and holdable as well as findable, as ridiculous and forbidden to children, as alive, as a stray kitten or a rabbit.

The children kept on going up the steep dark backstairs, so close on each other they prodded and nudged each other, both punishing and petting.

"Get back in bed like you were never out," Cassie advised. "Pull the beggarlice off you."

"But I think Mother saw me," he said over his shoulder, going.

Cassie didn't answer.

She shivered and walked into her room. There

was the scarf. It was an old friend, part enemy. She brought it to her face, touched her lips to it, breathed its smoky dye-smell, and passed it up her cheeks and over her eyes. She pressed it against her forehead. She might have lost it, might have run out with it . . . for she had visions of poor Miss Eckhart wearing it away over her head; of Virgie waving it, brazenly, in the air of the street; of too-knowing Jinny Love Stark asking, "Couldn't you keep it?"

"Listen and I'll tell you what Miss Nell served at the party," Loch's mother said softly, with little waits in her voice. She was just a glimmer at the foot of his bed.

"Ma'am."

"An orange scooped out and filled with orange juice, with the top put back on and decorated with icing leaves, a straw stuck in. A slice of pineapple with a heap of candied sweet potatoes on it, and a little handle of pastry. A cup made out of toast, filled with creamed chicken, fairly warm. A sweet peach pickle with flower petals around it of different-colored cream cheese. A swan made of a cream puff. He had whipped cream feathers, a pastry neck, green icing eyes. A pastry biscuit the size of a marble with a little date filling." She sighed abruptly.

"Were you hungry, Mama?" he said.

It was not really to him that his mother would be talking, but it was he who tenderly let her, as they watched and listened to the swallows just at dark. It was always at this hour that she spoke in this voice— not to him or to Cassie or Louella or to his father, or to the evening, but to the wall, more nearly. She bent seriously over him and kissed him hard, and swayed out of the room.

There was singing in the street. He saw Cassie, a lesser but similar gleam, go past his door. The hay wagon was coming up the street to get her. He heard the girls and boys hail her, and her greeting the same as theirs, as if nothing had happened up until now, heard them pull her up. Ran MacLain from MacLain Courthouse, or was it his brother Eugene, always called to Mrs. Morrison, teasing, "Come on! You come with us!" Did they really want to take her? He heard the wagon creak away. They were singing and playing on their ukuleles, some song of which he couldn't be sure.

Presently Loch lifted up and gazed through the same old leaves, dark once more, and saw the vacant house looking the same as it ever did. A cloud lighted anew, low in the deep sky, a single long wing. The mystery he had felt like a golden and aimless bird had waited until now to fly over. Until now, when all else had been driven out. His body shook. Perhaps the fever would go now, and the chill come.

But Louella brought him his supper and waited while he ate it, sitting quietly. She had made him chicken broth that sparkled like diamonds in the evening light, and then there would be the junket he hated, turning to water under his tongue.

"Louella, I don't want junket tonight. Louella, listen. Do you hear a thing ticking?"

"Hear it plain."

She took his tray and sat down again, and he lay on his back, looking upward. High in the sky the quarter moon was bright. "Reckon it's going to blow up in the night? You can see it. Look on the washstand." All by itself, of its own accord, it might let fly its little door and start up. He thought he heard it now. Or was it his father's watch in the next room, already laid on the dresser for the night?

"I 'spec' it will, Loch, if you wants it to," she said readily, and sat on in the dark. She added, "Blow up? If it do, I'll wrang your neck. Next time you scoot down that tree and come back draggin' sompm. Listen that big bullfrog in the swamp, you want to listen to sompm might blow up."

He listened, lying stretched and pointed in the four

directions. His heart pumping the secret anticipation that parted his lips, he fell into space and floated. Even floating, he felt the pressure of his frown and heard his growling voice and the gnashing of his teeth. He dreamed close to the surface, and his dreams were filled with a color and a fury that the daytime that summer never held.

Later, in her moonlit bed, Cassie lay thinking. Her hair and the inner side of her arms still smelled of hay; she tasted the sweet summer dryness in her mouth. In the distances of her mind the wagon still rocked, rocking its young girls' burden, the teasing anxiety, the singing, the moon and stars and the moving roof of leaves, Moon Lake brimming and the boat on it, the smiling drowse of boys, and the way she herself had let nobody touch even her hand. And she thought back to the sailor beginning to run down the street, as strange a sight with his clothes partly missing as a mer-man from the lake, and around again to Miss Eckhart and Virgie coming together on the deadquiet sidewalk. What she was certain of was the distance those two had gone, as if all along they had been making a trip (which the sailor was only starting). It had changed them. They were deliberately terrible. They looked at each other and neither wished to speak. They did not even horrify each other. No one could touch them now, either.

Danke schoen . . . That much was out in the open. Gratitude—like rescue—was simply no more. It was not only past; it was outworn and cast away. Both Miss Eckhart and Virgie Rainey were human beings terribly at large, roaming on the face of the earth. And there were others of them—human beings, roaming, like lost beasts.

Into her head flowed the whole of the poem she had found in that book. It ran perfectly through her head, vanishing as it went, one line yielding to the next, like a torch race. All of it passed through her head, through her body. She slept, but sat up in bed once and said aloud, *"'Because a fire was in my head.'"* Then she fell back unresisting. She did not see except in dreams that a face looked in; that it was the grave, unappeased, and radiant face, once more and always, the face that was in the poem.

3.

SIR RABBIT

He looked around first one side of the tree and then the other. And not a word!

"Oh-oh. I know you, Mr. King MacLain!" Mattie Will cried, but the impudence—which still seemed marvelous to her since she'd never laid eyes on him close or thought of opening her mouth to him—all the impudence was carried off on the batting spring wind. "I know the way you do." When it came down to it, scared or not, she wanted to show him she'd heard all about King MacLain and his way. And scared or not, the air made her lightheaded.

If it was Mr. King, he was, suddenly, looking around both sides of the tree at once—two eyes here and two eyes there, two little Adam's apples, and all those little brown hands. She shut her eyes, then her mouth. She planted her hoe in front of her toes and stood her ground by the bait can, too old—fifteen—to call out now that something was happening, but she took back what she'd said.

Then as she peeped, it was two MacLains that came out from behind the hickory nut tree. Mr. MacLain's twins, his sons of course. Who would have believed they'd grown up?—or almost; for they were scared. They must be as old as herself, thought Mattie Will. People aren't prepared for twins having to grow up like ordinary people but see them always miniature and young somewhere. And here they were coming—the very spit of Mr. King their father.

Mattie Will waited on them. She yawned—strangely, for she felt at that moment as though somewhere a little boat was going out on a lake, never to come back—to see two little meanies coming now that she'd never dreamed of, instead of the one that would have terrified her for the rest of her days.

Those twins were town boys. They had their own pop stand by the post office stile on Saturdays in summer. Out here in the country they had undone their knee buckles and came jingling. Their fair bangs lifted and fell in the soft downy light under the dark tree, with its flowers so few you could still count them, it was so early in spring. They trotted down and up through the little gully like a pony pair that could keep time to music in the Ringling Brothers', touching shoulders until the last.

They made a tinkling circle around her. They didn't give her a chance to begin her own commotion, only lifted away her hoe that she stretched out and leaned it on the big vines. They didn't have one smile between them; instead, little matching frowns were furring their foreheads, so that she wanted to press them out with the flat of her finger.

One of the twins took hold of her by the apron sash and the other one ran under and she was down. One of them pinned her arms and the other one jumped her bare, naked feet. Biting their lips, they sat on her. One small hand, smelling of a recent lightning-bug (so early in the year?), blindfolded her eyes. The strong fresh smell of the place—which she had found first—came up and they rolled over on the turned-up mold, where the old foolish worms were coming out in their blindness.

At moments the sun would take hold of their arms with a bold dart of light, or rest on their wetted, shaken hair, or splash over their pretty clothes like the torn petals of a sunflower. She felt the soft and babylike heads, and the nuzzle of little cool noses. Whose nose was whose? She might have felt more anger than confusion, except that to keep twins straight had fallen her lot. And it seemed to her that from now on, having a visit go the visitor's way would come before giving trouble. She who had kicked Old Man Flewellyn out of the dewberry patch, an old smiling man! She had set her teeth in a small pointed ear that had the fuzz of a peach, and did not bite. Then she rolled her head and dared the other twin, with her teeth at his ear, since they were all in this together, all in here equally now, where it had been quiet as moonrise to her, and now while one black crow after another beat his wings across a turned-over field no distance at all beyond.

When they sat up in a circle with their skinned knees propped up in the playing light that came down like a fountain, she and the MacLain twins ate candy —as many sticks of candy as they felt like eating out of one paper sack for three people. The MacLain twins had brought the sack away out here with them and had put it in a safe place ahead of time, as far from the scene as the pin oak—needlessly far. Their forethought cast a pall on all three as they sucked and held their candy in their mouths like old men's pipes. One crow hollered over their heads and they all got to their feet as though a clock struck.

"Now."

What did it matter which twin said that word, like a little bark? It was the parting word. There was her hoe held up in a grandfather vine, gone a little further in its fall, and there was her bucket. After they'd walked away from her—backwards for a piece—then she, jumping at them to chase them off, screamed into the veil of leaves, "I just did it because your mamma's a poor albino!"

She would think afterwards, married, when she had the time to sit down—churning, for instance— "Who had the least sense and the least care, for fifteen? They did. I did. But it wasn't fair to tease me.

To try to make me dizzy, and run a ring around me,
or make me think that first minute I was going to be
carried off by their pa. Teasing because I had to open
my mouth about Mr. King MacLain before I knew
what was coming."

Tumbling on the wet spring ground with the
goody-goody MacLain twins was something Junior
Holifield would have given her a licking for, just for
making such a story up, supposing, after she married
Junior, she had put anything in words. Or he would
have said he'd lick her for it if she told it *again*.

Poor Junior!

II.

"Oh, good afternoon, sir. Don't shoot me, it's King
MacLain. I'm in the habit of hunting these parts."

Junior had just knocked off a dead, double-headed
pine cone and Blackstone was aiming at the telephone wire when the light voice with the fast words
running together came out of the trees above the
gully.

"Thought I'd see if the birds around here still
tasted as sweet as they used to." And there he was—
that is, he showed for a minute and then was gone
behind a reddening sweetgum tree.

But fall coming or not, poor little quails weren't
any of his business, with him darting around tree
trunks in a starched white suit, even if he did carry a
gun for looks, Mattie Will thought. She studied the
empty arch between two trees with a far-sighted
look. If that was Mr. King MacLain, nobody was ever
going to shoot him. Shoot *him?* Let him go on ahead
in his Sunday best from one tree to another without
giving warning or being so fussy about wild shots
from the low scrub. He was Mr. King, all right. Up
there back of the leaves his voice laughed and made
fun this minute.

Junior looked up and said, "Well, we come out to

use up some old ammunition." He lifted his upper lip. He had another pine cone on his mind. He pinged it.

"You hear me?" said the voice.

"It sure did look like Mr. MacLain to me, Junior," Mattie Will whispered, pretending to be as slow as Junior was. She squinted against the small sun points that came at her cheeks through the braid of her hat. Then she pushed her way around her husband.

"Well. And we come out to shoot up some old ammunition on Saturday," Junior told her. "This *is* Saturday." He pulled her back.

"You boys been sighting any birds this way?" the white glimmer asked courteously, and then it passed behind another tree. "Seen my dog, then?" And the invisible mouth whistled, from east right around to west, they could hear the clean round of it. Mr. King even *whistled* with manners. And with familiarity. And what two men in the world whistle the same? Mattie Will believed she must have heard him and seen him closer-to than she thought. Nobody could have *told* her how sweet the old rascal whistled, but it didn't surprise her.

Wilbur, the Holifield dog, flailed his tail and took a single bound toward the bank. Of course he had been barking the whole time, answered tolerantly by some dogs in town who—as certainly as if you could see them—were lying in front of the barbershop.

"Sighted e'er bird? Just one cuckoo," Junior said now, with his baby-mouth drawn down as if he would cry, which meant he was being funny, and so Blackstone, his distance behind in the plum thicket, hopped on one foot for Junior, but Junior said, "Be still, Blackstone, no call for you to start cutting up yet."

"No, sir. Never pass by these parts without bringing down a few plump, juicy birds for my supper," said the voice. It was far-away for the moment; Mr. MacLain must have turned and looked at the view from the hilltop. You could see all Morgana from there, and he could have picked out his own house.

"My name is Holifield. We was just out using up some old ammunition on Saturday, me and a nigger. And as long as you don't get no closer to us, we ain't liable to hit you," said Junior.

That echoed a little. They both happened to get behind gum trees just then, Mr. MacLain and Junior. *Junior* was behind a tree! And she was between them. Mattie Will put her hand over her laughing mouth. Blackstone in the thicket broke a stick and chunked the pieces in the air. "And we won't pay no attention what you do in your part of the woods," Junior said, a dignified gaze on the falling chips.

"Suits me, sir!"

"Truth is—" Junior always kept right on! Just as he would do eating, at the table, and to his sorrow. "I ain't prepared to believe you come after birds, hardly, Mr. MacLain, if it is you. *We* are the ones come after what birds they is, if they is any birds. You're trespassing."

"Trespassing," said the voice presently. "Well— don't shoot me for that."

"Oho ho, Mr. Junior! Know what? *He* gawn shoot *us!* Shoot us!" In the ecstasy of knowing the end of it ahead of time, Blackstone flew out in the open and sang it like a bird, and beat his pants.

"You hush up, or if he don't shoot you, I will," Junior said. "Look, what happened to your gun, you lost it agin?"

Mr. MacLain was moving waywardly along, and sometimes got as completely hidden by even a skinny little wild cherry as if he'd melted into it.

Ping!

"One more redbird!" sighed Mattie Will.

"Ain't we two hunting men letting each other by and about their own business?" asked Mr. MacLain, suddenly loud upon them. They saw part of him, looking out there at the head of the gully, one hand on a knee. "Look—this is the stretch of woods I always did like the best. Why don't you try a different stretch?"

"*See there?*"

Mr. MacLain laughed agreeably at accusation.

"There's something else ain't what you think," Junior said in his most Holifield way. "Ain't e'er young lady folling after me, that you can catch a holt of—white or black."

Wilbur spraddled right up the bank to Mr. MacLain suddenly, before they knew it, and fawned on him before they got him back. He was named Wilbur after Mr. Morrison, who had printed Mattie Will's and Junior's marriage in the newspaper.

Mr. MacLain withdrew, and Junior was patting Wilbur, hammer-like.

"Junior," Mattie Will called softly through the cup of her hand. "Looks like you really scared that man away. Wonder who he was?"

"Bless God. Come out in the open, young lady. I can hear you but not see you," Mr. MacLain called, appearing immediately from the waist up.

So poor Junior had got one thing right. Mr. MacLain had been counting on it all the time—that young girl-wives not tied down yet could generally be found following after their husbands, if the husbands went out with a .22 on a nice enough day in October.

"Won't you come out and explain something mysterious to me, young lady?"

But it sounded as if he'd just thought of it, and called it mysterious.

Mattie Will, who was crouched to her knees, bent her head. She took a June bug off a leaf, a late June bug. She was thinking to herself, Mr. MacLain must be up in years, and they said he never did feel constrained to live in Morgana like other people and just visited Mrs. MacLain a little now and then. He roamed the country end on end, living up north and where-all, on funds; and might at any time appear and then, over night, disappear. Who could have guessed today he was this close?

"Show yourself, young lady. Are you a Holifield too? I don't think you are. Come out here and let me ask you something." But he went bobbing on to another tree while he was cajoling, bright as a lantern that swayed in a wind.

"Show yourself and I'll brain you directly, Mattie Will," Junior said. "You heard who he said he was and you done heard what he was, all your life, or you ain't a girl." Junior squeezed up to his .22 and trained it, immediately changing his voice to a little high singsong. "He's the one gits ever'thing he wants shootin' from around trees, like the MacLains been doing since Time. Killed folks trespassin' when he was growin' up, or his pa did, if it so pleased him. MacLains begun killin' when they begun settlin'. And don't nobody know how many chirren he has. Don't let him git no closer to me than he is now, you all."

Mattie Will ran the June bug up and down her arm and remembered once when she was little and her mother and father had both been taken with the prevalent sickness, and it was Mrs. MacLain from Morgana—who before that was known only by sight to her—who had come out to the farm and nursed and cooked for them, since there was nobody. She served them light-bread toast, and not biscuit, and didn't believe in molasses. She was not afraid of all the mud. She was in the congregation, always, a sweet-looking Presbyterian albino lady. Nothing was her fault. Mrs. MacLain came by herself to church, without boy or man, her lace collar fastened down by a cluster-pearl pin just like a little ice cream spoon, loaded. Going down the aisle she held up her head for the benefit of them all, while they considered Mr. MacLain a thousand miles away. And when they sang in church with her, they might as well have sung,

"A thousand miles away.
A thousand miles away."

It made church holier.

"I'll just start up that little bank till I see what he's after, Junior," Mattie Will said, rising.

Junior just looked at her stubbornly.

She pinched him. "Didn't you hear him ask me a question? Don't be so country: I'm going to answer it. And who's trespassing, if it's not us all three and a nigger? These whole woods belongs to you know who, Old Lady Stark. She'd like to see us all in Coventry this minute." She pointed overhead, without looking, where the signs said,

Posted.
No Pigs With or Without Rings.
No Hunting.
This Means You.
STARK

While he looked at those, and even Mr. MacLain looked at them, Mattie Will made her way up the bank.

"You see?" Junior cried again. "Yonder comes Mattie Will. It's just a good thing I got my gun too, Mr. MacLain. You're so smart. I didn't even know you was near enough to flush out, Mr. MacLain. You back to stay? Come on, Blackstone, let's me and you shoot him right now if he budges to catch a holt of Mattie Will, don't care what happens to us or who we hit, whether we both go to the 'lectric chair or not."

Mr. MacLain then looked out from a pin oak and fired a load of buckshot down, the way he'd throw a bone. Mattie Will's tongue ran out too, to show Junior how he'd acted in public.

Blackstone was howling out from his plum thicket, "Now it be's our turn and I found my old gun and we done used up every bit of ammunition we had on turtles an' trash! You see, you see."

Mattie Will looked up at Mr. MacLain and he beamed at her. He sent another load out, this one down over her where she held to some roots on the bank, and right over Junior's head.

It peppered his hat. Baby hole shamed it all over, blush-like. Junior threw away his gun.

Big red hand spread out on his shirt (he would always think he was shot through the heart if anybody's gun but his went off), Junior rose in the air and got a holler out. And then—he seemed determined about the way to come down, like Mister Holifield down from a ladder; no man more set in his ways than he, even Mister Holifield—he kicked and came down backwards. There was a fallen tree, a big fresh-cut magnolia some good-for-nothing had amused himself chopping down. Across that Junior decided to light, instead of on green moss—head and body on one side of the tree, feet and legs on the other. Then he went limp from the middle out, before their eyes. He was dead to the world; as immune as if asleep in his pew, but bent the opposite way.

Mr. MacLain appeared on top of the gully, wearing a yellowy Panama hat and a white linen suit with the sleeves as ridgy as two washboards. He looked like the preternatural month of June. He came light of foot and let his gunstock trail carefree through the periwinkle, which would bind it a little and then let go.

He went to Junior first, taking the bank in three or four knee-deep steps down.

He bent over and laid his ear to Junior. He thumped him, like a melon he tested, and let him lie —too green. As if lighting a match from his side, he drew a finger down Junior's brown pants leg, and stepped away. Mr. MacLain's linen shoulders, white as a goose's back in the sun, shrugged and twinkled in the glade.

To his back, he was not so very big, not so flashy and splendid as, for example, some brand-new evangelist come into the midst. He turned around and threw off his hat, and showed a thatch of straight, biscuit-colored hair. He smiled. His puckered face was like a little boy's, with square brown teeth.

Mattie Will slid down the bank. Mr. MacLain

stood with head cocked while the wind swelled and blew across the top of the ridge, turning over the green and gold leaves high up around them all, stirring along suspicions of burning leaves and gunpowder smoke and the juice of the magnolia, and then he dropped his gun flat in the vines. Mattie Will saw he was coming now.

"Turn *your* self around and start picking plums!" she called, joining her hands, and Blackstone turned around, just in time.

When she laid eyes on Mr. MacLain close, she staggered, he had such grandeur, and then she was caught by the hair and brought down as suddenly to earth as if whacked by an unseen shillelagh. Presently she lifted her eyes in a lazy dread and saw those eyes above hers, as keenly bright and unwavering and apart from her life as the flowers on a tree.

But he put on her, with the affront of his body, the affront of his sense too. No pleasure in that! She had to put on what he knew with what he did—maybe because he was so grand it was a thorn to him. Like submitting to another way to talk, she could answer to his burden now, his whole blithe, smiling, superior, frantic existence. And no matter what happened to her, she had to remember, disappointments are not to be borne by Mr. MacLain, or he'll go away again.

Now he clasped her to his shoulder, and her tongue tasted sweet starch for the last time. Her arms dropped back to the mossiness, and she was Mr. MacLain's Doom, or Mr. MacLain's Weakness, like the rest, and neither Mrs. Junior Holifield nor Mattie Will Sojourner; now she was something she had always heard of. She did not stir.

Then when he let her fall and walked off, when he was out of hearing in the woods, and the birds and woods-sounds and the wood-chopping throbbed clearly, she lay there on one elbow, wide awake. A dove feather came turning down through the light that was like golden smoke. She caught it with a dart of the hand, and brushed her chin; she was never displeased to catch anything. Nothing more fell.

But she moved. She was the mover in the family. She jumped up. Besides, she heard plums falling into the bucket—sounds of pure complaint by this time. She threw Blackstone a glance. He picked plums and had a lizard to play with, and his cap unretrieved from his first sailing delight still hung in a tree. The Holifield dog licked Blackstone on the seat patch and then trotted over and licked Junior on the stone-like hand, and looked back over his shoulder with the expression of a lady soloist to whose song nobody has really listened. For ages he might have been making a little path back and forth between Junior and Blackstone, but she could not think of his name, or would not, just as Junior would not wake up.

She wasn't going to call a one of them, man or dog, to his senses. There was Junior suspended dead to the world over a tree that was big enough around for two of him half as willful. He was hooped in the middle like the bridge over Little Chunky. Fools could set foot on him, walk over him. Even a young mule could run across him, the one he wanted to buy. His old brown pants hung halfway up his legs, and there in his poky middle pitifully gleamed the belt buckle anybody would know him by, even in a hundred years. J for Junior. A pang reached her and she took a step. It could be he was scared more than half to death—but no, not with that sleeping face, still with its look of "How come?", or its speckled lashes, quiet as the tails of sitting birds, in the shade of his brow.

"Let the church bells wake him!" said Mattie Will to Wilbur. "Ain't tomorrow Sunday? Blackstone, you have your cap to climb up after."

In the woods she heard sounds, the dry creek beginning to run or a strange man calling, one or the other, she thought, but she walked right up on Mr. MacLain again, asleep—snoring. He slept sitting up

with his back against a tree, his head pillowed in the
luminous Panama, his snorting mouth drawn round
in a perfect heart open to the green turning world
around him.

She stamped her foot, nothing happened, then she
approached softly, and down on hands and knees
contemplated him. Her hair fell over her eyes and she
steadily blew a part in it; her head went back and
forth appearing to say "No." Of course she was not
denying a thing in this world, but now had time to
look at anything she pleased and study it.

With her almost motherly sway of the head and
arms to help her, she gazed at the sounding-off, sleeping head, and the neck like a little porch column in
town, at the one hand, the other hand, the bent leg
and the straight, all those parts looking no more
driven than her man's now, or of any more use than a
heap of cane thrown up by the mill and left in the pit
to dry. But they were, and would be. He snored as if
all the frogs of spring were inside him—but to him
an old song. Or to him little balls, little bells for the
light air, that rose up and sank between his two
hands, never to be let fall.

His coat hung loosely out from him, and a letter
suddenly dropped a little way out from a pocket—
whiter than white.

Mattie Will subsided forward onto her arms. Her
rear stayed up in the sky, which seemed to brush it
with little feathers. She lay there and listened to the
world go round.

But presently Mr. MacLain leaped to his feet, bolt
awake, with a flourish of legs. He looked horrified—
that he had been seen asleep? and by Mattie Will?
And he did not know that there was nothing she
could or would take away from him—Mr. King Mac-
Lain?

> In the night time,
> At the right time,
> So I've understood,

'Tis the habit of Sir Rabbit
To dance in the wood—

That was all that went through Mattie Will's head.

"What you doing here, girl?" Mr. MacLain beat his snowy arms up and down. "Go on! Go on off! Go to Guinea!"

She got up and skedaddled.

She pressed through a haw thicket and through the cherry trees. With a tree-high seesawing of boughs a squirrel chase ran ahead of her through the woods —Morgan's Woods, as it used to be called. Fat birds were rocking on their perches. A little quail ran on the woods floor. Down an arch, some old cedar lane up here, Mattie Will could look away into the big West. She could see the drift of it all, the stretched land below the little hills, and the Big Black, clear to MacLain's Courthouse, almost, the Stark place plain and the fields, and their farm, everybody's house above trees, the MacLains'—the white floating peak —and even Blackstone's granny's cabin, where there had been a murder one time. And Morgana all in rays, like a giant sunflower in the dust of Saturday.

But as she ran down through the woods and vines, this side and that, on the way to get Junior home, it stole back into her mind about those two gawky boys, the MacLain twins. They were soft and jumpy! That day, with their brown, bright eyes popping and blinking, and their little aching Adam's apples—they were like young deer, or even remoter creatures . . . kangaroos. . . . For the first time Mattie Will thought they were mysterious and sweet—gamboling now she knew not where.

4.

MOON LAKE

From the beginning his martyred presence seriously affected them. They had a disquieting familiarity with it, hearing the spit of his despising that went into his bugle. At times they could hardly recognize what he thought he was playing. Loch Morrison, Boy Scout and Life Saver, was under the ordeal of a week's camp on Moon Lake with girls.

Half the girls were county orphans, wished on them by Mr. Nesbitt and the Men's Bible Class after Billy Sunday's visit to town; but all girls, orphans and Morgana girls alike, were the same thing to Loch; maybe he threw in the two councilors too. He was hating every day of the seven. He hardly spoke; he never spoke first. Sometimes he swung in the trees; Nina Carmichael in particular would hear him crashing in the foliage somewhere when she was lying rigid in siesta.

While they were in the lake, for the dip or the five-o'clock swimming period in the afternoon, he stood against a tree with his arms folded, jacked up one-legged, sitting on his heel, as absolutely tolerant as an old fellow waiting for the store to open, being held up by the wall. Waiting for the girls to get out, he gazed upon some undisturbed part of the water. He despised their predicaments, most of all their not being able to swim. Sometimes he would take aim and from his right cheek shoot an imaginary gun at something far out, where they never were. Then he resumed his pose. He had been roped into this by his mother.

At the hours too hot for girls he used Moon Lake. He dived high off the crosspiece nailed up in the big oak, where the American Legion dived. He went through the air rocking and jerking like an engine, splashed in, climbed out, spat, climbed up again, dived off. He wore a long bathing suit which stretched longer from Monday to Tuesday and from Tuesday to Wednesday and so on, yawning at the armholes toward infinity, and it looked black and formal as a mistrel suit as he stood skinny against the clouds as on a stage.

He came and got his food and turned his back and ate it all alone like a dog and lived in a tent by himself, apart like a nigger, and dived alone when the lake was clear of girls. That way, he seemed able to bear it; that would be his life. In early evening, in moonlight sings, the Boy Scout and Life Saver kept far away. They would sing "When all the little ships come sailing home," and he would be roaming off; they could tell about where he was. He played taps for them, invisibly then, and so beautifully they wept together, whole tentfuls some nights. Off with the whip-poor-wills and the coons and the owls and the little bobwhites—down where it all sloped away, he had pitched his tent, and slept there. Then at reveille, how he would spit into that cornet.

Reveille was his. He harangued the woods when the little minnows were trembling and running wizardlike in the water's edge. And how lovely and altered the trees were then, weighted with dew, leaning on one another's shoulders and smelling like big wet flowers. He blew his horn into their presence—trees' and girls'—and then watched the Dip.

"Good morning, Mr. Dip, Dip, Dip, with your water just as cold as ice!" sang Mrs. Gruenwald hoarsely. She took them for the dip, for Miss Moody said she couldn't, simply couldn't.

The orphans usually hung to the rear, and every

other moment stood swayback with knees locked, the shoulders of their wash dresses ironed flat and stuck in peaks, and stared. For swimming they owned no bathing suits and went in in their underbodies. Even in the water they would stand swayback, each with a fist in front of her over the rope, looking over the flat surface as over the top of a tall mountain none of them could ever get over. Even at this hour of the day, they seemed to be expecting little tasks, something more immediate—little tasks that were never given out.

Mrs. Gruenwald was from the North and said "dup." "Good morning, Mr. Dup, Dup, Dup, with your water just as cold as ice!" sang Mrs. Gruenwald, fatly capering and leading them all in a singing, petering-out string down to the lake. She did a sort of little rocking dance in her exhortation, broad in her bathrobe. From the tail end of the line she looked like a Shredded Wheat Biscuit box rocking on its corners.

Nina Carmichael thought, There is nobody and nothing named Mr. Dip, it is not a good morning until you have had coffee, and the water is the temperature of a just-cooling biscuit, thank Goodness. I hate this little parade of us girls, Nina thought, trotting fiercely in the center of it. It ruins the woods, all right. "Gee, we think you're mighty nice," they sang to Mr. Dip, while the Boy Scout, waiting at the lake, watched them go in.

"Watch out for mosquitoes," they called to one another, lyrically because warning wasn't any use anyway, as they walked out of their kimonos and dropped them like the petals of one big scattered flower on the bank behind them, and exposing themselves felt in a hundred places at once the little pangs. The orphans ripped their dresses off over their heads and stood in their underbodies. Busily they hung and piled their dresses on a cedar branch, obeying one of their own number, like a whole flock of ferocious little birds with pale topknots building themselves a nest. The orphan named Easter appeared in charge. She handed her dress wrong-side-out to a friend, who turned it and hung it up for her, and waited standing very still, her little fingers locked.

"Let's let the orphans go in the water first and get the snakes stirred up, Mrs. Guenwald," Jinny Love Stark suggested first off, in the cheerful voice she adopted toward grown people. "Then they'll be chased away by the time *we* go in."

That made the orphans scatter in their pantie-waists, outwards from Easter; the little gauzes of gnats they ran through made them beat their hands at the air. They ran back together again, to Easter, and stood excitedly, almost hopping.

"I think we'll all go in in one big bunch," Mrs. Gruenwald said. Jinny Love lamented and beat against Mrs. Gruenwald, Mrs. Gruenwald's solid, rope-draped stomach all but returning her blows. "All take hands—march! Into the water! *Don't* let the stobs and cypress roots break your legs! *Do* your best! Kick! Stay on top if you can and hold the rope if necessary!"

Mrs. Gruenwald abruptly walked away from Jinny Love, out of the bathrobe, and entered the lake with a vast displacing. She left them on the bank with her Yankee advice.

The Morgana girls might never have gone in if the orphans hadn't balked. Easter came to a dead stop at Moon Lake and looked at it squinting as though it floated really on the Moon. And mightn't it be on the Moon?—it was a strange place, Nina thought, un-likely—and three miles from Morgana, Mississippi, all the time. The Morgana girls pulled the orphans' hands and dragged them in, or pushed suddenly from behind, and finally the orphans took hold of one another and waded forward in a body, singing, "Good Morning" with their stiff, chip-like lips. None of them could or would swim, ever, and they just stood waist-deep and waited for the dip to be over. A few of them

reached out and caught the struggling Morgana girls
by the legs as they splashed from one barky post to
another, to see how hard it really was to stay up.

"Mrs. Gruenwald, look, they want to drown us."

But Mrs. Gruenwald all this time was rising and
sinking like a whale, she was in a sea of her own
waves and perhaps of self-generated cold, out in the
middle of the lake. She cared little that Morgana girls
who learned to swim were getting a dollar from
home. She had deserted them, no, she had never
really been with them. Not only orphans had she deserted. In the water she kept so much to the profile
that her single pushing-out eyeball looked like a little
bottle of something. It was said she believed in evolution.

While the Boy Scout in the rosy light under the
green trees twirled his horn so that it glittered and
ran a puzzle in the sun, and emptied the spit out of
it, he yawned, snappingly—as if he would bite the
day, as quickly as Easter had bitten Deacon Nesbitt's
hand on Opening Day.

"Gee, we think you're mighty nice," they sang to
Mr. Dip, gasping, pounding their legs in him. If they
let their feet go down, the invisible bottom of the lake
felt like soft, knee-deep fur. The sharp hard knobs
came up where least expected. The Morgana girls of
course wore bathing slippers, and the mud loved to
suck them off. The alligators had been beaten out of
this lake, but it was said that water snakes—pilots
—were swimming here and there; they would bite
you but not kill you; and one cottonmouth moccasin
was still getting away from the niggers—if the niggers
were still going after him; he would kill you. These
were the chances of getting sucked under, of being
bitten, and of dying three miles away from home.

The brown water cutting her off at the chest, Easter
looked directly before her, wide awake, unsmiling.
Before she could hold a stare like that, she would
have had to swallow something big—so Nina felt. It
would have been something so big that it didn't mat-

ter to her what the inside of a snake's mouth was lined with. At the other end of her gaze the life saver grew almost insignificant. Her gaze moved like a little switch or wand, and the life saver scratched himself with his bugle, raked himself, as if that eased him. Yet the flick of a blue-bottle fly made Easter jump.

They swam and held to the rope, hungry and waiting. But they had to keep waiting till Loch Morrison blew his horn before they could come out of Moon Lake. Mrs. Gruenwald, who capered before breakfast, believed in evolution, and put her face in the water, was quarter of a mile out. If she said anything, they couldn't hear her for the frogs.

II.

Nina and Jinny Love, with the soles of their feet shocked from the walk, found Easter ahead of them down at the spring.

For the orphans, from the first, sniffed out the way to the spring by themselves, and they could get there without stops to hold up their feet and pull out thorns and stickers, and could run through the sandy bottoms and never look down where they were going, and could grab hold with their toes on the sharp rutted path up the pine ridge and down. They clearly could never get enough of skimming over the silk-slick needles and setting prints of their feet in the bed of the spring to see them dissolve away under their eyes. What was it to them if the spring was muddied by the time Jinny Love Stark got there?

The one named Easter could fall flat as a boy, elbows cocked, and drink from the cup of her hand with her face in the spring. Jinny Love prodded Nina, and while they looked on Easter's drawers, Nina was opening the drinking cup she had brought with her, then collapsing it, feeling like a lady with a fan. That way, she was going over a thought, a fact: Half the people out here with me are orphans. Orphans. Orphans. She yearned for her heart to twist. But it didn't, not in time. Easter was through drinking—wiping her mouth and flinging her hand as if to break the bones, to get rid of the drops, and it was Nina's turn with her drinking cup.

Nina stood and bent over from the waist. Calmly, she held her cup in the spring and watched it fill. They could all see how it spangled like a cold star in the curling water. The water tasted the silver cool of the rim it went over running to her lips, and at moments the cup gave her teeth a pang. Nina heard her own throat swallowing. She paused and threw a smile about her. After she had drunk she wiped the cup on her tie and collapsed it, and put the little top on, and its ring over her finger. With that, Easter, one arm tilted, charged against the green bank and mounted it. Nina felt her surveying the spring and all from above. Jinny Love was down drinking like a chicken, kissing the water only.

Easter was dominant among the orphans. It was not that she was so bad. The one called Geneva stole, for example, but Easter was dominant for what she was in herself—for the way she held still, sometimes. All orphans were at once wondering and stoic —at one moment loving everything too much, the next folding back from it, tightly as hard green buds growing in the wrong direction, closing as they go. But it was as if Easter signaled them. Now she just stood up there, watching the spring, with the name Easter—tacky name, as Jinny Love Stark was the first to say. She was medium size, but her hair seemed to fly up at the temples, being cropped and wiry, and this crest made her nearly as tall as Jinny Love Stark. The rest of the orphans had hair paler than their tanned foreheads—straight and tow, the greenish yellow of cornsilk that dimmed black at the roots and shadows, with burnt-out-looking bangs like young boys' and old men's hair; that was from picking in the fields. Easter's hair was a withstanding gold. Around the back of her neck beneath the hair was a dark band on her skin like the mark a gold bracelet

leaves on the arm. It came to the Morgana girls with
a feeling of elation: the ring was pure dirt. They liked
to look at it, or to remember, too late, what it was—
as now, when Easter had already lain down for a
drink and left the spring. They liked to walk behind
her and see her back, which seemed spectacular from
crested gold head to hard, tough heel. Mr. Nesbitt,
from the Bible Class, took Easter by the wrist and
turned her around to him and looked just as hard at
her front. She had started her breasts. What Easter
did was to bite his right hand, his collection hand. It
was wonderful to have with them someone dangerous
but not, so far, or provenly, bad. When Nina's little
lead-mold umbrella, the size of a clover, a Cracker-
jack prize, was stolen the first night of camp, that was
Geneva, Easter's friend.

Jinny Love, after wiping her face with a handmade
handkerchief, pulled out a deck of cards she had
secretly brought in her middy pocket. She dropped
them down, bright blue, on a sandy place by the
spring. "Let's play cassino. Do they call you *Easter?*"

Down Easter jumped, from the height of the bank.
She came back to them. "Cassino, what's that?"

"All right, what do *you* want to play?"

"All right, I'll play you mumblety-peg."

"I don't know how you play that!" cried Nina.

"Who would ever want to know?" asked Jinny Love,
closing the circle.

Easter flipped out a jack-knife and with her sawed
fingernail shot out three blades.

"Do you carry that in the orphan asylum?" Jinny
Love asked with some respect.

Easter dropped to her scarred and coral-colored
knees. They saw the dirt. "Get down if you want to
play me mumblety-peg," was all she said, "and watch
out for your hands and faces."

They huddled down on the piney sand. The vivid,
hurrying ants were everywhere. To the squinted eye
they looked like angry, orange ponies as they rode
the pine needles. There was Geneva, skirting behind

a tree, but she never came close or tried to get in the game. She pretended to be catching doodlebugs. The knife leaped and quivered in the sandy arena smoothed by Easter's hand.

"I may not know how to play, but I bet I win," Jinny Love said.

Easter's eyes, lifting up, were neither brown nor green nor cat; they had something of metal, flat ancient metal, so that you could not see into them. Nina's grandfather had possessed a box of coins from Greece and Rome. Easter's eyes could have come from Greece or Rome that day. Jinny Love stopped short of apprehending this, and only took care to watch herself when Easter pitched the knife. The color in Easter's eyes could have been found somewhere, away—away, under lost leaves—strange as the painted color of the ants. Instead of round black holes in the center of her eyes, there might have been women's heads, ancient.

Easter, who had played so often, won. She nodded and accepted Jinny Love's barrette and from Nina a blue jay feather which she transferred to her own ear.

"I wouldn't be surprised if you cheated, and don't know what you had to lose if you lost," said Jinny Love thoughtfully but with an admiration almost fantastic in her.

Victory with a remark attached did not crush Easter at all, or she scarcely listened. Her indifference made Nina fall back and listen to the spring running with an endless sound and see how the July light like purple and yellow birds kept flickering under the trees when the wind blew. Easter turned her head and the new feather on her head shone changeably. A black funnel of bees passed through the air, throwing a funneled shadow, like a visitor from nowhere, another planet.

"We have to play again to see whose the drinking cup will be," Easter said, swaying forward on her knees.

Nina jumped to her feet and did a cartwheel.

Against the spinning green and blue her heart pounded as heavily as she touched lightly.

"You ruined the game," Jinny Love informed Easter. "You don't know Nina." She gathered up her cards. "You'd think it was made of fourteen-carat gold, and didn't come out of the pocket of an old suitcase, that cup."

"I'm sorry," said Nina sincerely.

As the three were winding around the lake, a bird flying above the opposite shore kept uttering a cry and then diving deep, plunging into the trees there, and soaring to cry again.

"Hear him?" one of the niggers said, fishing on the bank; it was Elberta's sister Twosie, who spoke as if a long, long conversation had been going on, into which she would intrude only the mildest words. "Know why? Know why, in de sky, he say 'Spirit? Spirit?' And den he dive *boom* and say 'GHOST'?"

"Why does he?" said Jinny Love, in a voice of objection.

"Yawl knows. *I* don't know," said Twosie, in her little high, helpless voice, and she shut her eyes. They couldn't seem to get on by her. On fine days there is danger of some sad meeting, the positive danger of it. "*I* don't know what he say dat for." Twosie spoke pitifully, as though accused. She sighed. "Yawl sho ain't got yo' eyes opem good, yawl. Yawl don't know what's out here in woods wid you."

"Well, what?"

"Yawl walk right by mans wid great big gun, could jump out at yawl. Yawl don't eem smellim."

"You mean Mr. Holifield? That's a flashlight he's got." Nina looked at Jinny Love for confirmation. Mr. Holifield was their handy man, or rather simply "the man to be sure and have around the camp." He could be found by beating for a long time on the porch of the American Legion boat house—he slept heavily. "He hasn't got a gun to jump out with."

"I know who you mean. I hear those boys. Just

some big boys, like the MacLain twins or somebody, and who cares about them?" Jinny Love, with her switch indented the thick mat of hair on Twosie's head and prodded and stirred it gently. She pretended to fish in Twosie's woolly head. "Why ain't *you* scared, then?"

"I is."

Twosie's eyelids fluttered. Already she seemed to be fishing in her night's sleep. While they gazed at her crouched, devoted figure, from which the long pole hung, so steady and beggarlike and ordained an appendage, all their passions flew home again and went huddled and soft to roost.

Back at the camp, Jinny Love told Miss Moody about the great big jack-knife. Easter gave it up.

"I didn't mean you couldn't *drink* out of my cup," Nina said, waiting for her. "Only you have to hold it carefully, it leaks. It's engraved."

Easter wouldn't even try it, though Nina dangled it on its ring right under her eyes. She didn't say anything, not even "It's pretty." Was she even thinking of it? Or if not, what did she think about?

"Sometimes orphans act like deaf-and-dumbs," said Jinny Love.

III.

"Nina!" Jinny Love whispered across the tent, during siesta. "What do you think you're reading?"

Nina closed *The Re-Creation of Brian Kent.* Jinny Love was already coming directly across the almost-touching cots to Nina's, walking on her knees and bearing down over Gertrude, Etoile, and now Geneva.

With Jinny Love upon her, Geneva sighed. Her sleeping face looked as if she didn't want to. She slept as she swam, in her pantie-waist, she was in running position and her ribs went up and down frantically —a little box in her chest that expanded and shut without a second's rest between. Her cheek was pearly with afternoon moisture and her kitten-like teeth pearlier still. As Jinny Love hid her and went over, Nina seemed to see her still; even her vaccination mark looked too big for her.

Nobody woke up from being walked over, but after Jinny Love had fallen in bed with Nina, Easter gave a belated, dreaming sound. She had not even been in the line of march; she slept on the cot by the door, curved shell-like, both arms forward over her head. It was an inward sound she gave—now it came again—of such wholehearted and fateful concurrence with the thing dreamed, that Nina and Jinny Love took hands and made wry faces at each other.

Beyond Easter's cot the corona of afternoon flared and lifted in an intensity that came through the eyelids. There was nothing but light out there. True, the black Negroes inhabited it. Elberta moved slowly through it, as if she rocked a baby with her hips, carrying a bucket of scraps to throw in the lake—to get hail Columbia for it later. Her straw hat spiraled rings of orange and violet, like a top. Far, far down a vista of intolerable light, a tiny daub of black cotton, Twosie had stationed herself at the edge of things, and slept and fished.

Eventually there was Exum wandering with his fish pole—he could dance on a dime, Elberta said, he used to work for a blind man. Exum was smart for twelve years old; too smart. He found that hat he wore—not a sign of the owner. He had a hat like new, filled out a little with peanut shells inside the band to correct the size, and he like a little black peanut in it. It stood up and away from his head all around, and seemed only following him—on runners, perhaps, like those cartridges for change in Spights' store.

Easter's sighs and her prolonged or half-uttered words now filled the tent, just as the heat filled it. Her words fell in threes, Nina observed, like the mourning-dove's call in the woods.

Nina and Jinny Love lay speechless, doubling for themselves the already strong odor of Sweet Dreams Mosquito Oil, in a trance of endurance through the hour's siesta. Entwined, they stared—orphan-like themselves—past Easter's cot and through the tent opening as down a long telescope turned on an incandescent star, and saw the spiral of Elberta's hat return, and saw Exum jump over a stick and on the other side do a little dance in a puff of dust. They could hear the intermittent crash, splash of Loch Morrison using their lake, and Easter's voice calling again in her sleep, her unintelligible words.

But however Nina and Jinny Love made faces at they knew not what, Easter concurred; she thoroughly agreed.

The bugle blew for swimming. Geneva jumped so hard she fell off her cot. Nina and Jinny Love were indented with each other, like pressed leaves, and jumped free. When Easter, who had to be shaken, sat up drugged and stupid on her cot, Nina ran over to her.

"Listen. Wake up. Look, you can go in in my bathing shoes today."

She felt her eyes glaze with this plan of kindness as she stretched out her limp red shoes that hung down like bananas under Easter's gaze. But Easter dropped back on the cot and stretched her legs.

"Never mind your shoes. I don't have to go in the lake if I don't want to."

"You do. I never heard of that. Who picked you out? You do," they said, all gathering.

"You make me."

Easter yawned. She fluttered her eyes and rolled them back—she loved doing that. Miss Moody passed by and beamed in at them hovered around Easter's passive and mutinous form. All along she'd been afraid of some challenge to her counselorship, from the way she hurried by now, almost too daintily.

"Well, *I* know," Jinny Love said, sidling up. "I know as much as you know, Easter." She made a chant, which drove her hopping around the tent pole in an Indian step. "You don't have to go, if you don't want

to go. And if it ain't so, you still don't have to go, if
you don't want to go." She kissed her hand to them.

Easter was silent—but if she groaned when she
waked, she'd only be imitating herself.

Jinny Love pulled on her bathing cap, which gave
way and came down over her eyes. Even in blindness,
she cried, "So you needn't think you're the only one,
Easter, not always. What do you say to that?"

"I should worry, I should cry," said Easter, lying
still, spread-eagled.

"Let's us run away from basket weaving," Jinny
Love said in Nina's ear, a little later in the week.

"Just as soon."

"Grand. They'll think we're drowned."

They went out the back end of the tent, barefooted; their feet were as tough as anybody's by this
time. Down in the hammock, Miss Moody was reading *The Re-Creation of Brian Kent* now. (Nobody
knew whose book that was, it had been found here,
the covers curled up like side combs. Perhaps anybody at Moon Lake who tried to read it felt cheated
by the title, as applying to camp life, as Nina did, and
laid it down for the next person.) Cat, the niggers'
cat, was sunning on a post and when they approached jumped to the ground like something
poured out of a bottle, and went with them, in front.

They trudged down the slope past Loch Morrison's tent and took the track into the swamp. There
they moved single file between two walls; by lifting
their arms they could have touched one or the other
pressing side of the swamp. Their toes exploded the
dust that felt like the powder clerks pump into new
kid gloves, as Jinny Love said twice. They were eye
to eye with the finger-shaped leaves of the castor bean
plants, put out like those gypsy hands that part the
curtains at the back of rolling wagons, and wrinkled
and coated over like the fortune-teller's face.

Mosquitoes struck at them; Sweet Dreams didn't

last. The whining lifted like a voice, saying "I don't want . . ." At the girls' shoulders Queen Anne's lace and elderberry and blackberry thickets, loaded heavily with flower and fruit and smelling with the melony smell of snake, overhung the ditch to touch them. The ditches had dried green or blue bottoms, cracked and glazed—like a dropped vase. "I hope we don't meet any nigger men," Jinny Love said cheerfully.

Sweet bay and cypress and sweetgum and live oak and swamp maple closing tight made the wall dense, and yet there was somewhere still for the other wall of vine; it gathered itself on the ground and stacked and tilted itself in the trees; and like a table in the tree the mistletoe hung up there black in the zenith. Buzzards floated from one side of the swamp to the other, as if choice existed for them—raggedly crossing the sky and shadowing the track, and shouldering one another on the solitary limb of a moon-white sycamore. Closer to the ear than lips could begin words came the swamp sounds—closer to the ear and nearer to the dreaming mind. They were a song of hilarity to Jinny Love, who began to skip. Periods of silence seemed hoarse, or the suffering from hoarseness, otherwise inexplicable, as though the world could stop. Cat was stalking something at the black edge of the ditch. The briars didn't trouble Cat at all, it was they that seemed to give way beneath that long, boatlike belly.

The track serpentined again, and walking ahead was Easter. Geneva and Etoile were playing at her side, edging each other out of her shadow, but when they saw who was coming up behind them, they turned and ran tearing back towards camp, running at angles, like pullets, leaving a cloud of dust as they passed by.

"Wouldn't you know!" said Jinny Love.

Easter was going unconcernedly on, her dress stained green behind; she ate something out of her hand as she went.

"We'll soon catch up—don't hurry."

The reason orphans were the way they were lay first in nobody's watching them, Nina thought, for she felt obscurely like a trespasser. They, they were not answerable. Even on being watched, Easter remained not answerable to a soul on earth. Nobody cared! And so, in this beatific state, something came out of *her*.

"Where are you going?"

"Can we go with you, Easter?"

Easter, her lips stained with blackberries, replied, "It ain't my road."

They walked along, one on each side of her. Though they automatically stuck their tongues out at her, they ran their arms around her waist. She tolerated the closeness for a little while; she smelled of orphan-starch, but she had a strange pure smell of sweat, like a sleeping baby, and in her temple, so close then to their eyes, the skin was transparent enough for a little vein to be seen pounding under it. She seemed very tender and very small in the waist to be trudging along so doggedly, when they had her like that.

Vines, a magnificent and steamy green, covered more and more of the trees, played over them like fountains. There were stretches of water below them, blue-black, netted over with half-closed waterlilies. The horizontal limbs of cypresses grew a short, pale green scruff like bird feathers.

They came to a tiny farm down here, the last one possible before the muck sucked it in—a patch of cotton in flower, a house whitewashed in front, a cleanswept yard with a little iron pump standing in the middle of it like a black rooster. These were white people—an old woman in a sunbonnet came out of the house with a galvanized bucket, and pumped it full in the dooryard. That was an excuse to see people go by.

Easter, easing out of the others' clasp, lifted her arm halfway and turning for an instant, gave two

waves of the hand. But the old woman was prouder
than she.

Jinny Love said, "How would you all like to live
there?"

Cat edged the woods onward, and at moments
vanished into a tunnel in the briars. Emerging from
other tunnels, he—or she—glanced up at them with
a face more mask-like than ever.

"There's a short-cut to the lake." Easter, breaking
and darting ahead, suddenly went down on her knees
and slid under a certain place in the barbed wire
fence. Rising, she took a step inward, sinking down
as she went. Nina untwined her arm from Jinny Love's
and went after her.

"I might have known you'd want us to go through
a barbed wire fence." Jinny Love sat down where she
was, on the side of the ditch, just as she would take
her seat on a needlepoint stool. She jumped up once,
and sat back. "Fools, fools!" she called. "Now I think
you've made me turn my ankle. Even if I wanted to
track through the mud, I couldn't!"

Nina and Easter, dipping under a second, unexpected fence, went on, swaying and feeling their feet
pulled down, reaching to the trees. Jinny Love was
left behind in the heartless way people and incidents
alike are thrown off in the course of a dream, like the
gratuitous flowers scattered from a float—rather in
celebration. The swamp was now all-enveloping, dark
and at the same time vivid, alarming—it was like being inside the chest of something that breathed and
might turn over.

Then there was Moon Lake, a different aspect altogether. Easter climbed the slight rise ahead and
reached the pink, grassy rim and the innocent open.
Here it was quiet, until, fatefully, there was one soft
splash.

"You see the snake drop off in the water?" asked
Easter.

"Snake?"

"Out of that tree."

"You can have him."

"There he is: coming up!" Easter pointed.

"That's probably a different one," Nina objected in the voice of Jinny Love.

Easter looked both ways, chose, and walked on the pink sandy rim with its purpled lip, her blue shadow lolling over it. She went around a bend, and straight to an old gray boat. Did she know it would be there? It was in some reeds, looking mysterious to come upon and yet in place, as an old boat will. Easter stepped into it and hopped to the far seat that was over the water, and dropping to it lay back with her toes hooked up. She looked falling over backwards. One arm lifted, curved over her head, and hung till her finger touched the water.

The shadows of the willow leaves moved gently on the sand, deep blue and narrow, long crescents. The water was quiet, the color of pewter, marked with purple stobs, although where the sun shone right on it the lake seemed to be in violent agitation, almost boiling. Surely a little chip would turn around and around in it. Nina dropped down on the flecked sandbar. She fluttered her eyelids, half closed them, and the world looked struck by moonlight.

"Here I come," came Jinny Love's voice. It hadn't been long. She came twitching over their tracks along the sandbar; her long soft hair blowing up like a skirt in a play of the breeze in the open. "But I don't choose to sit myself in a leaky boat," she was calling ahead. "I choose the land."

She took her seat on the very place where Nina was writing her name. Nina moved her finger away, drawing a long arrow to a new place. The sand was coarse like beads and full of minute shells, some shaped exactly like bugles.

"Want to hear about my ankle?" Jinny Love asked. "It wasn't as bad as I thought. I must say you picked a queer place, I saw an *owl*. It smells like the school basement to me—peepee and old erasers." Then she stopped with her mouth a little open, and was quiet, as though something had been turned off inside her. Her eyes were soft, her gaze stretched to Easter, to the boat, the lake—her long oval face went vacant.

Easter was lying rocked in the gentle motion of the boat, her head turned on its cheek. She had not said hello to Jinny Love anew. Did she see the drop of water clinging to her lifted finger? Did it make a rainbow? Not to Easter: her eyes were rolled back, Nina felt. Her own hand was writing in the sand. Nina, Nina, Nina. Writing, she could dream that her self might get away from her—that here in this faraway place she could tell her self, by name, to go or to stay. Jinny Love had begun building a sand castle over her foot. In the sky clouds moved no more perceptibly than grazing animals. Yet with a passing breeze, the boat gave a knock, lifted and fell. Easter sat up.

"Why aren't we out in the boat?" Nina, taking a strange and heady initiative, rose to her feet. "Out there!" A picture in her mind, as if already furnished from an eventual and appreciative distance, showed the boat floating where she pointed, far out in Moon Lake with three girls sitting in the three spaces. "We're coming, Easter!"

"Just as I make a castle. *I'm* not coming," said Jinny Love. "Anyway, there's stobs in the lake. We'd be upset, ha ha."

"What do I care, I can swim!" Nina cried at the water's edge.

"You can just swim from the first post to the second post. And that's in front of camp, not here."

Firming her feet in the sucking, minnowy mud, Nina put her weight against the boat. Soon her legs were half hidden, the mud like some awful kiss pulled at her toes, and all over she tautened and felt the sweat start out of her body. Roots laced her feet, knotty and streaming. Under water, the boat was caught too, but Nina was determined to free it. She saw that there was muddy water in the boat too,

which Easter's legs, now bright pink, were straddling.
Suddenly all seemed easy.

"It's coming loose!"

At the last minute, Jinny Love, who had extracted
her foot from the castle with success, hurried over
and climbed to the middle seat of the boat, scream-
ing. Easter sat up swaying with the dip of the boat;
the energy seemed all to have gone out of her. Her
lolling head looked pale and featureless as a pear
beyond the laughing face of Jinny Love. She had not
said whether she wanted to go or not—yet surely she
did; she had been in the boat all along, she had discovered the boat.

For a moment, with her powerful hands, Nina held
the boat back. Again she thought of a pear—not the
everyday gritty kind that hung on the tree in the backyard, but the fine kind sold on trains and at high
prices, each pear with a paper cone wrapping it
alone—beautiful, symmetrical, clean pears with thin
skins, with snow-white flesh so juicy and tender that
to eat one baptized the whole face, and so delicate
that while you urgently ate the first half, the second
half was already beginning to turn brown. To all
fruits, and especially to those fine pears, something
happened—the process was so swift, you were never
in time for them. It's not the flowers that are fleeting,
Nina thought, it's the fruits—it's the time when things
are ready that they don't stay. She even went through
the rhyme, "Pear tree by the garden gate, How much
longer must I wait?"—thinking it was the pears that
asked it, not the picker.

Then she climbed in herself, and they were rocking
out sideways on the water.

"Now what?" said Jinny Love.

"This is all right for me," said Nina.

"Without oars?—Ha ha."

"Why didn't you tell me, then!—But I don't care
now."

"You never are as smart as you think."

"Wait till you find out where we get to."

"I guess you know Easter can't swim. She won't even touch water with her foot."

"What do you think a *boat's* for?"

But a soft tug had already stopped their drifting. Nina with a dark frown turned and looked down.

"A chain! An old mean chain!"

"That's how smart you are."

Nina pulled the boat in again—of course nobody helped her!—burning her hands on the chain, and kneeling outward tried to free the other end. She could see now through the reeds that it was wound around and around an old stump, which had almost grown over it in places. The boat had been chained to the bank since maybe last summer.

"No use hitting it," said Jinny Love.

A dragonfly flew about their heads. Easter only waited in her end of the boat, not seeming to care about the disappointment either. If this was their ship, she was their figurehead, turned on its back, sky-facing. She wouldn't be their passenger.

"You thought we'd all be out in the middle of Moon Lake by now, didn't you?" Jinny Love said, from her lady's seat. "Well, look where we are."

"Oh, Easter! Easter! I wish you still had your knife!"

"—But let's don't go back yet," Jinny Love said on shore. "I don't think they've missed us." She started a sand castle over her other foot.

"You make me sick," said Easter suddenly.

"Nina, let's pretend Easter's not with us."

"But that's what *she* was pretending."

Nina dug into the sand with a little stick, printing "Nina" and then "Easter."

Jinny Love seemed stunned, she let sand run out of both fists. "But how could you ever know what Easter was pretending?"

Easter's hand came down and wiped her name clean; she also wiped out "Nina." She took the stick out of Nina's hand and with a formal gesture, as if she would otherwise seem to reveal too much, wrote for herself. In clear, high-waisted letters the word "Esther" cut into the sand. Then she jumped up.

"Who's that?" Nina asked.

Easter laid her thumb between her breasts, and walked about.

"Why, I call that 'Esther.' "

"Call it 'Esther' if you want to, I call it 'Easter.' "

"Well, sit down. . . ."

"And I named myself."

"How could you? Who let you?"

"I let myself name myself."

"Easter, I believe you," said Nina. "But I just want you to spell it right. Look—E-A-S—"

"I should worry, I should cry."

Jinny Love leaned her chin on the roof of her castle to say, "I was named for my maternal grandmother, so my name's Jinny Love. It couldn't be anything else. Or anything better. You see? Easter's just not a real name. It doesn't matter how she spells it, Nina, nobody ever had it. Not around here." She rested on her chin.

"I have it."

"Just see how it looks spelled right." Nina lifted the stick from Easter's fingers and began to print, but had to throw herself bodily over the name to keep Easter from it. "Spell it right and it's real!" she cried.

"But right or wrong, it's tacky." said Jinny Love. "You can't get me mad over it. All I can concentrate on out here is missing the figs at home."

" 'Easter' is real beautiful!" Nina said distractedly. She suddenly threw the stick into the lake, before Easter could grab it, and it trotted up and down in a crucible of sun-filled water. "I thought it was the day you were found on a doorstep," she said sullenly—even distrustfully.

Easter sat down at last and with slow, careful movements of her palms rubbed down the old bites on her legs. Her crest of hair dipped downward and she rocked a little, up and down, side to side, in a rhythm. Easter never did intend to explain anything unless she had to—or to force your explanations. She just had hopes. She hoped never to be sorry. Or did she?

"I haven't got no father. I never had, he ran away. I've got a mother. When I could walk, then my mother took me by the hand and turned me in, and I remember it. I'm going to be a singer."

It was Jinny Love, starting to clear her throat, who released Nina. It was Jinny Love, escaping, burrowing her finger into her castle, who was now kind, pretending Easter had never spoken. Nina banged Jinny Love on the head with her fist. How good and hot her hair was! Like hot glass. She broke the castle from her tender foot. She wondered if Jinny Love's head would break. Not at all. You couldn't learn anything through the head.

"Ha, ha, ha!" yelled Jinny Love, hitting back.

They were fighting and hitting for a moment. Then they lay quiet, tilted together against the crumbled hill of sand, stretched out and looking at the sky where now a white tower of cloud was climbing.

Someone moved; Easter lifted to her lips a piece of cross-vine cut back in the days of her good knife. She brought up a kitchen match from her pocket, lighted up, and smoked.

They sat up and gazed at her.

"If you count much on being a singer, that's not a very good way to start," said Jinny Love. "Even boys, it stunts their growth."

Easter once more looked the same as asleep in the dancing shadows, except for what came out of her mouth, more mysterious, almost, than words.

"Have some?" she asked, and they accepted. But theirs went out.

Jinny Love's gaze was fastened on Easter, and she dreamed and dreamed of telling on her for smoking, while the sun, even through leaves, was burning her pale skin pink, and she looked the most beautiful of all: she felt temptation. But what she said was, "Even after all this is over, Easter, I'll always remember you."

Off in the thick of the woods came a fairy sound, followed by a tremulous silence, a holding apart of the air.

"What's that?" cried Easter sharply. Her throat quivered, the little vein in her temple jumped.

"That's Mister Loch Morrison. Didn't you know he had a horn?"

There was another fairy sound, and the pried-apart, gentle silence. The woods seemed to be moving after it, running—the world pellmell. Nina could see the boy in the distance, too, and the golden horn tilted up. A few minutes back her gaze had fled the present and this scene; now she put the horn blower into his visionary place.

"Don't blow that!" Jinny Love cried out this time, jumping to her feet and stopping up her ears, stamping on the shore of Moon Lake. "You shut up! We can hear!—Come on," she added prosaically to the other two. "It's time to go. I reckon they've worried enough." She smiled. "Here comes Cat."

Cat always caught something; something was in his—or her—mouth, a couple of little feet or claws bouncing under the lifted whiskers. Cat didn't look especially triumphant; just through with it.

They marched on away from their little boat.

IV.

One clear night the campers built a fire up above the spring, cooked supper on sticks around it, and after stunts, a recitation of "How They Brought the Good News from Ghent to Aix" by Gertrude Bowles, and the ghost story about the bone, they stood up on the ridge and poured a last song into the woods—"Little Sir Echo."

The fire was put out and there was no bright point to look into, no circle. The presence of night was be-

side them—a beast in gossamer, with no shine of outline, only of ornament—rings, ear-rings. . . .

"March!" cried Mrs. Gruenwald, and stamped down
the trail for them to follow. They went single file on
the still-warm pine needles, soundlessly now. Not far
away there were crackings of twigs, small, regretted
crashes; Loch Morrison, supperless for all they knew,
was wandering around by himself, sulking, alone.

Nobody needed light. The night sky was pale as a
green grape, transparent like grape flesh over each
tree. Every girl saw moths—the beautiful ones like
ladies, with long legs that were wings—and the little
ones, mere bits of bark. And once against the night,
just before Little Sister Spights' eyes, making her cry
out, hung suspended a spider—a body no less mysterious than the grape of the air, different only a little.

All around swam the fireflies. Clouds of them, trees
of them, islands of them floating, a lower order of
brightness—one could even get into a tent by mistake. The stars barely showed their places in the
pale sky—small and far from this bright world. And
the world would be bright as long as these girls held
awake, and could keep their eyes from closing. And
the moon itself shone—taken for granted.

Moon Lake came in like a flood below the ridge;
they trailed downward. Out there Miss Moody
would sometimes go in a boat; sometimes she had a
late date from town, "Rudy" Spights or "Rudy"
Loomis, and then they could be seen drifting there
after the moon was up, far out on the smooth bright
surface. ("And she lets him hug her out there," Jinny
Love had instructed them. "Like this." She had seized,
of all people, Etoile, whose name rhymed with tinfoil.
"Hands off," said Etoile.) Twice Nina had herself
seen the silhouette of the canoe on the bright water,
with the figures at each end, like a dark butterfly
with wings spread open and still. Not tonight!

Tonight, it was only the niggers, fishing. But their
boat must be full of silver fish! Nina wondered if it
was the slowness and near-fixity of boats out on the

water that made them so magical. Their little boat in
the reeds that day had not been far from this one's
wonder, after all. The turning of water and sky, of
the moon, or the sun, always proceeded, and there
was this magical hesitation in their midst, of a boat.
And in the boat, it was not so much that they drifted,
as that in the presence of a boat the world drifted,
forgot. The dreamed-about changed places with the
dreamer.

Home from the wild moonlit woods, the file of little
girls wormed into the tents, which were hot as cloth
pockets. The candles were lighted by Miss Moody,
dateless tonight, on whose shelf in the flare of nightly
revelation stood her toothbrush in the glass, her hand-
painted celluloid powder box, her Honey and Al-
mond cream, her rouge and eyebrow tweezers, and at
the end of the line the bottle of Compound, contain-
ing true and false unicorn and the life root plant.

Miss Moody, with a fervent frown which precluded
interruption, sang in soft tremolo as she rubbed the
lined-up children with "Sweet Dreams."

> "Forgive me
> O please forgive me
> I didn't mean to make
> You cry!
> I love you and I need you—"

They crooked and bent themselves and lifted night-
gowns to her silently while she sang. Then when she
faced them to her they could look into the deep tan-
gled rats of her puffed hair and at her eyebrows
which seemed fixed for ever in that elevated line of
adult pleading.

> "Do anything but don't say good-bye!"

And automatically they almost said, "Good-bye!" Her
hands rubbed and cuffed them while she sang, pulling to her girls all just alike, as if girlhood itself were
an infinity, but a commodity. ("I'm ticklish," Jinny
Love informed her every night.) Her look of pleading

seemed infinitely perilous to them. Her voice had the sway of an aerialist crossing the high wire, even while she sang out of the nightgown coming down over her head.

There were kisses, prayers. Easter, as though she could be cold tonight, got into bed with Geneva. Geneva like a little June bug hooked onto her back. The candles were blown. Miss Moody ostentatiously went right to sleep. Jinny Love cried into her pillow for her mother, or perhaps for the figs. Just outside their tent, Citronella burned in a saucer in the weeds —Citronella, like a girl's name.

Luminous of course but hidden from them, Moon Lake streamed out in the night. By moonlight sometimes it seemed to run like a river. Beyond the cry of the frogs there were the sounds of a boat moored somewhere, of its vague, clumsy reaching at the shore, those sounds that are recognized as being made by something sightless. When did boats have eyes —once? Nothing watched that their little part of the lake stayed roped off and protected; was it there now, the rope stretched frail-like between posts that swayed in mud? That rope was to mark how far the girls could swim. Beyond lay the deep part, some bottomless parts, said Moody. Here and there was the quicksand that stirred your footprint and kissed your heel. All snakes, harmless and harmful, were freely playing now; they put a trailing, moony division between weed and weed—bright, turning, bright and turning.

Nina still lay dreamily, or she had waked in the night. She heard Gertrude Bowles gasp in a dream, beginning to get her stomach ache, and Etoile begin, slowly, her snore. She thought: Now I can think, in between them. She could not even feel Miss Moody fretting.

The orphan! she thought exultantly. The other way to live. There were secret ways. She thought, Time's really short, I've been only thinking like the others.

It's only interesting, only worthy, to try for the fiercest secrets. To slip into them all—to change. To change for a moment into Gertrude, into Mrs. Gruenwald, into Twosie—into a boy. To *have been* an orphan.

Nina sat up on the cot and stared passionately before her at the night—the pale dark roaring night with its secret step, the Indian night. She felt the forehead, the beaded stars, look in thoughtfully at her.

The pondering night stood rude at the tent door, the opening fold would let it stoop in—it, him—he had risen up inside. Long-armed, or long-winged, he stood in the center there where the pole went up. Nina lay back, drawn quietly from him. But the night knew about Easter. All about her. Geneva had pushed her to the very edge of the cot. Easter's hand hung down, opened outward. Come here, night, Easter might say, tender to a giant, to such a dark thing. And the night, obedient and graceful, would kneel to her. Easter's callused hand hung open there to the night that had got wholly into the tent.

Nina let her own arm stretch forward opposite Easter's. Her hand too opened, of itself. She lay there a long time motionless, under the night's gaze, its black cheek, looking immovably at her hand, the only part of her now which was not asleep. Its gesture was like Easter's, but Easter's hand slept and her own hand knew—shrank and knew, yet offered still.

"Instead . . . me instead. . . ."

In the cup of her hand, in her filling skin, in the fingers' bursting weight and stillness, Nina felt it: compassion and a kind of competing that were all one, a single ecstasy, a single longing. For the night was not impartial. No, the night loved some more than others, served some more than others. Nina's hand lay open there for a long time, as if its fingers would be its eyes. Then it too slept. She dreamed her hand was helpless to the tearing teeth of wild beasts. At reveille she woke up lying on it. She could not move it. She hit it and bit it until like a cluster of bees it stung back and came to life.

v.

They had seen, without any idea of what he would do—and yet it was just like him— little old Exum toiling up the rough barky ladder and dreaming it up, clinging there monkeylike among the leaves, all eyes and wrinkled forehead.

Exum was apart too, boy and nigger to boot; he constantly moved along an even further fringe of the landscape than Loch, wearing the man's stiff straw hat brilliant as a snowflake. They would see Exum in the hat bobbing along the rim of the swamp like a fisherman's cork, elevated just a bit by the miasma and illusion of the landscape he moved in. It was Exum persistent as a little bug, inching along the foot of the swamp wall, carrying around a fishing cane and minnow can, fishing around the bend from their side of the lake, catching all kinds of things. Things, things. He claimed all he caught, gloating —dangled it and loved it, clasped it with suspicious glee—wouldn't a soul dispute him that? The Boy Scout asked him if he could catch an electric eel and Exum promised it readily—a gift; the challenge was a siesta-long back-and-forth across the water.

Now all rolling eyes, he hung on the ladder, too little to count as looking—too everything-he-was to count as anything.

Beyond him on the diving-board, Easter was standing—high above the others at their swimming lesson. She was motionless, barefooted, and tall with her outgrown, printed dress on her and the sky under her. She had not answered when they called things up to her. They splashed noisily under her callused, coral-colored foot that hung over.

"How are you going to get down, Easter!" shouted Gertrude Bowles.

Miss Moody smiled understandingly up at Easter. How far, in the water, could Miss Parnell Moody be transformed from a schoolteacher? They had wondered. She wore a canary yellow bathing cap lumpy over her hair, with a rubber butterfly on the front. She wore a brassiere and bloomers under her bathing suit because, said Jinny Love, that was exactly how good she was. She scarcely looked for trouble, immediate trouble—though this was the last day at Moon Lake.

Exum's little wilted black fingers struck at his lips as if playing a tune on them. He put out a foolishly long arm. He held a green willow switch. Later they every one said they saw him—but too late. He gave Easter's heel the tenderest, obscurest little brush, with something of nigger persuasion about it.

She dropped like one hit in the head by a stone from a sling. In their retrospect, her body, never turning, seemed to languish upright for a moment, then descend. It went to meet and was received by blue air. It dropped as if handed down all the way and was let into the brown water almost on Miss Moody's crown, and went out of sight at once. There was something so positive about its disappearance that only the instinct of caution made them give it a moment to come up again; it didn't come up. Then Exum let loose a girlish howl and clung to the ladder as though a fire had been lighted under it.

Nobody called for Loch Morrison. On shore, he studiously hung his bugle on the tree. He was enormously barefooted. He took a frog dive and when he went through the air they noticed that the powdered-on dirt gave him lavender soles. Now he swam destructively into the water, cut through the girls, and began to hunt Easter where all the fingers began to point.

They cried while he hunted, their chins dropping into the brown buggy stuff and their mouths sometimes swallowing it. He didn't give a glance their way. He stayed under as though the lake came down a lid on him, at each dive. Sometimes, open-mouthed, he appeared with something awful in his hands, showing not them, but the world, or himself—long ribbons of green and terrible stuff, shapeless black matter, nobody's shoe. Then he would up-end and go down, hunting her again. Each dive was a call on Exum to scream again.

"Shut up! Get out of the way! You stir up the lake!" Loch Morrison yelled once—blaming them. They looked at one another and after one loud cry all stopped crying. Standing in the brown that cut them off where they waited, ankle-deep, waist-deep, knee-deep, chin-deep, they made a little V, with Miss Moody in front and partly obscuring their vision with her jerky butterfly cap. They felt his insult. They stood so still as to be almost carried away, in the pictureless warm body of lake around them, until they felt the weight of the currentless water pulling anyhow. Their shadows only, like the curled back edges of a split drum, showed where they each protruded out of Moon Lake.

Up above, Exum howled, and further up, some fulsome, vague clouds with uneasy hearts blew peony-like. Exum howled up, down, and all around. He brought Elberta, mad, from the cook tent, and surely Mrs. Gruenwald was dead to the world—asleep or reading—or she would be coming too, by now, capering down her favorite trail. It was Jinny Love, they realized, who had capered down, and now stood strangely signaling from shore. The painstaking work of Miss Moody, white bandages covered her arms and legs; poison ivy had appeared that morning. Like Easter, Jinny Love had no intention of going in the lake.

"Ahhhhh!" everybody said, long and drawn out, just as he found her.

Of course he found her, there was her arm sliding through his hand. They saw him snatch the hair of Easter's head, the way a boy will snatch anything he wants, as if he won't have invisible opponents snatching first. Under the water he joined himself to her. He spouted, and with engine-like jerks brought her in.

There came Mrs. Gruenwald. With something like
a skip, she came to a stop on the bank and waved her
hands. Her middy blouse flew up, showing her
loosened corset. It was red. They treasured that up.
But her voice was pre-emptory.

"This minute! Out of the lake! Out of the lake, out-
out! Parnell! Discipline! March them out."

"One's drowned!" shrieked poor Miss Moody.

Loch stood over Easter. He sat her up, folding, on
the shore, wheeled her arm over, and by that
dragged her clear of the water before he dropped
her, a wrapped bundle in the glare. He shook himself
in the sun like a dog, blew his nose, spat, and shook
his ears, all in a kind of leisurely trance that kept
Mrs. Gruenwald off—as though he had no notion that
he was interrupting things at all. Exum could now be
heard shrieking for Miss Marybelle Steptoe, the lady
who had had the camp last year and was now married and living in the Delta.

Miss Moody and all her girls now came out of the
lake. Tardy, drooping, their hair heavy-wet and their
rubber shoes making wincing sounds, they edged the
shore.

Loch returned to Easter, spread her out, and then
they could all get at her, but they watched the water
lake in her lap. The sun like a weight fell on them.
Miss Moody wildly ran and caught up Easter's ankle
and pushed on her, like a lady with a wheelbarrow.
The Boy Scout looped Easter's arms like sashes on
top of her and took up his end, the shoulders. They
carried her, looking for shade. One arm fell, touching
ground. Jinny Love, in the dazzling bandages, ran
up and scooped Easter's arm in both of hers. They
proceeded, zigzag, Jinny Love turning her head toward the rest of them, running low, bearing the arm.

They put her down in the only shade on earth,
after all, the table under the tree. It was where they
ate. The table was itself still mostly tree, as the ladder and diving board were half tree too; a camp
table had to be round and barky on the underside,

and odorous of having been chopped down. They knew that splintery surface, and the ants that crawled on it. Mrs. Gruenwald, with her strong cheeks, blew on the table, but she might have put a cloth down. She stood between table and girls; her tennis shoes, like lesser corsets, tied her feet solid there; and they did not go any closer, but only to where they could see.

"I got her, please ma'am."

In the water, the life saver's face had held his whole impatience; now it was washed pure, blank. He pulled Easter his way, away from Miss Moody—who, however, had got Easter's sash ends wrung out—and then, with a turn, hid her from Mrs. Gruenwald. Holding her folded up to him, he got her clear, and the next moment, with a spread of his hand, had her lying there before him on the table top.

They were silent. Easter lay in a mold of wetness from Moon Lake, on her side; sharp as a flatiron her hipbone pointed up. She was arm to arm and leg to leg in a long fold, wrong-colored and pressed together as unopen leaves are. Her breasts, too, faced together. Out of the water Easter's hair was darkened, and lay over her face in long fern shapes. Miss Moody laid it back.

"You can tell she's not breathing," said Jinny Love.

Easter's nostrils were pinched-looking like an old country woman's. Her side fell slack as a dead rabbit's in the woods, with the flowers of her orphan dress all running together in some antic of their own, some belated mix-up of the event. The Boy Scout had only let her go to leap onto the table with her. He stood over her, put his hands on her, and rolled her over; they heard the distant-like knock of her forehead on the solid table, and the knocking of her hip and knee.

Exum was heard being whipped in the willow clump; then they remembered Elberta was his

mother. "You little black son-a-bitch!" they heard
her yelling, and he howled through the woods.

Astride Easter the Boy Scout lifted her up between
his legs and dropped her. He did it again, and she
fell on one arm. He nodded—not to them.

There was a sigh, a Morgana sigh, not an orphans'. The orphans did not press forward, or claim
to own or protect Easter any more. They did nothing
except mill a little, and yet their group was delicately
changed. In Nina's head, where the world was still
partly leisurely, came a recollected scene: birds on a
roof under a cherry tree; they were drunk.

The Boy Scout, nodding, took Easter's hair and
turned her head. He left her face looking at them.
Her eyes were neither open nor altogether shut but
as if her ears heard a great noise, back from the time
she fell; the whites showed under the lids pale and
slick as watermelon seeds. Her lips were parted to
the same degree; her teeth could be seen smeared
with black mud.

The Boy Scout reached in and gouged out her
mouth with his hand, an unbelievable act. She did
not alter. He lifted up, screwed his toes. and with a
groan of his own fell upon her and drove up and
down upon her, into her, gouging the heels of his
hands into her ribs again and again. She did not
alter except that she let a thin stream of water out
of her mouth, a dark stain down the fixed cheek. The
children drew together. Life-saving was much worse
than they had dreamed. Worse still was the carelessness of Easter's body.

Jinny Love volunteered once more. She would
wave a towel over things to drive the mosquitoes, at
least, away. She chose a white towel. Her unspotted
arms lifted and criss-crossed. She faced them now;
her expression quietened and became ceremonious.

Easter's body lay up on the table to receive anything that was done to it. If *he* was brutal, her self,
her body, the withheld life, was brutal too. While the

Boy Scout as if he rode a runaway horse clung momently to her and arched himself off her back, dug
his knees and fists into her and was flung back ca-
reening by his own tactics, she lay there.

Let him try and try!

The next thing Nina knew was a scent of home, an
adult's thumb in her shoulder, and a cry, "Now
what?" Miss Lizzie Stark pushed in front of her,
where her hips and black purse swung to a full stop,
blotting out everything. She was Jinny Love's mother
and had arrived on her daily visit to see how the
camp was running.

They never heard the electric car coming, but
usually they saw it, watched for it in the landscape, as
out of place as a piano rocking over the holes and
taking the bumps, making a high wall of dust.

Nobody dared tell Miss Lizzie; only Loch Morrison's grunts could be heard.

"Some orphan get too much of it?" Then she said
more loudly, "But what's *he* doing to her? Stop that."

The Morgana girls all ran to her and clung to her
skirt.

"Get off me," she said. "Now look here, everybody.
I've got a weak heart. You all know that.—Is that
Jinny Love?"

"Leave me alone, Mama," said Jinny Love, waving
the towel.

Miss Lizzie, whose hands were on Nina's shoulders,
shook Nina. "Jinny Love Stark, come here to me,
Loch Morrison, get off that table and shame on you."

Miss Moody was the one brought to tears. She
walked up to Miss Lizzie holding a towel in front of
her breast and weeping. "He's our life saver, Miss
Lizzie. Remember? Our Boy Scout. Oh, mercy, I'm
thankful you've come, he's been doing that a long
time. Stand in the shade, Miss Lizzie."

"Boy Scout? Why, he ought to be—he ought to be
—I can't stand it, Parnell Moody."

"Can't any of us help it, Miss Lizzie. Can't any of us. It's what he came for." She wept.

"That's Easter," Geneva said. "That is."

"He ought to be put out of business," Miss Lizzie Stark said. She stood in the center of them all, squeezing Nina uncomfortably for Jinny Love, who flouted her up in front, and Nina could look up at her. The white rice powder which she used on the very front of her face twinkled on her faint mustache. She smelled of red pepper and lemon juice—she had been making them some mayonnaise. She was valiantly trying to make up for all the Boy Scout was doing by what she was thinking of him: that he was odious. Miss Lizzie's carelessly flung word to him on sight—the first day—had been, "You little rascal, I bet you run down and pollute the spring, don't you?" "Nome," the Boy Scout had said, showing the first evidence of his gloom.

"Tears won't help, Parnell," Miss Lizzie said. "Though some don't know what tears are." She glanced at Mrs. Gruenwald, who glanced back from another level; she had brought herself out a chair. "And our last afternoon. I'd thought we'd have a treat."

They looked around as here came Marvin, Miss Lizzie's yard boy, holding two watermelons like a mother with twins. He came toward the table and just stood there.

"Marvin. You can put those melons down, don't you see the table's got somebody on it?" Miss Lizzie said. "Put 'em down and wait."

Her presence made this whole happening seem more in the nature of things. They were glad Miss Lizzie had come! It was somehow for this that they had given those yells for Miss Lizzie as Camp Mother. Under her gaze the Boy Scout's actions seemed to lose a good deal of significance. He was reduced almost to a nuisance—a mosquito, with a mosquito's proboscis. "Get him off her," Miss Lizzie repeated, in her rich and yet careless, almost humorous voice, knowing it was no good. "Ah, get him off her." She stood hugging the other little girls, several of them, warmly. Her gaze only hardened on Jinny Love; they hugged her all the more.

She loved them. It seemed the harder it was to get out here and the harder a time she found them having, the better she appreciated them. They remembered now—while the Boy Scout still drove up and down on Easter's muddy back—how they were always getting ready for Miss Lizzie; the tents even now were straight and the ground picked up and raked for her, and the tea for supper was already made and sitting in a tub in the lake; and sure enough, the niggers' dog had barked at the car just as always, and now here she was. She could have stopped everything; and she hadn't stopped it. Even her opening protests seemed now like part of things—what she was supposed to say. Several of the little girls looked up at Miss Lizzie instead of at what was on the table. Her powdered lips flickered, her eyelids hooded her gaze, but she was there.

On the table, the Boy Scout spat, and took a fresh appraisal of Easter. He reached for a hold on her hair and pulled her head back. No longer were her lips faintly parted—her mouth was open. It gaped. So did his. He dropped her, the head with its suddenness bowed again on its cheek, and he started again.

"Easter's dead! Easter's d—" cried Gertrude Bowles in a rowdy voice, and she was slapped rowdily across the mouth to cut off the word, by Miss Lizzie's hand.

Jinny Love, with a persistence they had not dreamed of, deployed the towel. Could it be owing to Jinny Love's always being on the right side that Easter mustn't dare die and bring all this to a stop? Nina thought, It's I that's thinking. Easter's not thinking at all. And while not thinking, she is not dead, but unconscious, which is even harder to be. Easter had come among them and had held herself untouchable and intact. Of course, for one little touch could smirch her, make her fall so far, so deep.—Except that by that time they were all saying the nigger deliberately poked her off in the water, meant her to drown.

"Don't touch her," they said tenderly to one another.

"Give up! Give up! Give up!" screamed Miss Moody—she who had rubbed them all the same, as if she rubbed chickens for the frying pan. Miss Lizzie without hesitation slapped her too.

"Don't touch her."

For they were crowding closer to the table all the time.

"If Easter's dead, I get her coat for winter, all right," said Geneva.

"Hush, orphan."

"Is she then?"

"You shut up." The Boy Scout looked around and panted at Geneva. "You can ast *me* when I ast you to ast me."

The niggers' dog was barking again, had been barking.

"Now who?"

"A big boy. It's old Ran MacLain and he's coming."

"He would."

He came right up, wearing a cap.

"Get away from me, Ran MacLain," Miss Lizzie called toward him. "You and dogs and guns, keep away. We've already got all we can put up with out here."

She put her foot down on his asking any questions, getting up on the table, or leaving, now that he'd come. Under his cap bill, Ran MacLain set his gaze—he was twenty-three, his seasoned gaze—on Loch and Easter on the table. He could not be prevented from considering them all. He moved under the tree. He held his gun under his arm. He let two dogs run loose, and almost imperceptibly, he chewed gum. Only Miss Moody did not move away from him.

And pressing closer to the table, Nina almost walked into Easter's arm flung out over the edge. The arm was turned at the elbow so that the hand opened upward. It held there the same as it had held when the night came in and stood in the tent, when it had come to Easter and not to Nina. It was the one hand, and it seemed the one moment.

"Don't touch her."

Nina fainted. She woke up to the cut-onion odor of Elberta's under-arm. She was up on the table with Easter, foot to head. There was so much she loved at home, but there was only time to remember the front yard. The silver, sweet-smelling paths strewed themselves behind the lawn mower, the four-o'clocks blazed. Then Elberta raised her up, she got down from the table, and was back with the others.

"Keep away. Keep away, I told you you better keep away. Leave me alone," Loch Morrison was saying with short breaths. "I dove for her, didn't I?"

They hated him, Nina most of all. Almost, they hated Easter.

They looked at Easter's mouth and at the eyes where they were contemplating without sense the back side of the light. Though she had bullied and repulsed them earlier, they began to speculate in another kind of allurement: was there danger that Easter, turned in on herself, might call out to them after all, from the other, worse, side of it? Her secret voice, if soundless then possibly visible, might work out of her terrible mouth like a vine, preening and sprung with flowers. Or a snake would come out.

The Boy Scout crushed in her body and blood came out of her mouth. For them all, it was like being spoken to.

"Nina, you! Come stand right here in my skirt," Miss Lizzie called. Nina went and stood under the big bosom that started down, at the neck of her dress, like a big cloven white hide.

Jinny Love was catching her mother's eye. Of course she had stolen brief rests, but now her white arms lifted the white towel and whipped it bravely. She looked at them until she caught their eye—as if in the end the party was for *her*.

Marvin had gone back to the car and brought two more melons, which he stood holding.

"Marvin. We aren't ready for our watermelon. I told you."

"Oh, Ran. How could you? Oh, Ran."

That was Miss Moody in still a third manifestation.

By now the Boy Scout seemed for ever part of Easter and she part of him, he in motion on the up-and-down and she stretched across. He was dripping, while her skirt dried on the table; so in a manner they had changed places too. Was time moving? Endlessly, Ran MacLain's dogs frisked and played, with the niggers' dog between.

Time was moving because in the beginning Easter's face—the curve of her brow, the soft upper lip and the milky eyes—partook of the swoon of her fall —the almost forgotten fall that bathed her so purely in blue for that long moment. The face was set now, and ugly with that rainy color of seedling petunias, the kind nobody wants. Her mouth surely by now had been open long enough, as long as any gape, bite, cry, hunger, satisfaction lasts, any one person's grief, or even protest.

Not all the children watched, and their heads all were beginning to hang, to nod. Everybody had forgotten about crying. Nina had spotted three little shells in the sand she wanted to pick up when she could. And suddenly this seemed to her one of those moments out of the future, just as she had found one small brief one out of the past; this was far, far ahead of her—picking up the shells, one, another, another, without time moving any more, and Easter abandoned on a little edifice, beyond dying and beyond being remembered about.

"I'm so tired!" Gertrude Bowles said. "And hot. Ain't you tired of Easter, laying up there on that table?"

"My arms are about to break, you all," and Jinny Love stood and hugged them to her.

"I'm so tired of Easter," Gertrude said.

"Wish she'd go ahead and die and get it over with," said Little Sister Spights, who had been thumb-sucking all afternoon without a reprimand.

"I give up," said Jinny Love.

Miss Lizzie beckoned, and she came. "I and Nina and Easter all went out in the woods, and I was the only one that came back with poison ivy," she said, kissing her mother.

Miss Lizzie sank her fingers critically into the arms of the girls at her skirt. They all rose on tiptoe. Was Easter dead then?

Looking out for an instant from precarious holds, they took in sharply for memory's sake that berated figure, the mask formed and set on the face, one hand displayed, one jealously clawed under the waist, as if a secret handful had been groveled for, the spread and spotted legs. It was a betrayed figure, the betrayal was over, it was a memory. And then as the blows, automatic now, swung down again, the figure itself gasped.

"Get back. Get back." Loch Morrison spoke between cruel, gritted teeth to them, and crouched over.

And when they got back, her toes webbed outward. Her belly arched and drew up from the board under her. She fell, but she kicked the Boy Scout.

Ridiculously, he tumbled backwards off the table. He fell almost into Miss Lizzie's skirt; she halved herself on the instant, and sat on the ground with her lap spread out before her like some magnificent hat that has just got crushed. Ran MacLain hurried politely over to pick her up, but she fought him off.

"Why don't you go home—now!" she said.

Before their eyes, Easter got to her knees, sat up,

and drew her legs up to her. She rested her head on her knees and looked out at them, while she slowly pulled her ruined dress downward.

The sun was setting. They felt it directly behind them, the warmth flat as a hand. Easter leaned slightly over the table's edge, as if to gaze down at what might move, and blew her nose; she accomplished that with the aid of her finger, like people from away in the country. Then she sat looking out again; in another moment her legs dropped and hung down. The girls looked back at her, through the yellow and violet streams of dust—just now reaching them from Ran MacLain's flivver—the air coarse as sacking let down from the tree branches. Easter lifted one arm and shaded her eyes, but the arm fell in her lap like a clod.

There was a sighing sound from them. For the first time they noticed there was an old basket on the table. It held their knives, forks, tin cups and plates.

"Carry me." Easter's words had no inflection. Again, "Carry me."

She held out her arms to them, stupidly.

Then Ran MacLain whistled to his dogs.

The girls ran forward all together. Mrs. Gruenwald's fists rose in the air as if she lifted—no, rather had lowered—a curtain and she began with a bleating sound, "Pa-a-ack—"

"—up your troubles in your old kit bag
And smile, smile, smile!"

The Negroes were making a glorious commotion, all of them came up now, and then Exum escaped them all and ran waving away to the woods, dainty as a loosened rabbit.

"Who was he, that big boy?" Etoile was asking Jinny Love.

"Ran MacLain, slow-poke."

"What did he want?"

"He's just waiting on the camp. *They're* coming

out tomorrow, hunting. I heard all he said to Miss Moody."

"Did Miss Moody *know* him?"

"Anybody knows him, and his twin brother too."

Nina, running up in the front line with the others, sighed—the sigh she gave when she turned in her examination papers at school. Then with each step she felt a defiance of her own. She screamed, "Easter!"

In that passionate instant, when they reached Easter and took her up, many feelings returned to Nina, some joining and some conflicting. At least what had happened to Easter was out in the world, like the table itself. There it remained—mystery, if only for being hard and cruel and, by something Nina felt inside her body, murderous.

Now they had Easter and carried her up to the tent, Mrs. Gruenwald still capering backwards and leading on,

"—in your old kit bag!
Smile, girls-instead-of-boys, that's the style!"

Miss Lizzie towered along darkly, groaning. She grabbed hold of Little Sister Spights, and said, "Can *you* brush me off!" She would be taking charge soon, but for now she asked for a place to sit down and a glass of cold water. She did not speak to Marvin yet; he was shoving the watermelons up onto the table.

Their minds could hardly capture it again, the way Easter was standing free in space, then handled and turned over by the blue air itself. Some of them looked back and saw the lake, rimmed around with its wall-within-walls of woods, into which the dark had already come. There were the water wings of Little Sister Spights, floating yet, white as a bird. "I know another Moon Lake," one girl had said yesterday. "Oh, my child, Moon Lakes are all over the world," Mrs. Gruenwald had interrupted. "I know of one in Austria . . ." And into each fell a girl, they dared, now, to think.

The lake grew darker, then gleamed, like the water of a rimmed well. Easter was put to bed, they sat quietly on the ground outside the tent, and Miss Lizzie sipped water from Nina's cup. The sky's rising clouds lighted all over, like one spread-out blooming mimosa tree that could be seen from where the trunk itself should rise.

VI.

Nina and Jinny Love, wandering down the lower path with arms entwined, saw the Boy Scout's tent. It was after the watermelon feast, and Miss Lizzie's departure. Miss Moody, in voile and tennis shoes, had a date with old "Rudy" Loomis, and Mrs. Gruenwald was trying to hold the girls with a sing before bedtime. Easter slept; Twosie watched her.

Nina and Jinny Love could hear the floating songs, farewell-like, the cheers and yells between. An owl hooted in a tree, closer by. The wind stirred.

On the other side of the tent wall the slats of the Boy Scout's legs shuttered open and shut like a fan when he moved back and forth. He had a lantern in there, or perhaps only a candle. He finished off his own shadow by opening the flap of his tent. Jinny Love and Nina halted on the path, quiet as old campers.

The Boy Scout, little old Loch Morrison, was undressing in his tent for the whole world to see. He took his time wrenching off each garment; then he threw it to the floor as hard as he would throw a ball; yet that seemed, in him, meditative.

His candle—for that was all it was—jumping a little now, he stood there studying and touching his case of sunburn in a Kress mirror like theirs. He was naked and there was his little tickling thing hung on him like the last drop on the pitcher's lip. He ceased or exhausted study and came to the tent opening again and stood leaning on one raised arm, with his weight on one foot—just looking out into the night, which was clamorous.

It seemed to them he had little to do!

Hadn't he surely, just before they caught him, been pounding his chest with his fists? Bragging on himself? It seemed to them they could still hear in the beating air of night the wild tattoo of pride he must have struck off. His silly, brief, overriding little show they could well imagine there in his tent of separation in the middle of the woods, in the night. Minnowy thing that matched his candle flame, naked as he was with that, he thought he shone forth too. Didn't he?

Nevertheless, standing there with the tent slanting over him and his arm knobby as it reached up and his head bent a little, he looked rather at loose ends.

"We can call like an owl," Nina suggested. But Jinny Love thought in terms of the future. "I'll tell on him, in Morgana tomorrow. He's the most conceited Boy Scout in the whole troop; and's bowlegged.

"You and I will always be old maids," she added.

Then they went up and joined the singing.

5.

THE WHOLE WORLD KNOWS

Father, I wish I could talk to you, wherever you are right now.

Mother said, *Where have you been, son?*—Nowhere, Mother.—*I wish you wouldn't sound so unhappy, son. You could come back to MacLain and live with me now.*—I can't do that, Mother. You know I have to stay in Morgana.

When I slammed the door of the bank I rolled down my sleeves and stood for some time looking out at the cotton field behind Mr. Wiley Bowles' across the street, until it nearly put me to sleep and then woke me up like a light turned on in my face. Woodrow Spights had been gone a few minutes or so. I got in my car and drove up the street, turned around at the foot of Jinny's driveway (yonder went Woody) and drove down again. I turned around in our old driveway, where Miss Francine had the sprinkler running, and made the same trip. The thing everybody does every day, except not by themselves.

There was Maideen Sumrall on the drugstore step waving a little green handkerchief. When I didn't remember to stop, I saw the handkerchief pulled down. I turned again, to pick her up, but she'd caught her ride with Red Ferguson.

So I went to my room. Bella, Miss Francine

Murphy's little dog, panted all the time—she was
sick. I always went out in the backyard and spoke to
her. Poor Bella, how do you do, lady? Is it hot, do
they leave you alone?

Mother said on the phone, *Have you been out
somewhere, son?*—Just to get a little air.—*I can
tell you're all peaked. And you keep things from
me, I don't understand. You're as bad as Eugene
Hudson. Now I have two sons keeping things from
me.*—I haven't been anywhere, where would I go?—
*If you came back with me, to MacLain Courthouse,
everything would be all right. I know you won't
eat at Miss Francine's table, not her biscuit.*—It's as
good as Jinny's, Mother.

But Eugene's safe in California, that's what we
think.

When the bank opened, Miss Perdita Mayo came
up to my window and hollered, "Randall, when are
you going back to your precious wife? You forgive
her, now you hear? That's no way to do, bear
grudges. Your mother never bore your father a single
grudge in her life, and he made her life right hard. I
tell you, how do you suppose he made her life? She
don't bear him a grudge. We're all human on earth.
Where's little old Woodrow this morning, late to work
or you done something to him? I still think of him a
boy in knee britches and Buster Brown bob, riding
that pony, that extravagant pony, cost a hundred
dollars. Woodrow: a little common but so smart.
Felix Spights never overcharged a customer, and Miss
Billy Texas amounted to a good deal before she got
like she is now; and Missie could always play the
piano better than average; Little Sister too young to
tell yet. Ah, I'm a woman that's been clear around
the world in my rocking chair, and I tell you we all
get surprises now and then. But you march on back
to your wife, Ran MacLain. You hear? It's a thing of
the flesh not the spirit, it'll pass. Jinny'll get over this

in three four months. You hear me? And you go back
nice."

"Still hotter today, isn't it?"

I picked up Maideen Sumrall and we rode up and
down the street. She was from the Sissum community.
She was eighteen years old. "Look! Citified," she
said, and pushed both hands at me; she had new
white cotton gloves on. Maideen would ride there
by me and talk about things I didn't mind hearing
about—the Seed and Feed where she clerked and
kept the books, Old Man Moody that she worked for,
the way working in Morgana seemed after the country and junior college. Her first job: her mother still
didn't like the idea. And people could be so nice:
getting a ride home with me sometimes like this, instead of with Red Ferguson in the Coca-Cola truck.
So she told me now. "And I didn't think you were
going to see me at first, Ran. I saved my gloves to
wear riding home in a car."

I told her my eyes had gone bad. She said she was
sorry. She was country-prim and liked to have something to put in words that she could be sorry about.
I drove, idling along, up and down a few times
more. Mr. Steptoe was dragging the mail sack into
the postoffice—he and Maideen waved. In the Presbyterian church Missie Spights was playing "Will
There Be Any Stars in My Crown?", and Maideen
listened. And on the street the same ones stood in
doorways or rode in their cars, and waved at my car.
Maideen's little blue handkerchief was busy waving
back. She waved at them as she did at me.

"I wouldn't be surprised if it *wasn't* hard on the
eyes, to be cooped up and just count money all day,
Ran"—to say something to me.

She knew what anybody in Morgana told her; and
for four or five afternoons after the first one I picked
her up and took her up and down the street a few
turns, bought her a coke at Johnny Loomis's, and

drove her home out by Old Forks and let her out, and she never said a word except a kind one, like about counting money. She was kind; her company was the next thing to being alone.

I drove her home and then drove back to Morgana to the room I had at Miss Francine Murphy's.

Next time, there at the end of the pavement, I turned up the cut to the Starks'. I couldn't stand it any longer.

Maideen didn't say a word till we reached the head of the drive and stopped.

"Ran?" she said. She wasn't asking anything. She meant just to remind me I had company, but that was what I knew. I got out and went around and opened her door.

"You want to take me in yonder?" she said. "Please, I'd just as soon you wouldn't." Her head hung. I saw the extra-white part in her hair.

I said, "Sure. Let's go in and see Jinny. Why not?" I couldn't stand it any longer, that was why.

"I'm going and taking you."

It wasn't as if Mr. Drewsie Carmichael didn't say to me every afternoon, "Come on home with me, boy"—argue, while he banged that big Panama—like yours, Father—down on his head, "no sense in your not sleeping cool, with one of our fans turned on you. Mamie's mad at you for roasting in that room across the street from us—you could move in five minutes. Well, Ran, look: Mamie has something to say to you: I don't." And he'd wait a minute in the door before he left. He'd stand and hold his cane —the one Woody Spights and I had bought him together when he was elected Mayor—up by his head, to threaten me with comfort, till I answered him, "No thanks, sir."

Maideen was at my side. We walked across the Starks' baked yard to the front porch, passing under the heavy heads of those crape myrtles, the too

bright blooms that hang down like fruits that might
drop. My wife's mother—Miss Lizzie Morgan, Father
—put her face to her bedroom window first thing.
She'd know it first if I came back, all right. Parting
her curtains with a steel crochet hook, she looked
down at Randall MacLain coming to her door, and
bringing who-on-earth with him.

"What are you doing here, Ran MacLain?"

When I didn't look up, she rapped on the window
sill with her hook.

"I've never been inside the Stark home," Maideen
said, and I began to smile. I felt curiously light-
hearted. Lilies must have been in bloom somewhere
near, and I took a full breath of their ether smell:
consciousness could go or not. I pulled open the
screen door. From above, inside somewhere, Miss
Lizzie was calling, "Jinny Love!" like Jinny had a
date.

Jinny—not out playing croquet—stood with her
legs apart, cutting off locks of her hair at the hall
mirror. The locks fell at her feet. She had on straw
sandals, the kind that would have to be ordered,
boy's shorts. She looked up at me, short range, and
said "Just in time, to tell me when to stop." She'd cut
bangs. Her smile reminded me of the way a child
will open its mouth all right, but not let out the cry
till it sees the right person.

And turning to the mirror she cut again. "Obey
that impulse—" She had seen Maideen then, and
she went right on cutting her hair with those stork-
shaped scissors. "Come in too, take off your gloves."

That's right: she would know, with her quickness
like foreknowledge, first that I would come back
when the summer got too much for me, and second
that I'd just as soon bring a stranger if I could find
one, somebody who didn't know any better, to come
in the house with me when I came.

Father, I wished I could go back.

I looked at Jinny's head with the ragged points all
over it, and there was Miss Lizzie coming down; she

had just stopped to change her shoes, of course. For
the kind that came down stairs like a march. As we
all fell in together, we were leaving where we met
too, starting down the hall with nobody pairing, and
over each other's names or whatever we said, Jinny's
voice hollered at Tellie for cokes. She counted us
with her finger. That lightness came right back. Just
to step on the matting, that billows a little anyway,
and with Jinny's hair scattered like feathers on it, I
could have floated, risen and floated.

In rockers—we sat on the back porch—we were
all not rocking. The chairs, white wicker, had a new
coat of paint—their thousandth-and-first, but one
new coat since I left Jinny. The outside—a sheet of
white light—was in my eyes. The ferns close around
us were hushing on their stands, they had just been
watered. I could listen to women and hear pieces of
the story, of what happened to us, of course—but I
listened to the ferns.

No matter, it was being told. Not in Miss Lizzie's
voice, which wouldn't think of it, certainly not in
Jinny's, but in the clear voice of Maideen where it
had never existed—all the worse for the voice not
even questioning what it said—just repeating, just
rushing, old—the town words.

Telling what she was told she saw, repeating what
she listened to—young girls are outlandish little birds
that talk. They can be taught, some each day, to
sing a song *people* have made. . . . Even Miss Lizzie
put her head on one side, to let Maideen be.

He walked out on her and took his clothes down
to the other end of the street. Now everybody's waiting to see how soon he'll go back. They say Jinny
MacLain invites Woody out there to eat, a year
younger than she is, remember when they were
born. Invites, under her mama's nose. Sure, it's Woodrow Spights she invites. Who else in Morgana would
there be for Jinny Stark after Ran, with even Eugene
MacLain gone? She's kin to the Nesbitts. They don't
say when it started, can anybody tell? At the Circle,

at Miss Francine's, at Sunday School, they say, they say she will marry Woodrow: Woodrow'd jump at it but Ran will kill somebody first. And there's Ran's papa and the way he was and is, remember, remember? And Eugene gone that could sometimes hold him down. Poor Snowdie, it's her burden. He used to be sweet but too much devil in him from Time was, that's Ran. He'll do something bad. He won't divorce Jinny but he'll do something bad. Maybe kill them all. They say Jinny's not scared of that. Maybe she drinks and hides the bottle, you know her father's side. And just as prissy as ever on the street. And oh, don't you know, they run into each other every day of the world, all three. Sure, how could they help it if they wanted to help it, how could you get away from it, right in Morgana? You can't get away in Morgana. Away from anything at all, you know that.

Father! You didn't listen.

And Tellie was mad at all of us. She still held the tray, she held it about an inch and a half too high. When Maideen took her coke in her white glove, she said to Miss Lizzie, "I look too tacky and mussed when I work in the store all day to be coming in anybody's strange house."

"You're by far the freshest one here, my dear."

Who else had Maideen ever known to talk about but herself?

But she looked like Jinny. She was a child's copy of Jinny. Jinny's first steady look at me, coming just then, made that plain all at once. (Oh, her look always made contamination plain. Or plainer.) That resemblance I knew *post-mortem*, so to speak—and it made me right pleased with myelf. I don't mean there was any mockery in Maideen's little face—no— but there was something of Maideen in Jinny's, that went back early—to whatever I knew my Jinny would never be now.

The slow breeze from that ceiling fan—its old white blades frosted like a cake, with the flies riding on it—lifted the girls' hair like one passing hand,

Maideen's brown hair shoulder-long and Jinny's brown hair short, ruined—she ruined it herself, as she liked doing. Maideen was even more polite than she'd ever been to me, and making intervals in the quiet, like the ferns dripping, she talked about herself and the Seed and Feed; but she glowed with something she didn't know about, yet, there in the room with Jinny. And Jinny sat not rocking, yet, with her clever, not-listening smile.

I looked from Jinny to Maideen and back to Jinny, and almost listened for some compliment—a compliment from somewhere—Father!—for my good eyes, my vision. It took me, after all, to bring it out. There was nothing but time between them.

There were those annoying sounds keeping on out there—people and croquet. We finished the cokes. Miss Lizzie just sat there—hot. She still held the crochet hook, straight up like a ruler, and nobody was rapped, done to death. Jinny was on her feet, inviting us out to play croquet.

But it had been long enough.

They were slowly moving across the shade of the far backyard—Woody, Johnnie and Etta Loomis, Nina Carmichael and Jinny's cousin Junior Nesbitt, and the fourteen-year-old child that they let play— with Woody Spights knocking his ball through a wicket. He was too young for me—I'd never really looked at him before this year; he was coming up in the world. I looked down through the yard and the usual crowd seemed to have dwindled a little, I could not think who was out. Jinny went down there. It was myself.

Mother said, *Son, you're walking around in a dream.*

Miss Perdita came and said, "I hear you went back yesterday and wouldn't open your mouth, left again. Might as well not go at all. But no raring up now and doing anything we'll all be sorry to hear about. I know vou won't. I knew your father, was crazy about your father, glad to see him come every time, sorry to see him go, and love your mother. Sweetest people in the world, most happily mated people in the world, long as he was home. Tell your mother I said so, next time you see her. And you march back to that precious wife. March back and have you some chirren. My Circle declares Jinny's going to divorce you, marry Woodrow. I said, Why? Thing of the flesh, I told my Circle, won't last. Sister said you'd kill him, and I said Sister, who are you talking about? If it's Ran MacLain that I knew in his buggy, I said, he's not at all likely to take on to that extent. And little Jinny. Who's going to tell Lizzie to spank her, though? I couldn't help but laugh at Jinny: she says, It's my own business! We was in Hardware, old Holifield just scowling his head off. I says, How did it happen, Jinny, tell old Miss Perdita, you monkey, and she says, Oh, Miss Perdita, do like *me*. Do like *me*, she says, and just go on like nothing's happened. I declare, and she says I have to write my checks on the Morgana bank, and Woody Spights works in it, there's just him and Ran, so I go up to Woody and cash them. And I says, Child—how could you all get away from each other if you tried? You couldn't. It's a pity you had to run to a Spights, though. Oh, if there'd just been some Carmichael *boys*, I often say! No matter who you are, though, it's an endless circle. That's what a thing of the flesh is, endless circle. And you won't get away from that in Morgana. Even our little town.

"All right, I said to Old Man Moody while ago, look. Jinny was unfaithful to Ran—that's the up-and-down of it. There you have what it's all *about*. That's the brunt of it. Face it, I told Dave Moody. Like Lizzie Stark does, she's brave. Though she's seven miles south of here, Snowdie MacLain's another brave one. Poor Billy Texas Spights is beyond knowing. You're just a seed and feed man and the marshal here, you don't form opinions enough to suit me.

"Jinny was never scared of the Devil himself as a

growing girl, so she certainly shouldn't be now, she's twenty-five. She's Lizzie's own. And Woodrow Spights won't ever quit at the bank, will he? It's so much cleaner than the store, and he'll get the store too. So it's up to you, Ran, looks like.

"And I'd go back to my lawful spouse!" Miss Perdita puts both hands on the bars of my cage and raises her voice. "You or I or the Man in the Moon got no business sleeping in that little hot upstairs room with a western exposure at Miss Francine Murphy's for all the pride on earth, not in August! And even if it is the house you grew up in, it's a different room. And listen here to me. Don't you ruin a *country* girl in the bargain. Make what you will of that."

She backs away leaving her hands out, pulling-like at the air, like I'm floating on my ear suspended, hypnotized, and she can leave. But she just goes as far as the next window—Woody Spights'.

I went back to the room I had at Miss Francine Murphy's. Father, it used to be the trunk room. It had Mother's pieced quilts and her wedding dress and all the terrible accumulation of a long time you wouldn't have known about.

After work I would cut the grass or something in Miss Francine's backyard so it would be cooler for Bella. It kept the fleas away from her to some extent. It didn't do much good. The heat held on.

I tried going to Jinny's a little later in the afternoon. The men were playing, still playing croquet with a little girl, and the women had taken off to themselves, on the porch. I tried without Maideen.

It was the long Mississippi evening, the waiting till it was cool enough to eat. The voice of Miss Lizzie carried. Like the hum of the gin, it was there, but the evening was still quiet, still very hot and quiet.

Somebody called to me, "You're dead on Woody." It was just a little Williams girl in pigtails.

I may have answered with a joke. I felt lightheaded, not serious at all, really doing it for a child when I lifted my mallet—the one with the red band that had always been mine. But I brought Woody Spights down with it. He toppled and shook the ground. I felt the air rush up. Then I beat on him. I went over his whole length, and cracked his head apart with that soft girl's hair and all the ideas, beat on him without stopping till every bone, all the way down to the numerous little bones in the foot, was cracked in two. I didn't have done with Woody Spights till then. And I proved the male human body—it has a too positive, too special shape, you know, not to be hurt—it could be finished up pretty fast. It just takes one good loud blow after another— Jinny should be taught that.

I looked at Woodrow down there. And his blue eyes were just as unharmed. Just as unharmed as bubbles a child blows, the most impervious things— you've seen grass blades go through bubbles and they still reflect the world, give it back unbroken. Woodrow Spights I declare was dead. "Now you watch," he said.

He spoke with no sign of pain. Just that edge of competition was in his voice. He was ever the most ambitious fool. To me ambition's always been a mystery, but now it was his try to deceive us—me and him both. I didn't know how it could open again, the broken jawbone of Woody Spights, but it could. I heard him say, "Now you watch."

He was dead on the ruined grass. But he had risen up. Just to call attention to it, he gave the fat little Williams girl a spank. I could see the spank, but I couldn't hear it—the most familiar sound in the world.

And I should have called out *then*—All is disgrace! Human beings' cries could swell if locusts' could, in the last of evening like this, and cross the grass in a backyard, if only they enough of them cried. At our feet the shadows faded out light into no shadows left and the locusts sang in long waves, O-E, O-E, and the gin ran on. Our grass in August is like the floor of the sea, and we walk on it slowly playing, and the sky turns green before dark, Father, as you know. The sweat ran over my back and down my arms and legs, branching, like an upside-down tree.

Then, "You all come in!" They were calling from the porch—the well-known lamps suddenly all went on. They called us in their calling women's voices, of disguise, all but Jinny. "Fools, you're playing in the dark!" she said. "Supper's ready, if anybody cares."

The bright porch across the dark was like a boat on the river to me; an excursion boat I wasn't going on. I was going to Miss Francine Murphy's, as everybody knew.

Each evening to avoid Miss Francine and the three school teachers, I ran through the porch and hall both like a man through a burning building. In the backyard, with fig trees black, otherwise moonlit, Bella opened her eyes and looked at me. Her eyes both showed the moon. If she drank water, she vomited it up—yet she went with effort to her pan and drank again, for me. I held her. Poor Bella. I thought she suffered from a tumor, and stayed with her most of the night.

Mother said, *Son, I was glad to see you but I noticed that old pistol of your father's in your nice coat pocket, what do you want with that? Your father never cared for it, went off and left it. Not any robbers coming to the Morgana bank that I know of. Son, if you'd just saved your money you could take a little trip to the coast. I'd go with you. They always have a breeze at Gulfport, nearly always.*

Where the driveway ends at Jinny's, there are Spanish daggers and the bare front yard with the forked tree with the seat around it—like some old playground of a consolidated school, with the school back out of sight. Just the sharp, overgrown Spanish daggers, and the spiderwebs draped over them like clothes-rags. You can go under trees to the house by

going all around the yard and opening the old
gate by the summerhouse. Somewhere back in the
shade there's a statue from Morgan days, of a dancing
girl with her finger to her chin, all pockmarked, with
some initials on her legs.

Maideen liked the statue but she said, "Are you
taking me back in? I thought maybe now you weren't
going to."

I saw my hand on the gate and said, "Now you
wait. I've lost a button." I held out my sleeve to
Maideen. All at once I felt so unlike myself I was
ready to shed tears.

"A button? Why, I'll sew you one on, if you come
on and take me home," Maideen said. That's what I
wanted her to say, but she touched my sleeve. A
chameleon ran up a leaf, and held there panting.
"Then Mama can meet you. She'd be glad to have
you stay to supper."

I unlatched the little old gate. I caught a whiff of
the sour pears on the ground, the smell of August.
I'd never told Maideen I was coming to supper, at any
time, or would see her mama, of course; but also I
kept forgetting about the old ways, the eternal politeness of the people you hope not to know.

"Oh, Jinny can sew it on now," I said.

"Oh, I can?" Jinny said. She'd of course been listening all the time from the summerhouse. She came out,
alone, with the old broken wicker basket full of
speckled pears. She didn't say go back and shut the
gate.

I carried the rolling basket for her and we went
ahead of Maideen but I knew she was coming
behind; she wouldn't know very well how not to.
There in the flower beds walked the same robins.
The sprinkler dripped now. Once again we went
into the house by the back door. Our hands touched.
We had stepped on Tellie's patch of mint. The yellow cat was waiting to go in with us, the door handle
was as hot as the hand, and on the step, getting under
the feet of two people who went in together, the

Mason jars with the busy cuttings in water—"Watch out for Mama's—!" A thousand times we'd gone in like that. As a thousand bees had droned and burrowed in the pears that lay on the ground.

Miss Lizzie shrank with a cry and started abruptly up the back stairs—bosom lifted—her shadow trotted up the boarding beside her like a bear with a nose. But she couldn't get to the top; she turned. She came down, carefully, and held up a finger at me. She needed to be careful. That stairs was the one Mr. Comus Stark fell down and broke his neck on one night, going up the back way drunk. Did I call it to attention?—Jinny got away.

"Randall. I can't help but tell you about a hand I held yesterday. My partner was Mamie Carmichael and you know she always plays her own hand with no more regard for her partner than you have. Well, she opened with a spade and Etta Loomis doubled. I held: a singleton spade, five clubs to the king-queen, five hearts to the king, and two little diamonds. I said two clubs. Parnell Moody said two diamonds, Mamie two spades, all passed. And when I laid down my hand Mamie said, Oh, *partner!* Why didn't you bid your hearts! I said, Hardly. At the level of three with the opponents doubling for a takeout. It developed of course she was two-suited—six spades to the ace-jack and four hearts to the ace-jack-ten, also my ace of clubs. Now, Randall. It would have been just as easy for Mamie to bid three hearts on that second go-round. But no! She could see only her own hand and took us down two, and we could have made five hearts. Now do *you* say I should have bid three hearts?"

I said, "You were justified not to, Miss Lizzie."

She began to cry on the stairs. Tears stood on her powdered face. "You men. You got us beat in the end. May be I'm getting old. Oh no, that's not it. Because I can tell you where you got us beat. We'd know you through and through except we never know what ails you. Don't you look at me like that. Of course I see what Jinny's doing, the fool, but you ailed first. You just got her answer to it, Ran." Then she glared again, turned, and went back upstairs.

And what ails me I don't know, Father, unless maybe you know. All through what she had to say I stood holding the cooking-pears. Then I set the basket on the table.

Jinny was in the little back study, "Mama's office," with the landscape wallpaper and Mr. Comus's old desk full-up with U.D.C. correspondence and plat maps that cracked like thunder when the fan blew them. She was yelling at Tellie. Tellie came in with the workbasket and then just waited, eyeing her.

"Put it down, Tellie, I'll use it when I get ready. Now you go on. Pull your mouth in, you hear?"

Tellie put down the basket and Jinny flicked it open and fished in it. The stork scissors fell out. She found a button that belonged to me, and waited on Tellie.

"I hear you's a mess." Tellie went out.

Jinny looked at me and didn't mind. I minded. I fired pointblank at Jinny—more than once. It was close range—there was barely room between us suddenly for the pistol to come up. And she only stood frowning at the needle I had forgotten the reason for. Her hand never deviated, never shook from the noise. The dim clock on the mantel was striking—the pistol hadn't drowned that out. I was watching Jinny and I saw her pouting childish breasts, excuses for breasts, sprung full of bright holes where my bullets had gone. But Jinny didn't feel it. She threaded her needle. She made her little face of success. Her thread always went straight in the eye.

"Will you hold still."

She far from acknowledged pain—anything but sorrow and pain. When I couldn't give her something she wanted she would hum a little tune. In our room, her voice would go low and soft to complete disparagement. Then I loved her a lot. The little cheat. I waited on, while she darted the needle and pulled at my sleeve, the sleeve to my helpless hand. It was like counting my breaths. I let out my fury and breathed the pure disappointment in: that she was not dead on earth. She bit the thread—magnificently. When she took her mouth away I nearly fell. The cheat.

I didn't dare say good-bye to Jinny any more. "All right, now you're ready for croquet," she told me. She went upstairs too.

Old Tellie spat a drop of nothing into the sɤve and clanged the lid down as I went out through ɯe kitchen. Maideen was out in the swing, sitting. I ɯld her to come on down to the croquet yard, where we all played Jinny's game, without Jinny.

Going to my room, I saw Miss Billy Texas Spights outdoors in her wrapper, whipping the flowers to make them bloom.

Father! Dear God wipe it clean. Wipe it clean, wipe it out. Don't let it be.

At last Miss Francine caught hold of me in the hall. "Do me a favor, Ran. Do me a favor and put Bella out of her misery. None of these school teachers any better at it than I'd be. And my friend coming to supper too tenderhearted. You do it. Just do it and don't tell us about it, hear?"

Where have you been, Son, it's so late.—Nowhere, Mother, nowhere.—*If you were back under my roof,* Mother said, *if Eugene hadn't gone away too. He's gone and you won't listen to anybody.*—It's too hot to sleep, Mother.—*I stayed awake by the telephone. The Lord never meant us all to separate. To go and be cut off. One from the other, off in some little room.*

"I remember your wedding," old Miss Jefferson Moody said at my window, nodding on the other side of the bars. "Never knew it would turn out like this, the prettiest and longest wedding I ever saw. Look! If all that money belonged to you, you could leave town."

And I was getting tired, oh so tired, of Maideen waiting on me. I felt cornered when she told me, still as kind as ever, about the Seed and Feed. Because ever since I was born, Old Man Moody lined his sidewalk with pie pans full of shelled corn and stuff like bird-shot. The window used to be so clouded up it looked like stained glass. She'd scrubbed it for him, and exposed the barrels and cannisters and the sacks and bins of stuff inside, and Old Man Moody in an eyeshade sitting on a stool, making cat's-cradles; and her poking food at the bird. There were cotton blooms across the window and door, and then it would be sugarcane, and she told me she was thinking already about the Christmas tree. No telling what she was going to string on Old Man Moody's Christmas tree. And now I was told her mother's maiden name. God help me, the name Sojourner was laid on my head like the top teetering crown of a pile of things to remember. Not to forget, never to forget the name of Sojourner.

And then always having to take the little Williams girl home at night. She was the bridge player. That was a game Maideen had never learned to play. Maideen: I never kissed her.

But the Sunday came when I took her to Vicksburg.

Already on the road I began to miss my bridge. We could get our old game now, Jinny, Woody, myself, and either Nina Carmichael or Junior Nesbitt, or both and sit in. Miss Lizzie of course would walk out on us now, never be our fourth, holding no brief for what a single one of us had done; she couldn't stand the Nesbitts to begin with. I always won—Nina used to win, but anybody could see she was pressed too much about Nesbitt to play her cards, and sometimes she didn't come to play at all, or Nesbitt either, and we had to go get the little Williams girl and take her home.

Maideen never put in a word to our silence now. She sat holding some women's magazine. Every now and then she'd turn over a page, moistening her finger first, like my mother. When she lifted her eyes to me,

I didn't look up. Every night I would take their money. Then at Miss Francine's I would be sick, going outdoors so the teachers wouldn't wonder.

"Now you really must get these two home. Their mothers will be wondering." Jinny's voice.

Maideen would stand up with the little Williams girl to leave, and I thought whatever I let her in for, I could trust her.

She would get stupefied for sleep. She would lean farther and farther over in the Starks' chair. She would never have a rum and coke with us, but would be simply dead for sleep. She slept sitting up in the car going home, where her mama, now large-eyed, maiden name Sojourner, sat up listening. I'd wake Maideen and tell her where we were. The little Williams girl would be chatting away in the back seat, there and as far as her house wide awake as an owl.

Vicksburg: nineteen miles over the gravel and the thirteen little bridges and the Big Black. And suddenly all sensation returned.

Morgana I had looked at too long. Till the street was a pencil mark on the sky. The street was there just the same, red-brick scallops, two steeples and the water tank and the branchy trees, but if I saw it, it was not with love, it was a pencil mark on the sky that jumped with the shaking of the gin. If some indelible red false-fronts joined one to the other like a little toy train went by, I didn't think of my childhood any more. I saw Old Man Holifield turn his back, his suspenders looked cross, very cross.

In Vicksburg, I stopped my car at the foot of the street under the wall, by the canal. There was that dazzling light, water-marked light. I woke Maideen and asked her if she was thirsty. She smoothed her dress and lifted her head at the sounds of a city, the traffic on cobblestones just behind the wall. I watched the water taxi come to get us, chopping over the canal strip, babyish as a rocking horse.

"Duck your head," I told Maideen.

"In here?"

It was sunset. The island was very near across the water—a waste of willows, yellow and green strands loosely woven together, like a basket that let the light spill out uncontrollably. We all stood up and bent our heads under the ceiling in the tiny cabin, and shaded our eyes. The Negro who ran the put-put never said a word, "Get in" or "Get out." "Where is this we're going?" Maideen said. In two minutes we were touching the barge.

Nobody was inside but the barkeep—a silent, relegated place like a barn, old and tired. I let him bring some rum cokes out to the card table on the back where the two cane chairs were. It was open back there. The sun was going down on the island side while we sat, and making Vicksburg all picked out on the other. East and West were in our eyes.

"Don't make me drink it. I don't want to drink it," Maideen said.

"Go on and drink it."

"You drink it if you like it. Don't make me drink it."

"You drink it too."

I looked at her take some of it, and sit shading her eyes. There were wasps dipping from a nest over the old screen door and skimming her hair. There was a smell of fish and of the floating roots fringing the island, and of the oilcloth top of our table, and endless deals. A load of Negroes came over on the water taxi and stepped out sulphur-yellow all over, coated with cottonseed meal. They disappeared in the colored barge at the other end, in single file, carrying their buckets, like they were sentenced to it.

"Sure enough, I don't want to drink it."

"Look, you drink it and then tell me if it tastes bad, and I'll pour 'em both in the river."

"It will be too late."

Through the screen door I could see into the dim saloon. Two men with black cocks under their arms

had come in. Without noise they each set a muddy
boot on the rail and drank, the cocks absolutely
still. They got off the barge on the island side and
were lost in a minute in a hot blur of willow trees.
They might never be seen again.

The heat shook on the water and on the other side
shook along the edges of the old white buildings
and the concrete slabs and the wall. From the barge
Vicksburg looked like an image of itself in some old
mirror—like a portrait at a sad time of life.

A short cowboy and his girl came in, walking
alike. They dropped a nickel in the nickelodeon, and
came together.

There weren't any waves visible, yet the water did
tremble under our chairs. I was aware of it like the
sound of a winter fire in the room.

"You don't ever dance, do you," Maideen said.

It was a long time before we left. A good many
people had come out to the barge. There was old
Gordon Nesbitt, dancing. When we left, the white
barge and the nigger barge had both filled up, and
it was good-dark.

The lights were far between on shore—sheds and
warehouses, long walls that needed propping. High
up on the ramparts of town some old iron bells were
ringing.

"Are you a Catholic?" I asked her suddenly, and
she shook her head.

Nobody was a Catholic but I looked at her—I
made it plain she disappointed some hope of mine,
and she had, standing there with a foreign bell ringing on the air.

"We're all Baptists. Why, are you a Catholic? Is
that what you are?"

Without touching her except by accident with my
knee I walked her ahead of me up the steep uneven way to where my car was parked listing down-
hill. Inside, she couldn't shut her door. I stood outside and waited, the door hung heavily and she had

drunk all I had made her drink. Now she couldn't
shut her door.

"Shut it."

"I'll fall out. I'll fall in your arms. If I fall, catch
me."

"No. Shut it. You have to shut it. I can't. All your
might."

At last. I leaned against her shut door, and held on
for a moment.

I grated up the steep hills, turned and followed the
river road along the bluff, turned again off into a
deep rutted dirt way under shaggy banks, Father,
dark and circling and rushing down.

"Don't lean on me," I said. "Better to sit up and
get air."

"Don't want to."

"Pull up your head." I could hardly understand
what she said any more. "You want to lie down?"

"Don't want to lie down."

"You get some air."

"Don't want to do a thing, Ran, do we, from now
and on till evermore."

We circled down. The sounds of the river tossing
and teasing its great load, its load of trash, I could
hear through the dark now. It made the noise of a
moving wall, and up it fishes and reptiles and up-
rooted trees and man's throw-aways played and
climbed all alike in a splashing like innocence. A
great wave of smell beat at my face. The track had
come down here deep as a tunnel. We were on the
floor of the world. The trees met and their branches
matted overhead, the cedars came together, and
through them the stars of Morgana looked sifted
and fine as seed, so high, so far. Away off, there was
the sound of a shot.

"Yonder's the river," she said, and sat up. "I see it
—the Mississippi River."

"You don't see it. You only hear it."

"I see it, I see it."

"Haven't you ever seen the river before? You baby."

"I thought we were on it on the boat. Where's this?"

"The road's ended. You can see that."

"Yes, I can. Why does it come this far and stop?"

"How should I know?"

"What do they come down here for?"

"There're all kinds of people in the world." Far away, somebody was burning something.

"You mean bad people? Niggers?"

"Oh, fishermen. River men. See, you're waked up."

"I think we're lost," she said.

Mother said, *If I thought you'd ever go back to that Jinny Stark, I couldn't stand it.—*No, Mother, I'm not going back.—*The whole world knows what she did to you. It's different from when it's the man.*

"You dreamed we're lost. That's all right, you can lie down a little."

"You can't get lost in Morgana."

"After you lie down a little you'll be all right again. We'll go somewhere where you can lie down good."

"Don't want to lie down."

"Did you know my car would back up a hill as steep as this?"

"You'll be killed."

"I bet nobody ever saw such a crazy thing. Do you think anybody ever saw such a crazy thing?"

We were almost straight up and down, Father, hanging on the wall of the bluff, and the rear end of the car bumping and rising like something that wanted to fly, lifting and dropping us. At last we backed back over the brink, like a bee pulling out of a flower cup, and skidded a little. Without that last drink, maybe I wouldn't have made it at all.

We drove a long way then. All through the dark part, the same old statues and stances, the stone rifles at point again and again on the hills, lost and the same. The towers they've condemned, the lookout towers, lost and the same.

Maybe I didn't have my bearings, but I looked for the moon, due to be in the last quarter. There she was. The air wasn't darkness but faint light and floating sound. It was the breath of all the people in the world who were breathing out into the late night looking at the moon, knowing her quarter. And all along I knew I rode in the open world and took bearings by the stars.

We rode in wildernesses under the lifting moon. Maideen was awake because I heard her sighing, faintly, as if she longed for something for herself. A coon, white as a ghost, pressed low like an enemy, crossed over the road.

We crossed a highway and there a light burned in a white-washed tree. Under hanging moss it showed a half-circle of white-washed cabins, dark, and all along it a fence of pale palings. A little nigger boy leaned on the gate where our lights moved on him; he was wearing a train engineer's cap. Sunset Oaks.

The little nigger hopped on the runningboard, and I paid. I guided Maideen by the shoulders. She had been asleep after all.

"One step up," I told her at the door.

We fell dead asleep in our clothes across the iron bed.

The naked light hung far down into the room and our sleep, a long cord with the strands almost untwisted. Maideen got up after some time and turned the light off, and the night descended like a bucket let down a well, and I woke up. It was never dark enough, the enormous sky flashing with August light rushing into the emptiest rooms, the loneliest windows. The month of falling stars. I hate the time of year this is, Father.

I saw Maideen taking her dress off. She bent over all tender toward it, smoothing its skirt and shaking it and laying it, at last, on the room's chair; and tenderly like it was any chair, not that one. I propped myself up against the rods of the bed with my back pressing them. I was sighing—deep sigh after deep sigh. I heard myself. When she turned back to the bed, I said, "Don't come close to me."

And I showed I had the pistol. I said, "I want the whole bed." I told her she hadn't needed to be here. I got down in the bed and pointed the pistol at her, without much hope, the way I used to lie cherishing a dream in the morning, and she the way Jinny would come pull me out of it.

Maideen came into the space before my eyes, plain in the lighted night. She held her bare arms. She was disarrayed. There was blood on her, blood and disgrace. Or perhaps there wasn't. For a minute I saw her double. But I pointed the gun at her the best I could.

"Don't come close to me," I said.

Then while she spoke to me I could hear all the noises of the place we were in—the frogs and night-birds of Sunset Oaks, and the little idiot nigger running up and down the fence, up and down, as far as it went and back, sounding the palings with his stick.

"Don't, Ran. Don't do that, Ran. Don't do it, please don't do it." She came closer, but when she spoke I wasn't hearing what she said. I was reading her lips, the conscientious way people do through train windows. Outside, I thought the little nigger at the gate would keep that up for ever, no matter what I did, or what anyone did—running a stick along the fence, up and then down, to the end and back again.

Then that stopped. I thought, he's still running. The fence stopped, and he ran on without knowing it.

I drew back the pistol, and turned it. I put the pistol's mouth to my own. My instinct is always quick and ardent and hungry and doesn't lose any time. There was Maideen still, coming, coming in her petticoat.

"Don't do it, Ran. Please don't do it." Just the same. I made it—made the awful sound.

And *she* said, "Now you see. It didn't go off. Give
me that. Give that old thing to me, I'll take care of
it."

She took it from me. Dainty as she always was, she
carried it over to the chair; and prissy as she was, like
she knew some long-tried way to deal with a gun,
she folded it in her dress. She came back to the bed
again, and dropped down on it.

In a minute she put her hand out again, differently,
and laid it cold on my shoulder. And I had her so
quick.

I could have been asleep then. I was lying there.

"You're so stuck up," she said.

I lay there and after a while I heard her again. She
lay there by the side of me, weeping for herself. The
kind of soft, patient, meditative sobs a child will ven-
ture long after punishment.

So I slept.

How was I to know she would go and hurt herself?
She cheated, she cheated too.

Father, Eugene! What you went and found, was
it better than this?

And where's Jinny?

6.

MUSIC FROM SPAIN

One morning at breakfast Eugene MacLain was opening his paper and without the least idea of why he did it, when his wife said some innocent thing to him—"Crumb on your chin" or the like—he leaned across the table and slapped her face. They were in their forties, married twelve years—she was the older: she was looking it now.

He waited for her to say "Eugene MacLain!" The oven roared behind her—the second pan of toast was under the flame. Almost leisurely—that is, he sighed —Eugene rose and walked out of the kitchen, holding on to his paper; usually he put it in Emma's hand as he gave her the good-bye kiss.

He listened for "Eugene?" to follow him into the chill of the hall and wait for "Yes, dear?" He saw his face go past the mirror with a smile on it; that was a memory of little Fan's fly-away habit of answering her mother—and the sticking out of her two pigtails behind her as she ran off, the fair hair screwed up to the first tightenings of vanity—"That's my name." She had now been dead a year.

He put on his raincoat and hat, and secured his paper flat under his arm. Emma was still sitting propped back in her chair between table and stove, with the parrot-tailed housecoat just now settling in a series of puffs about her, and her too small, fat feet, as if *they* had been the most outraged, propped out before her. He knew the way Emma was looking in the kitchen behind him not because he had ever struck anyone before but because, with her, it was like having eyes in the back of his head. (*Only* in the back of his head!) Why, now, drawing her breath fast in the only warm room, she sat self-hypnotized in her own domain, with her "Get-out-of-my-kitchen" and "Come-here-do-you-realize-what-you've-done," all her stiffening and wifely glaze running sweet and finespun as sugar threads over her.

But Eugene went down the hall—now he heard like an echo her wounded cry and the shriek of the toast-pan—and pulled the apartment door locked behind him. He never could bear the sound of his own name called out in public, and she could still fling open the door and cry "Eugene Hudson Mac-Lain, come here to me!" down the stairs.

A tremor ran through his arm as it struggled with the front door, and he stepped through to the outside and the perfectly still, foggy morning. He let his breath out, and there it was: he could see it. The air, the street, a sea gull, all the same soft gray, were in the same degree visible and seemed to him suddenly as pure as his own breath was.

The sea gull like a swinging pearl came walking across Jones Street as if to join him. "Our sea gulls have become so immured to San Francisco life," he would remark on walking in Bertsingers'—for you came in to work with a humorous remark—"they even cross the streets at the intersections now." He couldn't have hurt Emma. There couldn't be a mark on her.

She was stronger than he was, 150 pounds to 139, he could inform old Mr. Bertsinger Senior, who liked to press for figures. He and Emma MacLain could at any time be printed in the paper where all could see, side by side naked and compared, in those testimonial silhouettes; maybe had been. Emma knew he hadn't hurt her; better than he knew, Emma knew.

He sighed gently. By now—for she did take things in slowly—the rosy mole might be riding the pulse in her throat as it did long after the telephone rang late in the night and was the wrong number—"Why, it might have been a *thousand* things." Pretty soon, with her middle finger she would start touching her hairpins, one by one, going over her head as though in finishing her meditations she was sewing some precautionary cap on.

Eugene was walking down the habitual hills to Bertsingers', Jewelers, and with sharp sniffs that as always rather pained him after breakfast he was taking note of the day, its temperature, fog condition, and prospects of clearing and warming up, all of which would be asked him by Mr. Bertsinger Senior who would then tell him if he was right. Why, in the name of all reason, had he struck Emma? His act—with that, proving it had been a part of him —slipped loose from him, turned around and looked at him in the form of a question. At Sacramento Street it skirted through traffic beside him in sudden dependency, almost like a comedian pretending to be an old man.

If Eugene had not known he could do such a thing as strike Emma, he was even less prepared for having done it. Down hill the eucalyptus trees seemed bigger in the fog than when the sun shone through them, they had the fluffiness of birds in the cold; he had the utterly strange and unamiable notion that he could hear their beating hearts. Walking down a very steep hill was an act of holding back; he had never seen it like that or particularly noticed himself reflected in these people's windows. His head and neck jerked in motions like a pigeon's; he looked down, and when he saw the fallen and purple eucalyptus leaves underfoot, his shoes suddenly stamped them hard as hooves.

A quarrel couldn't even grow between him and Emma. And she would be unfair, beg the question, if a quarrel did spring up; she would cry. That was a

thing a stranger might feel on being introduced to
Emma, even though Emma never proved it to anybody: she had a waterfall of tears back there. He
walked on. The sun, smaller than the moon, rolled
like a little wheel through the fog but gave no light
yet.

Why strike her even softly? They weren't very lov-
ingly inclined these days, with the heart taken out of
them by sorrow; violence was out of place to begin
with. *Why not strike her? And if she thought he
would stay around only to hear her start tuning up,
she had another think coming. Let her take care and
go about her business, he might do it once more and
not so kindly.*

If he had had time to think about it, he might simply have refused to eat his breakfast. He knew that
she minded. Ever since Emma was a landlady calling
"Come on quick, Mr. MacLain!" and he was an anxious roomer, he had known where she was *sensitive*.
Actually, of course, he wouldn't have dared not eat
—under any circumstances. If he had wanted to
kill her, he would have had to eat everything on her
table first, and praise it. She had had a first husband,
the mighty Mr. Gaines, and she would love forever a
compliment on her food. "Sit down and tell me what
you see" was what Emma would say.

The present fact was that she'd said something innocent—innocent but personal, personal but not dear
—to him, which she might have said a thousand times
in twelve years of marriage, and simply taking the
prerogative of a wife was leaning over to remove some
offense of his with her own motherly finger, and he
had slapped her face today. Why slap her today? The
question prodded him locally now, in the back of
one knee as nearly as he could tell. It accommodated
itself like the bang of a small bell to the stiff pull of
his shanks.

He struck her because she was a fat thing. Absurd,
she had always been fat, at least plump ("Your little
landlady's forever busy with something nice!"),

plump when he married her. *Always was is no reason
for its being absurd even yet to—* But couldn't it be
his reason for hitting her, and not hers? *He struck her
because he wanted another love. The forties. Psychol-
ogy.*

Nevertheless a face from nowhere floated straight
into that helpless irony and contemplated the world
of his inward gaze, a dark full-face, obscure and obe-
dient-looking as a newsprint face, looking outward
from its cap of dark hair and a dark background—all
shadow and softness, like a blurred spot on Jones
Street. *Miss Dimdummie Dumwiddie,* he could the
same as read underneath, in the italics of poetry. A
regardful look. Should he suspect? She had died, was
that the story? *Then too late to love you now. Too
late to verify this story of yours . . .* in the paper,
though he was carrying the paper for any such possible reference, pinned there by his right arm. This
morning it had become too late to love the young
and dead Miss Dumwiddie, and he had struck his
wife with the flat of his hand.

Eugene slowed his step obediently here; at the
jobbing butcher's he was habitually caught. Without
warning red and white beeves were volleyed across
the sidewalk on hooks, out of a van. The butchers,
stepped outside for a moment in their bloody aprons,
made a pause for ladies sometimes, but never for
men. The beeves were moving across, all right, and
on the other side a tramp leaned on a cane to watch,
leering like a dandy at each one of the carcasses as it
went by; it could have been some haughty and spurn-
ing woman he kept catching like that.

At the go-ahead from the butcher, made with a
knife, Eugene took one step, but stopped suddenly.
It was out of the question—that was all of a sudden
beautifully clear—that he should go to work that day.

And things were a great deal more serious than he
had thought.

Delicately and slowly as if he had been dared,

Eugene felt with his hand under his raincoat, touching coat and vest and silver pencil. He clung to one small revelation: that today he was not able to take those watches apart.

He had only reached California Street. He stood without moving at the brink of the great steepness, looking down. He had struck Emma and when he struck, her face had met his blow with blankness, a wide-open eye. It had been like kissing the cheek of the dead.

She could still bite his finger, couldn't she? and some mischievous, teasing spirit looked at him, mouthing joy before darting ahead. But he looked down at the steepness, shocked and almost numb. A passerby gave him a silent margin. The slap had been like kissing the cheek of the dead.

What would Mr. Bertsinger Senior, down at the shop, have to say about this, Eugene wondered, what lengthy thing? His watch opened in the palm of his hand, and then he was walking on again with protest and speed down the hill, the street like the sag of a rope that disappeared into fog. The world was the old man's subject, but he knew yours.

II.

Below in Market Street the fog ran high overhead and the bustle of life was revealed. Eugene could imitate his hurry. Could it seem at all sad or absurd to the others, he wondered—with his head seeming to float above his long steps—that Market had with the years become a street of trusses, pads, braces, false bosoms, false teeth, and glass eyes? And of course of jewelry stores. He passed the health food store where the shark liver oil pellets were displayed (really attractively, to tell the truth) on a paper lacy as a Valentine. How amazing it all was. Wasn't it? A sailor in the penny arcade was having his girl photographed in the arms of a stuffed gorilla. Eugene would like to show that to somebody.

He read the second story level of signs across the street, Joltz Nature System, Honest John Trusses, No Toothless Days. A lady carrying a streetcar transfer slip and a bunch of daisies wrapped in newspaper was coming down the stairs from the No Toothless Days door; would she dare smile, supposing she heard of a little joke, horseplay, would there be any use in telling her?

In the flyblown window of a bookstore a dark photograph that looked at first glance like Emma (Emma, he could bet, still sat on at the table composing herself, as carefully as if she had been up to the ceiling and back)˙ was, he read below, Madame Blavatsky. Every other store on Market Street was, pursuing some necessity, a jewelry store; so that if you wore a Strictform No Give Brace you could wear at the same time a butterfly breast pin or a Joy watch band, "Nothing but Gold to Touch the Flesh." It could all make a man feel shame. The kind of shame one had to jump up in the air, kick his heels, to express—whirl around!

Just on the other side of Bertsingers' there was a crowded market. Eugene could hear all day as he worked at his meticulous watches the glad mallet of the man who cracked the crabs. He could hear it more plainly now, mixed with the street noises, like the click and caw of a tropical bird, and the doorway there shimmered with the blue of Dutch iris and the mixed pink and white of carnations in tubs, and the bright clash of the pink, red, and orange azaleas lined up in pots. Oh, to have been one step further on, and grown flowers!

There was Bertsingers'.

Compunction gave Eugene a little elderly-like rap, and he recognized that Bertsingers' was more respectable than most of the jewelry stores: Mr. Bertsinger Senior was on hand. Bertsingers' did carry its brand of the rhinestone Pegasus and ruby swordfish, its tray of charms; and the diamond rings filling the window did each bear a neat card saying "With Full Trade-in

Privilege." But the cards were in Mr. Bertsinger Senior's handwriting—fine and with shaded loops. And Bertsingers' never had a neon sign over his cage in the repair department. There was some dignity left to everything, if you knew where to find it. And Eugene passed by the door.

Bertie Junior was up front and on the lookout for what he might miss, of course—Eugene took a chance. Bertie Junior's thumbs bent softly back, he had little ducktails at the back of his head, he looked privileged as well as young. He'd put a chip diamond in his Army discharge button, for the hell of it—he said. Even in the dark rear of the shop his gleam and his eagerness could be detected from the street, and there was an equal chance he might detect Eugene going by, his target on any occasion. But he came to the door with head lifted high at that moment, watching a fist fight come out of a barber shop. He gleamed even to the sideways glance, wearing two fountain pens, their clips forking tongue-like out of his still-soldierly breast. Eugene got by.

He was not called back, either, or discovered pausing so near, at the market. The fish windows were decorated like a holiday show. There was a double row of salmon steaks placed fan-wise on a tray, and filets of sole fixed this way and that down another tray as in a plait, like cut-off golden hair. When Eugene set his eyes on an arrangement of amber-red caviar in the shape of a large anchor, "They are fish eggs, sir," a young, smocked clerk said, "and personally I think it's a perfect *pity* that they should be allowed to take them." He stood arms akimbo in the market entrance and did not recognize Mr. MacLain who had repaired his watch at all, *that* little drudge. A yearning for levity took hold of the little drudge, he tipped his hat and bowed like a Southerner, to the fish eggs.

There was a soft gleam. Above, blue slides of sky were cutting in on the fog. The sun, as with a spurt of motion, came out. The streetcars, taking on banana colors, drove up and down, the line of movie houses fluttered streamers and flags as if they were going to sea. Eugene moved into the central crowd, which seemed actually to increase its jostling with the sunshine, like the sea with wind.

A little old tramp woke up on the street, and rubbed his eyes. He began scattering crumbs to the descending pigeons and sea gulls. They walked about him fussing like barnyard chickens, and he stood as if flattered by their transformation and their greed, pressing his knees together in the posture of a saint or a lady of the house and looking up to smile at the world. Eugene walked among crumbs and pigeons and crossed over the wide trashy street and when he looked to the right he could see, quite clearly just now, the twin brown-green peaks at the end of the view, the houses bright in their sides, while the lifted mass of blue and gray fog swayed as gently over them as a shade tree.

The lift of fog in the city, that daily act of revelation, brought him a longing now like that of vague times in the past, of long ago in Mississippi, to see the world—there were places he longed for the sight of whose names he had forgotten. And while now it was doubtful that he would ever see the Seven Wonders of the World, he had suggested to Emma that they take a simple little pleasure trip—modestly, on the bus—down the inexpensive side of the Peninsula; but it had been his luck to mention it on the anniversary of Fan's death and she had slammed the door in his face.

It was womanlike; he understood it now. The inviolable grief she had felt for a great thing only widened her capacity to take little things hard. Mourning over the same thing she mourned, he was not to be let in. For letting in was something else. How cold to the living hour grief could make you! Her eye was quite marble-like at the door crack.

There had been a time, too, when she was a soft woman, just as he had been a kind man, soft unto innocence—soft like little Fan, and he saw the child at bedtime letting her hair ripple down and all around, with it almost meeting under her chin like a little golden rain hat, and he wanted to say, "Oh, stay, wait." Just as the other thing was there too: Fan from the age she could walk to it was standing with her back to the fire (they kept an open fireplace then) and with that gesture like a curtsey was lifting up her gown to warm her backside, like any woman in the world.

Now, too late when the city opened out so softly in beauty and to such distances, it awoke a longing for that careless, patched land of Mississippi winter, trees in their rusty wrappers, slow-grown trees taking their time, the lost shambles of old cane, the winter swamp where his own twin brother, he supposed, still hunted. Eugene looked askance at a flower seller: where had the seasons gone? Too cheap, bewilderingly massed together, the summerlike, winterlike, springlike flowers tied up in bunches made him glance disparately at the old man marking down the price on a jug of tulips, and at three turbaned Hindus who bought nothing but in calm turn smelled the bouquets until they stood there with all their six eyes closed, translated into still another world.

"*Open the door, Richard!*" sang a hoarse, nigger voice from a pitch-black bar. A small Chinese girl, all by herself, with her hair up in aluminum curlers, went around Eugene, swinging a little silky purse. He all but put out a staying hand. When a stocky boy with a black pompadour went by him wearing taps on his shoes, some word waited unspoken on Eugene's lips. His chance for speaking tapped rhythmically by. He frowned in the street, the more tantalized, somehow, by seeing at the last minute that the stranger was tattooed with a butterfly on the inner side of his wrist; an intimate place, the wrist appeared to be.

Eugene saw the butterfly plainly enough to recognize it again, when this unfamiliar, callused hand of San Francisco put a flame to a bitten cigarette. In blue ink the double wings spanned the veins and the two feelers reached into the fold at the base of the hand; the spots were so deep they seemed to have come perilously near to piercing the skin.

It was then that Eugene—withdrawing one step in his thoughts, to where old Mr. Bertsinger Senior in his jeweler's glass doddered around, the most critical and slowest to appraise of men, and Bertie Junior waited, knowing without being told (nobody surer than a young man)—felt sure in some absolute way that no familiar person could do him any good. After the step he had taken, the thing he had done, he couldn't stop at all, he had to go on, go in this new direction. Friends: no help there.

In panic—and, it struck him, in exultation—seek a stranger. *Hi, mate. Just lammed the little wifey over the puss.—Horray!—That's what I did.—Sure, not a bad idea once ever so often. Take it easy.* They would be perched up at a bar having a beer together. And the other man would turn out to have done a whole lot worse; in fact, something should be done about *him.*

A tortoise-shell cat pillowed in apples gazed at him from a grocer's window. She pulled her round eyes closed as on little drawstrings. Eugene recollected that one street back a plaster bull dog, cerise with blue rings around the eyes, which ordinarily sat in the ground floor window of a hotel between the drawn shade and the glass, had this morning been taken away. Eugene had missed it—been cheated of it. As the cat opened her eyes again he had a moment of believing he would know anything that happened, anything that threatened the moral way, or transformed it, even, in the city of San Francisco that day: as if he and the city were watching each other—without accustomed faith. But with interest . . . boldness . . . recklessness, almost.

III.

Eugene proceeded down Market, his stride as brisk, businesslike, and concealing as though he had not already left Bertsingers' far behind. Bright mist bathed this end of the street and hid the tower of the Ferry Building; but as he walked he saw, going ahead of him and in the same direction, a tall and distinct figure that he recognized. It was the Spaniard he had heard play the guitar at Aeolian Hall the evening before. Imagine him walking along here! And as far as Eugene could make out over the heads of people intervening, he was walking along by himself.

Eugene had no doubts about that identity. Last night—though it seemed long enough ago now to make the recognition clever—Emma had come out with Eugene to a music hall, and it had turned out that this Spaniard performed, in solo recital. (No, she would not go with him to Half Moon Bay, but she would consent to a little music in one of the smaller halls, she said, and added, "Though you don't appreciate music." He patted her shoulder; they must have been thinking it together: his failure to respect music was part of the past, a night with little Fan at the Symphony, her treat. When the music began the child had held out her little arms, saying Pierre Monteaux came out of *Babar* and she wanted him down here and would spank him. Emma, honestly shocked, had pulled down her daughter's arms, and Eugene had laughed out loud, not then but in the middle of the next piece.) . . . He could not think of the Spaniard's name, but it was pretty observant the way he recognized the man at this distance and from the back, after seeing him only the one time and then over the bird of a lady's hat.

He was alluring, up ahead—the perfect being to catch up with. Eugene walked steadily and looked steadily at him, a stranger and yet not a stranger, going along measuredly and sedately before, the only

black-clad figure on this Western street, head and
shoulders above all the rest.

And the very next moment, something terrible almost happened.

The guitarist reached the curb and in entering the
traffic—really, he was quite provocatively slow, moving through this city street—he almost walked beneath the wheels of an automobile.

With the other's sudden danger, a gate opened to
Eugene. That was all there was to it. He did not have
time to think, but sprang forward as if to protect his
own. His paper flew away from him piecemeal and
as he ran he felt his toes pointing out behind him. This
did not surprise him, for he had been noted for his
running when he was a boy back home; in Morgana,
Mississippi, he was still little old Scooter MacLain.

He seized hold of the Spaniard's coat—which had
him weighing it, smelling it, and feeling the sun warm
on it—and pulled. So out of breath he was laughing,
he pulled in the big Spaniard—who for all his majestic weight proved light on his feet, like a big
woman who turns graceful once she's on the dance
floor. For a moment Eugene kept him at tow there,
on the safe curb, breathing his faint smoke-smell or
travel-smell; but he could not think of that long Spanish name, and he didn't say a word.

Well, what did that matter, when he was so re-
lieved, so delighted, that he had reached the big old
person in time—as delighted as with the surprise of a
gift? Eugene drew both hands away lightly, as if he
were publicly disclosing something, unveiling a huge
statue. But in the next moment, rescuer and rescuee
shook hands, and even in that self-conscious greeting
Eugene discovered something that made him want to
turn his back and say "Damn it all!" The Spaniard
could not speak English.

At least he smiled and *did* not. Proof, wasn't it?
Eugene felt overwhelmed, cut off—disappointed in
the man's very life. He pumped the substantial arm,
taking an extra moment to recover himself, not to

appear quite this disconcerted, or so rejected; he had entirely surprised himself.

Then the order of things seemed to be that the two men should stroll on together down the street. That came out of the very helplessness of not being able to speak—to thank or to deprecate. As he walked, Eugene sent out shy, still respectful glances, those of a man not quite sure his new pet knows who has just come into possession. Now that he thought back, the big fellow had walked out in front of the automobile almost tempting it to try and get him, with all the aplomb of—certainly, a bull fighter. There was another kind of Spaniard! Eugene looked up at his prize again, quite closely. The artist, who now smoked a cigarette, was wholly as imperturbable, if not quite as large bodily, as he had seemed on the Aeolian Hall stage the evening before.

At that time, he appeared carrying ahead of him a guitar, majestic and seeming in his walk years older than his thick black hair would show. He walked across the stage without a glance at the audience—an enormous man in an abundant dress suit with long, heavy tails. As he reached the center front of the stage and turned gravely—he seemed serious as a doctor —his head looked weighty too, long and broad together, with black-rimmed glasses circling his eyes and his hair combed back to hang behind him almost to his shoulders, like an Indian, or the old senator from back home.

He lowered himself to the straight chair that was the only furnishing of the stage except for an oblong object covered in black cloth that had been placed before it. Then he sat there like a mountain. This was just the sort of preliminary to-do that Emma liked; Eugene felt her draw herself up in the kind of bodily indignation that was her quickest expression of pleasure when she was out in public.

The guitarist began to play only after many tender and prolonged attentions to his instrument. He tuned it so softly that only he could hear. Then he gave some care to his extended right foot, which the black oblong object was there to accommodate as a rest, and care most of all to his fingers—flexing all ten of them, stretching them leisurely upon his thighs like a cat testing her claws on a cushion.

His face in the stage light, dark-skinned, smooth, with two deep folds from his nose down the sides of his mouth, was unmoved or even affronted in its stage expression. It did not change while he played or during the applause that came after each song. Only at the very last of the applause after the last song, a smile was seen to have come on his face—and to be enjoying itself there; it had the enchanted presence of a smile on the face of a beast. It lasted just so long, like an act of strength—as long as a strong man might hold a lifted weight. Yet it had been as clear and gradual a change as the light goes through at sunset. It hinted of ordeal, but the smile showed that like the audience, after all, he loved the extraordinary thing. His fingernails were painted bright red.

"Red fingernails," Eugene had whispered, just at the moment when Emma turned her head and gave him a look. It was meant to be a meaningful look from under the brim of the blue hat in which she had that night emerged from public-mourning.

The blueness of the hat even in the light of the dim hall ("Emma's blue," her sister called it) and the blank shine of her new glasses which hid her eyes, and her cheek with a little tear offered on it, all held his head turned toward her as though she had bidden it, but did not distract him from a deep lull in his spirit that was as enfolding as love. He turned his head gently back toward the stage, where an encore was being played. A most unexpected kind of music was being struck off the guitar.

He felt a lapse of all knowledge of Emma as his wife, and of comprehending the future, in some visit to a vast present-time. The lapse must have endured for a solid minute or two, and afterwards he could recollect it. It was as positively there and as defined at the edges as a spot or stain, and it affected him like a secret.

Now out here in the everyday and the open, Eugene was aware, as at the racing of the pulse, of the dark face by his, the Spaniard going beside him, his life actually owing to him, Eugene MacLain. Again he felt fleet of foot, at the very heels of a secret in the day. Was it so strange, the way things are flung out at us, like the apples of Atalanta perhaps, once we have begun a certain onrush? With his hand, which could have stormed a gate, he touched the Spaniard's elbow. It responded like a swinging weight, a balance, in the calm black sleeve. Eugene's touch, his push, now seemed judicious; and he pushed forthrightly to propel the old fellow across the street at the next crossing.

Once, waiting for a traffic light to change, they stood beside a woman on whom Eugene let his gaze rest. There was such strange beauty about her that he did not realize for a few moments that she was birth-marked and would be considered disfigured by most people—by himself, ordinarily. She was a Negro or a Polynesian and marked as a butterfly is, over all her visible skin. Curves, scrolls, dark brown areas on light brown, were beautifully placed on her body, as if by design, with pools about the eyes, at the nape of her neck, at the wrist, and about her legs too, like fawn spots, visible through her stockings. She had the look of waiting in leafy shade.

She was dressed in humble brown, but her hat was an exotic one, with curving bright feathers about her head. Eugene felt an almost palpable aura of a disgrace or sadness that had to be as ever-present as the skin is, of hiding and flaunting together. It was so strong an aura that by softly whistling Eugene pretended to people around that the woman was not there, and tried to keep the Spaniard from seeing her. For he might pounce upon her; something made him afraid of the Spaniard at that moment.

After a little it seemed something of a favor, a privilege, to be unable to communicate any more than by smiles and signs. They strolled along together. The Spaniard appeared content enough to walk along in the soft, mild sun with the little man who undertook to pull him out of the way of wheels. He did not object. He neither hurried nor revealed a plan.

Three pink neon arrows flickered toward a bar. Where were they going, thought Eugene, he and his Spaniard? They were still walking down Market Street past the shoddy, catch-eye stores. And just now they were approaching a shabby spot only too familiar to Eugene; he had to pass it every day, since it was between Bertsingers' and the cafeteria where he daily ate lunch.

A side-show had opened to take its turn in the rundown building where previously some gypsies had been telling fortunes. There were posters in the dirty windows and a languid, enthroned man offering tickets and intoning all day long the words, "Have—you—seen—Em-ma?" in a voice so tired it gave the effect of downright menace. Bertie Junior thought it was terribly funny, with old MacLain's wife being named Emma. He came along with Eugene to lunch now, so he could hear it, and every morning he too asked, "Have—you—seen—Emma?" as Eugene came in, before he could get past.

An enlarged photograph showed the side-show Emma—enormously fat, blown, her small features bunched like a paper of violets in the center of her face. But in the crushed, pushed-together countenance there was a look; it was accusation, of course. The sight of a person to whom other people have been cruel can be the most formidable of all, Eugene thought as he was ready to pass it again. And it is so recognizable, the glance that meets all glances and holds, like a mother's: they done me wrong.

The photograph showed Emma as wearing lace panties, and opposite it a real pair of panties—faded red with no lace—was exhibited hung up by clothes-pins, vast and sagging, limp with dust and travel. In his childhood, Eugene recalled, there was a Thelma that he had paid his Sunday School collection money to see. Thelma was an optical illusion, a woman's head on top of a stepladder; and she had been golden-haired and young, and had smiled invitingly.

Eugene all at once felt himself the host. Should he invite the Spaniard to take a look at Emma, inside? It gave him an appalling moment.

But the Spaniard, cocking his head at Emma's full-sailed manifestation, simply pointed to his own breadth and opened his eyes on Eugene with one warm, brimming question of his own.

It was midday. The street beggars knew it, they sat light-drenched, the blind accordion player with his eyes wide open and his lips formed in a kiss.

"Come on. I'm inviting you, all right. We'll eat," Eugene said, and tipping his finger to his companion's elbow turned him right around.

IV.

Eugene thought—as if in the nick of time—that only a good restaurant would do. Besides, though the cafe-teria was economical and healthy, just now it had begun to be infested by those wiry, but unlucky, old men forever reading racing forms as they drank cof-fee; one particularly, in a belligerent pea-green sweater with yellow bands, seemed to change the whole tone of the place simply by always occupying the table anybody else would want. With a suitable indication of where they were going, perhaps, in his smile, Eugene pulled open the door to a restaurant in Maiden Lane.

The Spaniard, with the merest lift of his black brows, walked in shaking the floor around him and proceeded up the staircase, shaking it, to the little upper dining room, where Eugene, as a matter of fact, had never been in his life.

This Spaniard everywhere seemed to be too much at home. He placed his hat, a big floppy black one, carefully on the radiator in the upper hall, not only as if he was perfectly aware without testing it that there was no heat in the pipes, but also as if the radiator existed not to heat others but to hold his hat.

The head waiter couldn't have seated them more showily. They were given a table by the curtained window; its own lamp was instantly flicked on. Huge menus were set up like tents on a camp field between them.

To Eugene the room was somehow old-fashioned and boxy, like a scene in some old silent movie. The gesturing people, who seemed actually to be turning artificial smiles upon them, were enclosed by walls papered in an intrusive design of balls and bubbles, lights behind poppy shades. Filipinos wearing their boys' belts ran around in a constant, silent double-time looking like twins-on-twins themselves, clearing tables, laying cloths, smiling.

The guitar player with something like a false expression of grief on his face meditated upon what he would, or would not, eat. With his finger he caressed the air; he decided; and it was probably in French that he responded (like a worshiper in the Catholic Church) to the waiter.

When the food was brought, and then still brought, Eugene sat up straight, still pleased but shocked to some extent at all the Spanish guest had commanded. Was he so great? How great was he, how great did he think he was? How well did he think he played the guitar? These things, in fact, made real mysteries.

Eugene, who got veal, began to count up mentally the money in his billfold, only to lose track, start over, and get lost again. He chewed steadily on his veal in another wonder where he lost himself still further.

Last night, he had not been able to keep from wondering at moments all through the music: what would the artist be doing if he weren't performing? After the songs were finished, then would he be alone, for instance? Those things were not such idle questions. . . . The fact was, Eugene thought now, he had had speculations about a man on the stage exactly as if he had known he would meet him in closer fashion afterward. As if he had known that by morning he himself would have struck his wife that blow and found out something new, something entirely different about life.

Eugene had been easily satisfied of one thing—the formidable artist was free. There was no one he loved, to tell him anything, to lay down the law.

The Spaniard tossed a clam shell out of his plate and Eugene at once bent expectantly toward him. He was glad to feel himself in the role of companion and advisor to the artist—just as he had felt, in that prophetic way, his only audience last night. Now he would undertake to put forward an idea or two— suggest something they might do together.

Eugene lifted one hand, vaguely caressing the air in front of the Spaniard. He tried to bring up a woman before him. Perhaps the Spaniard could produce a beautiful mistress he had somewhere, one he enjoyed and always went straight to, while in San Francisco: the strangely marked Negress, wouldn't she exactly do? And Eugene envisioned some silent (and this time, foreign) movie with that never spoken-in-love word, "enjoy," dancing for an instant upon the bouquet of flowers he'd be taking her. His own hand held an invisible bouquet, but the Spaniard looked right through it.

Eugene sank his cheek on his hand and looked across at his guest, who was good-humoredly spitting out a bone. It was more probable that the artist remained alone at night, aware of being too hard to please—and practicing on his guitar.

Yet these moments seemed so precious!

Why waste them? Why not visit a gambling house?
A game of chance would be very interesting. With
those red-nailed fingers (only—and Eugene's hope
fell—they were not red now) the Spaniard would be
able to place their chips on lucky numbers, and with
his sharp and shaming ear listen to the delicate, cheat-
ing click of the ball in the wheel. Eugene usually only
pressed his lips together—to part them—at the idea
of such places, but with the Spaniard along—! For
them, as for young, unattached, dashing boys, or
renegade old men far gone, the roulette wheel all
evening in some smoke-filled but ascetic room . . .
how would it be?

Suppose he, Eugene, found himself in San Francisco for only a day and a night, say, and not for the
rest of his life? Suppose he was still in the process of
leaving Mississippi—not stopped here, but simply an
artist, touring through. Or, if he chanced not to play
the guitar or something, simply out looking: not for
anyone in particular; on the track, say, of his old
man? (God forbid he'd find him! Old Papa King Mac-
Lain was an old goat, a black name *he* had.)

From right here, himself stopped in San Francisco,
Eugene could have told the artist something. This
city . . . often it looked open and free, down
through its long-sighted streets, all in the bright,
washing light. But hill and hill, cloud and cloud, all
shimmering one back of the other like purities or
transparencies of clear idleness and blue smoke, lifting
and going down like the fire-sirens that forever curved
through the place, and traveling water-bright one
upon the other—they were any man's walls still.

And at the same time it would be terrifying if walls,
even the walls of Emma's and his room, the walls of
whatever room it was that closed a person in in the
evening, would go soft as curtains and begin to tremble. If like the curtains of the aurora borealis the walls
of rooms would give even the illusion of lifting—if
they would threaten to go up. That would be repeating the Fire—of course. That could happen any time

to San Francisco. It was a special threat out here. But
the thing he thought of wasn't really physical. . . .

Eugene slowly buttered the last crust of bread.
There was nothing to change his mind about the
Spaniard—to make him think that this sedate man,
installed on the lighted stage with his foot on a rest
the way he liked to present himself, hadn't a secret
practice of going out to a dark and shady place on
his own, and wouldn't seek out as a further preoccu-
pation in his life some stranger's disgrace or necessity,
some marked, designated house. For it was natural
to suppose, supposed Eugene, that the solidest of
artists were chameleons.

What mightn't this Spaniard be capable of?

Eugene felt untoward visions churning, the Spaniard with his great knees bent and his black slippers
turning as if on a wheel's rim, dancing in a red
smoky place with a lead-heavy alligator. The Spaniard turning his back, with his voluminous coat-tails
sailing, and his feet off the ground, floating bird-like
up into the pin-point distance. The Spaniard with his
finger on the page of a book, looking over his shoulder, as did the framed Sibyl on the wall in his father's
study—no! then, it was old Miss Eckhart's "studio"
—where he was muscular, but in a story-like way
womanly. And the Spaniard with horns on his head
—waiting—or advancing! And always the one, dark
face, though momently fire from his nostrils brimmed
over, with that veritable *waste* of life!

Eugene, unaccustomed to visions of people as they
were not, as unaccustomed as he was to the presence
of the Spaniard as he was, choked abruptly on his
crust. He had even forgotten all about old Miss Eckhart in Mississippi, and the lessons he and not Ran
had had on her piano, though perhaps it was natural
that he should remember her now, within the aura of
music. Experimentally he let down one by one the
touchy, nimble fingers of his left hand on the table,
then little finger and thumb see-sawed. The Spaniard
as if through a curtain still seemed about to breathe

fire. Across the table his incessant cigarette smoke came out of his nostrils in a double spout. It was this that was smelling so sweet . . . Eugene seemed to hear the extending cadence of "The Stubborn Rocking Horse," a piece of his he always liked, and could play very well. He saw the window and the yard, with the very tree. The thousands of mimosa flowers, little puffs, blue at the base like flames, seemed not to hold quite steady in this heat and light. His "Stubborn Rocking Horse" was transformed into drops of light, plopping one, two, three, four, through sky and trees to earth, to lie there in the pattern opposite to the shade of the tree. He could feel his forehead bead with drops and the pleasure run like dripping juice through each plodding finger, at such an hour, on such a day, in such a place. Mississippi. A humming bird, like a little fish, a little green fish in the hot air, had hung for a moment before his gaze, then jerked, vanishing, away.

He held his glass again to the Filipino's pitcher. Eugene saw himself for a moment as the kneeling Man in the Wilderness in the engraving in his father's remnant geography book, who hacked once at the Traveler's Tree, opened his mouth, and the water came pouring in. What did Eugene MacLain really care about the life of an artist, or a foreigner, or a wanderer, all the same thing—to have it all brought upon him now? That engraving itself, he had once believed, represented his father, King MacLain, in the flesh, the one who had never seen him or wanted to see him.

A Filipino dropped a dish which broke to pieces on the floor and sent the food spilling. Eugene felt his face growing pointed with derogatory, yet pitying, truly pitying sounds. He was laughing at the Filipino; and all the time, out of the whole room, perhaps, only he knew how excruciating this small mishap probably was.

But he had got his money mentally counted up. He found he could pay for this affair, almost exactly, with a few pennies left over. It made the awe of the thing settle a little and go down.

The Spaniard had attracted some attention from the room, spitting out the bones of his special dish, breaking the bread and clamping it in his teeth with the sound of firecrackers. His black eyes were amiably following a little fly now. Dishes, hats, ladies' noses, curtains at the window, were his little fly's lighting places, his little choices. The Spaniard seemed to be playing the mildest little game with himself.

This was what he was like when he was not playing the guitar. Yet—he was not so bad. When the waiter came with the bill, Eugene paid for the extravagance quite eagerly. The sight, the memory now, of the aloof and ravenous face opposite his, dark in the pearly window light, and the sorrowful mouth devouring the very best food until all had disappeared except for a pile of bones and a frill of paper—this filled him with a glow that began to increase while they smilingly nodded and rose. Like a peacock's tail the papered wall seemed lazily to extend now from the table at which they had sat. As they walked among the tables to leave, the Spaniard reaching out and gently taking a number of match packets, in a breeze of succession the women in their large hats leaned toward one another, the flowery brims touching, and murmured some name, and glanced. Eugene looked back at them and frowned in a deaf, possessive fashion.

They came out into the flat light of day and the noise, like a deception or a concealment of rage, of the ordinary afternoon stir. As they paused on the walk, a streetcar not far away roared down a crowded street. With the air of a fool or a traitor, so the crowd felt all together—there was a feeling like a concussion in the air—a dumpy little woman tripped forward on high heels in the street, swung her purse like a hatful of flowers, spilling everything, and sank in an outrageous-looking pink color in the streetcar's path. In a moment the streetcar struck her. She was pitched about, thrown ahead on the tracks, then let alone; she was not run over by the car, but she was dead. Eugene could tell that, as they all could, by the slow swinging walk of the pair of policemen who saw everything and now had to take charge. This pair saw no use in the world to hurry now.

"Accident!" Eugene said—repeated, that is. His voice must have told the Spaniard that this should be of special interest to him. The big man stood planted, his lower lip jutted out under his cigarette, his eyes squinting. It was unquestionably a very horrible thing. Nobody hurried.

"She's dead, I'm pretty sure," Eugene said, but determined to keep his single voice a cautious one. Other voices close by were speaking. The Spaniard was shaking his head.

"Why don't the ambulance come?"

"Look at the motorman. His fault."

"She had gray hair."

Shake of the head.

"Somebody ought to pick up all those things and get them back in her purse."

"Don't they cover them up?"

"I wonder who she was."

"Who will they know to tell?"

Shake of the head.

The Spaniard shook his head.

"Let's go." Two girls spoke, turning. "I'm ready when you are."

But an inner group, a hollow square of people, hid the victim. They flanked her, and not all the time, but at moments, looked down at her. They held their ranks closed, like valuable persons. They were going to have been there. The group, businessmen, lady shoppers and children, seemed to consider themselves gently floating like the passengers on a raft, a little way out. One youth, hand on hip, looked with deep, idle, inward gaze at a street sparrow by his foot, and then, beside the sparrow's little foot was the dead woman's open purse.

"Well—!"

They went around the corner, the Spaniard still shaking his head at moments. At a glance he looked as if he thought the place couldn't be any good, really.

Eugene led him to a big hotel. They entered the glitter and perfume of the lobby and through its entire maze before Eugene could discover the men's room, feeling the responsibility of the big black Spaniard like a parade he was leading.

As they stood in their caves with the echoing partition between, Eugene's head nodded and rolled once or twice rhythmically. . . .

Well, the music last night had not been what he had thought it would be. In prophesying that, Emma had known what she was talking about. It was not at all throbbing—and of course not nigger. It had not a great many chords, it was never loud. The Spaniard's songs were old—ancient, his program said; some of them were written for organs and for lutes; and yet, he, So-and-So, the guitarist, played them. Were the difficulties and challenges what he had sought for most? Vain old person. Yes, it is the *guitar* I am playing. Yes, I am a *guitar player*. What did you think I was?

He was in as overwhelming a degree as if he announced it from the stage—in English—an extremely careful old person, an extremely careful artist.

Eugene suddenly felt both impatient and offended with him. Not bothering to conceal his own absorption in what he was playing, the man took no notice or care that he pleased anyone else either. . . . No! And Eugene had not been carried away altogether by the Spaniard's music. Not by any means. Only when the man at last played very softly some unbearably rapid or subtle songs of his own country, so soft as to be almost without sound, only a beating on the

air like a fast wing—then was Eugene moved. Sometimes the sounds seemed shaken out, not struck, with
the unearthly faint crash of a tambourine.

In love songs as in the rest, the artist himself remained remote, as a conscientious black cloud from a
summer day. He only loomed. He ended the recital
with a formal bow—as though it had been taken for
granted by then that passion was the thing he had in
hand, love was his servant, and even despair was a
little tamed animal trotting about in plain view. The
bow had been consummate with grace, and when he
lifted up, he was so big he looked very close to the
eyes.

When Eugene came out, the Spaniard was weighing himself. The arrow trembled, the Spaniard gently
regarding it, filling himself with a sigh to make it
shake. Eugene frowned at the figure. Only 240. He
had supposed the Spaniard would weigh more than
that—250 or 255.

His guest looked at him as bright and fresh as a
daisy. "Where shall we go now?" he meant, as plain
as day.

Eugene ushered him to the street. On the step was
a band of sunlight soft and level as little Fan's hair
when she would go flying before him. The men began walking, the Spaniard with spirit—was this ex-
ercise? The square shone, and the façade of a steep
street like a great gray accordion spread over a knee
seemed about to stutter into the air.

v.

They walked city squares in the sun until some meditative mood between them bound them like consent-
ing speech. At a corner two old fellows, twins,
absurdly dressed alike in plaid jackets, the same
size and together still, were helping each other onto
the crowded step of a streetcar. Eugene and the Spaniard noticed them at the same moment and casting
each other amused glances, they stepped up too, as

the car began moving, and rode off on the step. It was like surf-boarding on waves. Behind them, the cow-catcher was a big basketful of children.

A Negro, his fan of hair so coarse as to look grainy, immediately rammed his head between Eugene's and the Spaniard's. His pop-eyes watched. The streetcar climbed, rolled, and descended, rocking through warming and ever-crowding streets, and finally turned straight into the West. Eugene, with his head turned away from the Negro's, tried to close his ears against the cries of the children, and read the tattered street signs to himself as they passed.

The conductor was a big fat Negro woman who yelled out all the street names with joy. "Divisadero! I say Divisadero!" At The Bug Used Records and Shoe Massage Parlor, and from the steep, fancy-fronted, engraved-looking houses with all the paint worn away—like the solitary houses over railroad cuts seen once—the conductor's friends hollered at her as they went by. Swinging out of the car she often called back. "Off at two A.M!" "See you at the Cat!"

The Negro head between Eugene and the Spaniard rolled its eyes. Once Eugene caught a glimpse of the Spaniard *smiling* as he traveled. Niggers would think he comprehended all their nigger-business—that he himself might be at the Cat at two. The basket of children swarmed over.

Eugene managed to reach the bell. He got the Spaniard off the streetcar, actually having to pull him by the waist to extricate him backwards. It was too much. They continued their direction on foot, still into the sun and still up into the last rim of hills.

It was by rights a sleepy hour, for people who didn't have to work. The city was so ugly at close quarters and so beautiful down its long distances. The hills, hills after hills that they walked over, the increasing freshness of the air, the warmth of the nearer sun, all made Eugene feel as if he were falling asleep. Because the very silence between the men was—at last—replete and dream-like, the hills were to Eugene increasingly like those stairs he climbed in dreams.

The hills with their uniform, unseparated houses repeated over and over again his hill on Jones Street; the houses occurred over and over—all built on the same day, all one age. There was all one destiny. Suppose another Fire were to rack San Francisco and topple it and he, Eugene MacLain out of Mississippi, had to put it all back together again. His eyes half closed upon the mountains of houses not wall-like, as houses were in other places, but swollen like bee-hives, and one hive succeeding another, mounting into tremendous steps of stairs—and alive inside, inwardly contriving. How could he put a watch back to-gether?

Here came the old woman down the hill—there was always one. In tippets and tapping their canes they slowly came down to meet you. Sometimes it seemed to Eugene that all the women in San Fran-cisco were walking those hills all their lives, with canes before they knew it, and when they got old, instead of dying they used two canes, or crutches. Emma's feet were dainty, but the round flesh came all the way down her legs like pantalettes. She said it had only been there since the birth of the child: she blamed little Fan with it. Out of the middle of her grief she could rise and put her unanswerable pink finger on Woman's Sacrifice.

"Your little girl," Eugene remarked aloud, "said, 'Mama, my throat hurts me,' and she was dead in three days. You expected her mother would watch a fever, while you were at the office, not go talk to Mrs. Herring. But you never spoke of it, did you. Never did."

Each rounded house contained a stair. Every form had its spiral or its tendril, outward or concealed. Outside were fire escapes. He gazed up at the intri-cacies of those things; sea gulls were sitting at their heads. How could he make a fire escape if he were required to? The laddered, tricky fire escapes, the mesh of unguarded traffic, coiling springs, women's

lace, the nests in their purses—he thought how the
making and doing of daily life mazed a man about,
eyes, legs, ladders, feet, fingers, like a vine. It twined
a man in, the very doing and dying and daring of the
world, the citified world. He could not set about making a fire escape to his flat in Jones Street, given all
the parts and the whole day off and the right instru-
ments, if Mr. Bertsinger and Emma too told him to go
ahead, and that his life depended on it. Should he be
ashamed?

"Open the door, Richard. *Ouvrez le fenêtre, Paul
ou Jacques,*" the demoniac voice of the comedian
sang on the record, and Eugene waited to hear it
again. He remembered away back: there was an old
Negro and everybody in Morgana knew when he was
in trouble at home; he walked into the store and
asked them to play him a record—"Rocks in My Bed
Number Two," by Blind Boy Fuller. Through a basement window he saw an upright piano and a big
colored woman plying the keys. She looked like a long
way from home. He could not hear her, and realized
that there was much noise outside here, in the streets.

"*I* don't get the sun in *my* eyes," said a little boy,
looking up at Eugene, who was holding one hand
slanted before his face.

"You don't, sonnie?" said Eugene gently. With one
hand he took away the other, as if the little boy had
asked him to stop using it. The boy gave him a sweet,
cocksure smile, which jumped with many suns in
Eugene's vision.

They were on a numbered avenue not far, now,
from the ocean. Seasoned with light like old invalids
the young bungalows looked into the West. The
Spaniard rather unexpectedly lunged forward, swung
his big body around, and gazed for himself at the
world behind and below where they had come. He
tenderly swept an arm. The whole arena was alight
with a fairness and blueness at this hour of afternoon;
all the gray was blue and the white was blue—the
laid-out city looked soft, brushed over with some sky-

feather. Then he dropped his hand, as though the city might retire; and lifted it again, as though to bring it back for a second time. He was really wonderful, with his arm raised.

They walked on, until the sky ahead was brilliant enough to keep the eyes dazzled. On the next hill two nuns in a sea of wind looked destructible as smokestacks on a flaming roof.

"Chances are"—Eugene had begun speaking again —"you didn't know you had it in you—to strike a woman. Did you?"

The Spaniard threw him a dark glance. But it was as if Eugene had said, "You are a guitar player" or "This is Presidio Avenue." Calmly he set his steps over a sprawled old winehead sleeping up here far away from his kind. Quite unheeding of legs overhead, the sleeper was stretched out of a little garden with his head in the anemones and the gray beard shining like spittle on his face.

"You wouldn't mind finding yourself like that," Eugene said, walking in the Spaniard's exact steps over the fallen legs.

And Eugene felt all at once an emotion that visited him inexplicably at times—the overwhelming, secret tenderness toward his twin, Ran MacLain, whom he had not seen for half his life, that he might have felt toward a lover. Was all well with Ran? How little we know! For considering that he might have done some reprehensible thing, then he would need the gravest and tenderest handling. Eugene's eyes nearly closed and he half fainted upon the body of the city, the old veins, the mottled skin of pavement. Perhaps the soft grass in which little daisies opened would hold his temples and put its eyes to his. He heard the murmuring slit of the cable track.

The Spaniard was holding him by the arm. His large face overhead flowed over with commiseration and pleasure. As if he were saying, "Why, of course. This is what we came for!" Eugene was half-lifted across the street. Then the Spaniard, still with a look of interest, made a gesture of examining him, patted him and straightened him up, gave him a little finishing shake, a cuff.

And rain fell on them. In the air a fine, caressing "precipitation" was shining. An open-eyed baby in his cart extended his little hands and held his thumbs and forefingers tight-shut: a hold on the bright mist. On the hill a cable car slid to a perch on the crest and sat there, home-like as a lawn swing, gay with girls' and boys' legs. Above, over cleared ground where a tree-cutting and excavation went on in the old graveyard—the Spanish tombs—two homemade kites in the sky jumped at each other and nodded like gossips. A sea wind blew the scent of alyssum from all the waste spaces. It waved the wispy white beard of an old Chinese gentleman who was running with the abandon of a school child for the car, which waited on him. This hilltop wind passed over Eugene with the refreshment that sometimes comes of a gentle sloughing off of a daydream or desire which takes even its memory with it. He looked up at his Spaniard and drew a breath also, perhaps not really a sympathetic one, but he seemed to increase in size. Eugene watched his great fatherly barrel of chest move, and had a momentary glimpse of his suspenders, which were pink trimmed in silver with little bearded animal faces on the buckles.

His face with its expression that might be solicitude still—and at the same time, meditation, amusement, sleepiness, or implacability when the whole was seen at such close quarters with the black circles, the shell rims, around the eyes—was directed for a round moment on Eugene. Then his head swung and with the long black hair bobbing behind, nodded a fraction at something. It struck Eugene that he looked like that Doctor Caligari in the old silent movie days, ringing his bell on the sideshow platform.

For he had nodded up at the undestroyed part of

the embankment, where some of the old graves, still to be ransacked by the shovels, stood here and there under the olive trees. In the foreground was a cat. In the deep grass she held a motionless and time-honored pose.

Her head was three-quarters turned toward them where they stood. It seemed to have womanly eyebrows. Her gaze came out of her face with the whole of animal comprehension; whether it was menace or alarm in the full-open eyes, her face made a burning-glass of looking. Her eyes seemed after so long a time to be holding her herself in their power. She crouched rigid with the devotion and intensity of her vision, and if she had caught fire there, still she could not, Eugene felt, have stirred out of the seizure. She would have been consumed twice over before she disregarded either what she was looking at or her own frenzy.

On the untidy embankment something else—the object of the gaze—presently showed itself by a motion in the grass. As if the sight pricked him to move, Eugene darted for a heavy pine twig with cones and threw it at the cat; it struck her side. She seemed not to feel it, since she did not waver.

He exclaimed. And all the while the Spaniard was standing there in a relaxed posture looking on—he might have been over in Paris, looking at the Seine! And yet that detachment, Eugene was not unaware, and it gave him some bitterness, had been the outer semblance of what passion in his music last night! Eugene watched stubbornly, and even felt his excitement grow as the whirring of a wing or the pulsing of a tongue, whatever it was, came at less frequent intervals. It was still too rapid for the eye to tell what made it. Which was happening: was the whirring spending itself out, or was the lure, on its side, becoming an old thing, taken for granted? This had a beginning and end.

"What's in the grass, a bird or a snake? What do you bet?" Eugene said softly.

But the Spaniard stood patiently planted there, while the terrible gaze ran fast as a humming wire between the cat and the other creature. Didn't it matter which poor, avid life took the gaze and which gave it? The cat's eyes big as watches shone tearlessly. Eugene thought all at once, It's all the same—it's a bestial thing, all of it, I don't care to know, thank you.

But he waited. The next minute he threw a stone, this time in the direction of the fluttering in the grass. It excited him; this, indeed, made the cat spit drily and tremble all over.

The Spaniard, when Eugene looked to him, was making a hideous face over the lighting of another cigarette. The muscles of his face grouped themselves in hideous luxuriousness, rippled once, then all cleared. His lips were grape-colored, and the smoke smelled sweet.

"Come on," Eugene said to him, and took his arm and pulled. "Come on, you Dago."

VI.

They had come down at the end to the beach: great emptiness. At first it seemed no one was there, so late on this uncertain day. Then crossing the middle distance toward the sea appeared a student with his pants rolled up, reading as he walked, and a man, who looked like a hermit, rather gracefully shouldering wood. Farther away still in the pale expanse two middle-aged ladies in steadily threatened hats materialized; they looked at their watches: waiting for sunset. One battered, sand-colored auto was in sight; it had been left by the sea wall gate, one door open, a horse's bleached skull hanging on the face of the radiator. A little dog sat inside. Black smoke moved on the air, fading; the day's casual fires along the beach had gone out, and a ship was disclosed at sea. Some sea gulls perched on the roller-coaster humps, some stood short-necked and unmoving in front of the shuttered-down food stands, and the blackbirds like little ladies walked about at their feet, keeping busy.

How could it have seemed so silent, because it was deserted? Just the way it had seemed deserted, at first, because the noise hadn't been taken in. There was actually a steady tinkling where the carousel went around, with no child riding, and there was the excited and unrelieved sound of laughter filling the midway. Eugene knew its source and pointed it out to the Spaniard, who swayed each way and smiled faintly. The shouting mechanical dummy of a woman, larger than life, dressed up and with a feather in her hat, stood beckoning on the upper gallery of the House of Mirth and producing her wound-up laughter. In every way she called for the attention; the motions of her head with its feather, and of her arms and hips, were as raucous and hilarious as the sound that was played in her insides. The boom of the ocean seemed to be bearing that small sound, too, on its back, supporting this one extra little chip.

Eugene walked down to the sands where the wind beat the laughter to pieces and the ripping sound of his own hat filled his ears. The Spaniard was already at the shore, facing the waves, and so immovably established that the esthetic ladies had withdrawn. Only a pair of lovers lay close by the wall—motionless also. His solid tracks in the sand were the only straight line on the beach, butting through wood gatherers', students', ladies', lovers', and all the vanished children's and dogs'. Eugene's now went around his, light and toeing out. Sea onions littered the beach; what night had the storm been? Now and then the crashing reach of water came to the European points of the other man's shoes, advancing at the last instant with pure little tongues, that minutely kissed and withdrew.

Eugene gently pulled the Spaniard's arm, and pointed up the beach to the cliffs there. "Land's End!" he shouted, while the waves' sound drowned him out. He pulled gently.

The Spaniard looked affirmative, but first disengaged himself and made water toward the sea, throwing up a rampart, a regular castle, in the sand.

So they turned and their walk could still go on along shore, past the black pits of fires and the ubiquitous, ugly, naked sea onions, until they reached rocks; then it led up to the overlooking wall. A little boy up there on a velocipede with his yellow hair blown in points came riding dreamily between the men, even he with a tied-on sea onion tail dragging six feet behind him. The Spaniard soberly bent over and gave the tail a carefree, lariat-like swing. The little boy looked back, eyes and mouth all round, and the next instant screamed with delighted outrage, as if he saw himself mocked. Beyond the car barn was a black scraggly wood, and then there was something of a road that followed along the cliff interminably, or once there had been.

For there had been an occasion when Eugene and Emma had come this far, and picnicked here. They had drunk several bottles of red wine and gone to sleep in the hot sun on the rocks, lying on their backs, knees up, heads tipped together. Emma's fair skin had turned pink as a rose. Where was little Fan then? That hadn't bothered them that day.

The men walked and climbed along this road with the sea exploding straight under them at times—no beach now, only the brown rocks. From time to time another rock would move a little, or there would be a little rain of pebbly sound somewhere. Occasional paths wandered off down the sharp slopes through grass or over the bare rock to the boulders at the water's edge. The little bushes whipped, and the Spaniard's black coat leaped and danced. Eugene felt the Pacific wind like a fortification, he could storm it or lean onto it, just the same; it could stop his breath and keep him from falling too.

It blew the sea gulls back. A flock of them, collected points of light halfway up the sky, made a turn all at one time, and showed the facets of their flight clear as a diamond. Eugene sucked in the air—now it was rapture. He watched the birds fly out, blow back.

(Down at the wharf, down out of the high heavens, they stood solid as housewives, one large plump one to each little fishing boat, almost moral-looking, ready to pronounce judgment. It seemed sometimes that all sea gulls could not be the same, that they must be two varieties of birdkind, or the birds themselves must have two lives. Was it the sun or the fog, the time of day, that most often changed things, by changing their appearances? He supposed he had a horror of closed-in places and of being shut in, but in late afternoon he had seen Alcatraz light as a lady's hat afloat on the water, looking inviting, and he would almost wish to go to that island himself, and say to people, "Convicts are Christ," or the like.)

"Will you go in front, or behind?" he asked, but the Spaniard was already going in front.

"You know what you did," Eugene said. "You assaulted your wife. Do you say you didn't know you had it in you?"

The Spaniard up ahead made his way forward without turning around. By now the path had grown wild and narrow; it made slow going, or rather, the Spaniard's leisurely gaining of the cliff set the pace, not Eugene's backslidings and precarious scramblings.

All the while, as if they were borne independently of legs of any kind beneath, the heads of the two men kept turning calmly outward, eyes traveling over the view. But as if to mock that too, once the Spaniard's hands met on top of his head to clamp his hat, his elbows bent outward. It was the lumpy pose of a woman, a "nude reclining."

The deepening sky was divided in half as it often was at this hour, by a kind of spinal cloud. Ahead, the north was clear and the south behind was thickened with white. Under the clear portion of sky the

sea rushed in dark to greenness and blackness, the
lips of the waves livid. ("Flounder, flounder in the
sea," he heard his mother read.) Under the cloudy
portion the sea burned silver and at moments entirely
white, and the waves coming in held their form until
the last minute and appeared still and limitless as
snow. The beach and the city where they had walked
were crossed with dust and mist, the scene flickered
like the banners and flying sand of distant battle
or a tumult in the past. Ahead, the extending rocks
were unqualifiedly clear, hard, and azure.

The steepness increased, the path after a certain
point appeared entirely out of use. Here and there a
boulder had lately fallen and lay in their path wet
within its fissures as if it began to live, and secrete,
and they had to climb around it, holding to brush.
Where there were not rocks it was sandy and grassy
and very wild. A fault of course lay all through the
land.

Sometimes Eugene was aware that he jerked like a
pigeon or rocked like a sailor, going down, or sagged
like an old poodle, going up; it was all the same. Once
he leaped, and almost without a care. His tiltings,
projections, slidings, working to keep up, all were
painless now, and a progress he kept to himself.
When pain did not hurt, and the world did, things
had got very strange—different.

The sun was low, and some of the fog bank had
detached itself in narrow clouds thin and delicate
as bone, with the red light beginning to come
through. The Spaniard went as sedately as ever along
the edge he walked; had he been here before too?
When he jumped on his slick black shoes, his footing
was sure. It was he who took the choice of paths, and
the choice was always a clever and difficult one.
Paths ran everywhere now, a network of threads
over waste and rock, with dancing, graybeard bushes
to hold to. Below, the wet boulders were now faintly

covered with light. Bathers in the distance, or por-
poises, rose and sank sky-colored; there are always
strangers who swim at sunset time.

Eugene went where the Spaniard went, but not
always everywhere he went. There were caves where
the paths dropped to the sea, and the Spaniard
went on his own to inspect them. Eugene ceased
crying directions, for it made him feel like a lost lamb
bleating. The huge fellow let himself down the steep
rocks and with hands and knees peered into the caves,
like a dentist into alluring mouths. Rats ran up the
bald surfaces. They were big rats—a size not of any
habitation anywhere but of away out here, of un-
visited geographical parts—as the world's wild dogs
and wild horses are unseen and sizeless. The Spaniard
glanced after the rats with his head inclined to one
side. Even he could not light his cigarettes in this
wind.

As it grew later the men made their way on, and
piercing the sound of the wind the little dark birds
that lived for neatness about the edge of the sea began to fill the air with twitterings, like birds ready to
nest in leafy trees in a little springtime town. There
had evidently been, without their knowing it, a
loss of the wish to go back. Perhaps this wish had ex-
pired. Eugene, who had once nearly drowned, remembered his discovery of the death of volition to
stay up in the water. Such things were always found
out no telling how long after it was too late.

The sun was dropping. It looked wetter than
water, then not so much a bright body as a red
body. It dropped and was gone in the blue mist that
was coming in over the sea. For a brief period the
water, brighter than air, turned smooth and calm and
the fog with wings spreading sank over it and was
skimming at Eugene's face.

"You heard me, all the time," he said.

But the Spaniard bent over with his back to Eugene, and was peering at some blotched wild lilies
that grew in the coarse grass there. He touched the

tips of his fingers deliberately under the soft pale petals and examined their hairy hearts. Eugene was waiting behind him as he turned with a flower in his hand. All at once the Spanish eyes looked wide awake, and the man smiled—like someone waking from a deep dream, the sleep of a month. He put up his little flower, and regarded it.

"*Mariposa,*" he said, making each syllable clearly distinct. He held up the little wild waving spotted thing, the common mariposa lily. "*Mariposa?*" He repeated the word encouragingly, even sweetly, making the sound of it beautiful.

"You assaulted your wife," Eugene said loudly.

The Spaniard still held his eyes open wide. If the staring smile was a slight, at the same time he was presenting his stupid flower.

"But in your heart," Eugene said, and then he was lost. It was a lifelong trouble, he had never been able to express himself at all when it came to the very moment. And now, on a cliff, in a wind, to . . .

Eugene thrust both hands forward and took hold of the other man, not half compassing the vast waist. But he recognized the weight that was so light on its feet, and he had only to make one move more, to unsettle that weight and let it go. Under his watchful eyes the flower went out of the other's loosening, softening hand: it lay on the wind, and sank. One more move and the man would go too, drop out of sight. He would go down below and it took only a touch.

Eugene clung to the Spaniard now, almost as if he had waited for him a long time with longing, almost as if he loved him, and had found a lasting refuge. He could have caressed the side of the massive face with the great pores in the loose, hanging cheek. The Spaniard closed his eyes.

Then a bullish roar opened out of him. He wagged his enormous head. What seemed to be utterances of the wildest order came from the wide mouth, together with the dinner's old reek. Eugene half expected more bones. He could see everything more

than plainly. The Spaniard's eyes also were open to
the widest, and his nostrils had the hairs raised erect
in them.

Eugene suddenly lost his balance and nearly fell,
so that he had to pull himself back by helplessly seiz-
ing hold of the big man. He listened on, perforce, to
the voice that did not stop.

It was a terrible recital. Eugene drew back as far
as possible and presently began to glare at him—a
man laying himself altogether bare like that, with no
shame, no respect. . . . What was he digging up to
confess to, making such a spectacle? To whom did he
think he prayed for relief? Eugene's hands waited
nerveless moment after moment, while his ears were
beaten upon, his whole body, indeed.

Abruptly—and causing silence as with a stopper—
the Spaniard's broad-brimmed hat shot up in the
wind and was blown—to sea? Landward. Eugene
felt compelled to: he let go the Spaniard and ran
hurrying to catch the hat and bring it back. Now it
lifted ahead, turned over, clung to a wall, flew up
again. Eugene had to climb a rather difficult part of
the cliff. He saw the hat, and reached it where it
danced about a bush, and got it in his hand.

Eugene lost his own hat in the chase; but inspira-
tion was with him now, and he put on the Spaniard's.
Knees bent on the pinnacle, raincoat whipping, he
reached up and set it on his head. It stayed on, and
at the same time it shadowed him. The band inside
was warm and fragrant still. Elation ran all through
his body, like the first runner that ever knew the way
to it. His hands shaking with extreme care, as particularly as if he could see himself again in Emma's
mirror with the little snapshot stuck in the corner, he
set the brim just so.

He returned over the rocks and placed himself and
looked back at the other man, eyes protected. It was
in all confidence that he took fresh hold of him, but
this time—how cruel!—he could not move him. He
could not budge him an inch. He stood there with

his hands in appeal on the Spaniard's silent arms. But this time the Spaniard had hold of him. It was a hold of hard, callused fingers like prongs.

And the Spaniard would have looked small down there, all the way down below. Suppose there were a little guitar, no bigger than a watch. Eugene stood waiting there as if he listened to sirens. Then within himself he felt a strange sensation, strange in itself but, alas, he recognized it. He had felt it before —always before when very tired, and always when lying in bed at night, with Emma asleep beside him. Something round would be in his mouth. But its size was the thing that was strange.

It was as if he were trying to swallow a cherry but found he was only the size of the stem of the cherry. His mouth received and was explored by some immensity. It became more and more immense while he waited. All knowledge of the rest of his body and the feeling in it would leave him; he would not find it possible to describe his position in the bed, where his legs were or his hands; his mouth alone felt and it felt enormity. Only the finest, frailest thread of his own body seemed to exist, in order to provide the mouth. He seemed to have the world on his tongue. And it had no taste—only size.

He held onto the Spaniard and once more, feebly, with an arm or a leg, he tried to move him, to break away. The fog flowed into his throat and made him laugh. His laugh was repeated, an uncertain distance away. Eugene heard, then by chance saw, a man and girl moving along by their own light, a flashlight, skirting the brink just above, ahead of the night falling. They circled near. He heard them laugh, and in the dusk he flung back his head and could look up into the gleam of their teeth—was that happiness? Teeth bared like the rats', the same as in hunger or stress?

As he gasped, the sweet and the salt, the alyssum and the sea affected him as a single scent. It lulled him slightly, blurring the moment. The now calming ocean, the pounding of a thousand gentlenesses, went on into darkness and obscurity. He felt himself lifted up in the strong arms of the Spaniard, up above the bare head of the other man. Now the second hat blew away from him too. He was without a burden in the world.

Pillowed on great strength, he was turned in the air. It was greatest comfort. It was too bad that circling in his mind the daylong foreboding had to return, that he had yet to open the door and climb the stairs to Emma. There she waited in the front room, shedding her tears standing up, like a bride, with the white curtains of the bay window hanging heavy all around her.

When his body was wheeled another turn, the foreboding like a spinning ball was caught again. This time the vision—some niche of clarity, some future—was Emma MacLain turning around and coming part way to meet him on the stairs. Still like a rumble, her light and young-like tread, that could cause his whole body to be shaken with tenderness and mystery, crossed the floor. She lifted both arms in the wide, aroused sleeves and brought them together around him. He had to sink upon the frail hall chair intended for the coats and hats. And she was sinking upon him and on his mouth putting kisses like blows, returning him awesome favors in full vigor, with not the ghost of the salt of tears.

If he could have spoken! It was out of this relentlessness, not out of the gush of tears, that there would be a child again. Could it be possible that everything now could wait? If he could have stopped everything, until that pulse, far back, far inside, far within now, could shake like the little hard red fist of the first spring leaf!

He was brought over and held by the knees in the posture of a bird, his body almost upright and his forearms gently spread. In his nostrils and relaxing eyes and around his naked head he could feel the reach of fine spray or the breath of fog. He was upborne, open-armed. He was only thinking, My dear love comes.

He heard a loud, emotional cry—a bellow—from some other throat than his own, and heard it sink to the deepest rumbling. That was his Spaniard.

And the next moment—"Oh, is he going to throw him over?" a feminine voice with some eagerness in it was crying. The sweethearts were coming, on a lower road. "Aren't you ashamed of yourself, teasing a little fellow like that, scaring him?" the girl's voice continued. "Put him down and pick up one your own size, or Billy will teach you."

Then, or even before then, Eugene was lowered and set down again. His dangling heels, one of which had gone to sleep, kicked at the rock and then his feet stood on it. In the purple of night there was struck a little pasteboard match. Two big common, toothy sweethearts stood there in its light, and the next moment vanished in the fog looking pleased with each other.

The mask face of the Spaniard, with hair swirling about it, was left shining there by matchlight. It turned one way and the other, looked up and down. It exuded sweat.

VII.

So now, the Spaniard took hold of Eugene's arm and guided him carefully by the instant's light of one match after another and the emergent light of the wreathed, racing moon. The world was not dark, but pale. The mist flowed from their fingers and rolled behind their heels. They looked together for the thread of the way back. They seized hands at perilous places and took mistaken hold of streaming thorn bushes with a chorus of outcries. They retreated at points and tried the way again. They both jumped at scuttling sounds, though the Spaniard made some inimitable Spanish noise that sounded as though it might have, before now, made

rats go back. When was it they came to the easy part
of the path, then to the road? Next, the whole
sound of the sea faded behind the windbreak of
trees, which in the wet fog smelled of black pepper.

When the trees opened out and they reached pavement, some city corner and its streetlight, they were
so cold it was foregone they should go in the nearest
café for coffee.

Eugene pulled away, combed back his hair, and
led the way now.

"Two coffees!" he said loudly to the bare room
when they were seated at the counter.

It was warm here. The Spaniard began to smoke,
and sat with eyes shut, even when the waitress came
out.

Large, middle-aged, big-boned, she moved up in a
loose, grand style. Her face was large. All her features were made to seem bigger than life by paint,
a pinkish mouth painted over her real mouth, eyebrows put on with brown grease in bands half an
inch wide with perfect curves. Her eyes were small,
so that with the mascara and the shadows painted
on their lids they looked like flopping black butterflies. She had hennaed hair, somewhat greasy. She
wore jewelry worth about eleven dollars and a quarter all together, Eugene saw—hoops of gold in her
ears, a lavalier around her neck, four bracelets, and
rings on both hands. There on her one body the il-
lusions of gold, of silver, and of diamonds were all
gone.

"One coffee with milk," Eugene said to her, "one
black," and she turned from him. Her way of
response was dramatic—soliloquy, and with an accent.

"Meelk, meelk, there is one who wants meelk," she
said, striding up and down behind the counter
but not going away or looking at her customers or
consulting further.

"And pastry."

"Oh, no. Pastry is no more." She had a resonant,

brooding voice—there was something likeable and understandable about her, with her unbelievable accent. "A long time too you will wait for sandwiches." She shook her head. "All people here tonight waiting, waiting.—If sandwiches, what kind of bread, too? It is imporrrtant for me to know this."

"Two coffees. One with milk," Eugene said. He nodded at her.

When the waitress brought the coffees, cups swimming in their saucers, she marched off without bringing any sugar. Eugene, remembering the three lumps the Spaniard used, glanced at him.

The Spaniard met his glance, and his great black brows slowly lifted and his eyes implored like the eyes of a dog. The shell-rimmed glasses, sanded and smeared, he took off and held in his hand a moment, then put back on. He gave another imploring look. But Eugene only sat there. The Spaniard tried to bring back the waitress with his Spanish, then with a wave of the arm. And at first she only looked at him dreamily without moving, there at the back with her arm propped against the curtain. But then, swinging her hips weightily, she came. He had clapped his hands together; it woke her right up, like applause. She brought in a sugar jar with a spout.

"It was *sugar* you wanted," she said to the Spaniard, with baby-talk on top of her accent, as though it had been sugar, sugar for a long time. She patted him on the head. "Go to hell," she said resonantly to Eugene. "In my country I have a husband. He too is a little man, and sits up as small as you. When he is bad, I peek him up, I stand him on the mantelpiece." She held out her palm; Eugene could not help but peek in it. He paid—his last penny; there was a streetcar token left—one.

"Well, that will be all," Eugene said, to nobody.

The Spaniard had crumbs, sand, sugar, and ashes on him. Outside, back on the corner, the two men turned to each other almost formally. Eugene could only think, in their parting moment, Suppose there had been pastry, would the Spaniard finally have lowered himself to pay? Then he flew out to catch a streetcar.

The Spaniard was left waiting, for what one never would know, alone in the night on a dark corner at the edge of the city. Perhaps he was not so proud now! At the last glance, he seemed to be looking in the sky for the little moon.

Eugene raced up the stairs to the flat and opened the door. There was the smell of strong hot chowder. Emma was in the kitchen but there was feminine talking-away—her great friend, Mrs. Herring from next door, had evidently come to stay for supper. Right away he thought he might as well not tell them anything.

"You've left your hat somewhere," Emma told him. "I'll be burying you next from pneumonia." Then, with a stamp of her foot, she showed him—and also Mrs. Herring, who was evidently seeing it for the second or third time—where the hot grease had splattered on her hand today.

There couldn't have been a peep out of Mr. Bertsinger, it occurred to Eugene as he threw off his raincoat. Maybe he was dead!

They sat on at the table after the big meal. Sawing idly at the cheese and to interrupt Mrs. Herring (in honor of Mrs. Herring, who had returned from a trip, they even had a little wine), Eugene felt called on to make one remark.

"Saw Long-Hair, the guitar player, today, saw him walking along the street just like you or me. What was his name, anyway?" he asked, as if he wondered now for the first time.

"Bartolome Montalbano," Emma said and popped a grape onto her extended tongue. She added, "I have the feeling he suffers from indigestion," and drummed her breast while she swallowed. ". . . He's a Spaniard."

"A Spaniard? There was a Spaniard at early church

this morning," Mrs. Herring offered, "that needed a haircut. He was next to a woman and he was laughing with her out loud—bad taste, *we* thought. It was before service began, it's true. He laughed first and then slapped her leg, there in Peter and Paul directly in front of me home from my trip."

Eugene tilted back in his chair, and watched Emma pop the grapes in.

"That would be him," said Emma.

THE WANDERERS

"How come you weren't here yesterday?" old Mrs. Stark asked her maid, looking up from her solitaire board—inlaid wood that gave off pistol-like reports under the blows of her shuffling cards. It was September and here in the hall she imagined she could feel October at her back.

"I didn' get back from my sisters' in the country."

"And poor Miss Katie Rainey dead. What were you so busy doing?"

"Showin' my teef."

Mrs. Stark raised her voice. "Only thing I can do for people any more, in joy or sorrow, is send 'em you. You know how Miss Jinny and Mr. Ran back out on me, then you go off. Now it's here next day. Fix my breakfast and yours and go on down there. Get in the kitchen and clean it up for Miss Virgie, don't pay any attention to her. Take that ham we haven't sliced into. Start cooking for the funeral, if others didn't beat you to it yesterday."

"Yes'm."

"Mind you learn to appreciate your good kitchen when you stand over a wood stove all day."

"I was comin' back. Sister's place a place once you get to it—hard time gettin' out."

Mrs. Stark snapped her fingers. "You and all your sisters!" She rose and walked, with her walk like a girl's, to the front door, looking down over her hill, the burned, patchy grass no better than Katie

Rainey's, and the thirsty shrubs; but the Morgan sweet olive, her own grandmother's age, her grandmother's tree, was blooming. She murmured over her shoulder, "I never had cause to set foot in the Rainey house for over five minutes in my life. And I don't suppose they need me now. But I hope I know what any old woman owes another old woman. It doesn't matter if it's too late. Do you hear me? Go back and put on a clean apron."

The Raineys, Miss Katie and her daughter Virgie, still held on to the house beyond the pavement, on the MacLain Road. There on the ridge the tin roof shed the light under the crape myrtle and privet, gone to trees, that edged the porch. The cannas with their scorched edges, together with the well, made the three familiar islands in the whitened grass of the yard. Across and back again, with effort but bobbin-like, had moved Miss Katie, Mrs. Fate Rainey, in her dress the hard blue of a morning-glory.

In old age Miss Katie showed what a neat, narrow head she had under the hair no longer disheveled and flyaway. When she came outdoors, her carefully dressed and carefully held head was as silver-looking as a new mail box. It was out of the autocracy of her stroke—she had suffered "a light stroke" five years ago, "while separating my cows and calves," she would recount it—that she'd begun ordering things done by set times. When it was time for Virgie to come home from work in the afternoon, Miss Katie fretted herself for fear she wouldn't be in time to milk before dark. She still had her two favorite Jerseys, pastured near. She stood out in the front yard, or moved the best way she could back and forth, waiting for Virgie.

A fiery streak of salvia that ran around the side of the house would turn darker in the leveling light. Though the shade broadened, she still walked her narrow path, not yielding even to the kind sun. She held up poorly there, propped by an old thornstick.

Bleaching down by the roadside was a chair, an old chair she sold things from once, under the borrowed shade of the chinaberry across the road; but she didn't seem to want to sit down any more, or to be quite that near the trafficking. Clear up where she was, she felt the world tremble; day and night the loggers went by, to and from Morgan's Woods. That wore her out too. While she lived, she was going to wait—and she did wait, standing up—until Virgie her daughter, past forty now and too dressed up, came home to milk Bossy and Juliette the way she should. Virgie worked for the very people that were out depleting the woods, Mr. Nesbitt's company.

Miss Katie couldn't spare her good hand to put up and shade her eyes; yet after you passed, you saw her in that position, in your vision if not in your sight. She looked ready to ward you off, too, in case of pity, there in her gathered old-lady dress, sometimes in an old bonnety church-hat. There's the old lady that watches the turn of the road, thought the old countrymen, Sissums and Sojourners and Holifields, passing in trucks or wagons on Saturday, going home, lifting their hats. Young courting people, Little Sister Spights' crowd, giggled at her, but small children and Negroes did not; they took her for granted like the lady on the Old Dutch Cleanser can.

The old people in Morgana she reminded of Snowdie MacLain, her neighbor once, who watched and waited for her husband so long. They were reminded vaguely of themselves, too, now that they were old enough to see it, still watching and waiting for something they didn't really know about any longer, wouldn't recognize to see it coming in the road.

As she looked out from her hill in the creeping shade, Miss Katie Rainey might have liked to be argued with and prevailed upon to go back in the house; at the last she might have suffered contradiction, but from whom? Not from Virgie.

"Where's my girl? Have you seen my girl?"

Miss Katie thought she called to the road, but she didn't; shame drew down her head, for she could still feel one thing if she could feel little else coming to her from the outside world: lack of chivalry.

Waiting, she heard circling her ears like the swallows beginning, talk about lovers. Circle by circle it twittered, church talk, talk in the store and post office, vulgar man talk possibly in the barbershop. Talk she could never get near now was coming to her.

"So long as the old lady's alive, it's all behind her back."

"Daughter wouldn't run off and leave her, she's old and crippled."

"Left once, will again."

"That fellow Mabry's been taking out his gun and leaving Virgie a bag o' quail every other day. Anybody can see him go by the back door."

"I declare."

"He told her the day she got tired o' quail, let him know and he'd quit and go on off, that's what I heard."

"Do tell."

"Furthermore, I reckon it would be possible for a human being, a woman, to live off them rich birds for the remaining space of time. Her ma can help her eat 'em. Her ma ain't lost her appetite!"

"Hush."

"Guess it wouldn't be polite for her or him neither one to stop on the quails. Even if he heard. Got to keep on now."

"Oh, sure. Fate Rainey's a clean shot, too."

"But ain't he heard?"

Not Fate Rainey at all; but Mr. Mabry. It was just that the talk Miss Katie heard was in voices of her girlhood, and some times they slipped.

Then, in an odd set way, for she lied badly, she would lie to Virgie when she came. "I asked Passing. And not one of 'em said they could tell me where you were, what kept you so long in town."

But it's my last summer, and she ought to get back
here and milk on time, the old lady thought, stubbornly and yet pityingly, the two ways she was.

"Look where the sun is," she called, as Virgie did
drive up in the yard in the old coupe Miss Katie kept
forgetting she had, the battered thing she took in
trade for the poor little calf.

"I see it, Mama."

Virgie's long, dark, too heavy hair swung this way
and that as she came up in her flowered voile dress,
on her high heels through the bearded grass.

"You have to milk before dark, after driving them
in, and there's four little quails full of shot for you to
dress, lying on my kitchen table."

"Come on back in the house, Mama. Come in with
me."

"I been by myself all day."

Virgie bent and gave her mother her evening kiss.

Miss Katie knew then that Virgie would drive the
cows home and milk and feed them and deliver the
milk on the road, and come back and cook the little
quails.

"It's a wonder, though," she thought. "A blessed
wonder to see the child mind."

The day Miss Katie died, Virgie was kneeling on
the floor of her bedroom cutting out a dress from
some plaid material. She was sewing on Sunday.

"There's nothing Virgie Rainey loves better than
struggling against a real hard plaid," Miss Katie
thought, with a thrust of pain from somewhere unexpected. Whereas, there was a simple line down
through her own body now, dividing it in half; there
should be one in every woman's body—it would
need to be the long way, not the cross way—that was
too easy—making each of them a side to feel and
know, and a side to stop it, to be waited on, finally.

But she wanted to drop to her knees there where
Virgie's plaid spread out like a pretty rug for her.

Her last clear feeling as she stood there, holding herself up, was that she wanted to be down and covered up, in, of all things, Virgie's hard-to-match-up plaid. But she turned herself around by an act of strength which tore her within and walked, striking her cane, the width of the hall and two rooms and lay down on her own bed.

"Stop and fan me a minute," she called aloud. She was thinking rapidly to herself, though, that Virgie had said, "I aim to get married on my bulb money."

Virgie, who worked in her gown, came in with pins in her mouth and her thumb marked green from the scissors, and stood over her. She brought a paper up and down over her mother's face. She fanned her with the *Market Bulletin*.

Dying, Miss Katie went rapidly over the list in it, her list. As though her impatient foot would stamp at each item, she counted it, corrected it, and yet she was about to forget the seasons, and the places things grew. Purple althea cuttings, true box, four colors of cannas for fifteen cents, moonvine seed by teaspoonful, green and purple jew. Roses: big white rose, little thorn rose, beauty-red sister rose, pink monthly, old-fashioned red summer rose, very fragrant, baby rose. Five colors of verbena, candlestick lilies, milk and wine lilies, blackberry lilies, lemon lilies, angel lilies, apostle lilies. Angel trumpet seed. The red amarylis.

Faster and faster, Mrs. Rainey thought: Red salvia, four-o'clock, pink Jacob's ladder, sweet geranium cuttings, sword fern and fortune grass, century plants, vase palm, watermelon pink and white crape myrtle, Christmas cactus, golden bell. White Star Jessamine. Snowball. Hyacinthus. Pink fairy lilies. White. The fairy white.

"Fan me. If you stop fanning, it's worse than if you never started."

And when Mama is gone, almost gone now, she meditated, I can tack on to my ad: the quilts! For sale, Double Muscadine Hulls, Road to Dublin, Starry Sky, Strange Spider Web, Hands All Around, Double Wedding Ring. Mama's rich in quilts, child.

Miss Katie lay there, carelessly on the counterpane, thinking, Crochet tablecloth, Sunburst design, very lacy. She knew Virgie stood over her, fanning her in rhythmic sweeps. Presently Miss Katie's lips shut tight.

She was thinking, Mistake. Never Virgie at all. It was me, the bride—with more than they guessed. Why, Virgie, go away, it was me.

She put her hand up and never knew what happened to it, her protest.

Virgie knelt, crouched there. She held her head, her mouth opened, and one by one the pins fell out on the floor. She was not much afraid of death, either of its delay or its surprise. As yet nothing in the place of fear came into her head; only something about her dress.

The bed, the headboard dark and ungiving as an old mirror on the wall, to her as a child a vast King Arthur shield that might have concealed a motto, cast its afternoon shadow down dark as muscadines, to her mother's waist. The old shadow, familiar as sleep the life long, always ran down over the bolster this time of year, the warm and knotty medallions of the familiar counterpane—the overworked, inherited, and personal pattern—from which her mother's black shoes now pointed up.

Behind the bed the window was full of cloudy, pressing flowers and leaves in heavy light, like a jar of figs in syrup held up. A humming bird darted, fed, darted. Every day he came. He had a ruby throat. The clock jangled faintly as cymbals struck under water, but did not strike; it couldn't. Yet a torrent of riches seemed to flow over the room, submerging it, loading it with what was over-sweet.

Virgie ran to the porch. Waiting on a passing Negro, she called, in a moment, "Go get me Dr.

Loomis out of church!" The Negro began to sprint in his Sunday clothes.

By mid-afternoon the house was filling with callers and helpers. Each one who came seemed stopped by the enormous dead boxwood, like a yellow sponge, that stood by the steps; it had to be gone around. Coffee was being kept on the stove and iced tea in the pitcher in the hall. Virgie was dressed, in the dress she had ironed that morning for Monday, and at the front of the house. Moving around her, a lady watered the ferns and evened the shades in the parlor, then watered and evened again, as if some obscure sums were being balanced and checked. Every seat in the parlor and Virgie's room was taken, the porch and the steps creaked under the men who stood outside.

Cassie Morrison, her black-stockinged legs seeming to wade among the impeding legs of the other women, crossed the parlor to where Virgie sat in the chair at the closed sewing machine. Cassie had chosen the one thin, gold-rimmed coffee cup for herself, and balanced it serenely.

"Papa sent his sympathy. Let me sit by you, Virgie." She kissed her. "You know I know what it's like."

"Excuse me," Virgie was saying. All at once she slept, straight in the cane chair. When she opened her eyes, she watched and listened to the even fuller roomful as carefully, and as carelessly, as vacillating as though she were on the point of departure. Through their murmur she heard herself circle the room to speak to them and be kissed. She made the steps of the walk they had to watch, head, breasts, and hips in their helpless agitation, like a rope of bells she started in their ears.

"She can't help it," Cassie Morrison was saying to the person beside her in the gentle tones of a verdict. "She can't take in what's happened quite yet and she doesn't really know us."

The unnaturally closed door led from Miss Katie's

room out to the parlor. Behind it, they all knew—
waiting as they were for it to open—Miss Snowdie
MacLain was laying Miss Katie out. She washed and
dressed her herself, tolerating only two old Loomis
Negroes to wait on her, and Miss Snowdie was
nearly seventy too, and had come seven miles from
MacLain. There was something about it nobody liked,
perhaps a break in custom. Miss Lizzie Stark, whose
place they felt it to be to supervise the house while
old Miss Emmy Holifield laid out the dead, had felt
too weak today, and sent word she had had to lie
down. And old Emmy herself was gone.

It was true that none of the callers except Miss
Snowdie had been inside the Rainey house since Mr.
Fate Rainey's funeral. No wonder Virgie looked at
them now, staring, at moments.

Always in a house of death, Virgie was thinking,
all the stories come evident, show forth from the
person, become a part of the public domain. Not the
dead's story, but the living's.

She could see Ran MacLain, standing at the door
shaking hands with Mr. Nesbitt who was coming in.
And didn't it show on Ran, that once he had taken
advantage of a country girl who had died a suicide?
It showed at election time as it showed now, and he
won the election for mayor over Mr. Carmichael, for
all was remembered in his middle-age when he
stood on the platform. Ran was smiling—holding
on to a countryman now. They had voted for him for
that—for his glamour and his story, for being a Mac-
Lain and the bad twin, for marrying a Stark and
then for ruining a girl and the thing she did. Old
Man Moody found her on the floor of his store—the
place she worked—and walked out into the street
with her in his arms. They voted for the revelation;
it had made their hearts faint, and they would assert
it again. Ran knew that every minute, there in the
door he stood it.

"Cheer up, now, cheer up," Mr. Nesbitt was saying to her, seeming to lift her to her feet by running

his finger under her chin. His eyes—so willed by him, she thought—ran tears and dried. "Come here," he called over his shoulder.

"Virgie, tell Mr. Thisbee who's your best friend in this town." He had brought the new man in the company.

"You, Mr. Bitts," Virgie said.

"Everybody in Morgana calls me Mr. Bitts, Thisbee; you can too. Now wait. Tell him who hired you when nobody else was in the hiring mood, Virgie. Tell him. And was always kind to you and stood up for you."

She never turned away until it was finished; today this seemed somehow brief and easy, a relief.

"Hurry up, Virgie. Got to cheer my daughter up next."

Nina Carmichael, Mrs. Junior Nesbitt heavy with child, was seated where he could see her, head fine and indifferent, one puffed white arm stretched along the sewing machine. He winked at her across the room.

"You, Mr. Bitts."

"Tell him how long you've been working for old Mr. Bitts."

"A long time."

"No, tell him how long it's been—my my my, tell him. I've been in three different businesses, Thisbee. How long?"

"Since 1920, Mr. Bitts."

"And if you ever made any mistakes in your letters and figgers, who was it stood behind you with the company?"

"I'm very sorry for you in your sorrow," Mr. Thisbee said suddenly, letting go her hand. She almost fell.

"But who? Who stood behind you?"

Mr. Nesbitt extended his arms overly wide, as he did when asking her to dance with him in Vicksburg. Abruptly he wheeled and went off; he was hurt, disappointed in her for the hundredth time. She saw

Mr. Nesbitt's fat, hurt back as he wandered as if lost and stood a long time contemplating and cheering up Nina Carmichael.

Food—two banana cakes and a baked ham, a platter of darkly deviled eggs, new rolls—and flowers kept arriving at the back, and the kitchen filled with women as the parlor now filled with men come farther in. Virgie went back once more to the kitchen, but again the women stopped what they were doing and looked at her as though something—not only today—should prevent her from knowing at all how to cook—the thing they knew. She went to the stove, took a fork, and turned over a piece or two of the chicken, to see Missie Spights look at her with eyes wide in a kind of wonder and belligerence.

Then she walked through them and stood on the quiet back porch to feel the South breeze. The packed freezer, wrapped in a croker sack, the old, golden stopper of newspaper hidden and waiting on tomorrow, stood in the dishpan. The cut flowers were plunged stem-down and head-down in shady water buckets. Virgie had a sudden recollection of recital night at Miss Eckhart's—the moment when she was to be called out. She was thirteen, waiting outside, on guard at a vast calming spectacle of turmoil, and saving it. A little drop spilled, she remembered it now: an anxiety which brought her to the point of sickness, that back in there they were laughing at her mother's hat.

She went back into the parlor. Like a forest murmur the waiting talk filled the room.

The door opened. Miss Snowdie stood against it, sideways, looking neither in nor out.

Immediately the ladies rose and filled the doorway; some of them went in. Only the end of the bed and Miss Katie's feet could be seen from within the parlor. There were soft cries. "Snowdie!" "Miss Snowdie! She looks beautiful!" Then the rest of the ladies tiptoed forward and could be seen bending over the bed as they would bend over the crib of a little kicking baby. They came out again.

"Come see your mother."

They pulled pre-emptorily at Virgie's arms, their voices bright.

"Don't touch me."

They pulled harder, still smiling but in silence, and Virgie pulled back. Her hair fell over her eyes. She shook it back. "Don't touch me."

"Honey, you just don't know what you lost, that's all."

They were all people who had never touched her before who tried now to struggle with her, their faces hurt. She was hurting them all, shocking them. They leaned over her, agonized, pleading with the pull of their hands. It was a Mrs. Flewellyn, pulling the hardest, who had caught the last breath of her husband in a toy balloon, by his wish, and had it at home still—most of it, until a Negro stole it.

Miss Perdita Mayo's red face looked over their wall. "Your mama was too fine for you, Virgie, too fine. That was always the trouble between you."

In that truth, Virgie looked up at them lightheadedly and they lifted her to her feet and drew her into the bedroom and showed her her mother.

She lay in the black satin. It had been lifted, heavy as a child, out of her trunk, the dress in which diminished, pea-sized mothballs had shone and rolled like crystals all Virgie's life, in waiting, taken out twice, and now spread out in full triangle. Her head was in the center of the bolster, the widow's place in which she herself laid it. Miss Snowdie had rouged her cheeks.

They watched Virgie, but Virgie gave them no sign now. She felt their hands smooth down her and leave her, draw away from her body and then give it a little shove forward, even their hands showing sorrow for a body that did not fall, giving back to hands what was broken, to pick up, smooth again.

For people's very touch anticipated the falling of the body, the own, the single and watchful body.

Later, back in the parlor, she cried. They said, "She used to set out yonder and sell muscadines, see out there? There's where she got rid of all her plums, the early and late, blackberries and dewberries, and the little peanuts you boil. Now the road goes the wrong way." Though that was like a sad song, it was not true: the road still went the same, from Morgana to MacLain, from Morgana to Vicksburg and Jackson, of course. Only now the wrong people went by on it. They were all riding trucks, very fast or heavily loaded, and carrying blades and chains, to chop and haul the big trees to mill. They were not eaters of muscadines, and did not stop to pass words on the season and what grew. And the vines had dried. She wept because they could not tell it right, and they didn't press for her reasons.

"Call Mr. Mabry now. She's let loose."

Mr. Mabry, fresh from the barbershop, took Virgie's hands and swung them, then dropped them. She dried her eyes instantly and withdrew, giving him permission to go into the other room. She wondered when she had seen him leave her on tiptoe before. Old country fellows in the hall began to speak of him now, respectfully, as he looked down at the dead with his face so rubylike, so recently complimented upon, that in the next moment it would fill with concern for itself.

"He aims to get closer to Ives. Where he don't have to use hoot owls for roosters and fox for yard dogs, is the way he put it to me."

"Then why on earth don't he come to Morgana? No nicer place than right here, 's what I think, if I wanted to be close in."

"He prefers Ives."

"I see."

But in the parlor it was generally felt polite now to consider Miss Katie as the center of conversation, since the door was now open.

"Virgie might get a little bit of dairyfood savings now, bet she'll spend it on something 'sides the house, hm?" A lady Virgie couldn't place said it halfway in her direction, leaning toward her now and then as she had been doing, with her full weight. "Her pretty quilts, she can't ship those to the Fair no more. What does Virgie care about housekeeping and china plates without no husband, hm? Wonder what Virgie'll do with the chickens, Katie always enjoyed a mixed yard. Wonder who Virgie'll give the deer to if she don't want it. That picture of the deer Miss Katie's mother hooked in Tishomingo with the mistletoe crown over the horns, and the oak leaves, Miss Katie considered it the prettiest thing in the world. The cloth doll with the china head and hands, that she used to let any and all play with—"

"Guinevere! Oh, I wish I had her now!" Cassie Morrison held out both gloved hands.

"Her fern stand. Virgie won't stay here to keep care of ferns, I bet. Her begonia, thirty-five years old. Not much older than Virgie, is it, Virgie? She left her recipes to the Methodist Church—I hope."

"She was a living saint," answered another lady, as if this would agree with everything.

"Look at my diamond."

Jinny MacLain, Ran's wife, was coming in. With her hand out, she showed a ring about the room on her way to Virgie. "I deserved me a diamond," she went on to say to Cassie Morrison, twisting her hand on its wrist. "That's what I told Ran." Softly, abruptly, she turned and kissed Virgie's cheek, whispering, "I don't have to see her—do I, Virgie?"

Then they all rose as Miss Snowdie came in.

"I don't have to see anybody!" whispered Jinny fiercely.

Virgie, still holding a cup of coffee, walked out and waited on the porch, for she knew Miss Snowdie would come outside. She could hear her in the parlor now, staying to take a certain amount of praise. Then Miss Snowdie came out, now as at all times a gentle lady, her face white and graciously folded, gently concerned but no more. She stood and looked out, at once shading her eyes, to the house across the road where she used to live. She kissed Virgie then, almost idly.

"I think she looks all right, Virgie."

Her albino's hands were cruelly reddened. But she never seemed really to feel their redness any more. Her soft black-and-white dotted dress smelled as freshly as always of verbena.

"I saw to her well as I knew how. If Emmy Holifield were still living, she might have thought of things I didn't."

But her eyes went past Virgie, across the road, where the old house was a ruin now. In between where the women were standing and the sight of the old place, in the Rainey yard, the children waiting for their parents stood still, fell still, at that moment, and not knowing where to look all at once, listened— listened to the locusts, perforce, which sounded like the sound of the world going around to them as they suddenly beat their cupped hands over their ears.

"Virgie? You know Lizzie Stark and I long ago made up. About Ran and Jinny's trouble; that's over, all over. But do you reckon, at such a time, it was old feelings rising up that kept her away?"

Miss Snowdie sighed, as if she had forgotten her question with the asking, as if a reply would interrupt her. Across there was a place where she had lived a long time, the old deserted time, when Virgie played with Ran and Eugene under her trees, on her porch, under her house, along the river bank, and in Morgan's woods. There were leggy cedars still lining the old property, their trunks white and knobbed like chicken bones. The old summer-house was still back there, lattices leaning inward and not matching at the joinings, in the shadow like a place where long ago something had been kept that could peep out now; in the sun like a little temple raised to it. The big chinaberry tree had been cut down with the other

lawn trees when the house burned, but its many suck-
ers sprayed up from the stump like a fountain.
Negroes had carried away most of the sides and roof
that remained of the house, but had hardly made
inroad on the chimney, surprisingly enough; it was
its full height still, visible from here, dove-pink
through the dust and leafiness. Little locusts and castor plants tall as a man had come up all around, the
altheas had come back and made trees, shaggy as
old giants holding twilit, flimsy little flowers up high.
Vines had taken the yard and the walk, the brick
cross of the foundation, and the trees and all.

Virgie removed herself from Miss Snowdie's arm
which had gone around her waist. The two women
stood quiet in the afternoon light.

"I said I'd want *her* to lay *me* out," the old lady
said. She trembled very slightly but did not go
back. She looked out still.

From around the big boxwood Mr. King MacLain,
treading so lightly they didn't hear him, came up the
steps.

"You know Virgie," Miss Snowdie murmured, still
motionless.

"And Katie Blazes, that's what we used to call your
mother," Mr. King nodded at Virgie. The little patch
of hair under his lip—not silky, coarse, a pinkish
white—shook in a ruminating way. Viola, their
Negro, had driven him over after giving him his dinner; she could be seen going to the back now, to visit
the kitchen.

"Sir?"

"I'll take that coffee if it's hot and you ain't drinking it. Katie Blazes. Didn't you ever hear your mother
tell how she never took a dare to put a match to her
stockings, girl? Whsst! Up went the blazes, up to her
knee! Sometimes both legs. Cotton stockings the girls
used to wear—fuzzy, God knows they were. Nobody
else among the girls would set fire to their legs. She
had the neighborhood scared she'd go up in flames
at an early age."

"Did you eat your dinner?" Miss Snowdie turned to him.

Virgie watched the black coffee beginning to shake in the little cup. There was something terrifying about that old man—he was too old.

"In flames!"

He left them and went into the hall of men.

"I don't know what to do with him," Miss Snowdie said, in a murmur as quiet as the world around them now. She did not know she had spoken. When her flyaway husband had come home a few years ago, at the age of sixty-odd, and stayed, they said she had never gotten over it—first his running away, then his coming back to her. "He didn't want to come at all. Now he has her mixed up with Nellie Loomis."

"Virgie, we've got enough ready to feed an army," Missie Spights called up the hall. She was coming, untying Miss Katie's apron from her dress, her arms shining red. "Ham, chickens, potato salad, deviled eggs, and all the cake and folderol people send besides."

"Does there have to be so much?" Virgie asked, going in to meet her.

"Watch. The out-of-town relatives are always hungry!"

Her busyness gave Missie an air of abandon, quite impregnable. Parnell Moody stood behind her, drying every circle of the potato masher with care. The others were clattering the dishes, putting them in stacks, talking.

"My husband's been waiting on me an hour."

"Mr. King MacLain took himself a nap pretty as you please. Viola had to shriek in his ear to get him up."

"We'll all be back early for the funeral, Virgie—wish you'd let us stay." Cassie drew her delicate brows, surveying the kitchen which she had never got to. "Everybody who would, I let stay with me."

"It's a good thing we cut all our flowers," Missie

called, fastening her corset behind the door. "Virgie, you haven't a solitary one."

She saw them all, except Miss Snowdie who stayed, get into their cars in the yard, or walk down the path and into the road. As they went, they seemed to drag some mythical gates and barriers away from her view. She looked at the lighted distance, the little last crescent of hills before the country of the river, and the fields. The world shimmered. Cotton fields look busy on Sunday even; while they are not being picked they push out their bloom the same. The frail screens of standing trees still measured, broke, divided—Stark from Loomis from Spights from Holifield, and the summer from the rain. Each tree like a single leaf, half hair-fine skeleton, half gauze and green, let the first suspicious wind through its old, pressed shape, its summertime branches. The air came smelling of what it was, the end of September.

Down the settling dust of the road came an ancient car. It would turn in here. Old Plez, up until his death, had stopped by to milk and feed the chickens for Miss Katie Rainey on his way to and from the Starks'. His grandchildren, still country people, would come today. The car pounded up the hill to her. It was cracked like some put-together puzzle of the globe of the world. Its cracks didn't meet from one side across to the other, and it was all held together with straightened-out baling wire, for today. Next day, next year, it would sit in the front yard for decoration, at rest on its axles, the four wheels gone and the tires divided up between women and children: two for flowerbeds and two for swings.

They had brought the flowers from their dooryard, princess feathers, snow-on-the-mountain. It took them a long time to turn around and get a start back. A little boy ran back with the pan of butterbeans and okra.

"All come to the funeral if you can get away!" she called after them, too late.

Virgie walked down the hill too, crossed the road,

and made her way through the old MacLain place
and the pasture and down to the river. She stood on
the willow bank. It was bright as mid-afternoon
in the openness of the water, quiet and peaceful. She
took off her clothes and let herself into the river.

She saw her waist disappear into reflectionless
water; it was like walking into sky, some impurity of
skies. All was one warmth, air, water, and her own
body. All seemed one weight, one matter—until as
she put down her head and closed her eyes and the
light slipped under her lids, she felt this matter a
translucent one, the river, herself, the sky all vessels
which the sun filled. She began to swim in the river,
forcing it gently, as she would wish for gentleness to
her body. Her breasts around which she felt the
water curving were as sensitive at that moment as
the tips of wings must feel to birds, or antenna to
insects. She felt the sand, grains intricate as little
cogged wheels, minute shells of old seas, and the
many dark ribbons of grass and mud touch her and
leave her, like suggestions and withdrawals of some
bondage that might have been dear, now dismember-
ing and losing itself. She moved but like a cloud in
skies, aware but only of the nebulous edges of her
feeling and the vanishing opacity of her will, the
carelessness for the water of the river through which
her body had already passed as well as for what was
ahead. The bank was all one, where out of the faded
September world the little ripening plums started.
Memory dappled her like no more than a paler light,
which in slight agitations came through leaves, not
darkening her for more than an instant. The iron taste
of the old river was sweet to her, though. If she
opened her eyes she looked at blue-bottles, the skating waterbugs. If she trembled it was at the smooth-
ness of a fish or snake that crossed her knees.

In the middle of the river, whose downstream or
upstream could not be told by a current, she lay on
her stretched arm, not breathing, floating. Virgie

ha𝑑 reached the point where in the next moment
she might turn into something without feeling it
shock her. She hung suspended in the Big Black
River as she would know to hang suspended in felic-
ity. Far to the west, a cloud running fingerlike over
the sun made her splash the water. She stood, walked
along the soft mud of the bottom and pulled herself
out of the water by a willow branch, which like warm
rain brushed her back with its leaves.

At a distance, two little boys lying naked in the
red light on the sandbar looked at her as she disappeared into the leaves. They did not move or speak.

The moon, while she looked into the high sky,
took its own light between one moment and the
next. A wood thrush, which had begun to sing,
hushed its long moment and began again. Virgie put
her clothes back on. She would have given much for
a cigarette, always wishing for a little more of what
had just been.

She went back to the pasture, where the enormous
ant hills shone, with long shadows, like pyramids on
the other side of the world, and drove the cows home.

The crape myrtle had a last crown of bloom on
top, once white, now faintly nutmegged. The
ground below was littered with its shed bark, and
the limbs shone like human limbs, lithe and warm,
pink.

She went out to milk and came back to the house.

From the hall she looked into her mother's room.
The window and the room were the one blue of first-
dark. Only the black dress, the density of skirt, was
stamped on it, like some dark chip now riding mid-
air on blue lakes.

Miss Snowdie MacLain had elected to "sit up" the
first hours of night. She slept in the bedroom rocker,
in the luminous veil of her dress, the cocoon of her
head hanging upon it, and the fan let fall from her
fingers.

II.

Virgie waked to see the morning star hanging over the fields. What had she meant to do so early? She made and drank her coffee, milked, drove the cows to pasture through mist, chopped wood, and at last she attacked the high grass in the yard. Yesterday cutting the Rainey grass in time for the funeral was considered a project so impossible that even if men could be spared and given scythes, success was never guaranteed. Virgie took her sewing scissors from the little bundle of plaid material in her room, and went outdoors. She crouched in the pink early light, clipping and sawing the heads off the grass— it had all gone to seed—a handful at a time. She could feel dimmed round Venus still, for she must feel some presence, there was always something, someone, and Venus watching her made the imperceptible work almost leisurely, then again fierce. The choked-out roses scratched, surprised her, drew blood drops on her legs. She had to come in when Miss Snowdie, whose presence she had forgotten, stepped out on the porch and called her. As though for a long time she had been extremely angry and had wept many tears, she allowed Miss Snowdie to drive her inside the house and cook her breakfast.

Then Miss Lizzie Stark's Juba arrived, followed by a little stairsteps of Negro children bearing curtain stretchers, and Miss Snowdie and Juba began taking down all the curtains. In half an hour these were out in the backyard, stretched and set forth like the tents in the big Bible's Wilderness of Kadesh. The ladies soon were everywhere, radiating once more from the kitchen.

"First thing," Missie Spights told Virgie, "you called me Missie Spights yesterday. I'm married."

"Oh. Yes, I remember."

"I'm Missie Spights Littlejohn and I've got three children. I married from off."

"I remember, Missie."

Some of Miss Katie's people arrived by noon, in good time for the funeral—big dark people named Mayhew, men and women alike with square, cleft chins and blue eyes. A little string of tow-headed children made a row behind, finishing some bananas. Virgie couldn't remember all the Mayhews or tell them apart; they all came upon her at once, after knocking on the porch to bring her out, all kissed her in greedy turn and begged before they got through the door for ice water or iced tea or both. They had ridden in in several trucks, now drawn up by the porch, from the Stockstill and Lastingwell communities near the Tennessee line. The first thing the largest Mayhew man did, once inside the house, was to catch up a little child of Missie Spights', who was swatting flies, and tickle her violently, speaking soberly over her screams, "Now wait: you don't know who I am."

Only the same old Rainey came from Louisiana who had come to Fate's funeral years ago and hadn't sent word since. Again he brought his own coffee. Again he offered to fix the front porch and in time, and again was prevented. He was the only Rainey that made the trip. The Raineys were mostly all died out, or couldn't leave the fields, or were too far to buy a ticket. The old man explained it all again, and told what had happened to the French name with all the years.

"Yes, some are missing," Miss Perdita Mayo told Virgie when she arrived and saw the lined-up kin. "But you got in touch, or I did for you. If the funeral's small we can't reproach ourselves."

Screams surrounded the house. The little Mac-Lain children and their nurse had gotten away from old Miss Lizzie, their grandmother, and come to play in the Rainey yard. Gradually other children, Loomis and Maloney, attracted by the magnetic Mac-Lains, played there too, all drunk with the attractions of an untried place, and a place sinister for the day.

The little Mayhews, every time they were gathered up and brought away from these into the house, cried. Blue jays were scolding the whole morning over the roof, and the logging trucks thundered by, shaking their chains and threatening the clean curtains.

Miss Perdita Mayo, who had got into the bedroom and formed a circle, was telling a story. "Sister couldn't get her new shoes back on after that funeral, because while she was in the cemetery—" Suddenly Miss Perdita appeared backing out of the room, thinking herself still telling her story, but mistaken. She had heard the coffin come, and ran to meet it. Mr. Holifield at the hardware store sent his grandsons, Hughie and Dewey Holifield, with it on their produce truck. The boys came inside and made it steady, the Mayhews watching.

"Where's all them Mayhews going to bed down?" old Mr. Rainey, with nothing to do, asked Virgie, indicating Mayhews with a thumb purpled like a fig.

"They won't stay. They're striking right out for Stockstill after the funeral, sir," said Virgie. "As soon as they've packed some lunch." And they were taking the bed, Katie's bed; they could set it right up in the truck, they said, looking at it detached from its owner who was lying on it; and the children could ride home on it instead of standing.

Mr. Rainey was shaking his head. "Pity. Never a chance to know those." He put up a little horned finger and touched a string on the old banjo of her father's, which hung on its nail in the hall, the head faintly luminous by morning light. But he didn't play the note. "*He* traveled around a bit," he said at length. "And settled hereabouts for the adventure of it."

The home-grown flowers came early, and the florist flowers late. Mr. Nesbitt sent word by the janitor in the barbership, who wore gold-rimmed spectacles, that he must be out of town during the funeral, the Negro then bringing out from behind his back a large

cross of gladiolas and ferns on a stand, evidently
from Vicksburg, with Mr. Nesbitt's card tied on. The
Mayhews moved upon it and placed it in front of all
the other flowers—now steadily being made into
wreaths on the back porch—where they could look
at it during the service, to remember. The Sunday
School chairs arrived by wagon, and the Mayhews
took them at the door and set them in cater-cornered
rows. Had Miss Lizzie Stark been able to come, people said, it wouldn't have happened quite the same
way.

Old Mr. King MacLain did not appear happy over
having to come to the Rainey house again today. He
fumed, and went back to visit in the kitchen.

"Little conversation with your mother in '18, or
along there," he said to Virgie, who was folding napkins with the Stark "S" on them. "You know in those
days I was able to make considerable trips off, and
only had my glimpses of the people back here."

Miss Snowdie had come to stand folding napkins
too.

"I'd come and I'd go again, only I ended up at the
wrong end, wouldn't you say?" He suddenly smiled,
rather fiercely, but at neither woman. He wore the
stiffest-starched white suit Virgie ever saw on any old
gentleman; it looked fierce too—the lapels alert as
ears. "Saw your mother in a pink sunbonnet. Rosy-
cheeked. 'Hello!'—'I declare, King MacLain, you
look to me as you ever did, strolling here in the road.
You rascal.'—'Just for that, what would you rather
have than anything? I'm asking because I'm going to
get it for you.'—'A swivel chair. So I can sit out front
and sell crochet and peaches, if my good-for-nothing
husband'll let me.' Ah, we all knew sweet old Fate,
he was a sweet man among us. 'Shucks, that's too
easy. Say something else. I'd have got you anything
your living heart desired.'—'Well, I told you. And
you mischief, I believe you.'

"Three niggers black as dirtdaubers up to the house

in a wagon, bang-up noon next day. Up to the door, pounding.

" 'Oh, King MacLain! You've brought it so quick-like!'

"But I! I was no telling where by that time. Looked to her, I know, like I couldn't wait long enough to hear her pleasure. So bent, so bent I was on all I had to do, on what was ahead of me.

"*She* told me how she flew around the yard. 'Watch out, now, don't set that down a minute till I tell you where it'll go!' Had niggers carrying here, carrying there. Then she put it spang by the road, close as she could get.

"And her chair always too big for her, little heels wouldn't touch ground. It was big enough for a man, big enough for Drewsie Carmichael, 'cause it was his. I prevailed on the widow. Oh, Katie Rainey was a sight, I saw her swing her chair round many's the time, to hear me coming down the road or starting out, waving her hand to me. And sold more eggs than you'd dream. Oh, then, she could see where Fate Rainey had fallen down, and a lovely man, too; never got her the thing she wanted. I set her on a throne!"

"Mr. King, I never knew the chair came from you," Virgie said, smiling.

He looked all at once inconsolable, but Miss Snowdie shook her head.

"Have a little refreshments, sir. There's ham and potato salad—"

"Oh, is there ham?"

Virgie led him down the hall. The Negroes stood by the table with fly swatters. She laid a little piccalilli with the ham on his plate, which he held for her as long as she'd help it.

When Virgie returned to the parlor, Jinny MacLain came forward to greet her: as if their positions were reversed.

Jinny, who in childhood had seemed more knowing than her years, was in her thirties strangely childlike; was it old perversity or further tactics? She too

arrived at close range, looked at the burns and scars
on Virgie's hands, as Missie Spights had done, making them stigmata of something at odds in her
womanhood.

"Listen. You should marry now, Virgie. Don't put it
off any longer," she said, making a face, any face, at
her own words. She was grimacing out of the iron
mask of the married lady. It appeared urgent with
her to drive everybody, even Virgie for whom she
cared nothing, into the state of marriage along with
her. Only then could she resume as Jinny Love Stark,
her true self. She was casting her eye around the
room, as if to pick Virgie some husband then and
there; and her eyes rested over Virgie's head on—Virgie knew it—Ran MacLain. Virgie smiled faintly; now
she felt, without warning, that two passionate people
stood in this roomful, with their indifferent backs to
each other.

A great many had gathered now. People sat inside
and outside, listening and not listening. Young people
held hands, all of them taking seats early to reserve
the back row. Then some of the Mayhews carried the
coffin into the parlor and placed it over the hearth on
the four chairs from around the table. The wreaths
were stood on edge to hide the chair legs.

"What are my children up to?" Jinny whispered
hurriedly, and swept a curtain aside to expose the
front yard. "My daughter has chosen today to catch
lizards. She's wearing lizard earrings! How can she
stand those little teeth in her!" Jinny laughed delightedly as she settled herself by the window.

"Sit by me, Virgie," said Cassie Morrison, who began to put her handkerchief to her eyes. "This is when
it's the worst, or almost."

There was a new arrival just before the service.
Brother Dampeer from Goodnight, whose father was
the preacher when Mrs. Rainey was a child and baptized her as a girl in Cold Creek, in North Mississippi, couldn't let her go without one more glimpse,

he said. Virgie had never seen Brother Dampeer; he
sized her up and kissed her. There was a tuning fork
in his shirt pocket that showed when he walked sideways back of the coffin and leaned over it full front
to scrutinize the body.

"Come up to my crossroads church some pretty
Sunday, ever' one of y'all," was all he said, straighten-
ing up and addressing the living. Why had he no com-
ment to make on the dead? they felt as a hushed
roomful—with him, it seemed marked, as if he found
nothing sufficiently remarkable about the body to give
him anything flattering to say. "I guarantee nobody'll
bite you if you put in at the collection for the piano,
either," he added, rocking sidewise off.

"Where were his manners! But of course, he
couldn't be turned away," Miss Snowdie, back of
Virgie, was whispering. "Coming was his privilege."
She drew her fan deeply back and forth, with the
pressure of a heavy tail on the air. "A perfect stranger,
and he handed out fans from Katie's deer horns out
there, because he was a preacher; gave one to everybody."

"It's not time for the Last Look," Parnell Moody
said in her natural, school voice. But the little Mayhews had to follow right behind Brother Dampeer.
There came the prompting voice of Mrs. Junie Mayhew, "Chirren? Want to see your cousin Kate? Go
look in, right quick. She raised your Uncle Berry.
Take hands and go now, while there's nobody else;
so you'll have her to remember." And they came in
dipping their heads and pulling one another. The
oldest little boy came hopping; it was remembered
that at one point during the day he had run a nail in
his foot.

"Brothers and sisters." Dr. Williams was facing the
room.

Virgie rose right up. In the pink china jar on the
mantel shelf, someone had placed her mother's old
stick—like a peach branch, as though it would flower.
Brother Dampeer cleared his throat: his work. Before

his eyes and everybody's she marched over, took the stick out of the vase, and carried it away to the hall, where she placed it in the ring on the hatrack. When she was back in her chair, Dr. Williams opened the book and held the service.

Every now and then Mr. King, his tender-looking old head cocked sidewise, his heels lifted, his right hand pricking the air, tiptoed down the hall to the table to pick at the ham—all as if nobody could see him. While Mamie C. Loomis, a child in peach, sang "O Love That Will Not Let Me Go," Mr. King sucked a little marrow bone and lifted his wobbly head and looked arrogantly at Virgie through the two open doors of her mother's bedroom. Even Weaver Loomis and Little Sister Spights, holding hands on the back row, were crying by now, listening to music, but Mr. King pushed out his stained lip. Then he made a hideous face at Virgie, like a silent yell. It was a yell at everything—including death, not leaving it out—and he did not mind taking his present animosity out on Virgie Rainey; indeed, he chose her. Then he cracked the little bone in his teeth. She felt refreshed all of a sudden at that tiny but sharp sound.

She sat up straight and touched her hair, which sprang to her fingers, as always. Turning her head, looking out of the one bright window through which came the cries of the little MacLains playing in the yard, she knew another moment of alliance. Was it Ran or King himself with whom she really felt it? Perhaps that confusion among all of them was the great wound in Ran's heart, she was thinking at the same time. But she knew the kinship for what it was, whomever it settled upon, an indelible thing which may come without friendship or even too early an identity, may come even despisingly, in rudeness, intruding in the middle of sorrow. Except in a form too rarefied for her, it lacked future as well as past; but she knew when even a rarefied thing had become a matter of loyalty and alliance.

"Child, you just don't know yet what you've lost," said Miss Hattie Mayo through the words of the service. It was the only thing Virgie remembered ever hearing Miss Hattie say; and then it was a thing others had been saying before her.

Miss Lizzie Stark—for she had, after all, been able to come to the funeral—waved her own little fan— black chiffon—at Virgie's cheeks from a jet chain. Miss Lizzie looked very rested, and had succeeded in exchanging seats with Cassie Morrison. She let a hand fall plumply on Virgie's thigh, and did not lift it again.

Down the hall, with the blue sky at his back, Mr. King MacLain sent for coffee, tasted it, and put out his tongue in the air to cool, a bright pink tongue wagging like a child's while they sang "Nearer, My God, to Thee."

"Go back," they told Virgie as they all moved out of the parlor. "Be alone with her before you come with us."

"You're the onliest one now," a Mayhew said. The Mayhews had asked to carry Katie home to Lastingwell Church to bury her, but acknowledged that Mr. Fate, whom the Raineys had wanted likewise to take back to their home place, was in Morgana ground, and Victor— "And so will you be," they had concluded to Virgie.

Virgie drew back while they marked time, and then she wasn't alone in the parlor. There was little Jinny MacLain, shoes and socks in hand, quietly bent over the coffin, looking boldly in. She had prized open the screen and climbed in the window. Green lizards hung like tiny springs at her ears, their eyes and jaws busy. At any other house today, Virgie knew, more care would have been exercised by them all; here, a child could slip through.

Jinny looked up at Virgie; the expression on her face was disappointment.

"Hi, Jinny."

"This doesn't look like a coffin. Did you have to use a bureau drawer?"

"They haven't put the lid down, that's all."

"Well, will you put the lid down for me?"

"Run on. Go the back way," said Virgie. "Wait—how is it that you make lizards catch on to your ears?"

"Press their heads," Jinny said languidly, over her shoulder. She walked out beating her shoes softly together with her hands.

Virgie walked over and pressed her forehead against the broken-into screen. She looked far out, over the fields, down to the far, low trees—the old vision belonging to this window. It was the paper serpent with the lantern lights through whose interior was flowing the Big Black.

"So here you are," said Miss Perdita Mayo.

The procession—the coffin passing through their ranks and now going before—marched humped and awkward down the path. They were like people waked by night, in the shimmering afternoon.

This was the children's dispensation: what they'd been waiting for. Little Jinny, her face bright and important, stood by little King, who—he was exactly timing the funeral—sucked a four-o'clock. "Move, Clara," she was saying to the nurse. They adored seeing beyond dodging aprons and black protecting arms (except Clara at the moment was smoking) the sight of grown people streaming tears and having to be held up. They liked coffins carried out because of the chance they could perceive that coffins might be dropped and the dead people spilled right out. But the chance would fade a little more with today. No dead people had ever been spilled while any of them watched, just as ·no freight train had ever wrecked while they prayed for it to, so they could get the bananas.

"But mainly, Mr. MacLain, you should remember to keep off rich food," Miss Snowdie said, leading her husband down a divergent path. They were not going to the cemetery with the rest; no one expected it of them. Their Negro girl chauffeur waited with their car turned the other way. "At home we've got that nice Moody fish from Moon Lake."

Virgie watched the mysterious, vulnerable back of the old man. Even as Miss Snowdie, unmysterious, led him away, he was eating still. At some moment today she had said, "Virgie, I spent all Mama and Papa had tracing after him. The Jupiter Detective Agency in Jackson. I never told. They never found or went after the right one. But I'll never forgive myself for tracing after him." Virgie had wanted to say, "Forgive yourself, yes," but could not speak the words. And they would not have mattered that much to Miss Snowdie.

"Granddaddy's almost a hundred," said little King clearly. "When you get to be a hundred, you pop."

The old people did not think to say good-bye. Mr. MacLain pressed ahead, a white inch of hair in the nape of his neck curling over in the breeze.

Virgie was again seized by both arms, as if, in the open, she might try to bolt. Her body ached from the firm hand of—in the long run—Miss Lizzie Stark. She was escorted to the Stark automobile parked in the road, where Ran now waited in the driver's seat. The line of cars and trucks had started.

"Poor Mr. Mabry, he didn't show up." Miss Perdita Mayo's flushed face appeared a moment at the window. "He's down with a cold. It came on him yesterday: I saw it coming."

They had to drive the length of Morgana to the cemetery. It was spacious and quiet within, once they rolled over the cattle-guard; yet wherever Virgie looked from the Starks' car window, she seemed to see the same gravestones again, Mr. Comus Stark, old Mr. Tim Carmichael, Mr. Tertius Morgan, like the repeating towers in the Vicksburg park. Twice she thought she saw Mr. Sissum's grave, the same stone pulled down by the same vines—the grave into which Miss Eckhart, her old piano teacher whom she had hated, tried to throw herself on the day of his funeral. And more than once she looked for the squat, dark

stone that marked Miss Eckhart's own grave; it would
turn itself from them, as she'd seen it do before, when
they wound near and passed. And a seated angel, first
visible from behind with the stone hair spread on the
shoulders, turned up later from the side, further away,
showing the steep wings.

'Do you like it?" Cassie was asking from the front
seat beside Ran (Jinny had to go home with the children).

So it was Mrs. Morrison's angel. After being so gay
and flighty always, Cassie's mother went out of the
room one morning and killed herself. "I was proud
of it," said Cassie. "It took everything I had."

"Where's Loch these days?" Ran asked.

"Ran, don't you remember he's in New York City?
Likes it there. He writes us."

Loch was too young for Virgie ever to have known
well in Morgana—always polite, "too good," "too
young," people said when he went to war, and she
remembered him only as walking up the wooden
staircase to his father's printing office. He gave a bent,
intent nod of the head, too young and already too
distant.—But he's not dead! she thought—it's something else.

"What did you say, Virgie?"

"Nothing, Cassie." Yet she must have hurt Cassie
some way, if only by that moment's imagining that
what was young was all gone—disappeared wholly.

Virgie leaned out to look for a certain blackened
lamb on a small hump of earth that was part of her
childhood. It was the grave of some lady's stillborn
child (now she knew it must have been that baby
sister of Miss Nell Loomis's), the lamb flattened by
rains into a little fairy table. There she had enter-
tained a large imaginary company with acorn cups,
then ridden away on the table.

"You staying on in Morgana, Virgie?" came Miss
Nell's undertone. She talked on—the same in a moving car as she was in a parlor.

"Going away. In the morning," Virgie was saying.

"Auction off everything?"

Virgie said nothing more; she had decided to leave
when she heard herself say so—decided by ear.

"Turn to the right and stop, Ran."

That was the first thing Miss Lizzie had said; perhaps she had felt too crowded in her own car to
break silence.

Ran stopped, and lifted the ladies out. The group
of three fat ones—Ran with Miss Lizzie and Miss Nell
in arm—moved in hobbled walk ahead. The Rainey
lot was well back under the trees. Cassie put her fingers in Virgie's. All around, the yuccas were full of
bells, the angels were reared and horsily dappled.
The magnolias' inflamed cones and their brown litter
smoldered in the tail of the eye. And also in the tail
of the eye was Miss Billy Texas Spights: they had let
her come. She wore purple—the costume she had
worn on election day.

"Thank goodness Snowdie's not here to see that,"
Miss Perdita remarked ahead to Miss Hattie. "Ran's
here, but nothing bothers Ran."

Virgie, as if nudged, knew they must be near the
poor little country girl's grave, with the words "Thy
Will Be Done" on the stone. She was buried here with
the Sojourners.

I hate her, Virgie thought calmly, not turning her
head. Hate her grave.

Mr. Holifield passed by, mowing the grass, and
raised his hat significantly. Virgie saw the familiar
stone of her father's grave, his name spelled out Lafa-
yette, and the red hole torn out beside it. In spite of
the flowers waiting, the place still smelled of the
sweat of Negro diggers and of a big cedar root
which had been cut through and glimmered wetly in
the bed of the grave. Victor was buried on the other
side. Perhaps there was nothing there. The box that
came back from the other war—who knew what had
been sent to the Raineys in that? Somewhere behind
her, Virgie could hear the hollow but apologetic
coughing of Mr. Mabry. Except that it could not be

he, of course; he had not been able to come, after all.

Brother Dampeer was with them still; with his weight thrown to one hip, he stood in front of them all, ahead of the row of Mayhews, and watched the success of the lowering of the coffin and the filling of the grave.

After Dr. Williams' prayer, little crumbs and clods ran down the mound, pellmell; the earth grew immediately vivacious and wild as a creature. Virgie never moved. People taking their turns went up and scattered the wreaths about and slowly stuck the clods with paper cornucopias of flowers with pins to hold them. The cornucopias were none of them perfectly erect but leaned to one side or the other, edging the swollen pink mound, monstrous, wider than it was long until it should "settle."

As the party moved away, one of the cornucopias fell over and spilled its weight of red zinnias. No one returned to right it. A feeling of the tumbling activity and promptitude of the elements had settled over people and stirred up, of all things, their dignity; they could not go back now.

They left the cemetery without looking at anything, and some parted with the company at the gate. Attrition was their wisdom. Already, tomorrow's rain pelted the grave with loudness, and made hasty streams run down its sides, like a mountain red with rivers, already settling the patient work of them all; not one little "made" flower holder, but all, would topple; and so had, or might as well have, done it already; this was the past now.

Brother Dampeer said good-bye and climbed on his mount. He had ridden twenty miles on a mule for this; he did not disclose whether, today, it had been worth it.

The evening fields were still moving, people busy, the sun gone yet busy, where their uneven cotton country tilted and fell riverward into the West. Most of the funeral party had returned to the Raineys' for refreshments. Virgie, with a slip from even Miss Lizzie's arm, which was tired, had not yet gone in.

Four little Mayhews waited for her, perched like birds on the old swivel chair. They hopped off, put their arms around her knees, and pleaded with her too to come in the house now. From the road the lighted-up house had a roof sheared sharp as a fold of paper. The serried leaves of the chinaberry trembled over the road, the branches spread winglike in a breeze that meant change. It was the last of the month of beautiful evening skies, of the lovely East, behind the dark double-twinkling of swallows.

Smells of ham, banana cake, and tuberoses came out and the longing children ran to meet it. Ferns seemed in the early alcoves of twilight to creep, or suddenly to descend like waterfalls in between the deserted porch chairs, and over old man Rainey sitting along the edge of the porch, feet dangling. Juba came running forth, saying Miss Lizzie said for Miss Virgie to come and eat with her company.

Virgie had often felt herself at some moment callous over, go opaque; she had known it to happen to others; not only when her mother changed on the bed while she was fanning her. Virgie had felt a moment in life after which nobody could see through her, into her—felt it young. But Mr. King MacLain, an old man, had butted like a goat against the wall he wouldn't agree to himself or recognize. What fortress indeed would ever come down, except before hard little horns, a rush and a stampede of the pure wish to live?

The feeling had been strong upon her from the moment she came home that she had lived the moment before; it was a moment that found Virgie too tender. She had needed a little time, she needed it now. On the path, with the funeral company at her heels, then surrounding her and passing her and now sitting down to her table without her, she strained against the feeling of the double coming-back.

"Take your time, Virge!" Old Man Rainey said

softly. He climbed to his feet and walked into the house without waiting for her.

At seventeen, coming back, she'd jumped the high step from the Y. & M. V. train. She had reached earth dazzled, the first moment, at its unrocked calm. Grass tufted like the back of a dog that had been rolling the moment before shone brown under the naked sprawled-out light of a still-stretching outer world. She heard nothing but the sigh of the vanished train and the single drumbeat of thunder on a bright July day. Across the train yard was Morgana, the remembered oaks like the counted continents against the big blue. Having just jumped from the endless, grinding interior of the slow train from Memphis, she had come back to something—and she began to run toward it, with her suitcase as light as a shoebox, so little had she had to go away with and now to bring back—the lightness made it easier.

"You're back at the right time to milk for me," her mother said when she got there, and untied her bonnet and dashed it to the floor between them, looking up at her daughter. Nobody was allowed weeping over hurts at her house, unless it was Mrs. Rainey herself first, for son and husband, both her men, were gone.

For Virgie, there were practical changes to begin at once with the coming back—no music, no picture show job any more, no piano.

But in that interim between train and home, she walked and ran looking about her in a kind of glory, by the back way.

Virgie never saw it differently, never doubted that all the opposites on earth were close together, love close to hate, living to dying; but of them all, hope and despair were the closest blood—unrecognizable one from the other sometimes, making moments double upon themselves, and in the doubling double again, amending but never taking back.

For that journey, it was ripe afternoon, and all about her was that light in which the earth seems to come into its own, as if there would be no more days, only this day—when fields glow like deep pools and the expanding trees at their edges seem almost to open, like lilies, golden or dark. She had always loved that time of day, but now, alone, untouched now, she felt like dancing; knowing herself not really, in her essence, yet hurt; and thus happy. The chorus of crickets was as unprogressing and out of time as the twinkling of a star.

Her fingers set, after coming back, set half-closed; the strength in her hands she used up to type in the office but most consciously to pull the udders of the succeeding cows, as if she would hunt, hunt, hunt daily for the blindness that lay inside the beast, inside where she could have a real and living wall for beating on, a solid prison to get out of, the most real stupidity of flesh, a mindless and careless and calling body, to respond flesh for flesh, anguish for anguish. And if, as she dreamed one winter night, a new piano she touched had turned, after the one pristine moment, into a calling cow, it was by her own desire.

After she had gone in and served her company and set the Mayhews ("You'd sure better come live with us. If it wasn't for leaving such a nice house," they murmured to her) on the right road (they had come clear around by Greenwood), and after Old Man Rainey had gone to bed in the old bedroom up under the roof, Virgie sat down in the uncleared kitchen and ate herself, while Juba ate near by—a little chicken, at first, then ham, then bacon and eggs. She drank her milk. Then she sent Juba home and turned out a fantastic number of lights.

After she was in bed and her own light out, there was a pre-emptory pounding on the porch floor.

She walked to the open front door, her nightgown blowing about her in the moist night wind. She was trembling, and put on a light in the hall. ·

From the gleam falling over the transom behind her she could see an old lady in a Mother Hubbard and clayed boots, holding out something white in a dark wrapping.

"It's you," the old lady said abruptly. "Child, you don't know me, but I know you and brought you somethin'. Mighty late, ain't it? My night-blooming cereus throwed a flower tonight, and I couldn't forbear to bring you it. Take it—unwrop it."

Virgie looked at the naked, luminous, complicated flower, large and pale as a face on the dark porch. For a moment she felt more afraid than she had coming to the door.

"It's for you. Keep it—won't do the dead no good. And tomorrow it'll look like a wrung chicken's neck. Look at it enduring the night."

A horse stamped and whimpered from the dark road. The old woman declined to come in.

"No, oh no. You used to play the pi-anna in the picture show when you's little and I's young and in town, dear love," she called, turning away through the dark. "Sorry about your mama: didn't suppose anybody make as pretty music as you *ever* have no trouble.—I thought you's the prettiest little thing ever was."

Virgie was still trembling. The flower troubled her; she threw it down into the weeds.

She knew that now at the river, where she had been before on moonlit nights in autumn, drunken and sleepless, mist lay on the water and filled the trees, and from the eyes to the moon would be a cone, a long silent horn, of white light. It was a connection visible as the hair is in air, between the self and the moon, to make the self feel the child, a daughter far, far back. Then the water, warmer than the night air or the self that might be suddenly cold, like any other arms, took the body under too, running without visibility into the mouth. As she would drift in the river, too alert, too insolent in her heart in those days, the mist might thin momentarily and brilliant jewel eyes would look out from the water-line and the bank.

Sometimes in the weeds a lightning bug would lighten, on and off, on and off, for as long in the night as she was there to see.

Out in the yard, in the coupe, in the frayed velour pocket next to the pistol, was her cache of cigarettes. She climbed inside and shielding the matchlight, from habit, began to smoke cigarettes. All around her the dogs were barking.

III.

"I'll sell the cows to the first white man I meet in the road," Virgie thought, waking up.

After she had milked them and driven them to pasture and come back, she saw Mrs. Stark's Juba back at the kitchen door.

"Leavin'? One thing, I seen your mama's ghost already," Juba said. She picked up a plate. As she began wrapping the china in newspaper, she explained that Virgie's goods must be packed in papers and locked in trunks before Virgie left, or Mrs. Stark would not think it fitting to the dead or to departure either. Virgie was to come up to the house and bid Mrs. Stark good-bye—before noon.

"Still in the house," Juba said. "Ghost be's."

"Well, I don't want to hear about ghosts," Virgie said. They were now crouched together over a shelf in the china closet.

"Don't?"

Juba courteously ignored Virgie's clashing two plates together. Things? Miss Virgie must despise things more than the meanest people, more than any throwing ghosts.

"I don't. I don't like ghosts."

"*Now!*" Juba said, by way of affirmation. "However, this'n, your mama, her weren't in two pieces, or floatin' upside down, or any those things yet. Her lyin' up big on a stuff davenport like a store window, three four *us* fannin' her."

"I still don't want to hear about it." Virgie said. "Just wrap everything up quick for Mrs. Stark and put it away, then you can go."

"Yes, ma'am. Her ghost restin'. Not stren'us-minded like some. I sees ghosts go walkin' and carryin' on. But your mama." To be the ghost, Juba laid her hand on her chest and put her head to one side, fluttering her eyelids tenderly and not breathing. "Yes'm. Yonder up the wall, is where her was. I says Juba, tell Miss Virgie, her would appreciate word of that."

"Did you come here to make me wrap stuff up and then get in my way?" Virgie said. "You know I'm in a hurry to shut up this house."

"Goin' off and leave all these here clean curtains?"

"Juba, when I was in my worst trouble, I scared everybody off, did you know that? Now I'm not scarey any more. Like Ran MacLain; he's not," Virgie said absently as they wrapped together.

Juba laughed in an obscure glee. "You'll scare 'em when you's a ghost."

"Hurry."

"I seen more ghosts than live peoples, round here. Black and white. I seen plenty both. Miss Virgie, some is given to see, some try but is not given. I seen that Mrs. Morrison from 'cross the road in long white nightgown, no head atall, in her driveway Saddy. Rackanize her freckle arms. You ever see her? I seen her here. She die in pain?"

Juba lowered her lids hypocritically.

"Pain a plenty and I don't ever want to see her." Virgie got to her feet. "Go on, go on back to Mrs. Stark. Tell her I can pack up better without you. Do I have to pack everything?"

"Yes'm. Her idea is," Juba said, "pack 'em up strong for the day the somebody come *unpack*. And I done bent over and stoop best I could. Held all them curlycue plates without spillin' one."

"Do that for Mrs. Stark."

Juba picked herself up. She shook her head at the

open cupboard, the dwindled and long-sugared jelly, the rusty cream of tartar box, the Mason jar of bay leaves, the spindly and darkened vanilla bottle, all the old confusion. Her eyes fastened and held to the twenty-year-old box of toothpicks, and Virgie, seeing, got it for her.

"Juba, take it all," she said then. "Plates, knives and forks, the plants on the porch, whatever you want, take. And what's in the trunks. You and Minerva divide." Then she had to burst out and say something to Juba. "And I saw Miverva! I saw her take Mama's hair switch—her young hair that was yellow and I never saw when it matched any more and she could do anything but keep it in that trunk, and I saw it put down in that paper sack. And my brother's baby clothes and my own, yellow and all the lace—I saw all stolen and put with Miverva's umbrella to take home, and I let them go. You tell that Negro. Tell her I know I was robbed, and that I don't care."

Juba nodded and changed the subject. "Thank you, Miss Virgie, for men's clothes. That salt-and-pepper of poor Mr. Rainey."

"Mama kept everything," Virgie said after a moment.

"Glory."

"Now you can go."

"Why, it's a-rainin'. Do hate rain."

Juba left. But she came back.

"That's it," she called softly, appearing once more in her fedora at the kitchen door. "That's right. Cry. Cry. Cry."

"Taking a trip? Think I might come along with you," said Old Man Rainey. "I always aimed to see the world." He looked at her closely.

"Please, sir, don't you come! Yes—I may go far—"

He gave her a hug before he turned to his coffee.

"Do you want to put our cows in your truck to take along?" She gave over to him everything she could think of, hoping he would accept something, something at least.

Virgie went out into the rainy morning and got into her car. She drove it, bumping, down the hill. In the road, the MacLains' old chinaberry tree brushed her window, enjoying the rain like a bird.

She drove through Morgana, hearing a horn blow from another car; it was Cassie Morrison. Cassie called out, driving abreast.

"I want you to come see Mama's Name in the Spring, Virgie. This morning before it rained I divided all the bulbs again, and it ought to be prettier than ever!"

"Always see it when I pass your yard," Virgie called back.

"Virgie! I know how you feel. You'll never get over it, never!"

They called from car to car, running parallel along the road with the loose gravel from the unpaved part knocking loudly, bounced from one car to the other.

"Well. You come."

"I guess it takes a lot of narcissus to spell Catherine," Virgie called, when Cassie still did not pass her.

"Two hundred and thirty-two bulbs! And then Miss Katie's hyacinthus all around those, and I've got it bordered in violets, you know, to tell me where it is in summer!" Cassie's voice, growing louder, grew at the same time more anxious and more reverent. She was not hurt, not suspecting, only anxious. But it was for Cassie that Virgie had turned her car toward town, to not let her see. "Now you come. We were friends that summer—" (Virgie remembered Cassie and herself in the revival tent, pulling light bugs off each other's shoulders while singing "Throw Out the Life Line.") "You could come play my piano, nobody does but my pupils."

Virgie, and Cassie too, circled the cemetery and drove back the length of Morgana. Then, "Where are you going? Are you going somewhere, Virgie?"

Virgie slowed for a minute as Cassie turned in at her own house. The Morrisons' looked the same as always, except, as the MacLain house had had before it—when Miss Eckhart was there—it now had a fly-like cluster of black mailboxes at its door; it had been cut up for road workers and timber people. In the upstairs corner room, where they tried to keep poor Mr. Morrison, the shade was still down, but she felt him look out through his telescope. Across the front yard stretched the violet frame in which Mama's Name was planted against the coming of spring.

Virgie lifted her hand, and the girls waved.

"You'll go away like Loch," Cassie called from the steps. "A life of your own, away—I'm so glad for people like you and Loch, I am really."

Virgie drove on, the seven winding miles to Mac-Lain and stopped the car in front of the courthouse.

She had often done this, if only to turn around and go right back after a rest of a few moments and a Coca-Cola standing up in Billy Hudson's drugstore MacLain pleased her—the uncrowded water tank, catching the first and last light; the old iron bell in the churchyard looking as heavy as a fallen meteor. The courthouse pleased her—space itself, with the columns standing away from its four faces, and the pea-green blinds flat to the wall, and the stile rising in pepper grass over the iron fence to it—and a quail just now running across the yard; and the live oaks —trunks flaky black and white now, as if soot, not rain, had once fallen from heaven on them, and the wet eyes of cut-off limbs on them; and the whole rain-lighted spread roof of green leaves that moved like children's lips in speech, high up.

Virgie left the car and running through the light drops reached the stile and sat down on it in the open shelter of trees. She touched the treads, worn not by feet so much as by their history of warm, spreading seats At this distance the Confederate soldier on the

shaft looked like a chewed-on candle, as if old gnashing teeth had made him. On past him, pale as a rainbow, the ancient circus posters clung to their sheds,
they no longer the defacing but the defaced.

There was nobody out in the rain. The land across
from the courthouse used to be Mr. Virgil MacLain's
park. He was old Mr. King's father; he used to keep
deer. Now like a callosity, a cataract of the eye over
what was once transparent and bright—for the park
racing with deer was an idea strangely transparent
to Virgie—was the line of store fronts and the Mac-
Lain Bijou, and the cemetery that was visible on the
cedar hill.

Here the MacLains buried, and Miss Snowdie's people, the Hudsons. Here lay Eugene, the only MacLain
man gone since her memory, after old Virgil himself. Eugene, for a long interval, had lived in another
part of the world, learning while he was away tha*
people don't have to be answered just because they
want to know. His very wife was never known here,
and he did not make it plain whether he had children
somewhere now or had been childless. His wife did
not even come to the funeral, although a telegram
had been sent. A foreigner? "Why, she could even be
a Dago and we wouldn't know it." His light, tuber-
cular body seemed to hesitate on the street of Morgana, hold averted, anticipating questions. Sometimes
he looked up in the town where he was young and
said something strangely spiteful or ambiguous (he
was never reconciled to his father, they said, was sar-
castic to the old man—all he loved was Miss Snowdie
and flowers) but he bothered no one. "He never did
bother a soul," they said at his graveside that day,
forgetting his childhood. And all Mr. King's family
lay over there, Cedar Hill was bigger than the Courthouse; his father Virgil in the Confederate section,
and his mother, his grandfather—who remembered
his name and what he did? The name was on the
stone.

Didn't he kill a man, or have to, and what would be the long story behind it, the vaunting and the wandering from it?

And Miss Eckhart was over there. When Miss Eckhart died, up in Jackson, Miss Snowdie had her brought here and buried in her lot. Her grave was there near to Eugene's. There was the dark, squat stone Virgie had looked for yesterday, confusing her dead.

Before her ran rain-colored tin and red brick, doors weathered down to the whorl and color of river water. The vine over the jail was deep as a bed with brown leaves. At the MacLain Bijou, directly across from Virgie on the stile, there was a wrinkled blue sheen of rain on the two posters and deeper in, the square of yellow card ("Deposit Required for Going In to Talk") hung always like a lighted window in a traveler's gloom. She had sometimes come alone to the MacLain Bijou after Mr. Nesbitt let her go in the afternoon.

Footsteps sounded on the walk, a white man's. It was Mr. Nesbitt, she thought at first, but then saw it was another man almost like him—hurrying, bent on something, furious at being in the rain, speechless. He was all alone out here. His round face, not pushed out now, away from other faces, looked curiously deep, womanly, dedicated. Mr. Nesbitt's twin passed close to her, and down the street he turned flamboyantly and entered what must have been his own door, splashing frantically through a puddle.

Virgie, picking the irresistible pepper grass, saw Mr. Mabry too. It was really himself, looking out under his umbrella for somebody. How wretchedly dignified and not quite yet alarmed he looked, and how his cold would last! Mr. Mabry imagined he was coming to her eventually, but was it to him that she had come, backward to protection? She'd have had to come backward, not simply stand still, to get from the wild spirit of Bucky Moffitt (and where was he?

Never under the ground! She smiled, biting the seed in the pepper grass), back past the drunk Simon Sojourner that didn't want her, and on to embarrassed Mr. Mabry, behind whom waited loud, harmless, terrifying Mr. Nesbitt who wanted to stand up for her. She had reached Mr. Mabry but she had passed him and it had not mattered about her direction, since here she was. She sat up tall on the stile, feeling that he would look right through her—Virgie Rainey on a stile, bereaved, hatless, unhidden now, in the rain—and he did. She watched him march by. Then she was all to herself.

Was she that? Could she ever be, would she be, where she was going? Miss Eckhart had had among the pictures from Europe on her walls a certain threatening one. It hung over the dictionary, dark as that book. It showed Perseus with the head of the Medusa. "The same thing as Siegfried and the Dragon," Miss Eckhart had occasionally said, as if explaining second-best. Around the picture—which sometimes blindly reflected the window by its darkness—was a frame enameled with flowers, which was always self-evident—Miss Eckhart's pride. In that moment Virgie had shorn it of its frame.

The vaunting was what she remembered, that lifted arm.

Cutting off the Medusa's head was the heroic act, perhaps, that made visible a horror in life, that was at once the horror in love, Virgie thought—the separateness. She might have seen heroism prophetically when she was young and afraid of Miss Eckhart. She might be able to see it now prophetically, but she was never a prophet. Because Virgie saw things in their time, like hearing them—and perhaps because she must believe in the Medusa equally with Perseus—she saw the stroke of the sword in three moments, not one. In the three was the damnation—no, only the secret, unhurting because not caring in itself—beyond the

beauty and the sword's stroke and the terror lay their
existence in time—far out and endless, a constellation
which the heart could read over many a night.

Miss Eckhart, whom Virgie had not, after all, hated
—had come near to loving, for she had taken Miss
Eckhart's hate, and then her love, extracted them, the
thorn and then the overflow—had hung the picture
on the wall for herself. She had absorbed the hero
and the victim and then, stoutly, could sit down to
the piano with all Beethoven ahead of her. With her
hate, with her love, and with the small gnawing feelings that ate them, she offered Virgie her Beethoven.
She offered, offered, offered—and when Virgie was
young, in the strange wisdom of youth that is accept-
ing of more than is given, she had accepted *the*
Beethoven, as with the dragon's blood. That was the
gift she had touched with her fingers that had drifted
and left her.

In Virgie's reach of memory a melody softly lifted,
lifted of itself. Every time Perseus struck off the Medusa's head, there was the beat of time, and the
melody. Endless the Medusa, and Perseus endless.

An old wrapped-up Negro woman with a red hen
under her arm came and sat down on the step below
Virgie.

"Mornin'."

Occasional drops of rain fell on Virgie's hair and her
cheek, or rolled down her arm, like a cool finger; only
it was not, as if it had never been, a finger, being the
rain out of the sky. October rain on Mississippi fields.
The rain of fall, maybe on the whole South, for all
she knew on the everywhere. She stared into its mag-
nitude. It was not only what expelled some shadow
of Mr. Bitts, and pressed poor Mr. Mabry to search
the street—it was the air's and the earth's fuming
breath, it could come and go. As if her own modesty
could also fall upon her now, freely and coolly, outside herself and on the everywhere, she sat a little
longer on the stile.

She smiled once, seeing before her, screenlike, the hideous and delectable face Mr. King MacLain had made at the funeral, and when they all knew he was next—even he. Then she and the old beggar woman, the old black thief, were there alone and together in the shelter of the big public tree, listening to the magical percussion, the world beating in their ears. They heard through falling rain the running of the horse and bear, the stroke of the leopard, the dragon's crusty slither, and the glimmer and the trumpet of the swan.